MATHEM &
MYSTIPHYSICS

featuring the

WANDERING STARS

VOLUME ONE:
THE PROBABILITIES OF PANDEMONIUM

Written by JAMES DAVIDGE
Drawn by JESSE DAVIDGE
Lettered by DEREK MAH

Rosencrantz Comics
A Division of Bayeux Arts

Mathemagick and Mystiphysics

Volume One: The Probabilities of Pandemonium

Published by: Bayeux Arts, Inc., 119 Stratton Crescent SW, Calgary, Canada T3H 1T7
www.bayeux.com

Cover image: Jesse Davidge

Library and Archives Canada Cataloguing in Publication

Davidge, James, 1973–
Mathemagick & mystiphysics volume 1 : the probabilities of pandemonium / James Davidge ; Jesse Davidge, illustrator.

ISBN 978-1-897411-19-3
I. Davidge, Jesse, 1982– II. Title. III. Title: Mathemagick and mystiphysics volume 1.

PN6733.D38M37 2010 j741.5'971 C2010-900535-X

First Printing: March 2010

Printed in Canada

Books published by Bayeux Arts/Rosencrantz are available at special quantity discounts to use a premiums and sales promotions, or for use in corporate training programs. For more information, pleas write to

Special Sales, Bayeux Arts, Inc., 119 Stratton Crescent SW, Calgary, Canada T3H 1T7.

The publishing activities of Bayeux/Rosencrantz are supported by the Canada Council for the Arts, th Alberta Foundation for the Arts, and by the Government of Canada through its Book Publishin Industry Development Program.

Canadian Heritage Patrimoine canadien

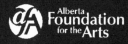

Alberta Foundation for the Arts

Canada Council for the Arts Conseil des Arts du Canada

BOOK ONE

A marvelous neutrality have these things mathematical, and also a strange participation between things supernatural, immortal, intellectual, simple and indivisible, and things natural, mortal, sensible, compounded and divisible.

~ John Dee, 1570

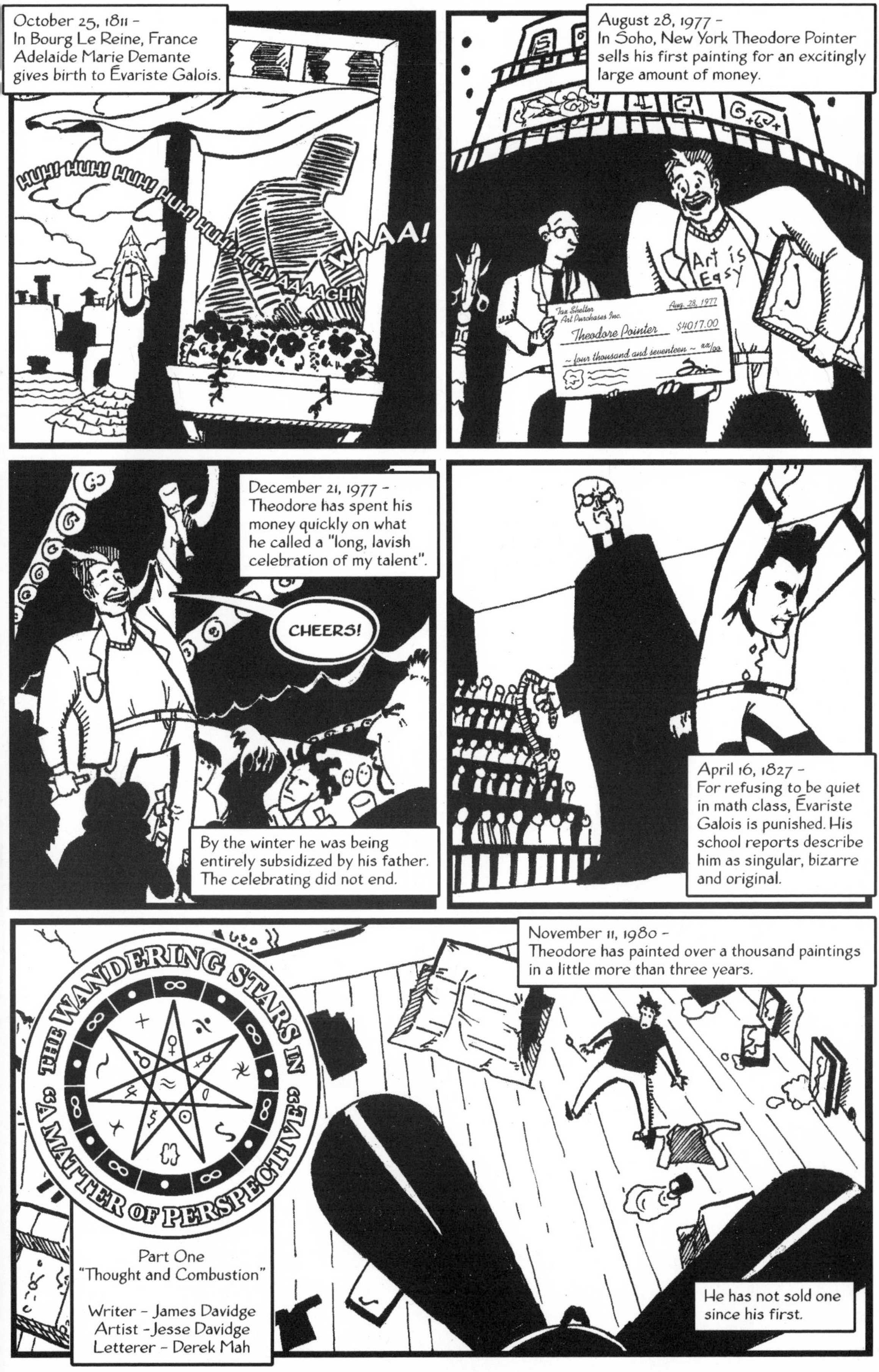
October 25, 1811 -
In Bourg Le Reine, France
Adelaide Marie Demante
gives birth to Évariste Galois.
HUH! HUH! HUH! HUH! HUH! HUH! AAAAGH!
WAAAA!
August 28, 1977 -
In Soho, New York Theodore Pointer
sells his first painting for an excitingly
large amount of money.
Art is Easy
Tax Shelter Art Purchases Inc.
Aug. 28, 1977
Theodore Pointer
$4017.00
four thousand and seventeen ~ xx/100
December 21, 1977 -
Theodore has spent his
money quickly on what
he called a "long, lavish
celebration of my talent".
CHEERS!
By the winter he was being
entirely subsidized by his father.
The celebrating did not end.
April 16, 1827 -
For refusing to be quiet
in math class, Évariste
Galois is punished. His
school reports describe
him as singular, bizarre
and original.
THE WANDERING STARS IN
"A MATTER OF PERSPECTIVE"
Part One
"Thought and Combustion"
Writer - James Davidge
Artist - Jesse Davidge
Letterer - Derek Mah
November 11, 1980 -
Theodore has painted over a thousand paintings
in a little more than three years.
He has not sold one
since his first.

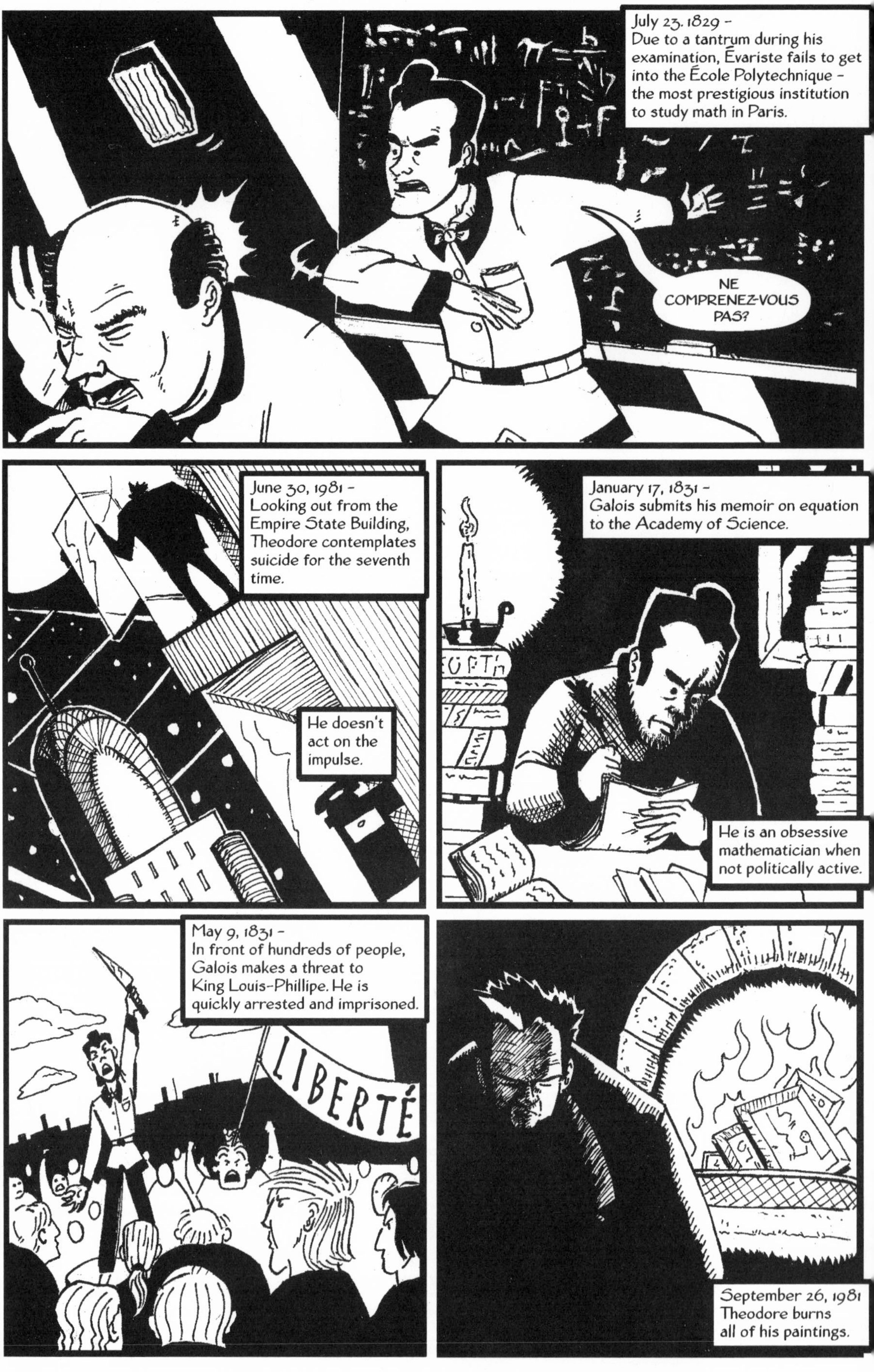
July 23, 1829 -
Due to a tantrum during his examination, Évariste fails to get into the École Polytechnique - the most prestigious institution to study math in Paris.
NE COMPRENEZ-VOUS PAS?
June 30, 1981 -
Looking out from the Empire State Building, Theodore contemplates suicide for the seventh time.
He doesn't act on the impulse.
January 17, 1831 -
Galois submits his memoir on equation to the Academy of Science.
He is an obsessive mathematician when not politically active.
May 9, 1831 -
In front of hundreds of people, Galois makes a threat to King Louis-Phillipe. He is quickly arrested and imprisoned.
LIBERTÉ
September 26, 1981
Theodore burns all of his paintings.

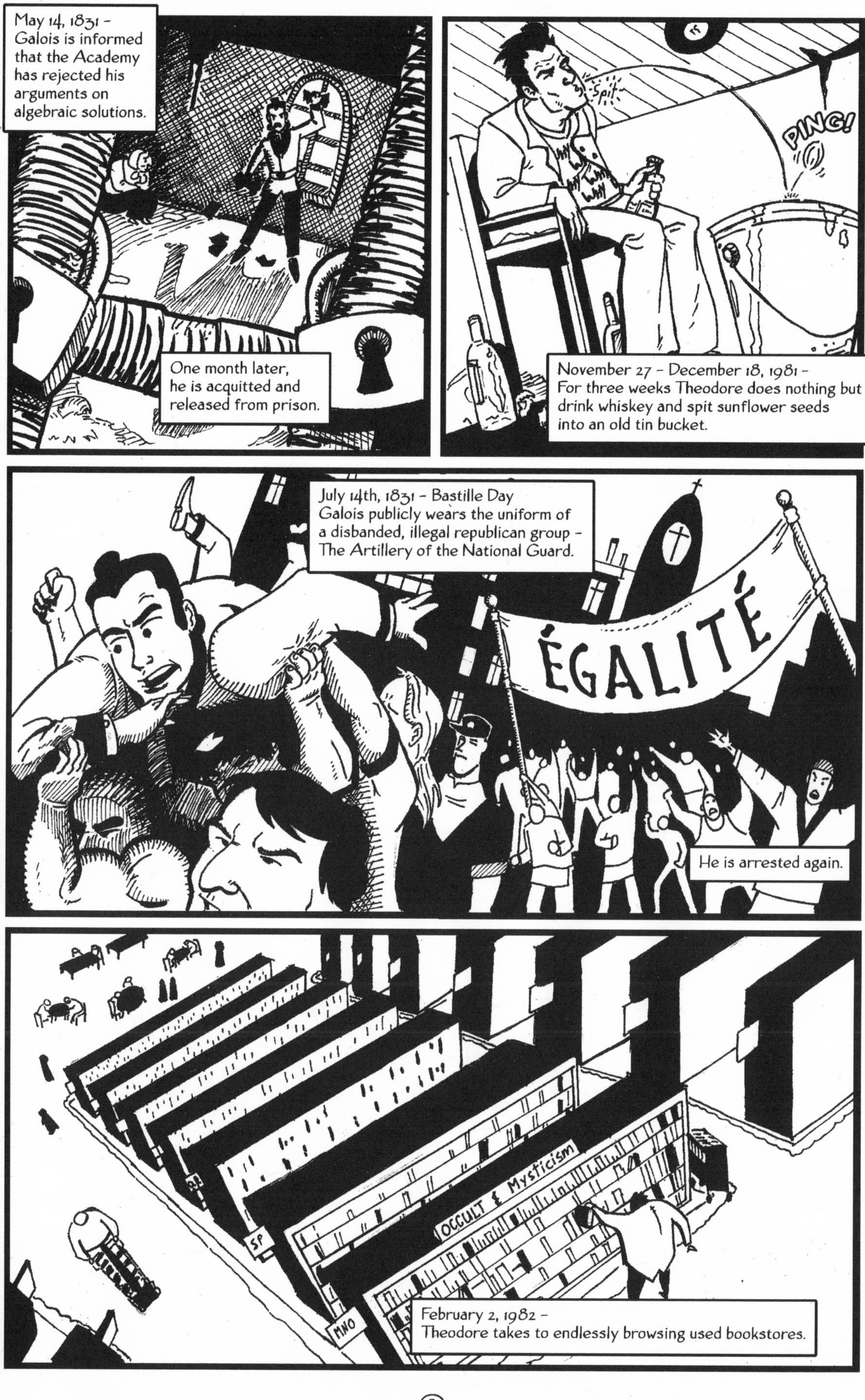
May 14, 1831 - Galois is informed that the Academy has rejected his arguments on algebraic solutions.
One month later, he is acquitted and released from prison.
Spit
PING!
November 27 - December 18, 1981 - For three weeks Theodore does nothing but drink whiskey and spit sunflower seeds into an old tin bucket.
July 14th, 1831 - Bastille Day Galois publicly wears the uniform of a disbanded, illegal republican group - The Artillery of the National Guard.
ÉGALITÉ
He is arrested again.
OCCULT & Mysticism
SP
MNO
February 2, 1982 - Theodore takes to endlessly browsing used bookstores.

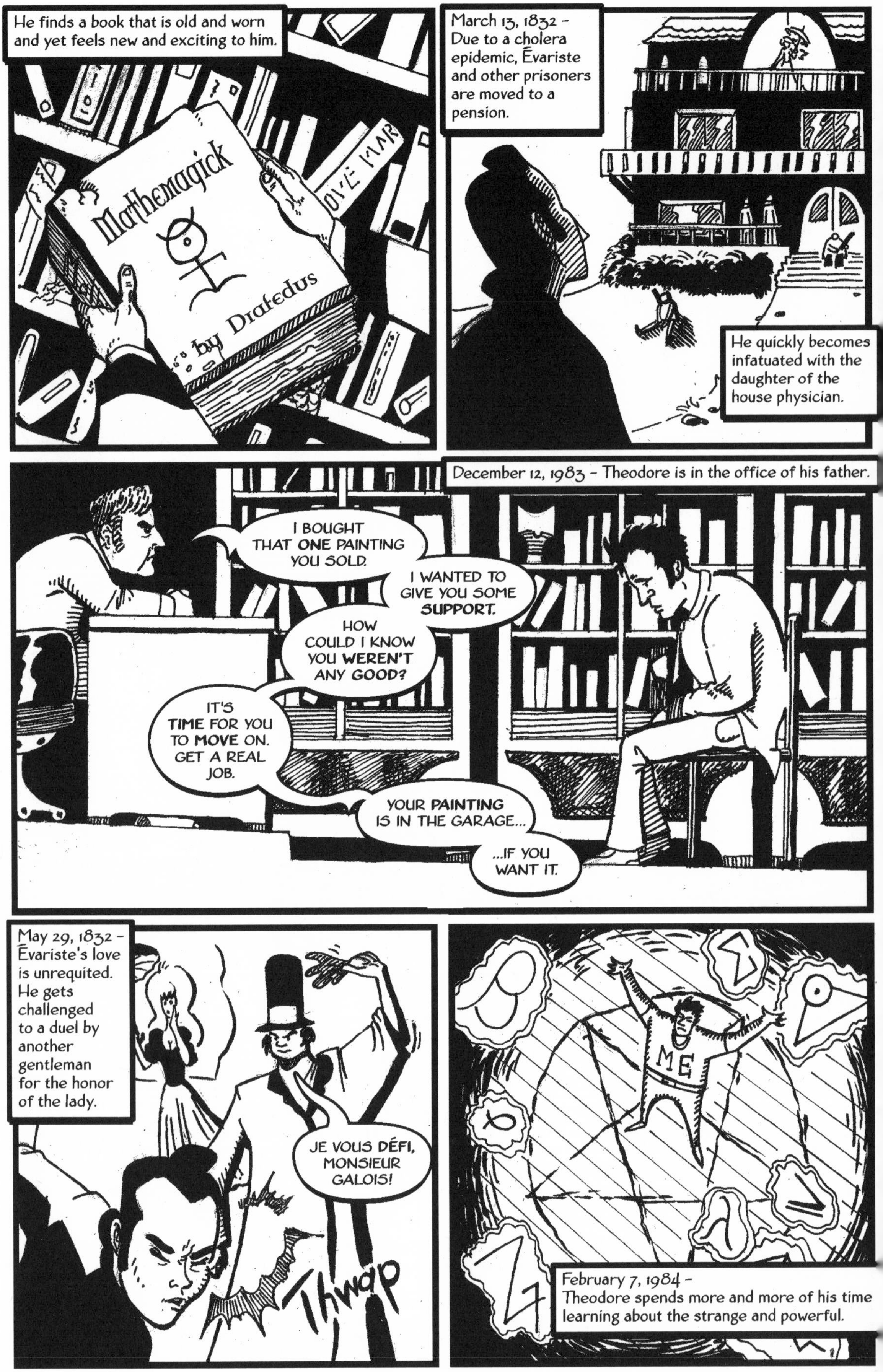
He finds a book that is old and worn and yet feels new and exciting to him.
Mathemagick
by Diatedus
March 13, 1832 - Due to a cholera epidemic, Évariste and other prisoners are moved to a pension.
He quickly becomes infatuated with the daughter of the house physician.
December 12, 1983 - Theodore is in the office of his father.
I BOUGHT THAT ONE PAINTING YOU SOLD.
I WANTED TO GIVE YOU SOME SUPPORT.
HOW COULD I KNOW YOU WEREN'T ANY GOOD?
IT'S TIME FOR YOU TO MOVE ON. GET A REAL JOB.
YOUR PAINTING IS IN THE GARAGE...
...IF YOU WANT IT.
May 29, 1832 - Évariste's love is unrequited. He gets challenged to a duel by another gentleman for the honor of the lady.
JE VOUS DÉFI, MONSIEUR GALOIS!
Thwap
ME
February 7, 1984 - Theodore spends more and more of his time learning about the strange and powerful.

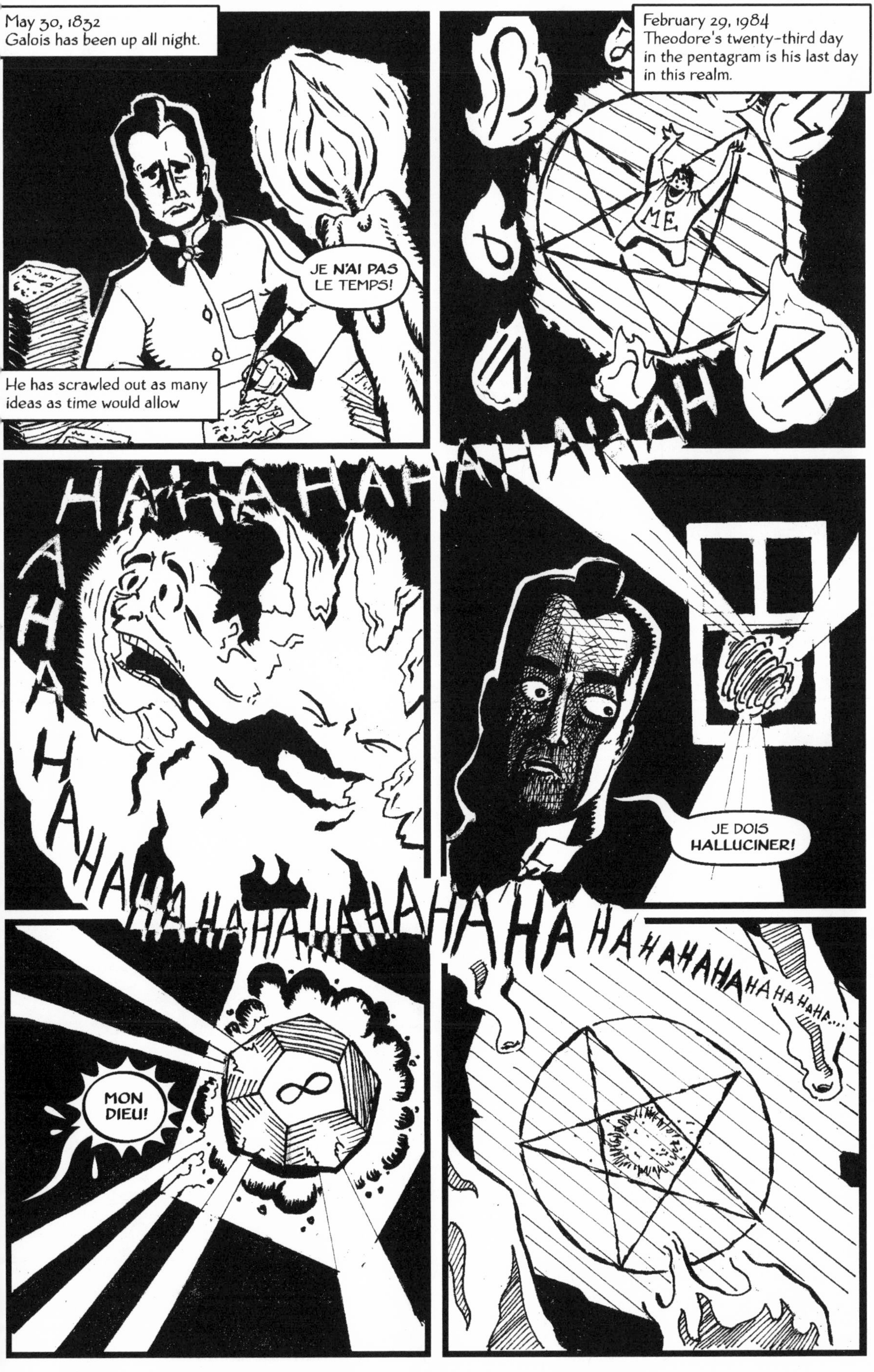
May 30, 1832
Galois has been up all night.
JE N'AI PAS LE TEMPS!
He has scrawled out as many ideas as time would allow
February 29, 1984
Theodore's twenty-third day in the pentagram is his last day in this realm.
ME
AHAHAH
HAHAHAHAHAH
JE DOIS HALLUCINER!
HA HA HA HAHAHAHA HA HA HAHA...
MON DIEU!

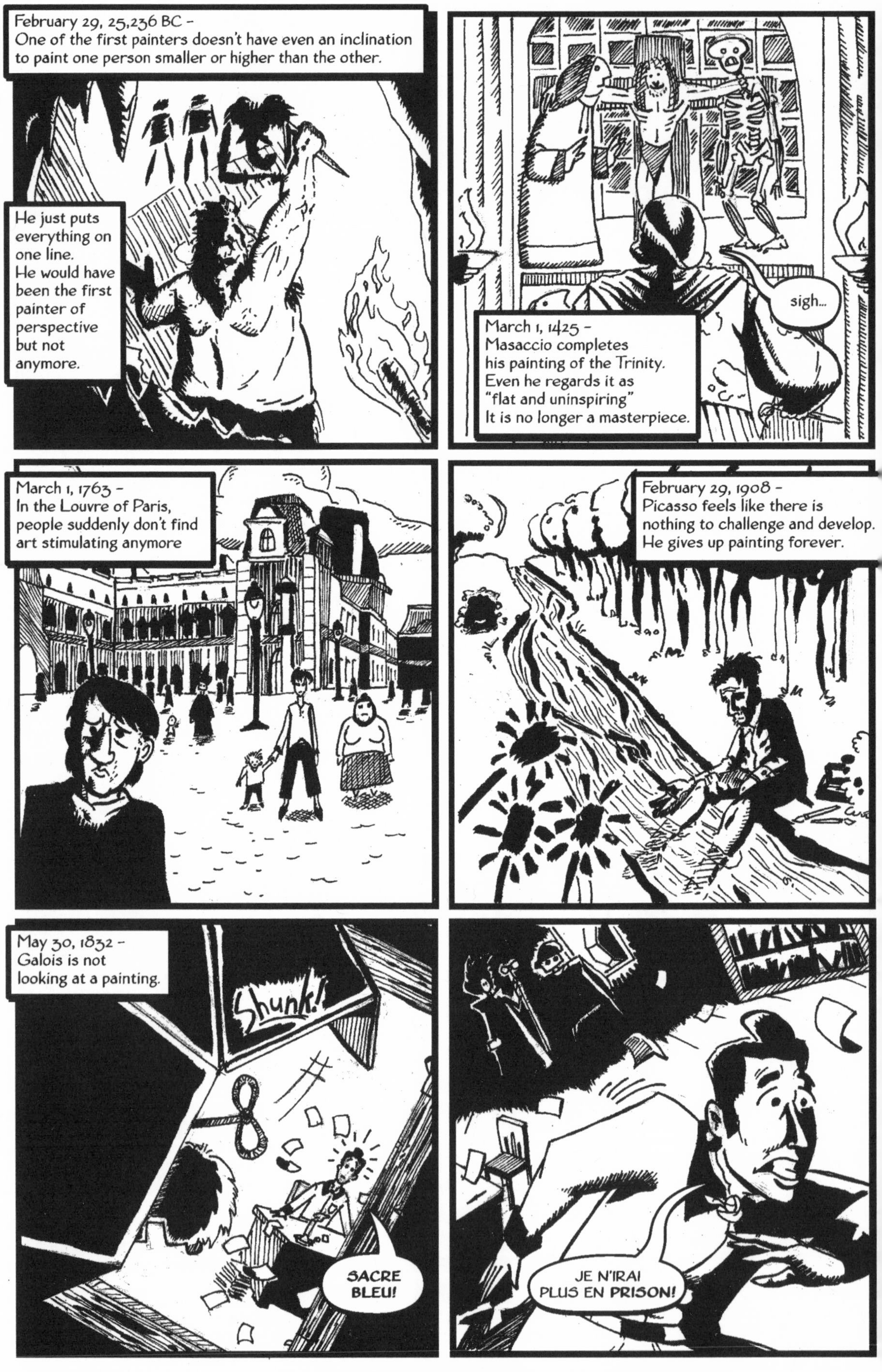
February 29, 25,236 BC –
One of the first painters doesn't have even an inclination to paint one person smaller or higher than the other.
He just puts everything on one line. He would have been the first painter of perspective but not anymore.
sigh...
March 1, 1425 –
Masaccio completes his painting of the Trinity. Even he regards it as "flat and uninspiring" It is no longer a masterpiece.
March 1, 1763 –
In the Louvre of Paris, people suddenly don't find art stimulating anymore
February 29, 1908 –
Picasso feels like there is nothing to challenge and develop. He gives up painting forever.
May 30, 1832 –
Galois is not looking at a painting.
Shunk!
SACRE BLEU!
JE N'IRAI PLUS EN PRISON!

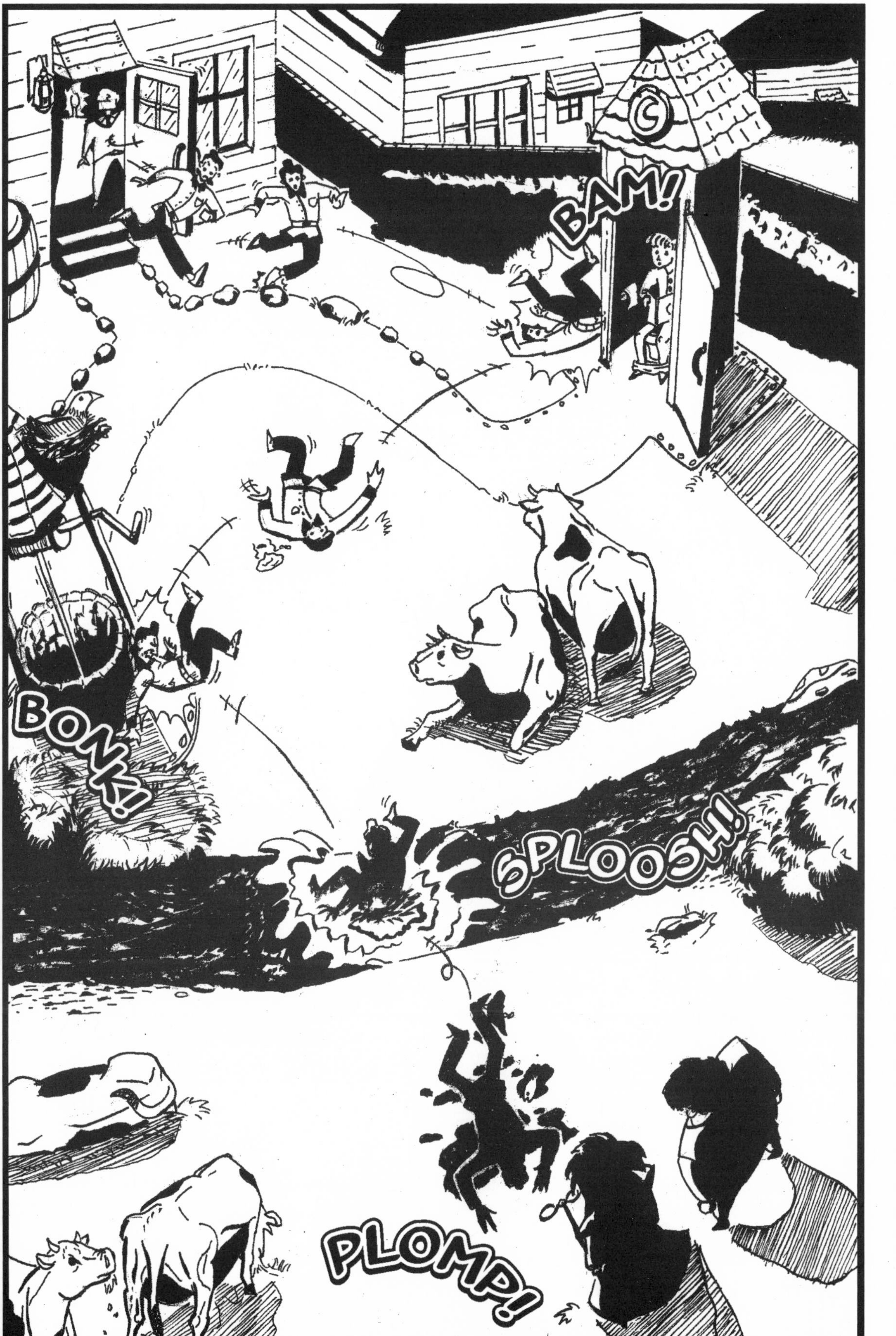
BAM!
BONK!
SPLOOSH!
PLOMP!

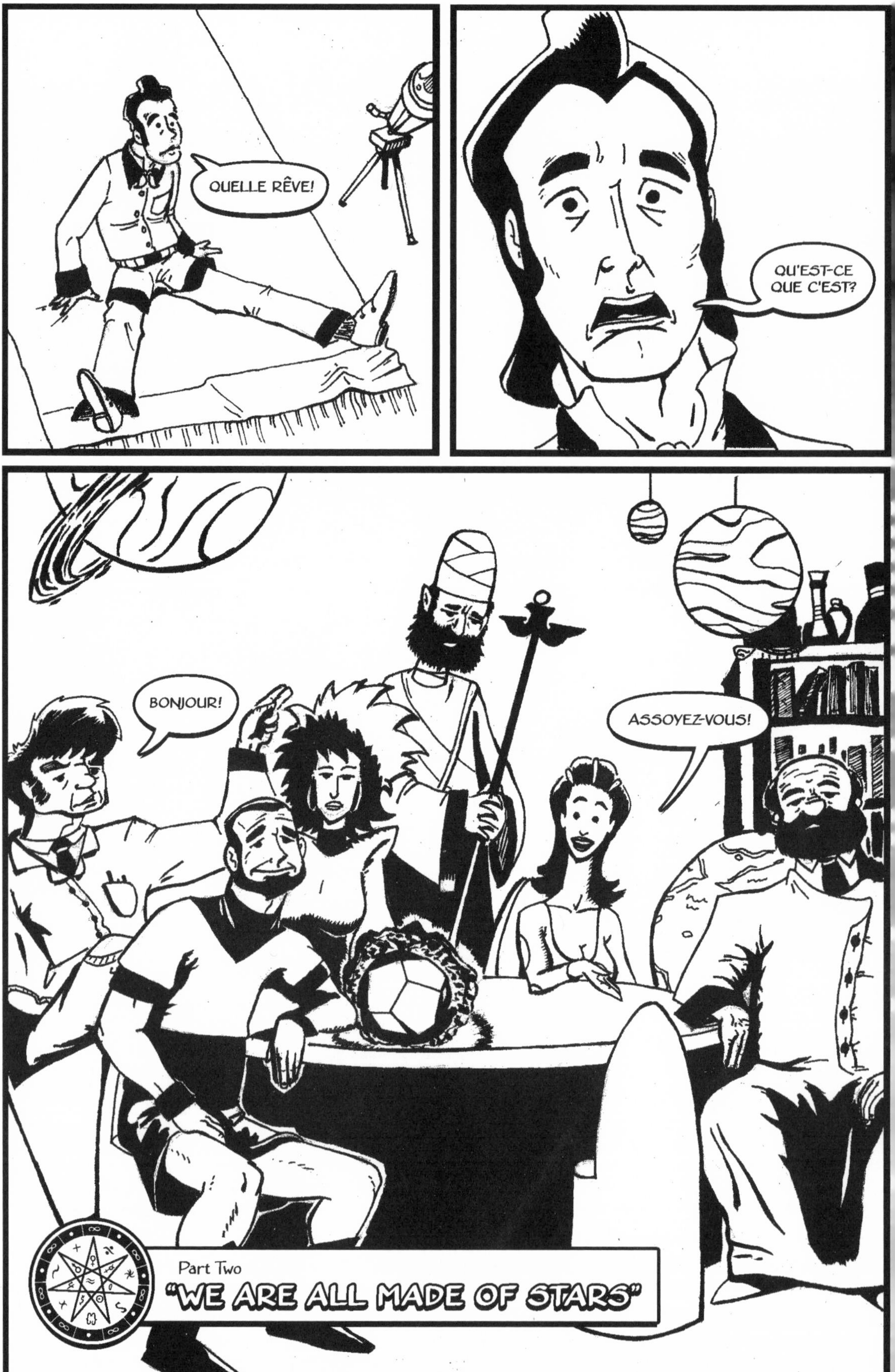
QUELLE RÊVE!
QU'EST-CE QUE C'EST?
BONJOUR!
ASSOYEZ-VOUS!
Part Two
"WE ARE ALL MADE OF STARS"

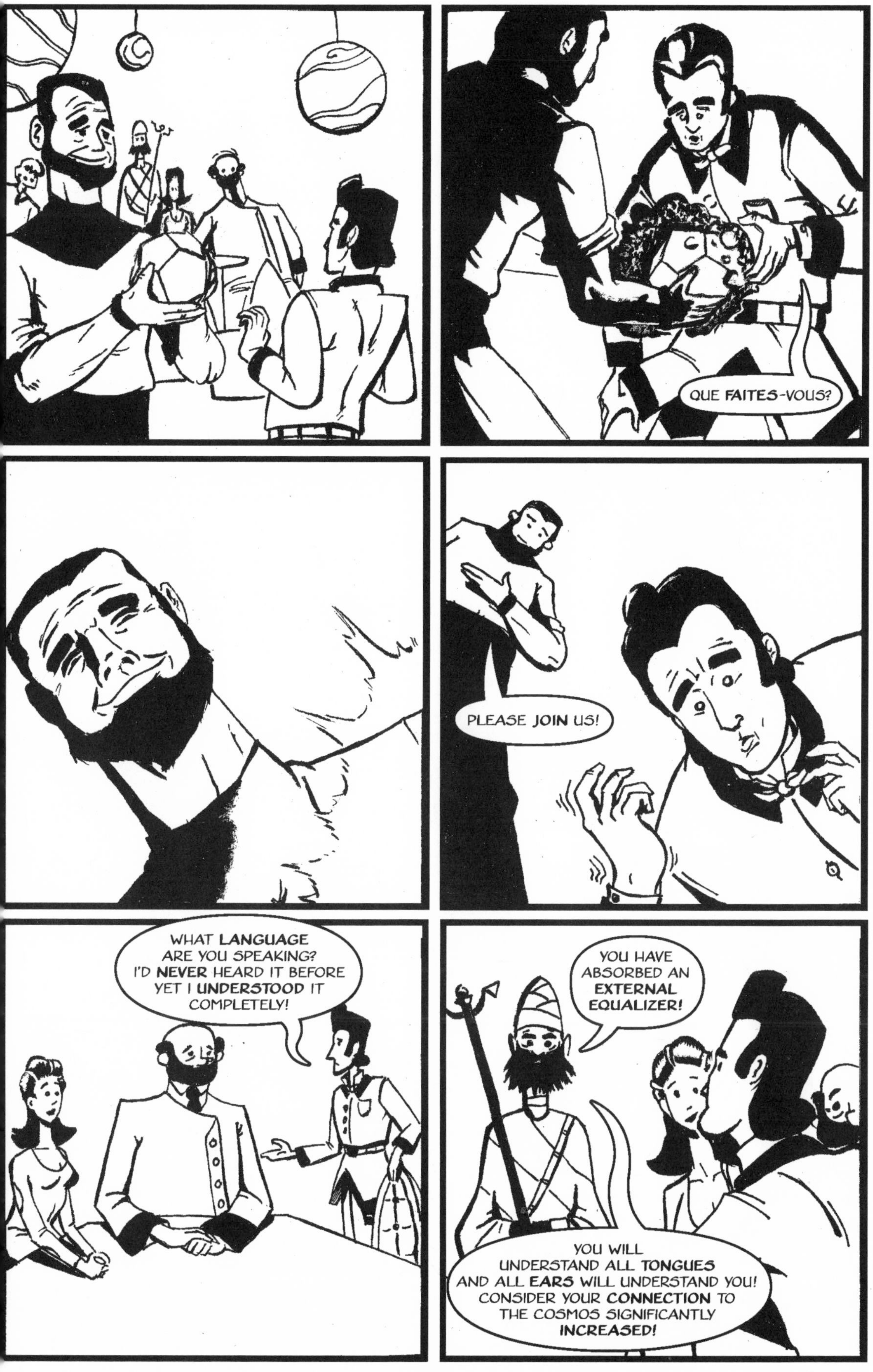
QUE FAITES-VOUS?
PLEASE JOIN US!
WHAT LANGUAGE ARE YOU SPEAKING? I'D NEVER HEARD IT BEFORE YET I UNDERSTOOD IT COMPLETELY!
YOU HAVE ABSORBED AN EXTERNAL EQUALIZER!
YOU WILL UNDERSTAND ALL TONGUES AND ALL EARS WILL UNDERSTAND YOU! CONSIDER YOUR CONNECTION TO THE COSMOS SIGNIFICANTLY INCREASED!

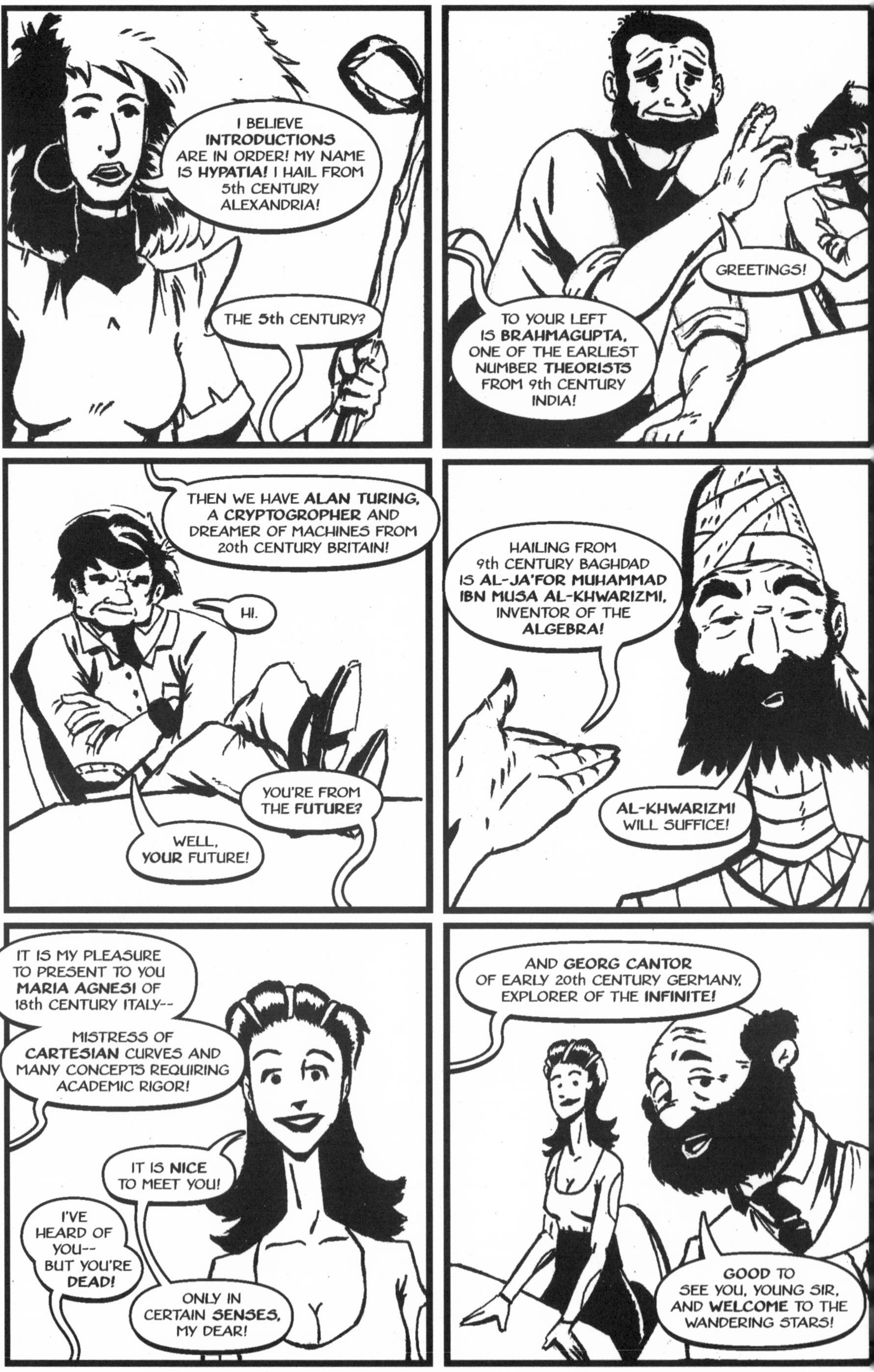
I BELIEVE INTRODUCTIONS ARE IN ORDER! MY NAME IS HYPATIA! I HAIL FROM 5th CENTURY ALEXANDRIA!
THE 5th CENTURY?
GREETINGS!
TO YOUR LEFT IS BRAHMAGUPTA, ONE OF THE EARLIEST NUMBER THEORISTS FROM 9th CENTURY INDIA!
THEN WE HAVE ALAN TURING, A CRYPTOGROPHER AND DREAMER OF MACHINES FROM 20th CENTURY BRITAIN!
HI.
YOU'RE FROM THE FUTURE?
WELL, YOUR FUTURE!
HAILING FROM 9th CENTURY BAGHDAD IS AL-JA'FOR MUHAMMAD IBN MUSA AL-KHWARIZMI, INVENTOR OF THE ALGEBRA!
AL-KHWARIZMI WILL SUFFICE!
IT IS MY PLEASURE TO PRESENT TO YOU MARIA AGNESI OF 18th CENTURY ITALY--
MISTRESS OF CARTESIAN CURVES AND MANY CONCEPTS REQUIRING ACADEMIC RIGOR!
IT IS NICE TO MEET YOU!
I'VE HEARD OF YOU-- BUT YOU'RE DEAD!
ONLY IN CERTAIN SENSES, MY DEAR!
AND GEORG CANTOR OF EARLY 20th CENTURY GERMANY, EXPLORER OF THE INFINITE!
GOOD TO SEE YOU, YOUNG SIR, AND WELCOME TO THE WANDERING STARS!

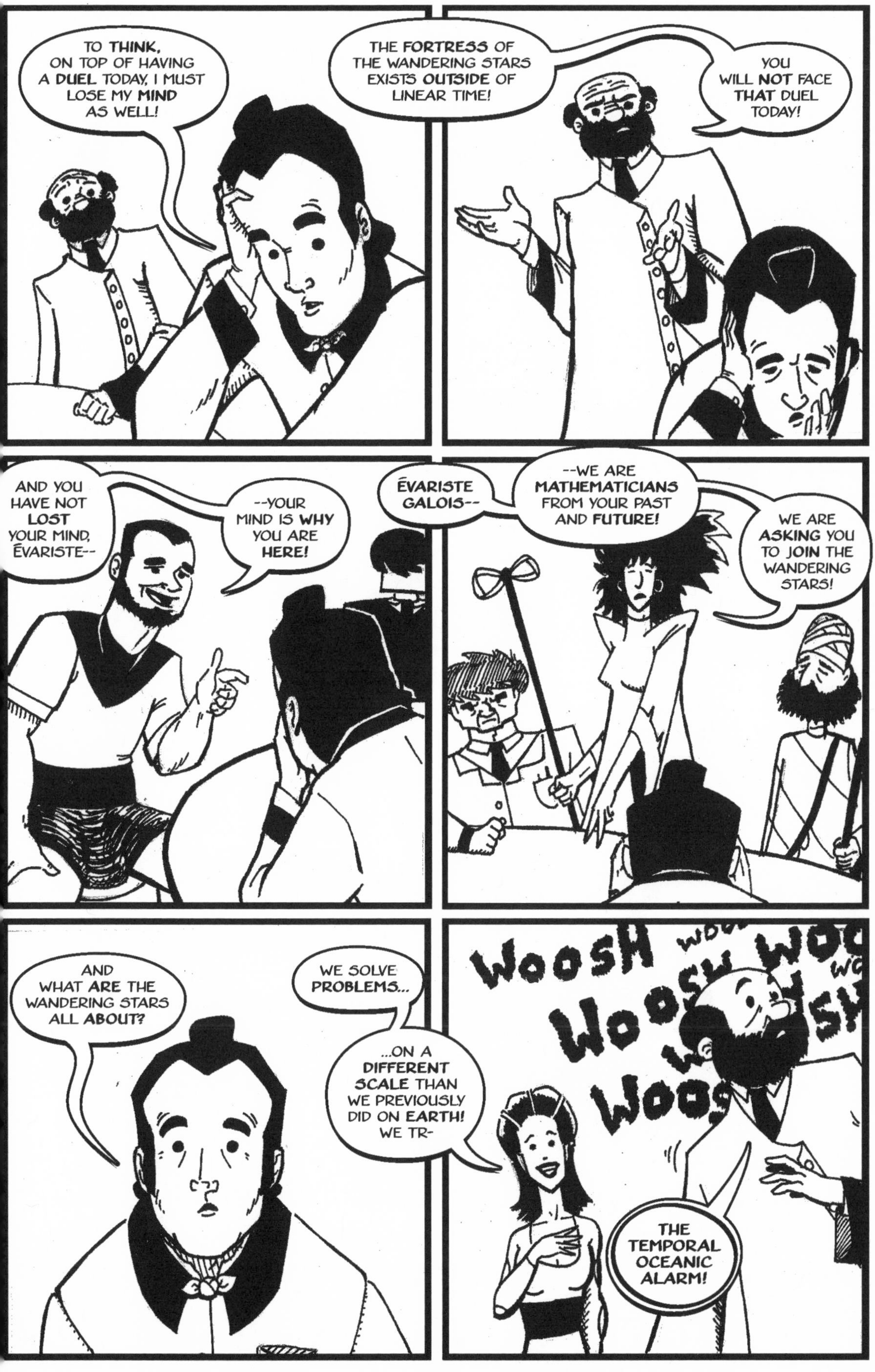
TO THINK, ON TOP OF HAVING A DUEL TODAY, I MUST LOSE MY MIND AS WELL!
THE FORTRESS OF THE WANDERING STARS EXISTS OUTSIDE OF LINEAR TIME!
YOU WILL NOT FACE THAT DUEL TODAY!
AND YOU HAVE NOT LOST YOUR MIND, ÉVARISTE--
--YOUR MIND IS WHY YOU ARE HERE!
ÉVARISTE GALOIS--
--WE ARE MATHEMATICIANS FROM YOUR PAST AND FUTURE!
WE ARE ASKING YOU TO JOIN THE WANDERING STARS!
AND WHAT ARE THE WANDERING STARS ALL ABOUT?
WE SOLVE PROBLEMS...
...ON A DIFFERENT SCALE THAN WE PREVIOUSLY DID ON EARTH! WE TR-
WOOSH
WOOSH
WOOS
THE TEMPORAL OCEANIC ALARM!

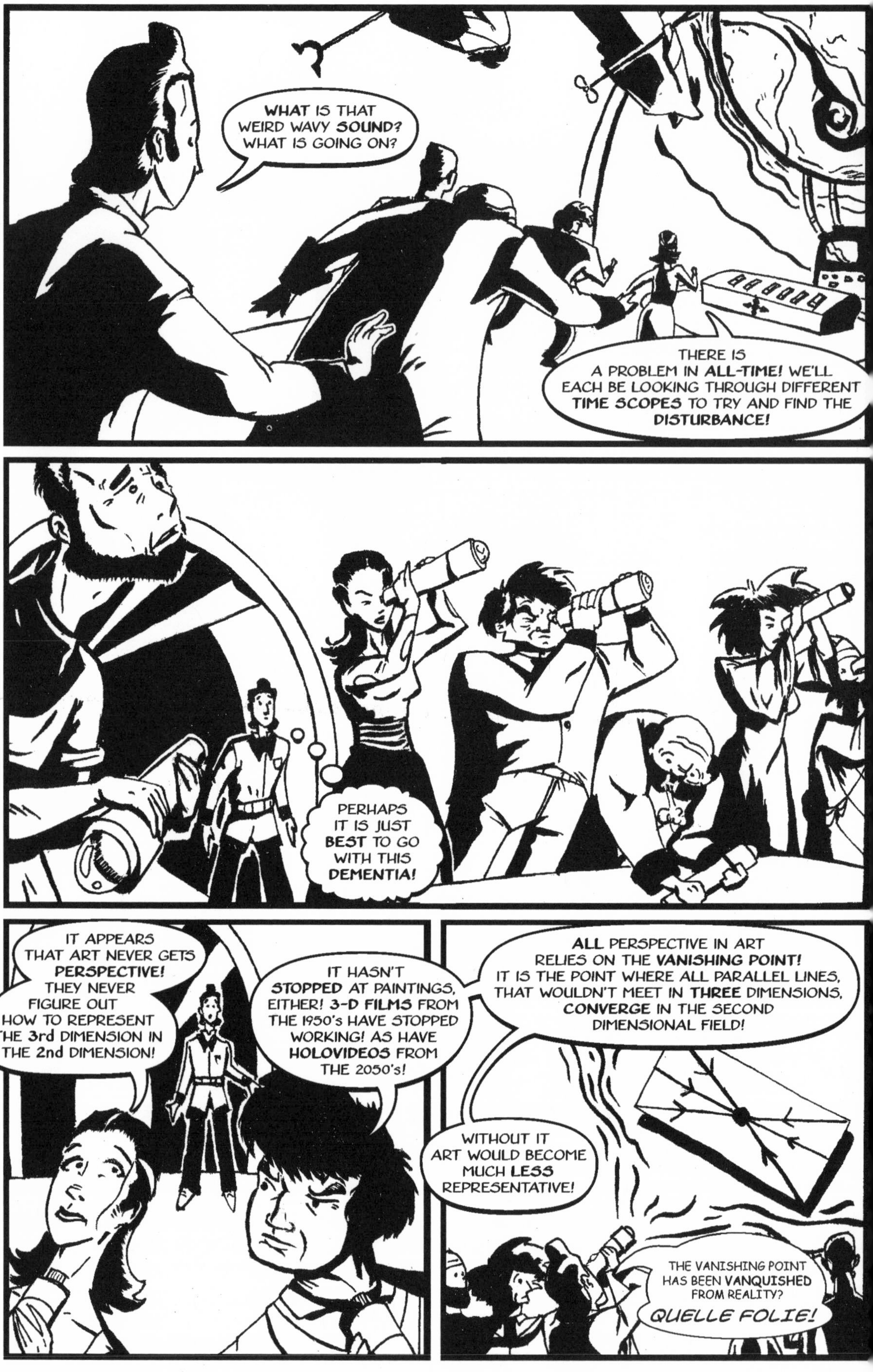
WHAT IS THAT WEIRD WAVY SOUND? WHAT IS GOING ON?
THERE IS A PROBLEM IN ALL-TIME! WE'LL EACH BE LOOKING THROUGH DIFFERENT TIME SCOPES TO TRY AND FIND THE DISTURBANCE!
PERHAPS IT IS JUST BEST TO GO WITH THIS DEMENTIA!
IT APPEARS THAT ART NEVER GETS PERSPECTIVE!
THEY NEVER FIGURE OUT HOW TO REPRESENT THE 3rd DIMENSION IN THE 2nd DIMENSION!
IT HASN'T STOPPED AT PAINTINGS, EITHER! 3-D FILMS FROM THE 1950's HAVE STOPPED WORKING! AS HAVE HOLOVIDEOS FROM THE 2050's!
ALL PERSPECTIVE IN ART RELIES ON THE VANISHING POINT! IT IS THE POINT WHERE ALL PARALLEL LINES, THAT WOULDN'T MEET IN THREE DIMENSIONS, CONVERGE IN THE SECOND DIMENSIONAL FIELD!
WITHOUT IT ART WOULD BECOME MUCH LESS REPRESENTATIVE!
THE VANISHING POINT HAS BEEN VANQUISHED FROM REALITY?
QUELLE FOLIE!

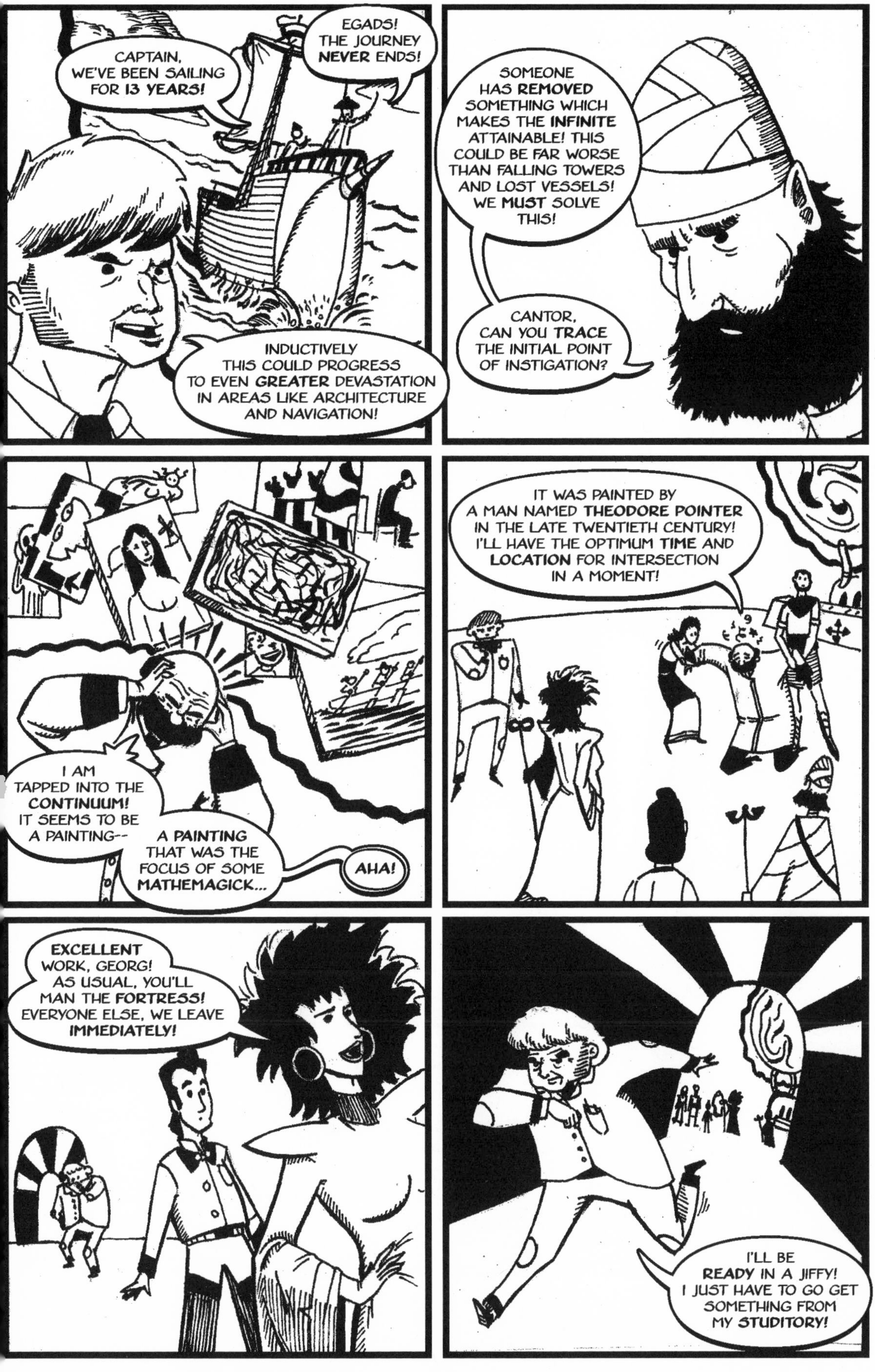
CAPTAIN, WE'VE BEEN SAILING FOR 13 YEARS!
EGADS! THE JOURNEY NEVER ENDS!
INDUCTIVELY THIS COULD PROGRESS TO EVEN GREATER DEVASTATION IN AREAS LIKE ARCHITECTURE AND NAVIGATION!
SOMEONE HAS REMOVED SOMETHING WHICH MAKES THE INFINITE ATTAINABLE! THIS COULD BE FAR WORSE THAN FALLING TOWERS AND LOST VESSELS! WE MUST SOLVE THIS!
CANTOR, CAN YOU TRACE THE INITIAL POINT OF INSTIGATION?
I AM TAPPED INTO THE CONTINUUM! IT SEEMS TO BE A PAINTING--
A PAINTING THAT WAS THE FOCUS OF SOME MATHEMAGICK...
AHA!
IT WAS PAINTED BY A MAN NAMED THEODORE POINTER IN THE LATE TWENTIETH CENTURY! I'LL HAVE THE OPTIMUM TIME AND LOCATION FOR INTERSECTION IN A MOMENT!
EXCELLENT WORK, GEORG! AS USUAL, YOU'LL MAN THE FORTRESS! EVERYONE ELSE, WE LEAVE IMMEDIATELY!
I'LL BE READY IN A JIFFY! I JUST HAVE TO GO GET SOMETHING FROM MY STUDITORY!

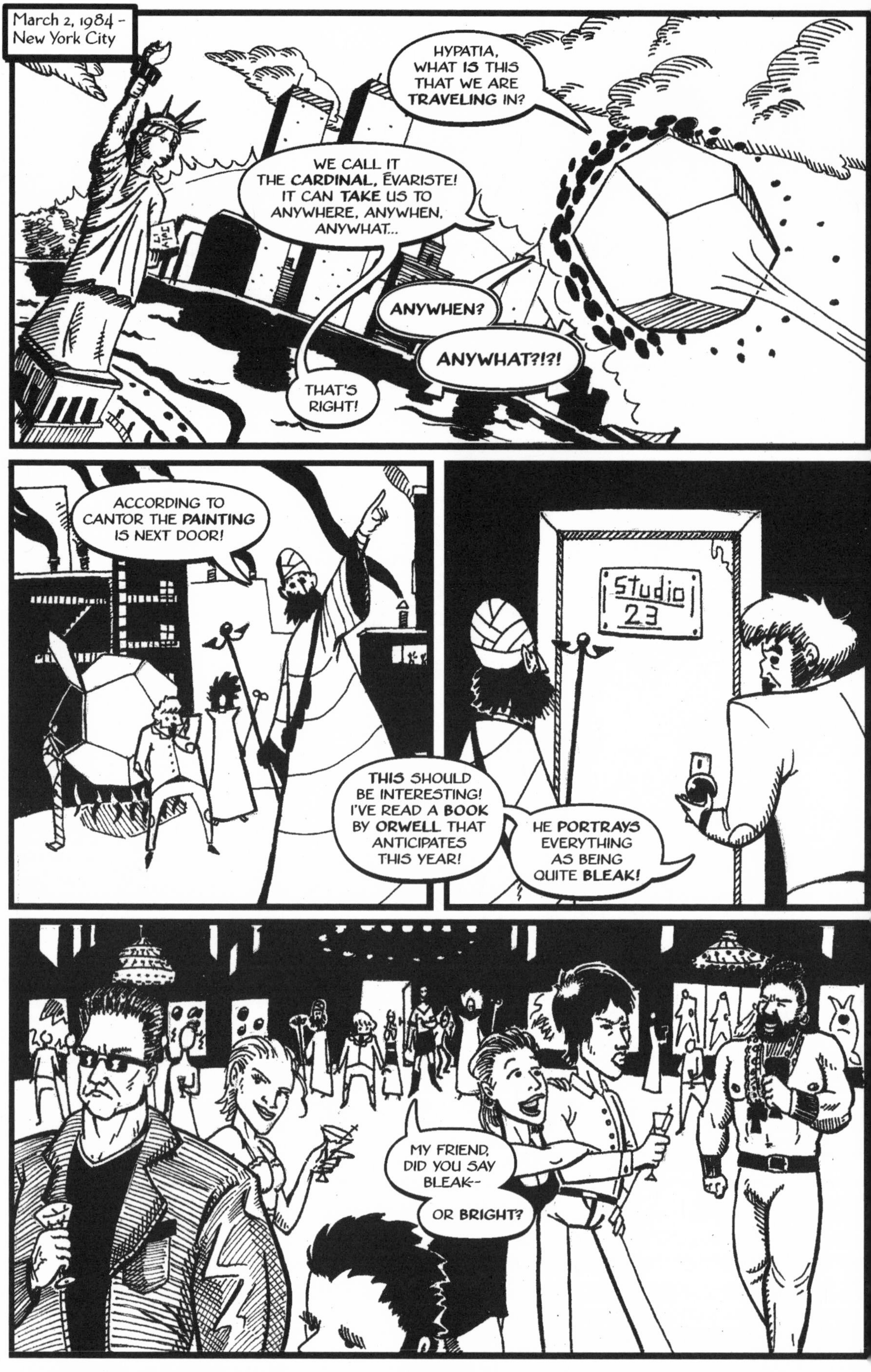
March 2, 1984 - New York City
HYPATIA, WHAT IS THIS THAT WE ARE TRAVELING IN?
WE CALL IT THE CARDINAL, ÉVARISTE! IT CAN TAKE US TO ANYWHERE, ANYWHEN, ANYWHAT...
ANYWHEN?
ANYWHAT?!?!
THAT'S RIGHT!
ACCORDING TO CANTOR THE PAINTING IS NEXT DOOR!
Studio 23
THIS SHOULD BE INTERESTING! I'VE READ A BOOK BY ORWELL THAT ANTICIPATES THIS YEAR!
HE PORTRAYS EVERYTHING AS BEING QUITE BLEAK!
MY FRIEND, DID YOU SAY BLEAK-
OR BRIGHT?

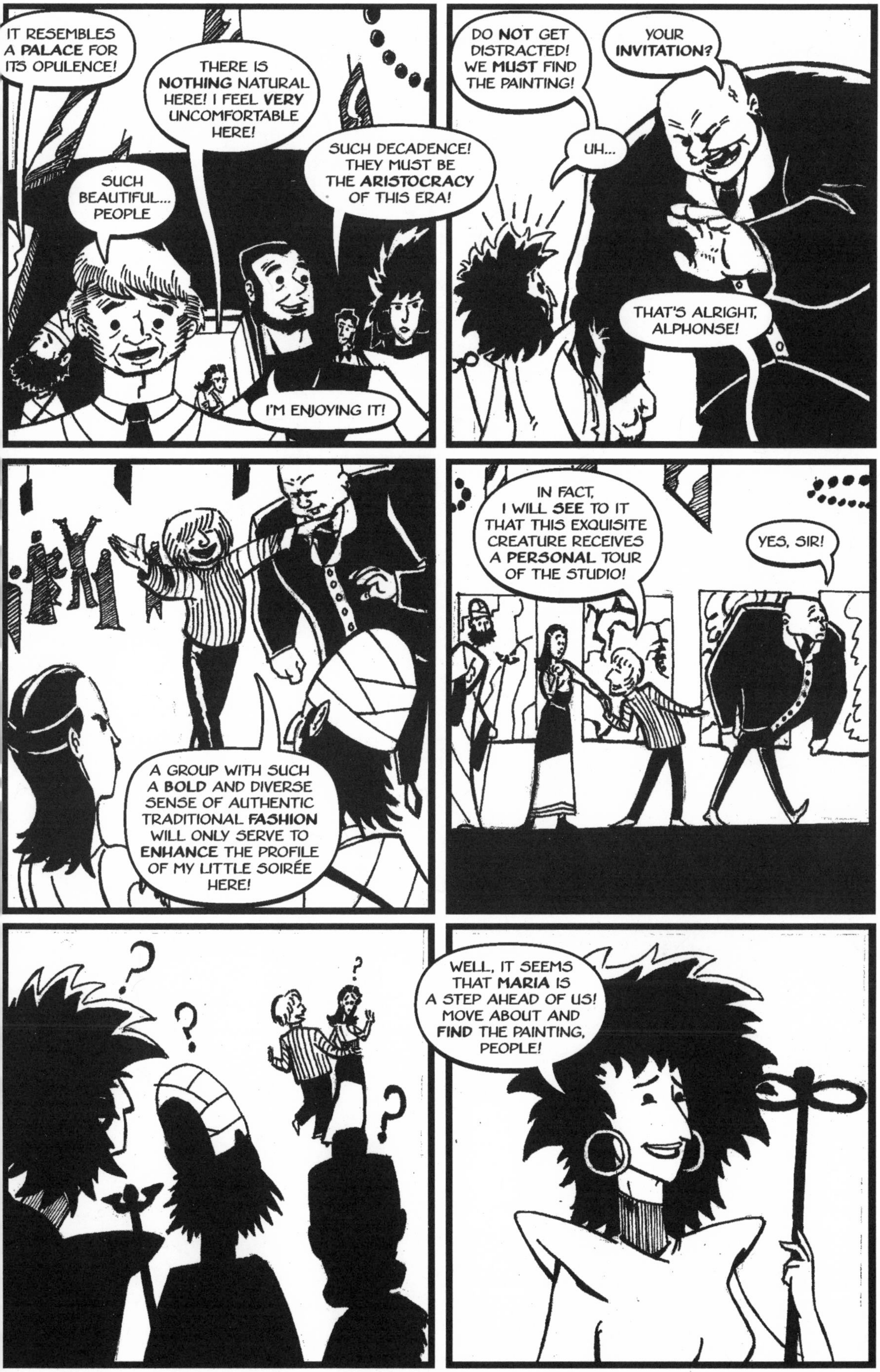
IT RESEMBLES A PALACE FOR ITS OPULENCE!
THERE IS NOTHING NATURAL HERE! I FEEL VERY UNCOMFORTABLE HERE!
SUCH BEAUTIFUL... PEOPLE
SUCH DECADENCE! THEY MUST BE THE ARISTOCRACY OF THIS ERA!
I'M ENJOYING IT!
DO NOT GET DISTRACTED! WE MUST FIND THE PAINTING!
YOUR INVITATION?
UH...
THAT'S ALRIGHT, ALPHONSE!
A GROUP WITH SUCH A BOLD AND DIVERSE SENSE OF AUTHENTIC TRADITIONAL FASHION WILL ONLY SERVE TO ENHANCE THE PROFILE OF MY LITTLE SOIRÉE HERE!
IN FACT, I WILL SEE TO IT THAT THIS EXQUISITE CREATURE RECEIVES A PERSONAL TOUR OF THE STUDIO!
YES, SIR!
?
?
?
?
WELL, IT SEEMS THAT MARIA IS A STEP AHEAD OF US! MOVE ABOUT AND FIND THE PAINTING, PEOPLE!

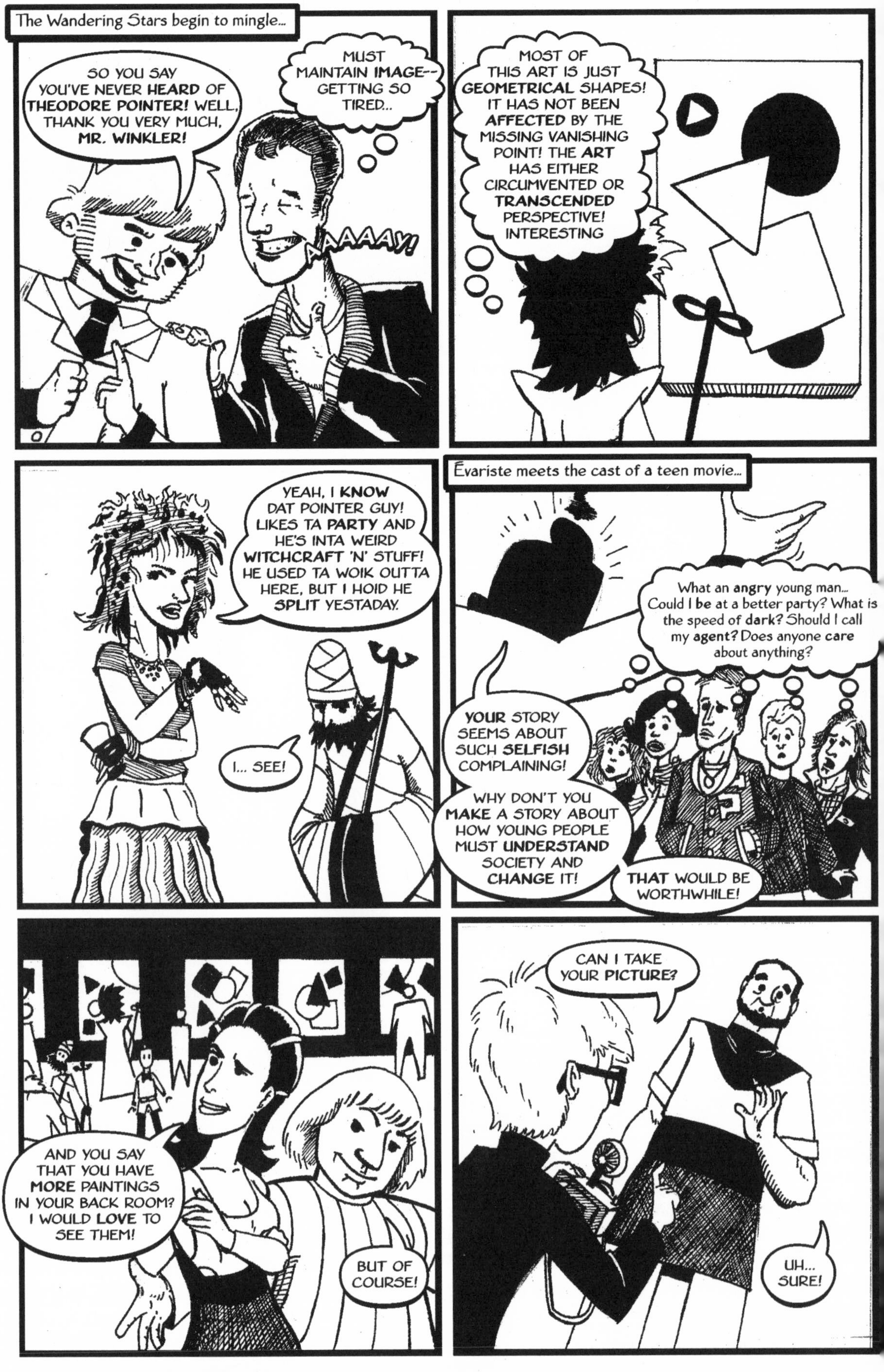
The Wandering Stars begin to mingle...
SO YOU SAY YOU'VE NEVER HEARD OF THEODORE POINTER! WELL, THANK YOU VERY MUCH, MR. WINKLER!
MUST MAINTAIN IMAGE-- GETTING SO TIRED...
AAAAAY!
MOST OF THIS ART IS JUST GEOMETRICAL SHAPES! IT HAS NOT BEEN AFFECTED BY THE MISSING VANISHING POINT! THE ART HAS EITHER CIRCUMVENTED OR TRANSCENDED PERSPECTIVE! INTERESTING
YEAH, I KNOW DAT POINTER GUY! LIKES TA PARTY AND HE'S INTA WEIRD WITCHCRAFT 'N' STUFF! HE USED TA WOIK OUTTA HERE, BUT I HOID HE SPLIT YESTADAY.
I... SEE!
Évariste meets the cast of a teen movie...
What an angry young man... Could I be at a better party? What is the speed of dark? Should I call my agent? Does anyone care about anything?
YOUR STORY SEEMS ABOUT SUCH SELFISH COMPLAINING!
WHY DON'T YOU MAKE A STORY ABOUT HOW YOUNG PEOPLE MUST UNDERSTAND SOCIETY AND CHANGE IT!
THAT WOULD BE WORTHWHILE!
AND YOU SAY THAT YOU HAVE MORE PAINTINGS IN YOUR BACK ROOM? I WOULD LOVE TO SEE THEM!
BUT OF COURSE!
CAN I TAKE YOUR PICTURE?
UH... SURE!

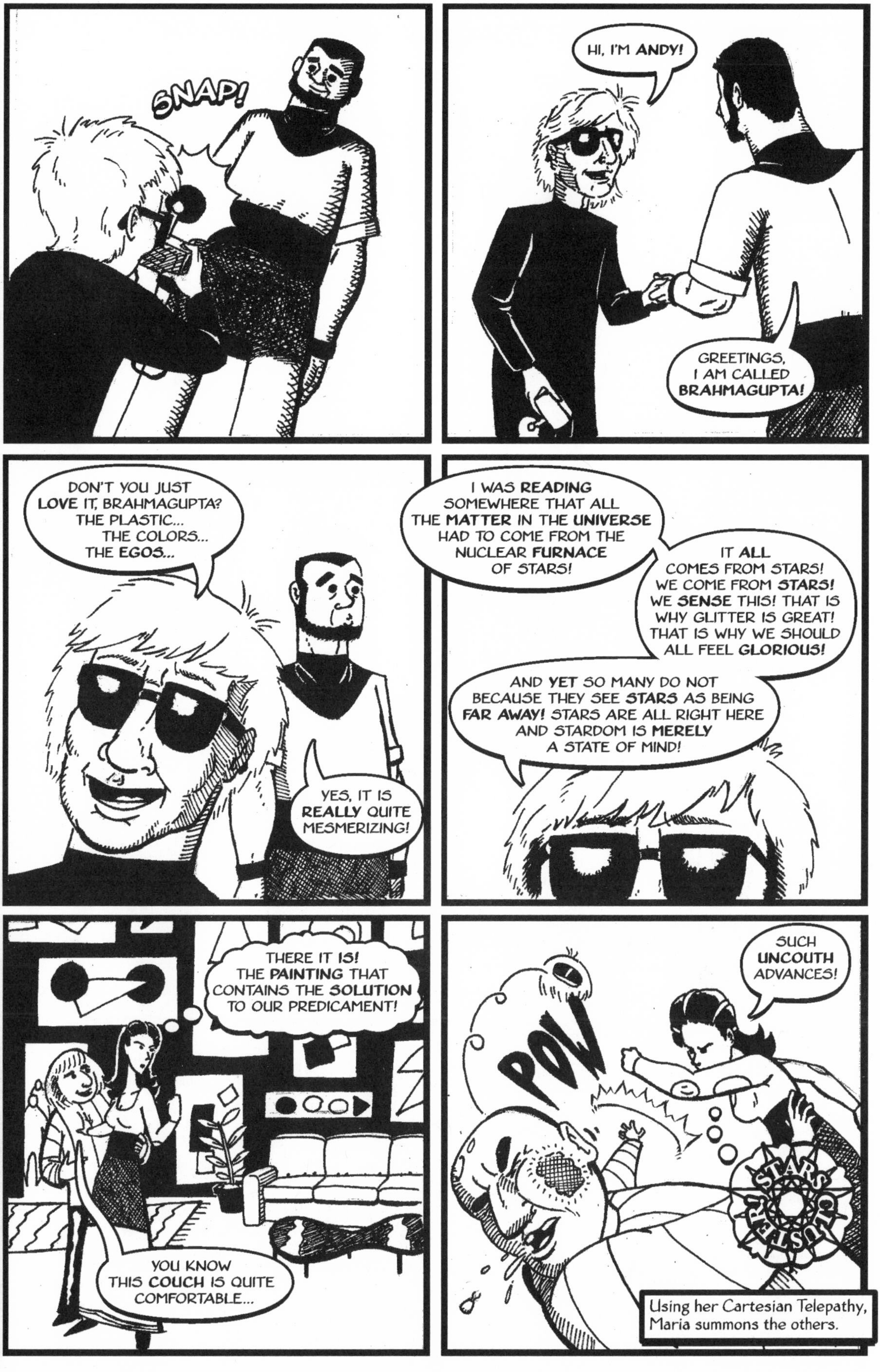
SNAP!
HI, I'M ANDY!
GREETINGS, I AM CALLED BRAHMAGUPTA!
DON'T YOU JUST LOVE IT, BRAHMAGUPTA? THE PLASTIC... THE COLORS... THE EGOS...
YES, IT IS REALLY QUITE MESMERIZING!
I WAS READING SOMEWHERE THAT ALL THE MATTER IN THE UNIVERSE HAD TO COME FROM THE NUCLEAR FURNACE OF STARS!
IT ALL COMES FROM STARS! WE COME FROM STARS! WE SENSE THIS! THAT IS WHY GLITTER IS GREAT! THAT IS WHY WE SHOULD ALL FEEL GLORIOUS!
AND YET SO MANY DO NOT BECAUSE THEY SEE STARS AS BEING FAR AWAY! STARS ARE ALL RIGHT HERE AND STARDOM IS MERELY A STATE OF MIND!
THERE IT IS! THE PAINTING THAT CONTAINS THE SOLUTION TO OUR PREDICAMENT!
YOU KNOW THIS COUCH IS QUITE COMFORTABLE...
SUCH UNCOUTH ADVANCES!
POW
Using her Cartesian Telepathy, Maria summons the others.

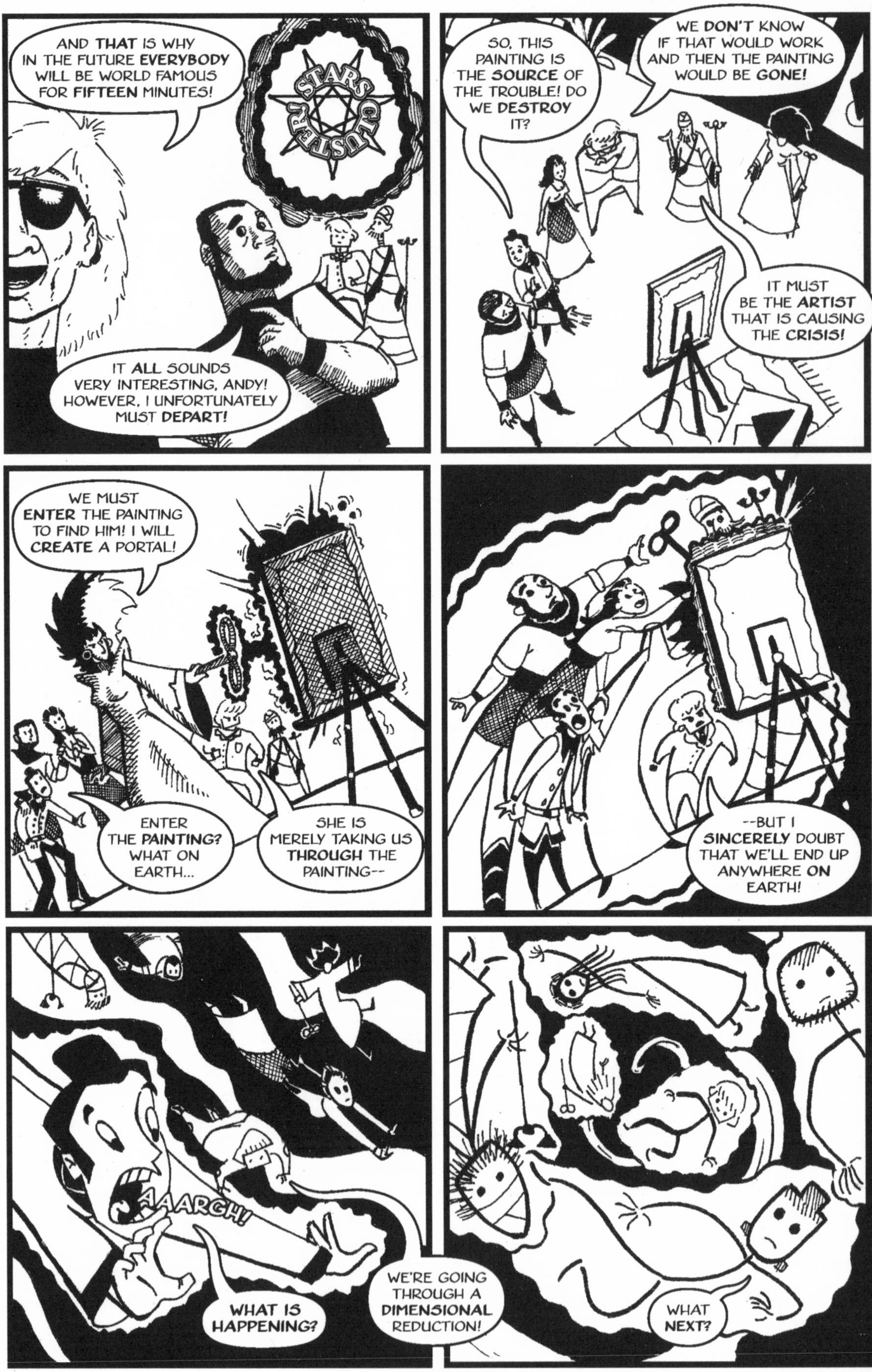
AND THAT IS WHY IN THE FUTURE EVERYBODY WILL BE WORLD FAMOUS FOR FIFTEEN MINUTES!
STARS CLUSTER!
IT ALL SOUNDS VERY INTERESTING, ANDY! HOWEVER, I UNFORTUNATELY MUST DEPART!
SO, THIS PAINTING IS THE SOURCE OF THE TROUBLE! DO WE DESTROY IT?
WE DON'T KNOW IF THAT WOULD WORK AND THEN THE PAINTING WOULD BE GONE!
IT MUST BE THE ARTIST THAT IS CAUSING THE CRISIS!
WE MUST ENTER THE PAINTING TO FIND HIM! I WILL CREATE A PORTAL!
ENTER THE PAINTING? WHAT ON EARTH...
SHE IS MERELY TAKING US THROUGH THE PAINTING--
--BUT I SINCERELY DOUBT THAT WE'LL END UP ANYWHERE ON EARTH!
AAARGH!
WHAT IS HAPPENING?
WE'RE GOING THROUGH A DIMENSIONAL REDUCTION!
WHAT NEXT?

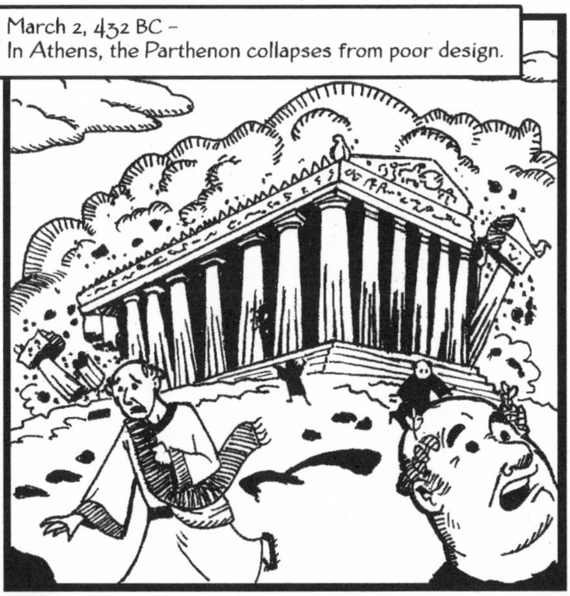
March 2, 432 BC –
In Athens, the Parthenon collapses from poor design.

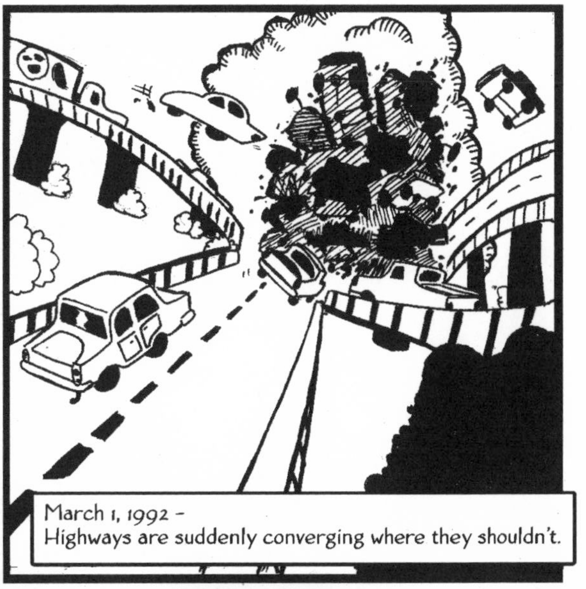
March 1, 1992 –
Highways are suddenly converging where they shouldn't.

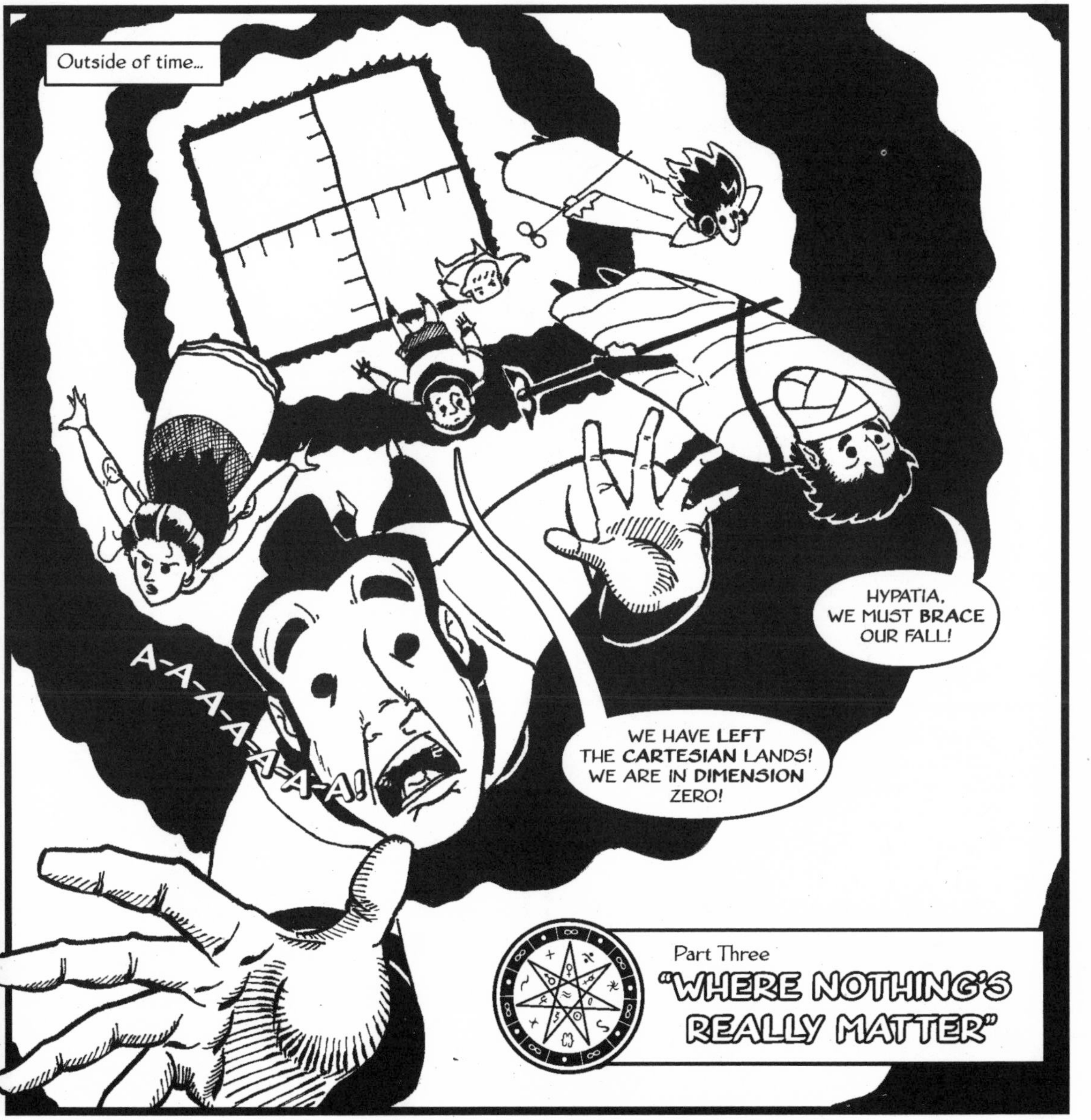
Outside of time...
HYPATIA, WE MUST BRACE OUR FALL!
A-A-A-A-A-A-A-A!
WE HAVE LEFT THE CARTESIAN LANDS! WE ARE IN DIMENSION ZERO!
Part Three
"WHERE NOTHING'S REALLY MATTER"

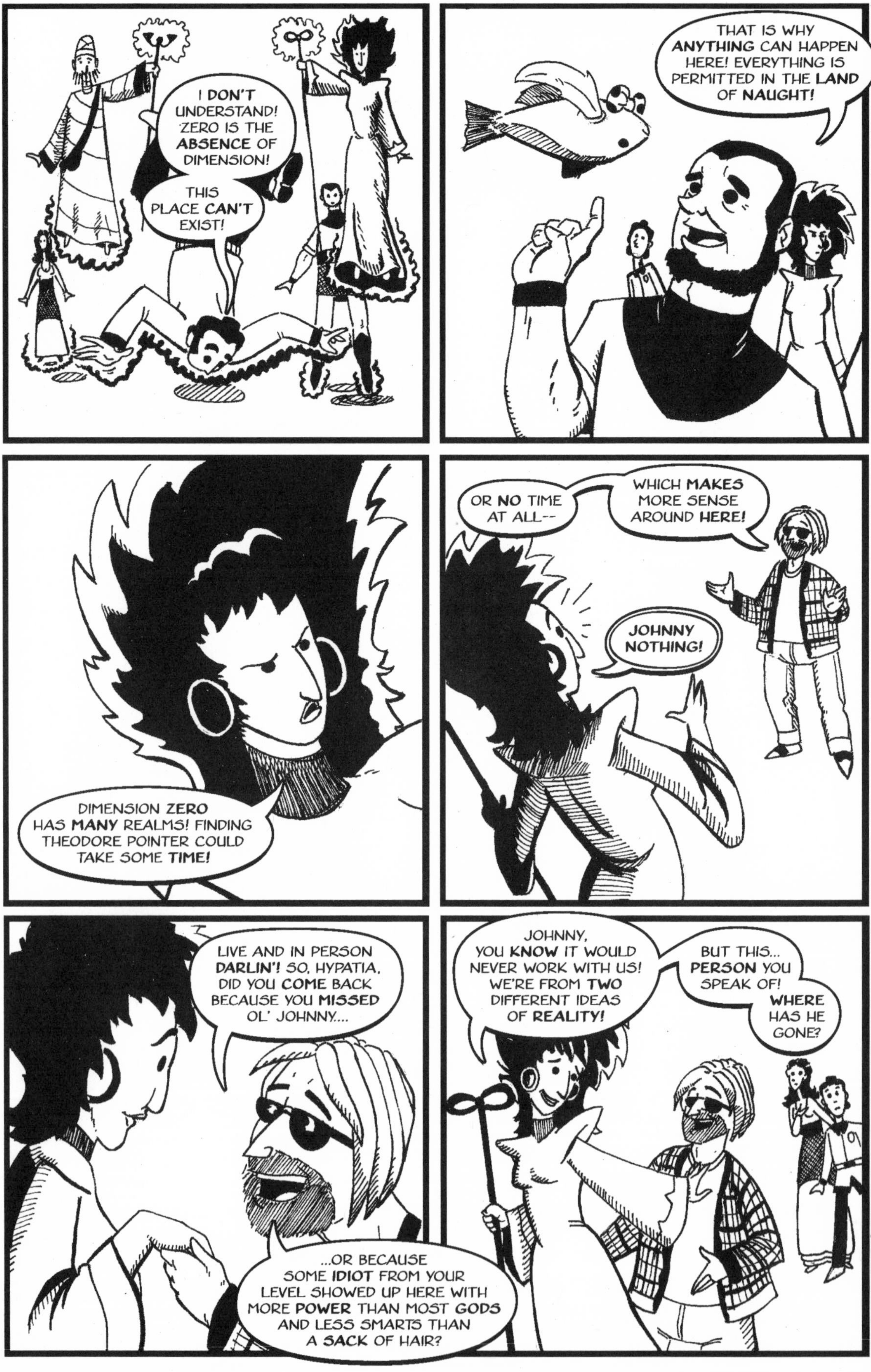
I DON'T UNDERSTAND! ZERO IS THE ABSENCE OF DIMENSION!
THIS PLACE CAN'T EXIST!
THAT IS WHY ANYTHING CAN HAPPEN HERE! EVERYTHING IS PERMITTED IN THE LAND OF NAUGHT!
DIMENSION ZERO HAS MANY REALMS! FINDING THEODORE POINTER COULD TAKE SOME TIME!
OR NO TIME AT ALL--
WHICH MAKES MORE SENSE AROUND HERE!
JOHNNY NOTHING!
LIVE AND IN PERSON DARLIN'! SO, HYPATIA, DID YOU COME BACK BECAUSE YOU MISSED OL' JOHNNY....
...OR BECAUSE SOME IDIOT FROM YOUR LEVEL SHOWED UP HERE WITH MORE POWER THAN MOST GODS AND LESS SMARTS THAN A SACK OF HAIR?
JOHNNY, YOU KNOW IT WOULD NEVER WORK WITH US! WE'RE FROM TWO DIFFERENT IDEAS OF REALITY!
BUT THIS... PERSON YOU SPEAK OF! WHERE HAS HE GONE?

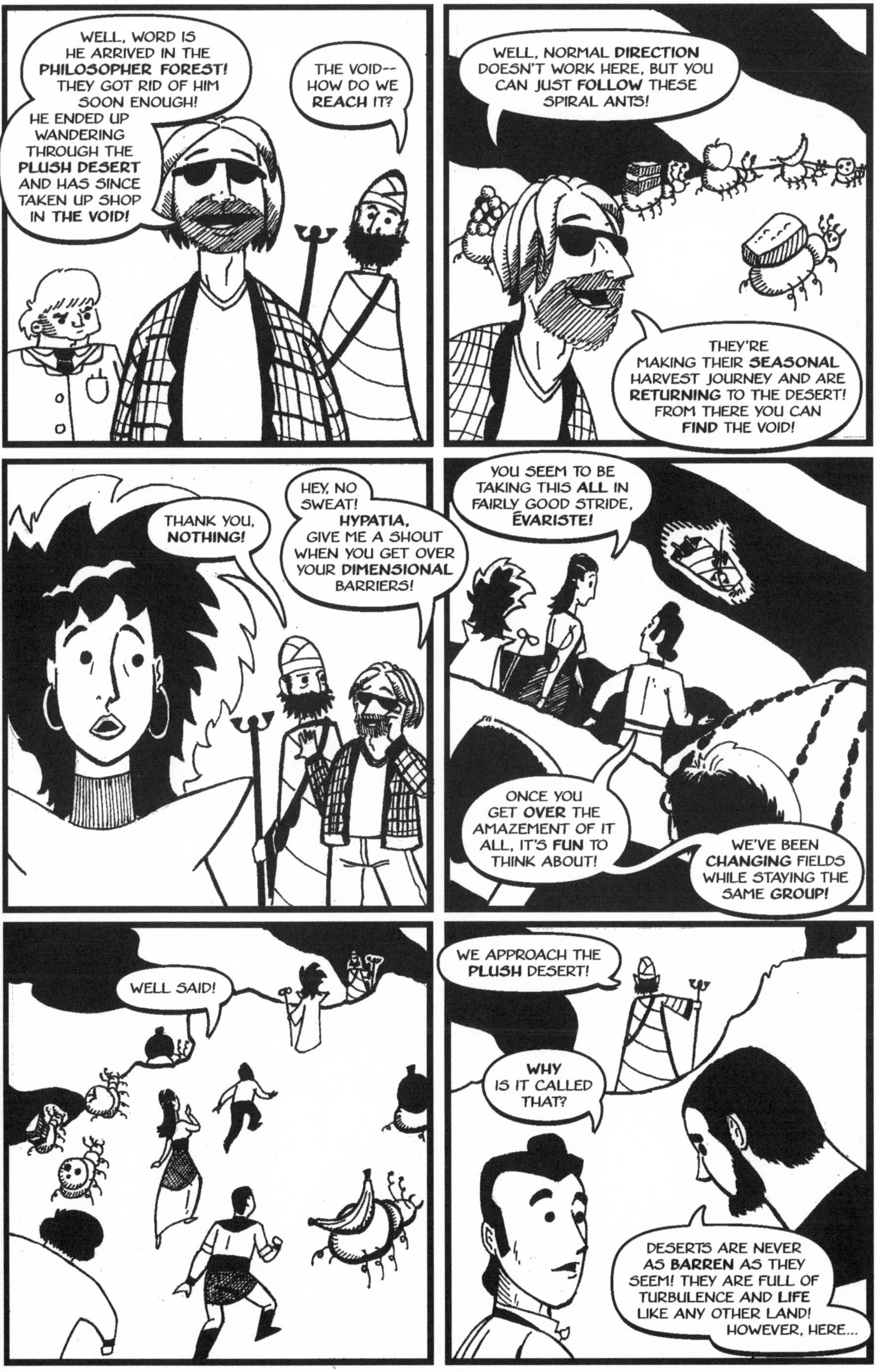

WELL, WORD IS HE ARRIVED IN THE PHILOSOPHER FOREST! THEY GOT RID OF HIM SOON ENOUGH!
HE ENDED UP WANDERING THROUGH THE PLUSH DESERT AND HAS SINCE TAKEN UP SHOP IN THE VOID!
THE VOID-- HOW DO WE REACH IT?
WELL, NORMAL DIRECTION DOESN'T WORK HERE, BUT YOU CAN JUST FOLLOW THESE SPIRAL ANTS!
THEY'RE MAKING THEIR SEASONAL HARVEST JOURNEY AND ARE RETURNING TO THE DESERT! FROM THERE YOU CAN FIND THE VOID!
THANK YOU, NOTHING!
HEY, NO SWEAT! HYPATIA, GIVE ME A SHOUT WHEN YOU GET OVER YOUR DIMENSIONAL BARRIERS!
YOU SEEM TO BE TAKING THIS ALL IN FAIRLY GOOD STRIDE, ÉVARISTE!
ONCE YOU GET OVER THE AMAZEMENT OF IT ALL, IT'S FUN TO THINK ABOUT!
WE'VE BEEN CHANGING FIELDS WHILE STAYING THE SAME GROUP!
WELL SAID!
WE APPROACH THE PLUSH DESERT!
WHY IS IT CALLED THAT?
DESERTS ARE NEVER AS BARREN AS THEY SEEM! THEY ARE FULL OF TURBULENCE AND LIFE LIKE ANY OTHER LAND! HOWEVER, HERE...

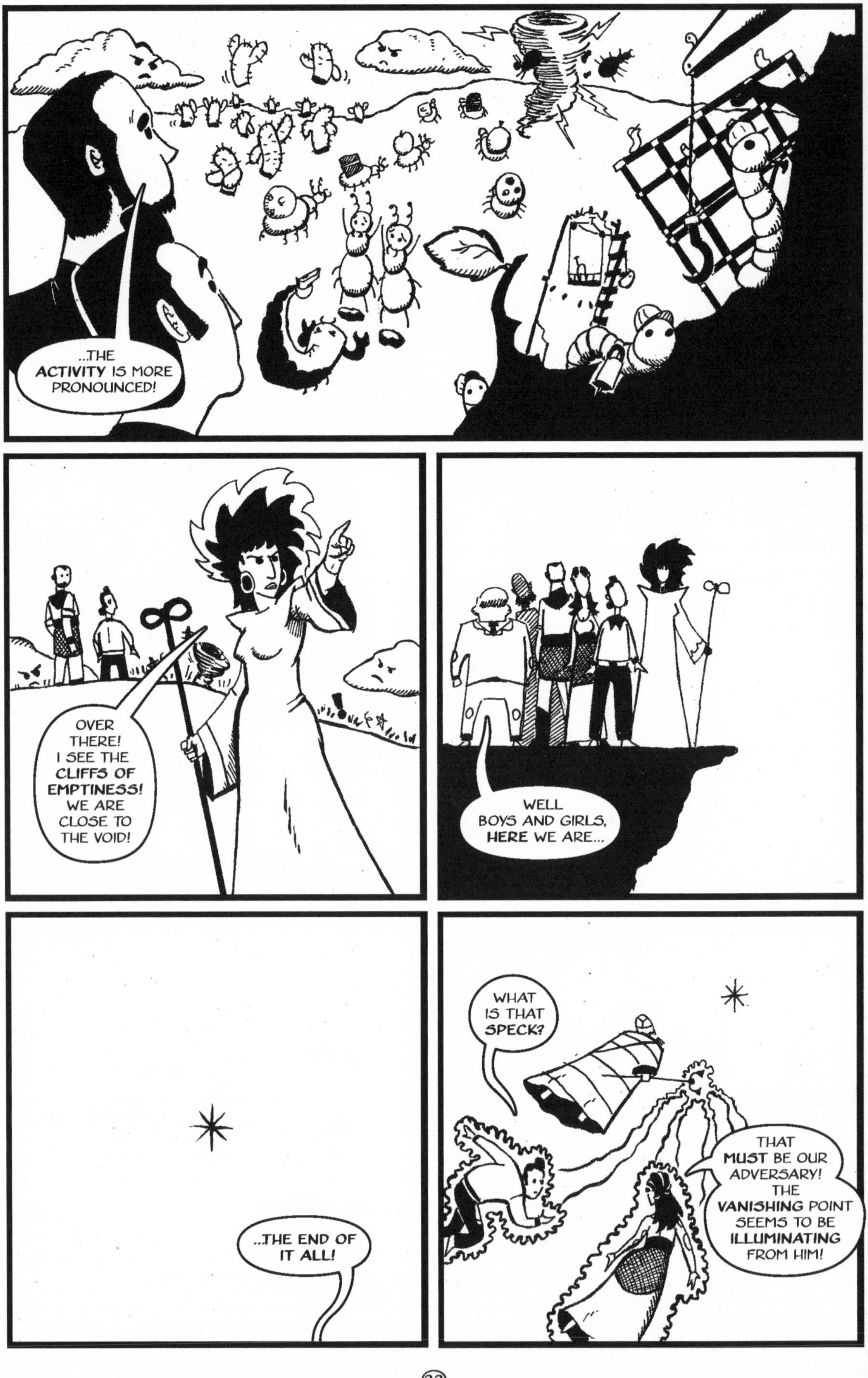
..THE ACTIVITY IS MORE PRONOUNCED!
OVER THERE! I SEE THE CLIFFS OF EMPTINESS! WE ARE CLOSE TO THE VOID!
WELL BOYS AND GIRLS, HERE WE ARE...
..THE END OF IT ALL!
WHAT IS THAT SPECK?
THAT MUST BE OUR ADVERSARY! THE VANISHING POINT SEEMS TO BE ILLUMINATING FROM HIM!

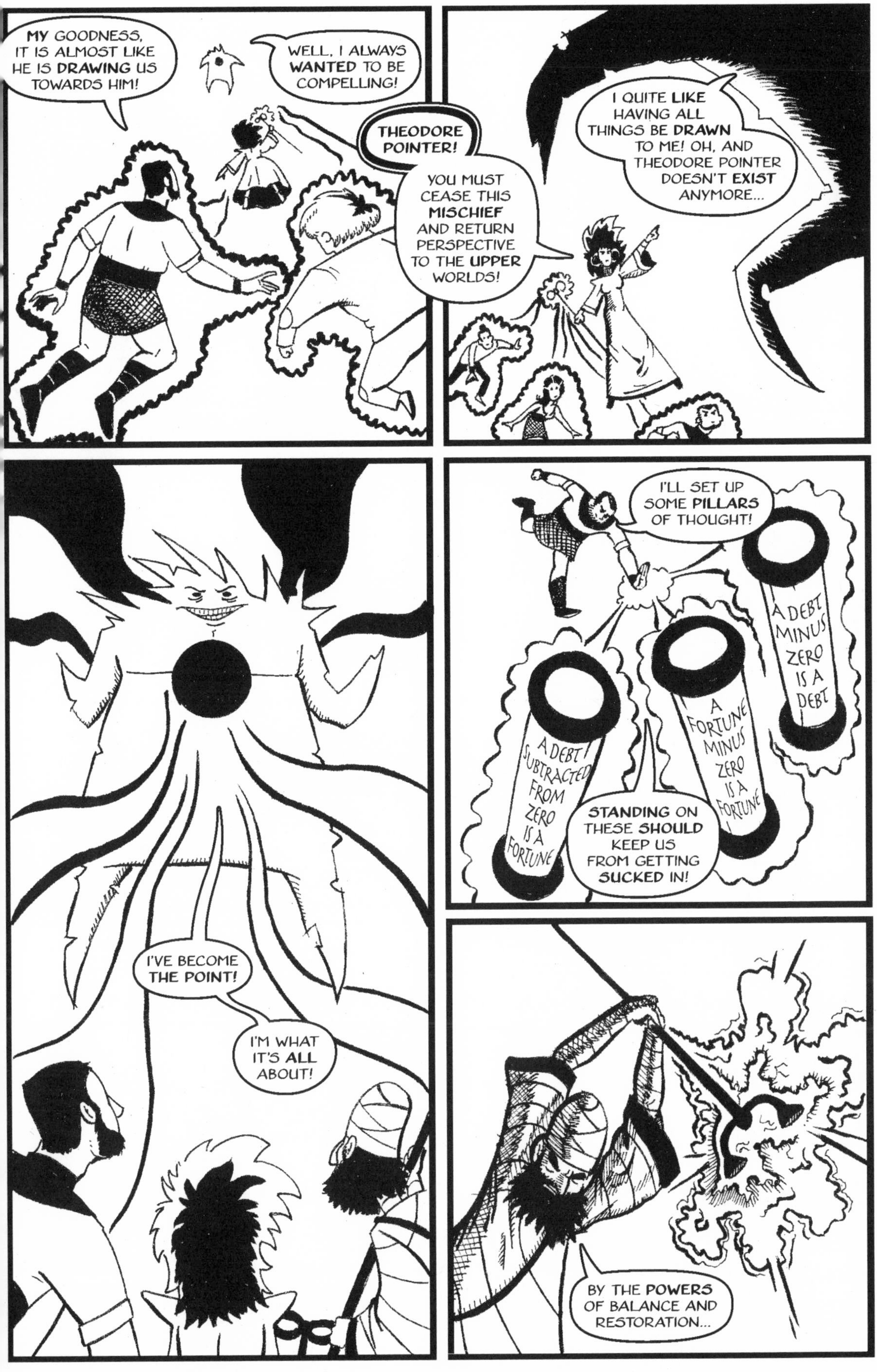
MY GOODNESS, IT IS ALMOST LIKE HE IS DRAWING US TOWARDS HIM!
WELL, I ALWAYS WANTED TO BE COMPELLING!
THEODORE POINTER!
YOU MUST CEASE THIS MISCHIEF AND RETURN PERSPECTIVE TO THE UPPER WORLDS!
I QUITE LIKE HAVING ALL THINGS BE DRAWN TO ME! OH, AND THEODORE POINTER DOESN'T EXIST ANYMORE...
I'VE BECOME THE POINT!
I'M WHAT IT'S ALL ABOUT!
I'LL SET UP SOME PILLARS OF THOUGHT!
A DEBT MINUS ZERO IS A DEBT
A FORTUNE MINUS ZERO IS A FORTUNE
A DEBT SUBTRACTED FROM ZERO IS A FORTUNE
STANDING ON THESE SHOULD KEEP US FROM GETTING SUCKED IN!
BY THE POWERS OF BALANCE AND RESTORATION...

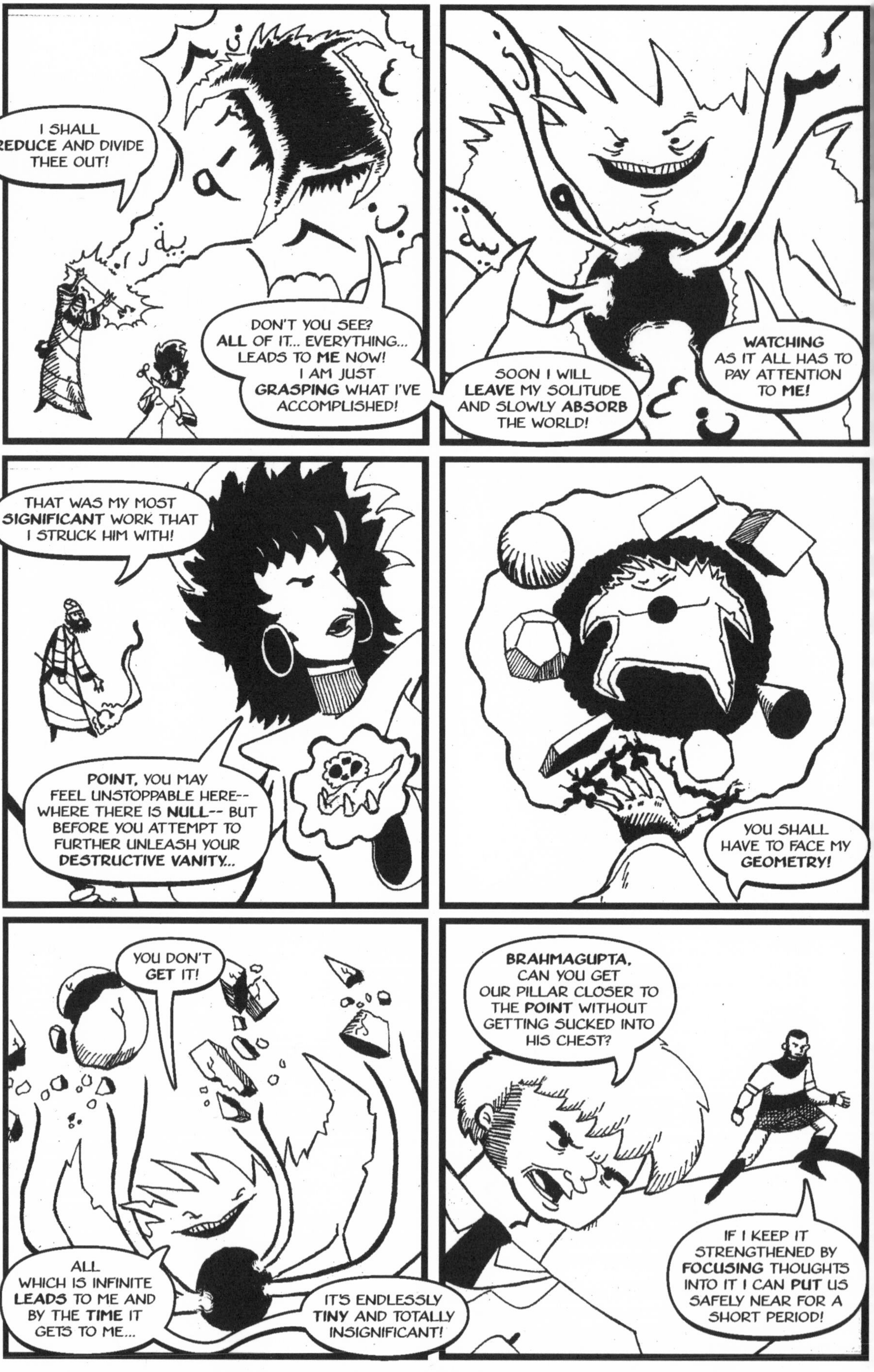

I SHALL REDUCE AND DIVIDE THEE OUT!
DON'T YOU SEE? ALL OF IT... EVERYTHING... LEADS TO ME NOW! I AM JUST GRASPING WHAT I'VE ACCOMPLISHED!
SOON I WILL LEAVE MY SOLITUDE AND SLOWLY ABSORB THE WORLD!
WATCHING AS IT ALL HAS TO PAY ATTENTION TO ME!
THAT WAS MY MOST SIGNIFICANT WORK THAT I STRUCK HIM WITH!
POINT, YOU MAY FEEL UNSTOPPABLE HERE-- WHERE THERE IS NULL-- BUT BEFORE YOU ATTEMPT TO FURTHER UNLEASH YOUR DESTRUCTIVE VANITY...
YOU SHALL HAVE TO FACE MY GEOMETRY!
YOU DON'T GET IT!
ALL WHICH IS INFINITE LEADS TO ME AND BY THE TIME IT GETS TO ME...
IT'S ENDLESSLY TINY AND TOTALLY INSIGNIFICANT!
BRAHMAGUPTA, CAN YOU GET OUR PILLAR CLOSER TO THE POINT WITHOUT GETTING SUCKED INTO HIS CHEST?
IF I KEEP IT STRENGTHENED BY FOCUSING THOUGHTS INTO IT I CAN PUT US SAFELY NEAR FOR A SHORT PERIOD!

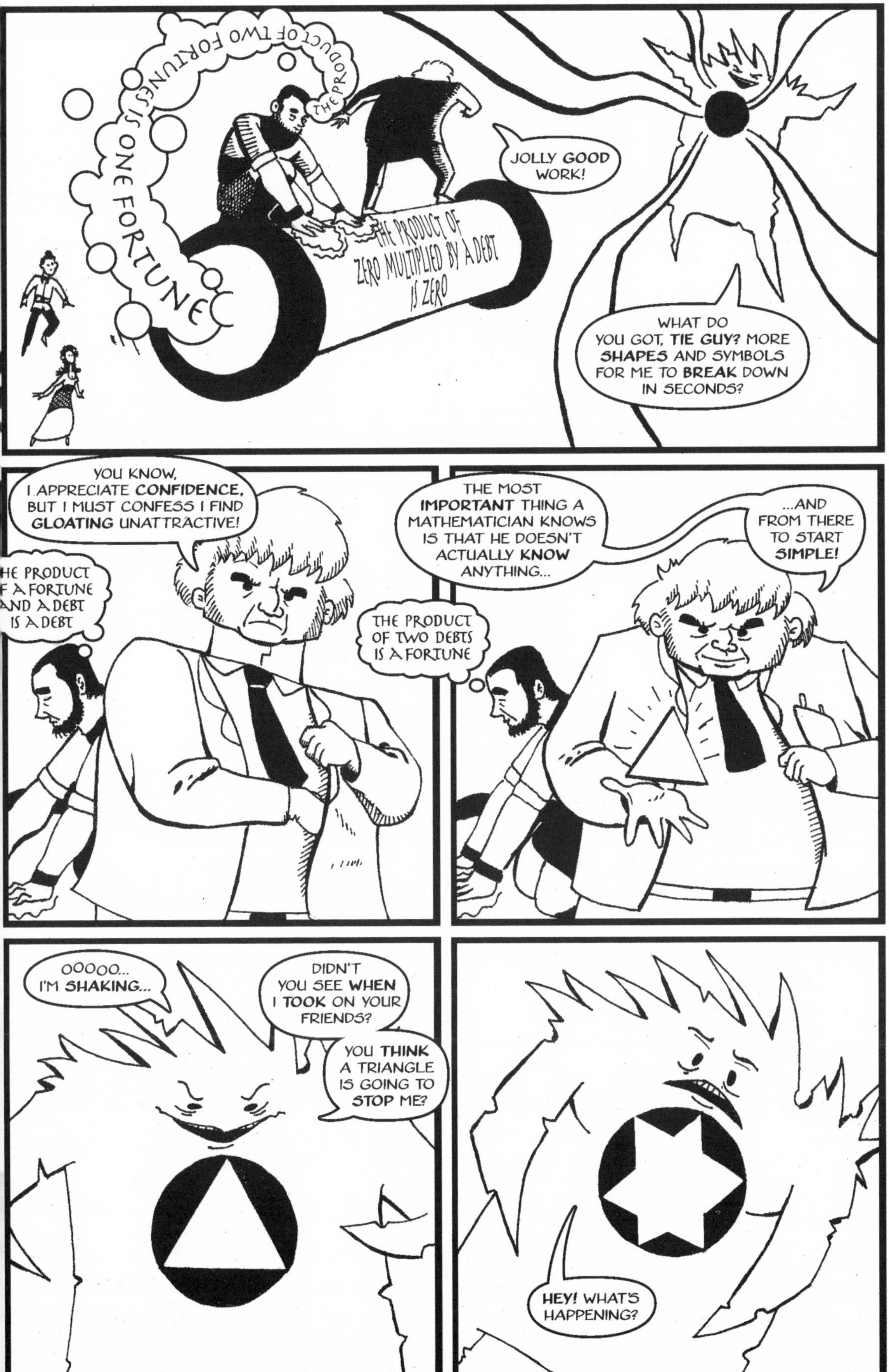
THE PRODUCT OF TWO FORTUNES IS ONE FORTUNE
THE PRODUCT OF ZERO MULTIPLIED BY A DEBT IS ZERO
JOLLY GOOD WORK!
WHAT DO YOU GOT, TIE GUY? MORE SHAPES AND SYMBOLS FOR ME TO BREAK DOWN IN SECONDS?
YOU KNOW, I APPRECIATE CONFIDENCE, BUT I MUST CONFESS I FIND GLOATING UNATTRACTIVE!
HE PRODUCT F A FORTUNE AND A DEBT IS A DEBT
THE PRODUCT OF TWO DEBTS IS A FORTUNE
THE MOST IMPORTANT THING A MATHEMATICIAN KNOWS IS THAT HE DOESN'T ACTUALLY KNOW ANYTHING...
...AND FROM THERE TO START SIMPLE!
OOOOO... I'M SHAKING...
DIDN'T YOU SEE WHEN I TOOK ON YOUR FRIENDS?
YOU THINK A TRIANGLE IS GOING TO STOP ME?
HEY! WHAT'S HAPPENING?

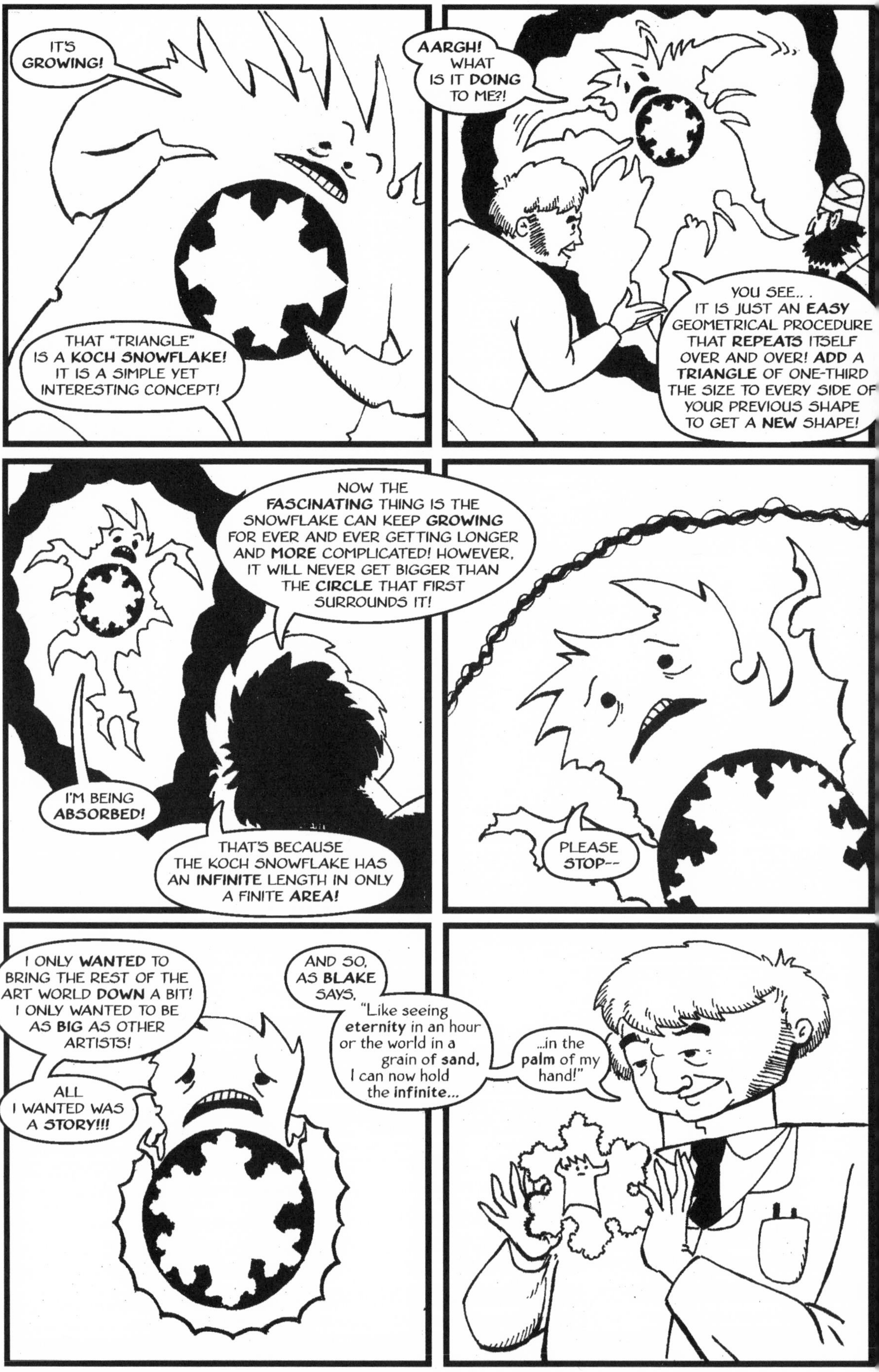
IT'S GROWING!
THAT "TRIANGLE" IS A KOCH SNOWFLAKE! IT IS A SIMPLE YET INTERESTING CONCEPT!
AARGH! WHAT IS IT DOING TO ME?!
YOU SEE.. . IT IS JUST AN EASY GEOMETRICAL PROCEDURE THAT REPEATS ITSELF OVER AND OVER! ADD A TRIANGLE OF ONE-THIRD THE SIZE TO EVERY SIDE OF YOUR PREVIOUS SHAPE TO GET A NEW SHAPE!
NOW THE FASCINATING THING IS THE SNOWFLAKE CAN KEEP GROWING FOR EVER AND EVER GETTING LONGER AND MORE COMPLICATED! HOWEVER, IT WILL NEVER GET BIGGER THAN THE CIRCLE THAT FIRST SURROUNDS IT!
I'M BEING ABSORBED!
THAT'S BECAUSE THE KOCH SNOWFLAKE HAS AN INFINITE LENGTH IN ONLY A FINITE AREA!
PLEASE STOP--
I ONLY WANTED TO BRING THE REST OF THE ART WORLD DOWN A BIT! I ONLY WANTED TO BE AS BIG AS OTHER ARTISTS!
ALL I WANTED WAS A STORY!!!
AND SO, AS BLAKE SAYS, "Like seeing eternity in an hour or the world in a grain of sand, I can now hold the infinite...
...in the palm of my hand!"

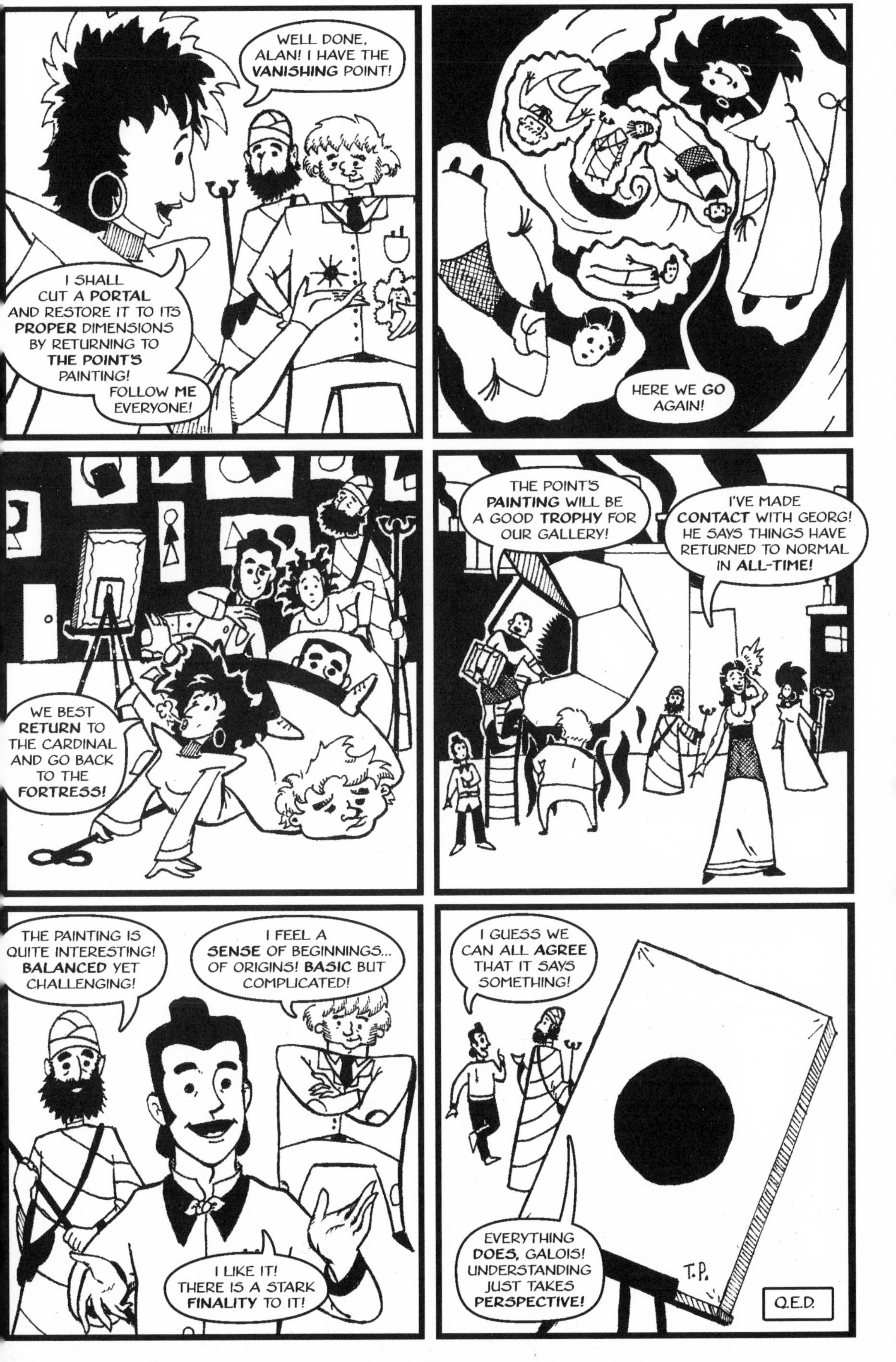
WELL DONE, ALAN! I HAVE THE VANISHING POINT!
I SHALL CUT A PORTAL AND RESTORE IT TO ITS PROPER DIMENSIONS BY RETURNING TO THE POINT'S PAINTING!
FOLLOW ME EVERYONE!
HERE WE GO AGAIN!
WE BEST RETURN TO THE CARDINAL AND GO BACK TO THE FORTRESS!
THE POINT'S PAINTING WILL BE A GOOD TROPHY FOR OUR GALLERY!
I'VE MADE CONTACT WITH GEORG! HE SAYS THINGS HAVE RETURNED TO NORMAL IN ALL-TIME!
THE PAINTING IS QUITE INTERESTING! BALANCED YET CHALLENGING!
I FEEL A SENSE OF BEGINNINGS... OF ORIGINS! BASIC BUT COMPLICATED!
I LIKE IT! THERE IS A STARK FINALITY TO IT!
I GUESS WE CAN ALL AGREE THAT IT SAYS SOMETHING!
EVERYTHING DOES, GALOIS! UNDERSTANDING JUST TAKES PERSPECTIVE!
T.P.
Q.E.D.

Wanderings

We hope you enjoyed the first story of The Wandering Stars.
Now, please join Alan Turing as he gives a brief lesson on the Koch Snowflake.

The Koch Snowflake demonstrates a simple yet fascinating relationship between the limited and the never ending.

Named after Niels Fabian Helge von Koch, a Swedish mathematician born in 1870, the basic idea of the Koch Snowflake starts with an equilateral triangle.

One then adds triangles that have sides a third of the length of the previous triangle to the middle of each side.

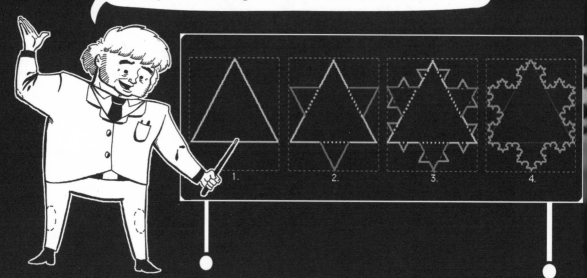

The first iteration makes the Star of David. Repeat this process on every side of the new shape. As the snowflake evolves with every iteration, a more and more intricate pattern forms while maintaining the initial triangle's three lines of symmetry.

The number of triangles that are added to each snowflake increases by a factor of four for each iteration (3,12,48…).

However, the area of each new set of triangles decreases significantly. The area's growth factor is ~1.333 for the first iteration while it is ~1.002 for the seventh iteration.

By the 23rd iteration the snowflake's area barely increases at all. In fact, the area will never grow larger than the circle defined by the three vertices of the first triangle.

The perimeter of the snowflake is not nearly as restrained. Each side is opened and a third of its length is added to make the new triangle on that side.

Therefore the distance around the snowflake will constantly increase by a third. Its rate of growth will never waiver at a stable factor of one and one third or ~1.333.

Imagining that the **Koch** Snowflake can forever increase in complexity, we can conceive of an **infinite** first dimensional length surrounding a **finite** two dimensional area. Such are the **dreams** of math.

~ approximately

BOOK TWO

Under capitalism, man exploits man.
Under communism, it's just the opposite.

- Old saying often attributed to
John Kenneth Galbraith, Economist
1908 – 2006

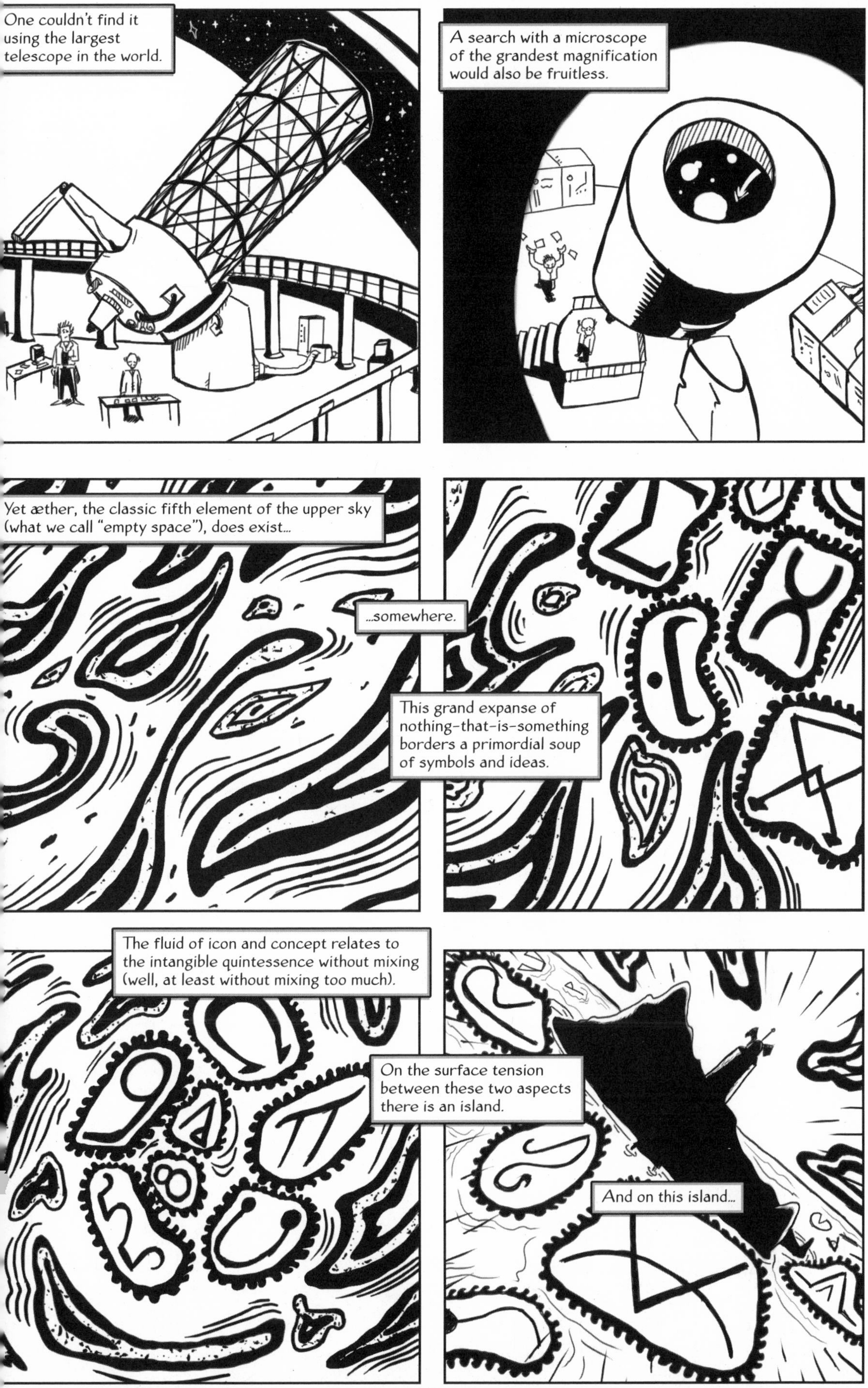
One couldn't find it using the largest telescope in the world.
A search with a microscope of the grandest magnification would also be fruitless.
Yet æther, the classic fifth element of the upper sky (what we call "empty space"), does exist...
...somewhere.
This grand expanse of nothing-that-is-something borders a primordial soup of symbols and ideas.
The fluid of icon and concept relates to the intangible quintessence without mixing (well, at least without mixing too much).
On the surface tension between these two aspects there is an island.
And on this island...

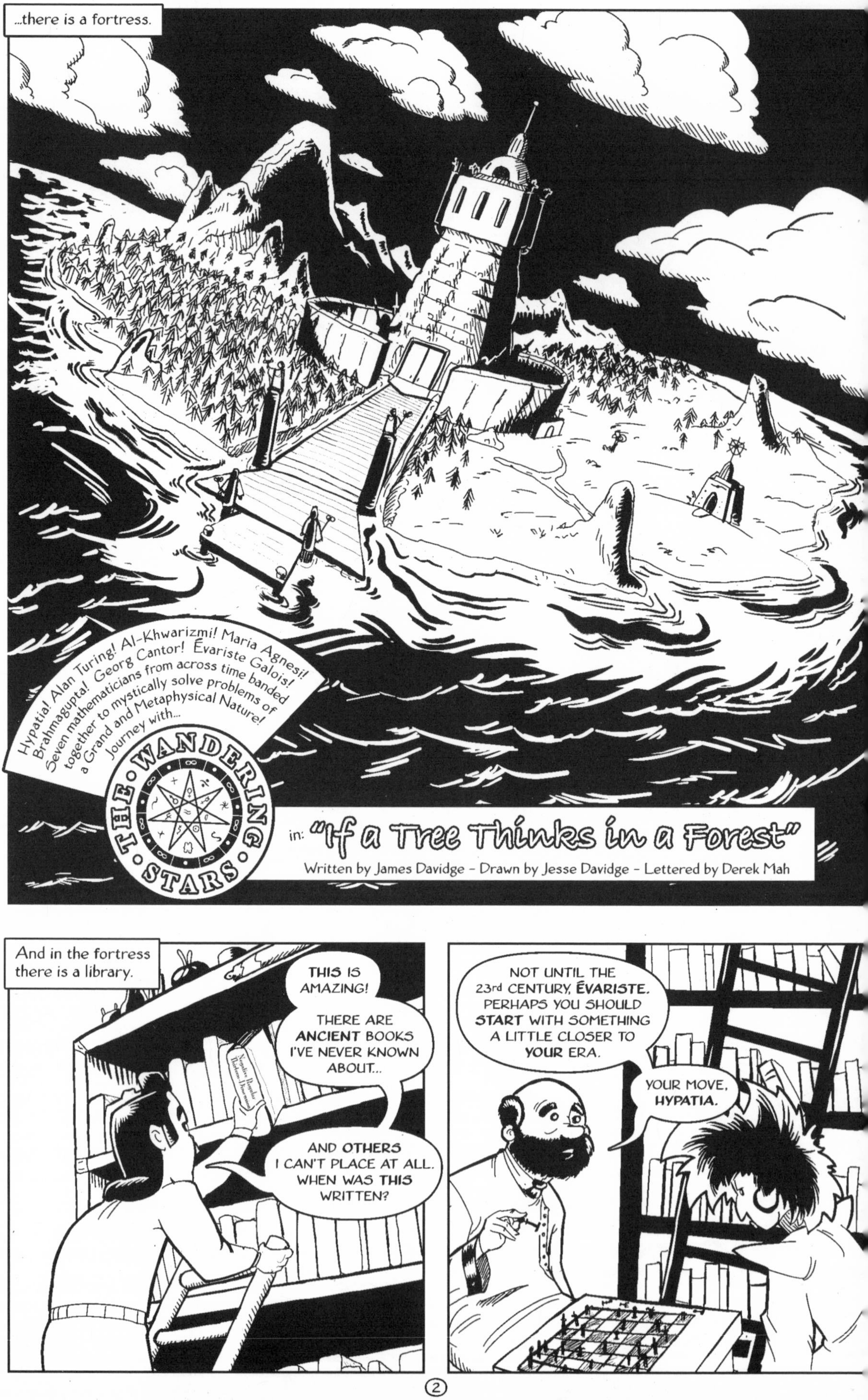
...there is a fortress.
Hypatia! Alan Turing! Al-Khwarizmi! Maria Agnesi! Brahmagupta! Georg Cantor! Évariste Galois! Seven mathematicians from across time banded together to mystically solve problems of a Grand and Metaphysical Nature! Journey with...
THE WANDERING STARS
in: "If a Tree Thinks in a Forest"
Written by James Davidge – Drawn by Jesse Davidge – Lettered by Derek Mah
And in the fortress there is a library.
THIS IS AMAZING!
THERE ARE ANCIENT BOOKS I'VE NEVER KNOWN ABOUT...
AND OTHERS I CAN'T PLACE AT ALL. WHEN WAS THIS WRITTEN?
NOT UNTIL THE 23rd CENTURY, ÉVARISTE. PERHAPS YOU SHOULD START WITH SOMETHING A LITTLE CLOSER TO YOUR ERA.
YOUR MOVE, HYPATIA.

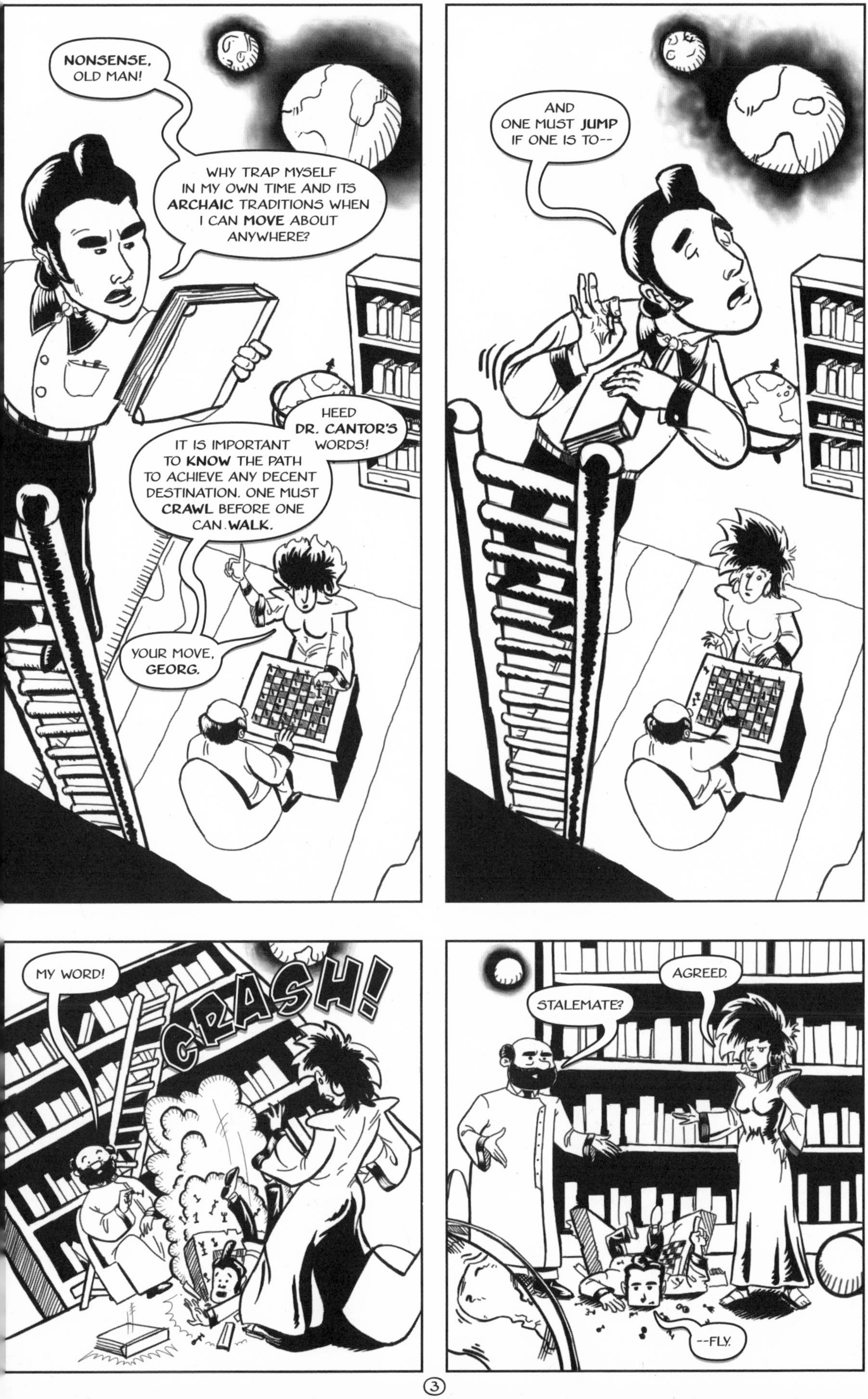
NONSENSE, OLD MAN!
WHY TRAP MYSELF IN MY OWN TIME AND ITS ARCHAIC TRADITIONS WHEN I CAN MOVE ABOUT ANYWHERE?
HEED DR. CANTOR'S WORDS!
IT IS IMPORTANT TO KNOW THE PATH TO ACHIEVE ANY DECENT DESTINATION. ONE MUST CRAWL BEFORE ONE CAN WALK.
YOUR MOVE, GEORG.
AND ONE MUST JUMP IF ONE IS TO--
MY WORD!
CRASH!
STALEMATE?
AGREED.
--FLY.

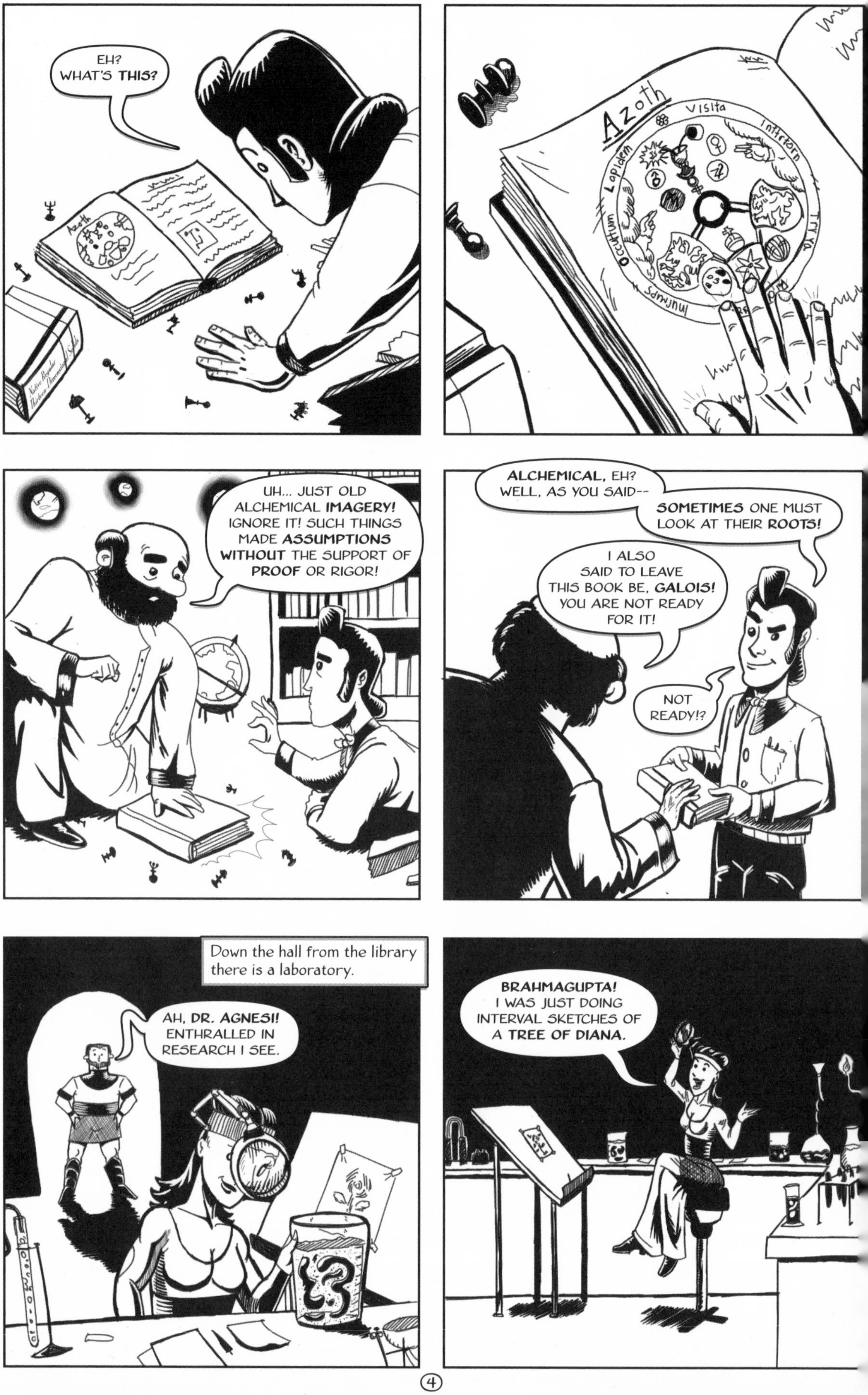
EH? WHAT'S THIS?
Azoth
Visita
UH... JUST OLD ALCHEMICAL IMAGERY! IGNORE IT! SUCH THINGS MADE ASSUMPTIONS WITHOUT THE SUPPORT OF PROOF OR RIGOR!
ALCHEMICAL, EH? WELL, AS YOU SAID--
SOMETIMES ONE MUST LOOK AT THEIR ROOTS!
I ALSO SAID TO LEAVE THIS BOOK BE, GALOIS! YOU ARE NOT READY FOR IT!
NOT READY!?
Down the hall from the library there is a laboratory.
AH, DR. AGNESI! ENTHRALLED IN RESEARCH I SEE.
BRAHMAGUPTA! I WAS JUST DOING INTERVAL SKETCHES OF A TREE OF DIANA.

TREE OF DIANA?

WATCH AS I PUT A **DROP** OF MERCURY INTO THIS NITRATE OF **SILVER!**

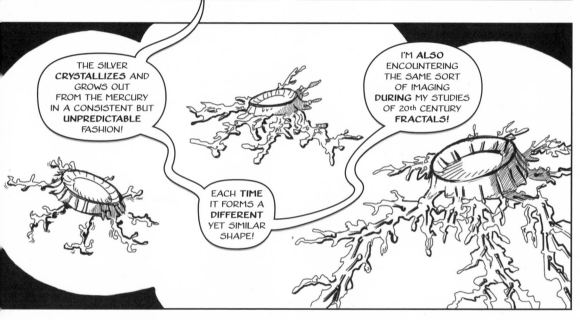

THE SILVER **CRYSTALLIZES** AND GROWS OUT FROM THE MERCURY IN A CONSISTENT BUT **UNPREDICTABLE** FASHION!

EACH **TIME** IT FORMS A **DIFFERENT** YET SIMILAR SHAPE!

I'M **ALSO** ENCOUNTERING THE SAME SORT OF IMAGING **DURING** MY STUDIES OF 20th CENTURY **FRACTALS!**

SO **MANY** IDEAS OF THE FUTURE TO LEARN! WHAT ARE FRACTALS, **MARIA?**

MATHEMATICAL PROCESSES THAT **REPEAT** OVER AND OVER AGAIN TO FORM **WONDERFUL** IMAGES.

THAT WHICH **SEEMS** COMPLEX OFTEN STEMS FROM THE MOST **BASIC** CONCEPT.

Not far from the laboratory is a garden.

I MUST SAY, **TURING,** I ALWAYS FIND IT REFRESHING TO GO FOR A WALK IN THE **BOTANICAL** GARDENS!

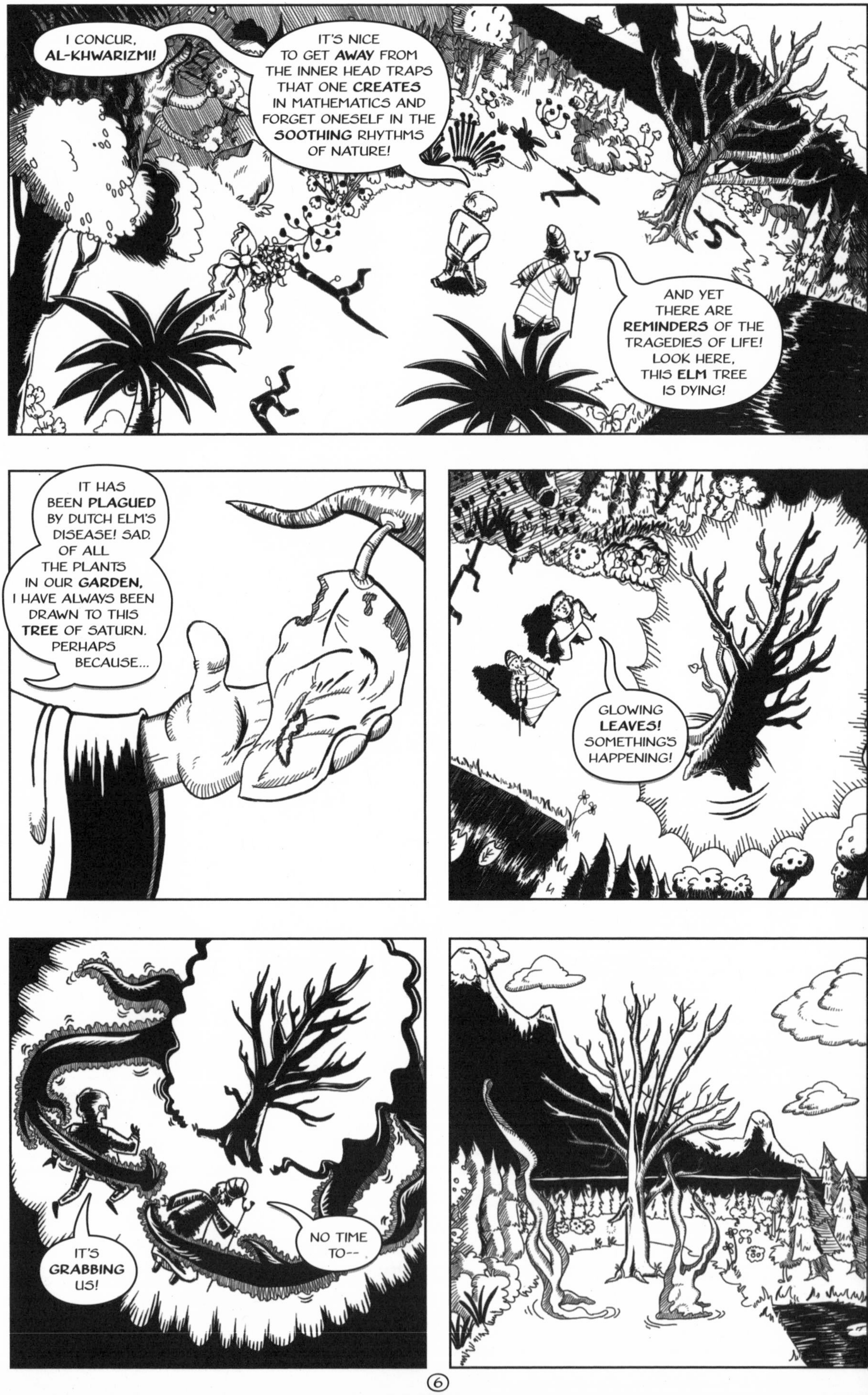
I CONCUR, AL-KHWARIZMI!
IT'S NICE TO GET AWAY FROM THE INNER HEAD TRAPS THAT ONE CREATES IN MATHEMATICS AND FORGET ONESELF IN THE SOOTHING RHYTHMS OF NATURE!
AND YET THERE ARE REMINDERS OF THE TRAGEDIES OF LIFE! LOOK HERE, THIS ELM TREE IS DYING!
IT HAS BEEN PLAGUED BY DUTCH ELM'S DISEASE! SAD. OF ALL THE PLANTS IN OUR GARDEN, I HAVE ALWAYS BEEN DRAWN TO THIS TREE OF SATURN. PERHAPS BECAUSE...
GLOWING LEAVES! SOMETHING'S HAPPENING!
IT'S GRABBING US!
NO TIME TO--

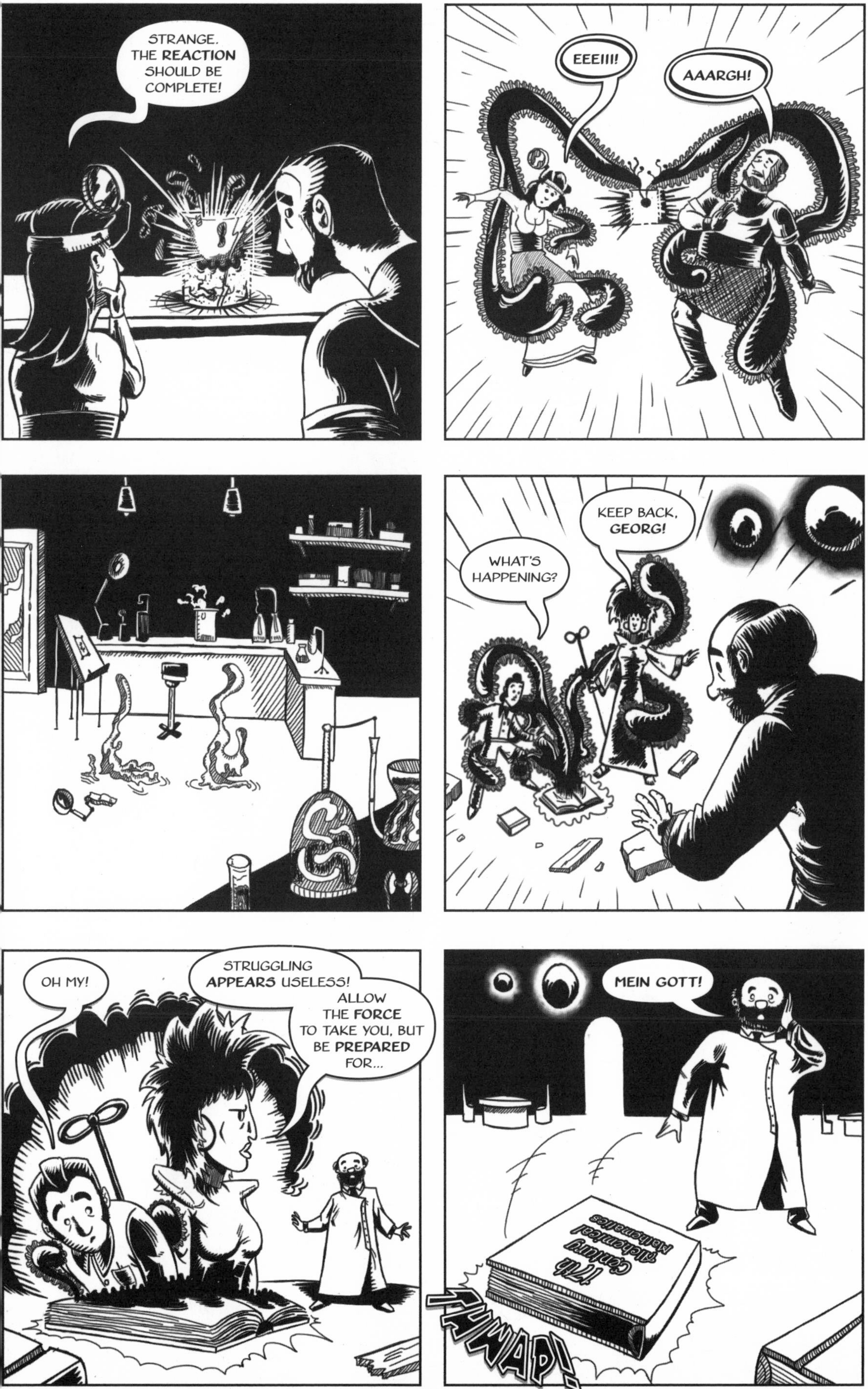
STRANGE. THE REACTION SHOULD BE COMPLETE!
EEEIII!
AAARGH!
WHAT'S HAPPENING?
KEEP BACK, GEORG!
OH MY!
STRUGGLING APPEARS USELESS! ALLOW THE FORCE TO TAKE YOU, BUT BE PREPARED FOR...
MEIN GOTT!
17th Century Alchemical Mathematics
THWAP!

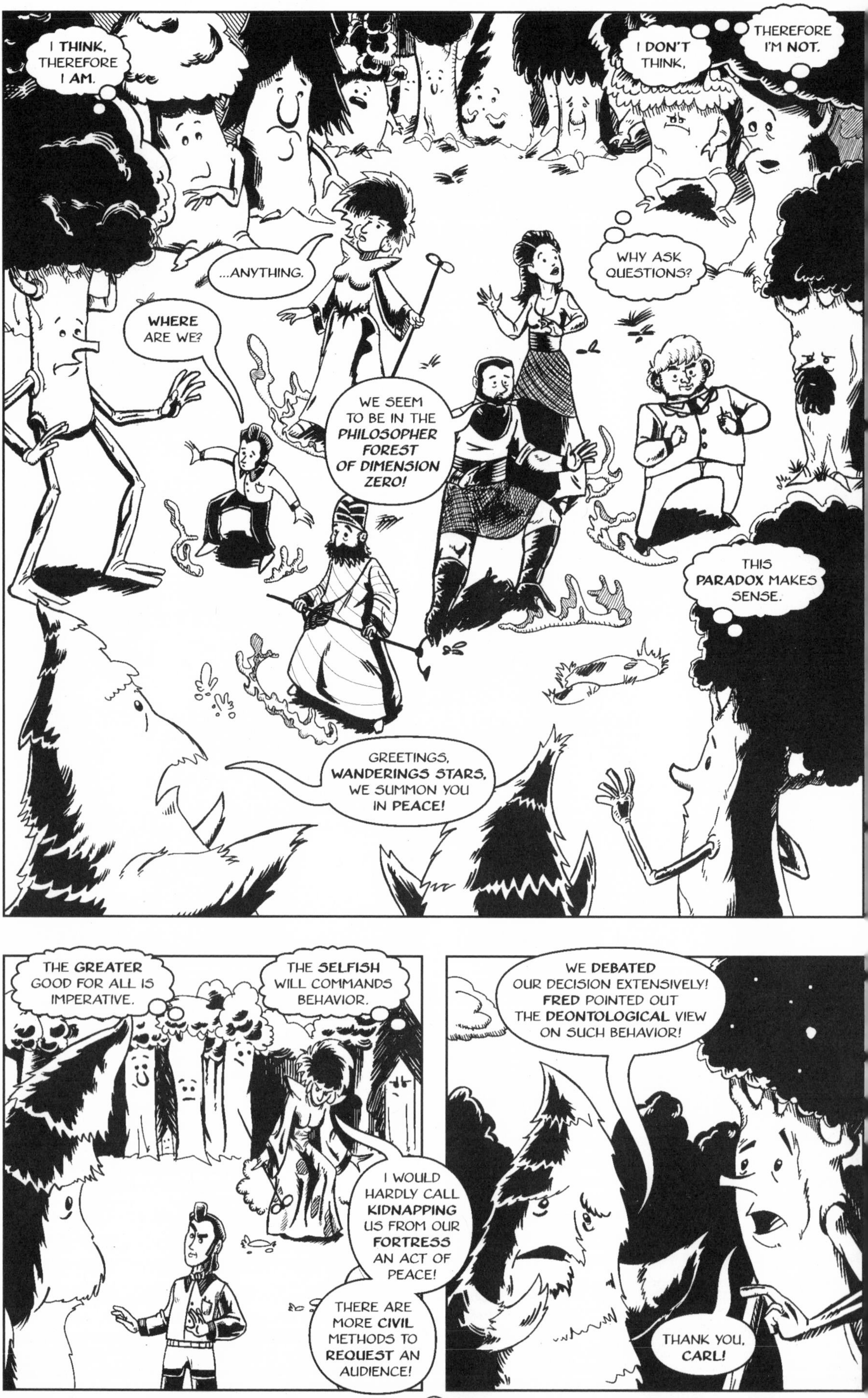
I THINK, THEREFORE I AM.
I DON'T THINK,
THEREFORE I'M NOT.
...ANYTHING.
WHY ASK QUESTIONS?
WHERE ARE WE?
WE SEEM TO BE IN THE PHILOSOPHER FOREST OF DIMENSION ZERO!
THIS PARADOX MAKES SENSE.
GREETINGS, WANDERINGS STARS, WE SUMMON YOU IN PEACE!
THE GREATER GOOD FOR ALL IS IMPERATIVE.
THE SELFISH WILL COMMANDS BEHAVIOR.
I WOULD HARDLY CALL KIDNAPPING US FROM OUR FORTRESS AN ACT OF PEACE!
THERE ARE MORE CIVIL METHODS TO REQUEST AN AUDIENCE!
WE DEBATED OUR DECISION EXTENSIVELY! FRED POINTED OUT THE DEONTOLOGICAL VIEW ON SUCH BEHAVIOR!
THANK YOU, CARL!

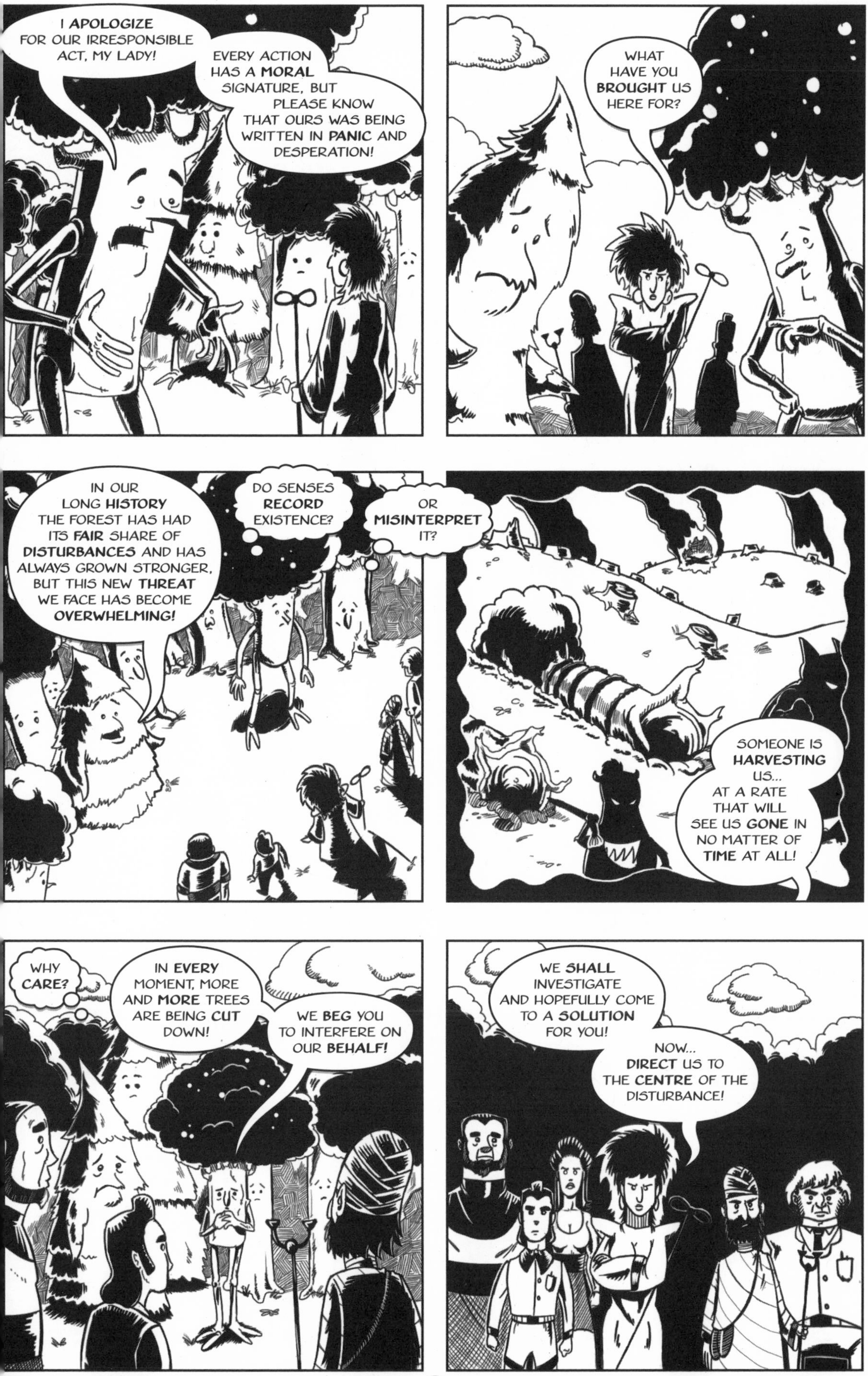
I APOLOGIZE FOR OUR IRRESPONSIBLE ACT, MY LADY!
EVERY ACTION HAS A MORAL SIGNATURE, BUT PLEASE KNOW THAT OURS WAS BEING WRITTEN IN PANIC AND DESPERATION!
WHAT HAVE YOU BROUGHT US HERE FOR?
IN OUR LONG HISTORY THE FOREST HAS HAD ITS FAIR SHARE OF DISTURBANCES AND HAS ALWAYS GROWN STRONGER, BUT THIS NEW THREAT WE FACE HAS BECOME OVERWHELMING!
DO SENSES RECORD EXISTENCE?
OR MISINTERPRET IT?
SOMEONE IS HARVESTING US... AT A RATE THAT WILL SEE US GONE IN NO MATTER OF TIME AT ALL!
WHY CARE?
IN EVERY MOMENT, MORE AND MORE TREES ARE BEING CUT DOWN!
WE BEG YOU TO INTERFERE ON OUR BEHALF!
WE SHALL INVESTIGATE AND HOPEFULLY COME TO A SOLUTION FOR YOU!
NOW... DIRECT US TO THE CENTRE OF THE DISTURBANCE!

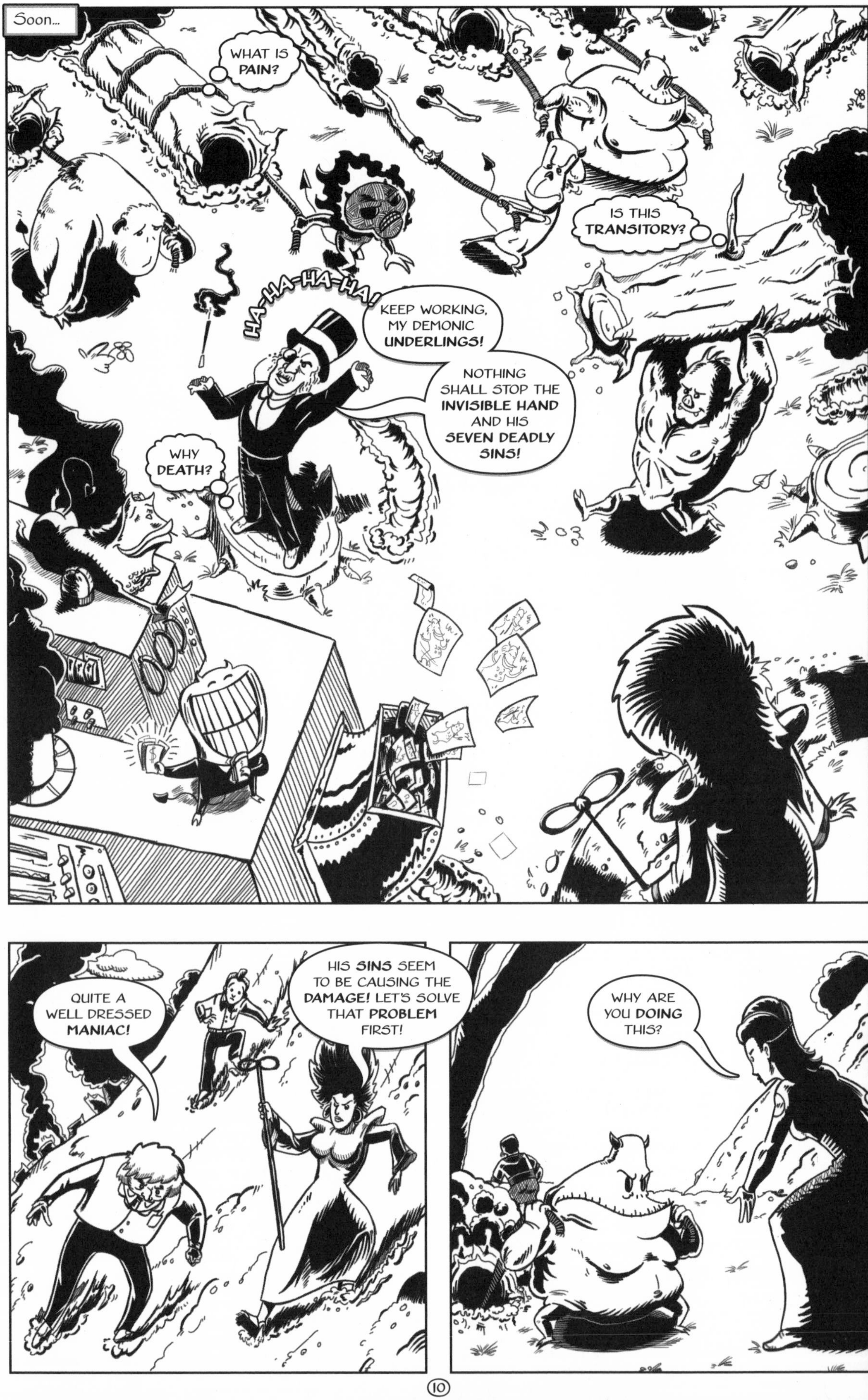
Soon...
WHAT IS PAIN?
HA-HA-HA-HA!
KEEP WORKING, MY DEMONIC UNDERLINGS!
NOTHING SHALL STOP THE INVISIBLE HAND AND HIS SEVEN DEADLY SINS!
IS THIS TRANSITORY?
WHY DEATH?
QUITE A WELL DRESSED MANIAC!
HIS SINS SEEM TO BE CAUSING THE DAMAGE! LET'S SOLVE THAT PROBLEM FIRST!
WHY ARE YOU DOING THIS?

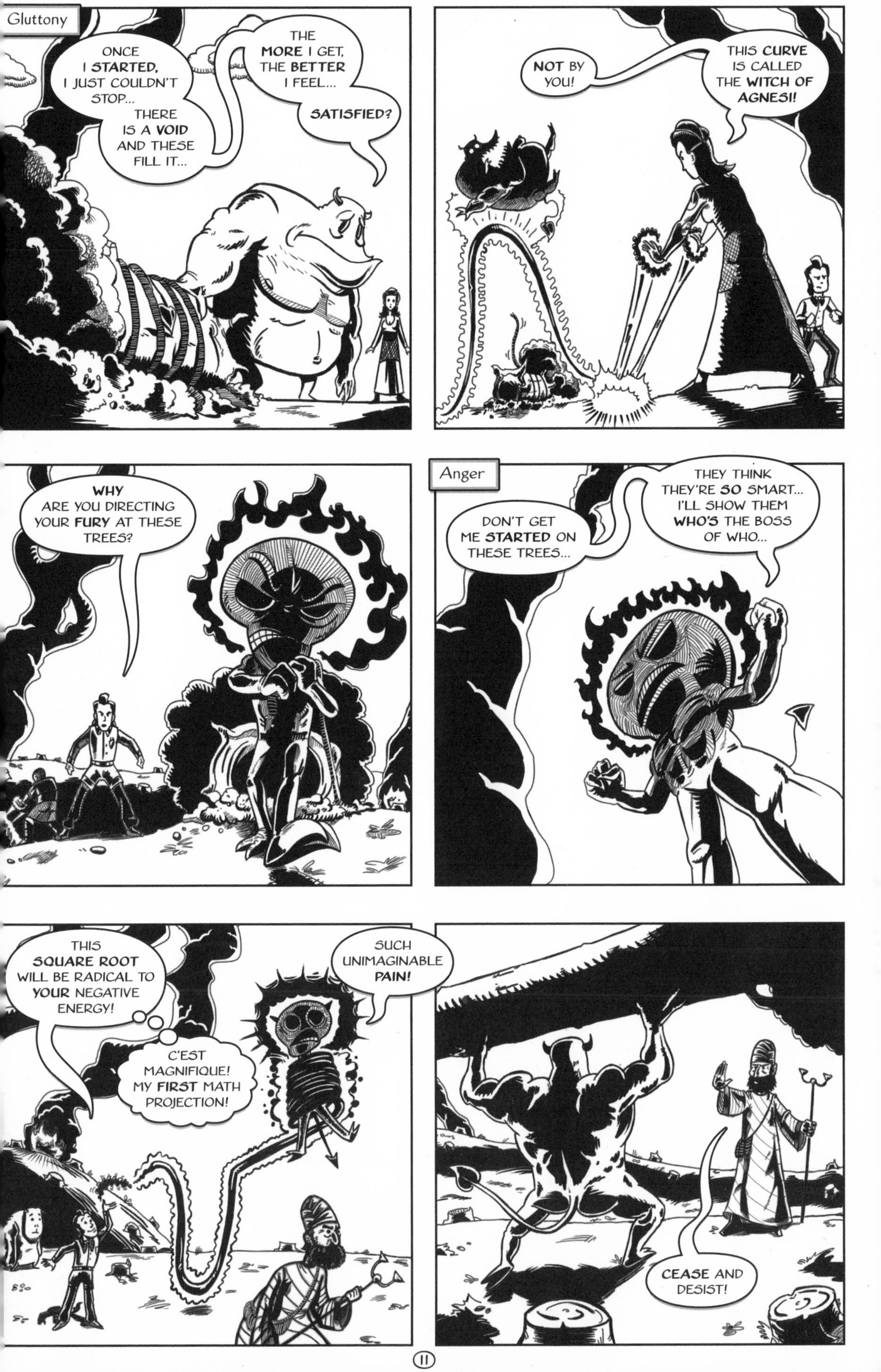
Gluttony
ONCE I STARTED, I JUST COULDN'T STOP... THERE IS A VOID AND THESE FILL IT...
THE MORE I GET, THE BETTER I FEEL...
SATISFIED?
NOT BY YOU!
THIS CURVE IS CALLED THE WITCH OF AGNESI!
WHY ARE YOU DIRECTING YOUR FURY AT THESE TREES?
Anger
DON'T GET ME STARTED ON THESE TREES...
THEY THINK THEY'RE SO SMART... I'LL SHOW THEM WHO'S THE BOSS OF WHO...
THIS SQUARE ROOT WILL BE RADICAL TO YOUR NEGATIVE ENERGY!
C'EST MAGNIFIQUE! MY FIRST MATH PROJECTION!
SUCH UNIMAGINABLE PAIN!
CEASE AND DESIST!

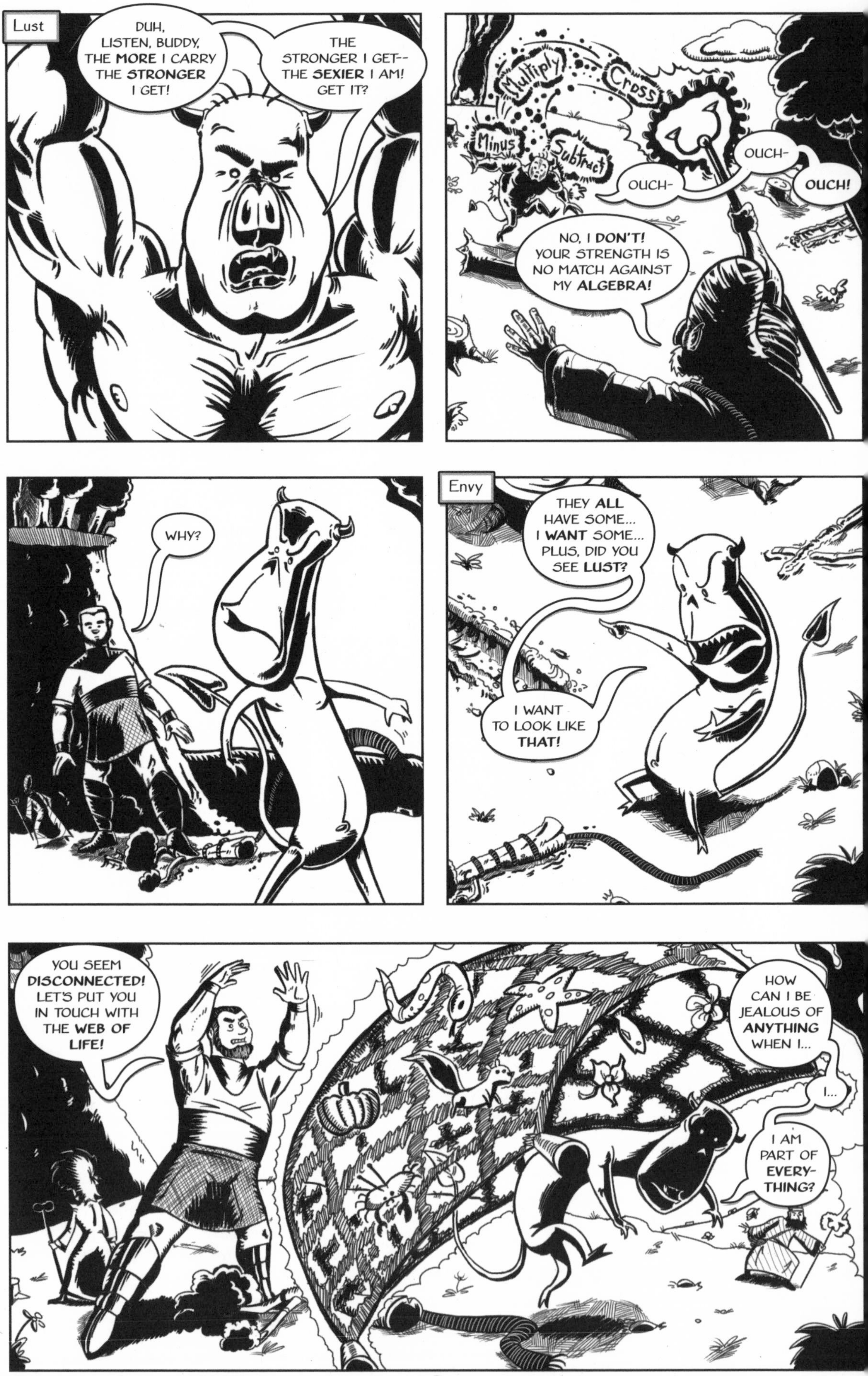
Lust
DUH, LISTEN, BUDDY, THE MORE I CARRY THE STRONGER I GET!
THE STRONGER I GET-- THE SEXIER I AM! GET IT?
Multiply
Cross
Minus
Subtract
OUCH-
OUCH-
OUCH!
NO, I DON'T! YOUR STRENGTH IS NO MATCH AGAINST MY ALGEBRA!
WHY?
Envy
THEY ALL HAVE SOME... I WANT SOME... PLUS, DID YOU SEE LUST?
I WANT TO LOOK LIKE THAT!
YOU SEEM DISCONNECTED! LET'S PUT YOU IN TOUCH WITH THE WEB OF LIFE!
HOW CAN I BE JEALOUS OF ANYTHING WHEN I...
I...
I AM PART OF EVERYTHING?

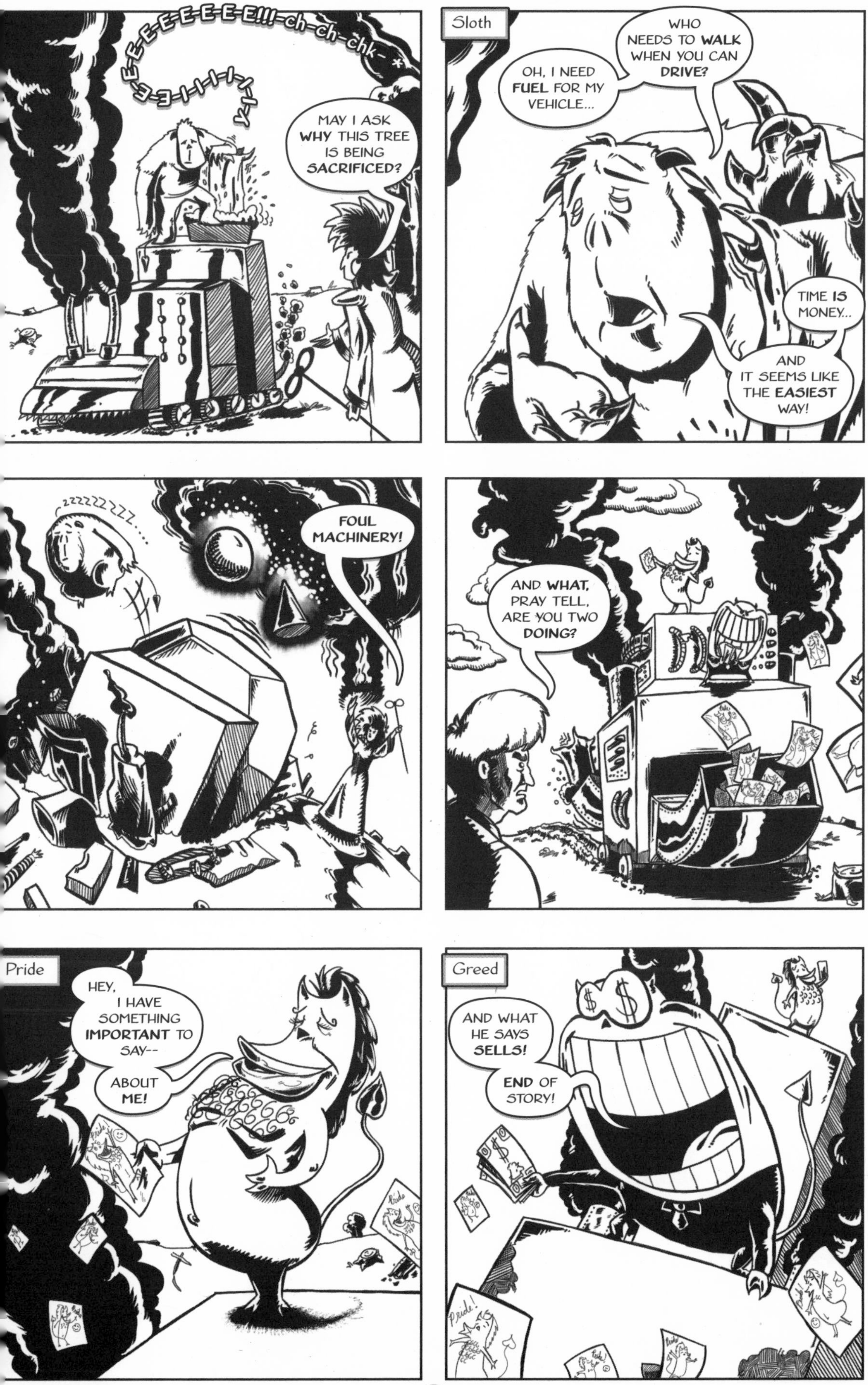
Y-I-I-I-I-I-I-E-E-E-E-E-E-E-E-E-E!!!-ch-ch-chk-*
MAY I ASK **WHY** THIS TREE IS BEING **SACRIFICED?**
Sloth
OH, I NEED **FUEL** FOR MY VEHICLE...
WHO NEEDS TO **WALK** WHEN YOU CAN **DRIVE?**
TIME **IS** MONEY...
AND IT SEEMS LIKE THE **EASIEST** WAY!
ZZZZZZZZ...
FOUL MACHINERY!
AND **WHAT,** PRAY TELL, ARE YOU TWO **DOING?**
Pride
HEY, I HAVE SOMETHING **IMPORTANT** TO SAY--
ABOUT **ME!**
Greed
AND WHAT HE SAYS **SELLS!**
END OF STORY!
Pride!

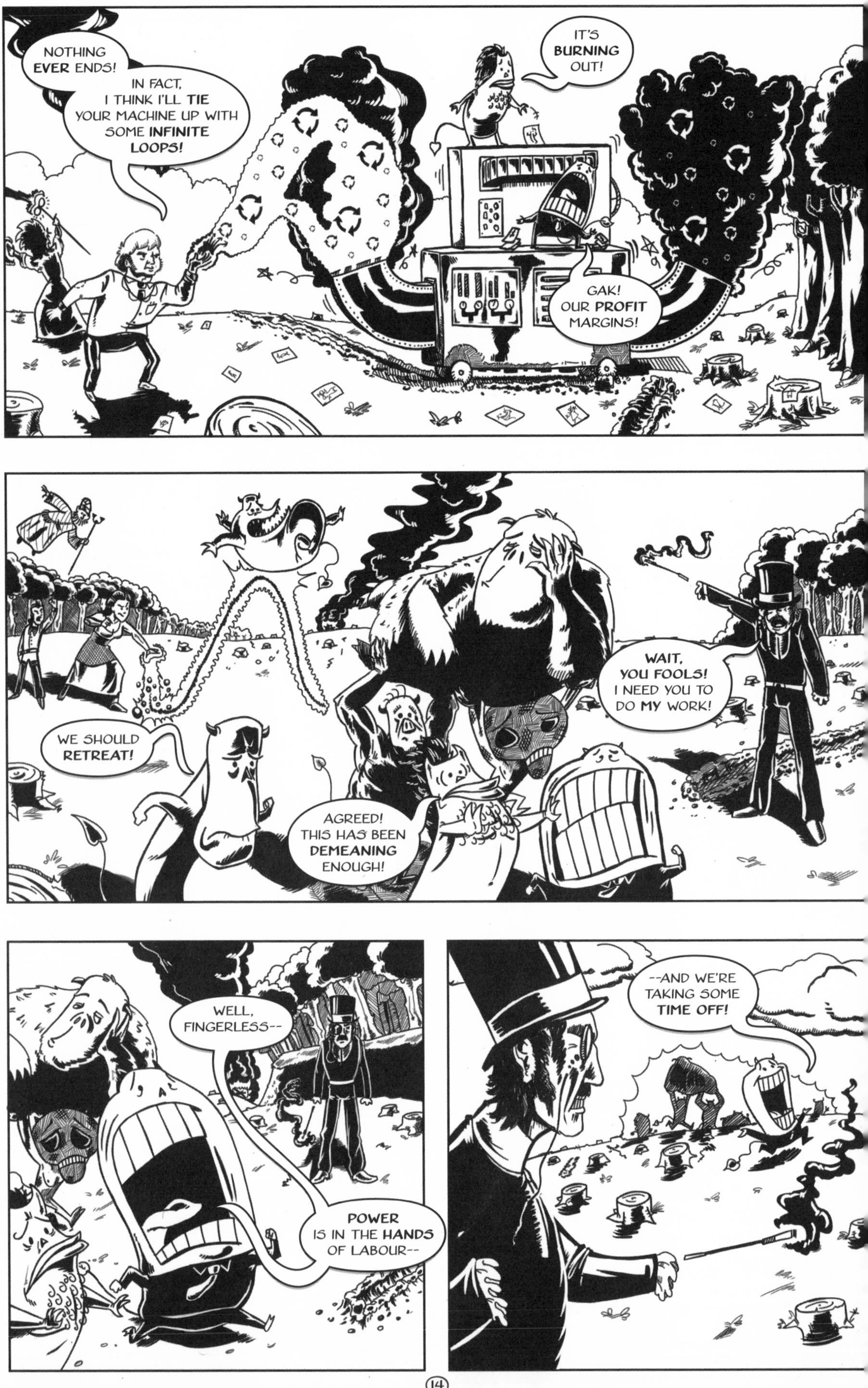
NOTHING EVER ENDS!
IN FACT, I THINK I'LL TIE YOUR MACHINE UP WITH SOME INFINITE LOOPS!
IT'S BURNING OUT!
GAK! OUR PROFIT MARGINS!
WAIT, YOU FOOLS! I NEED YOU TO DO MY WORK!
WE SHOULD RETREAT!
AGREED! THIS HAS BEEN DEMEANING ENOUGH!
WELL, FINGERLESS--
POWER IS IN THE HANDS OF LABOUR--
--AND WE'RE TAKING SOME TIME OFF!

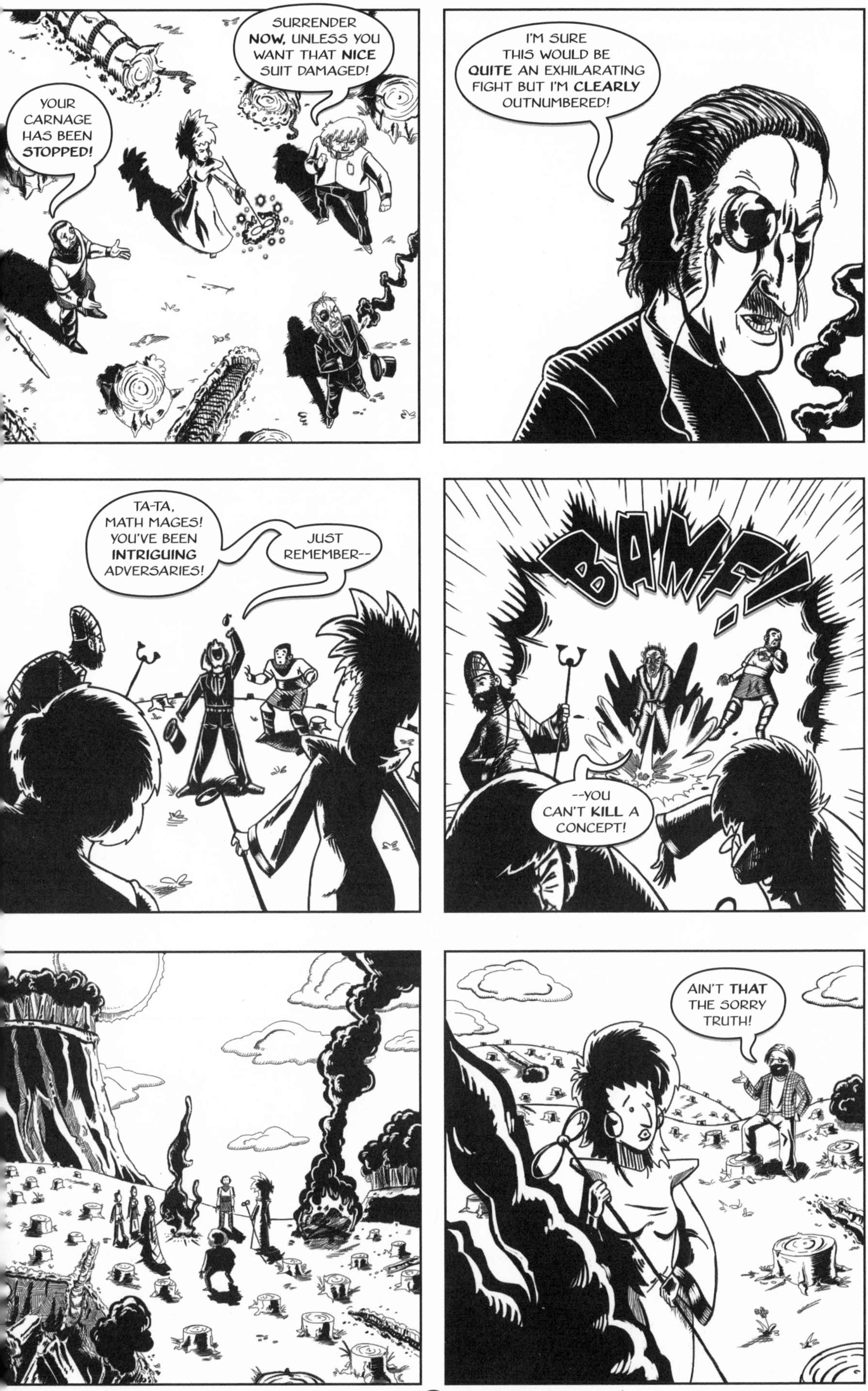
YOUR CARNAGE HAS BEEN STOPPED!
SURRENDER NOW, UNLESS YOU WANT THAT NICE SUIT DAMAGED!
I'M SURE THIS WOULD BE QUITE AN EXHILARATING FIGHT BUT I'M CLEARLY OUTNUMBERED!
TA-TA, MATH MAGES! YOU'VE BEEN INTRIGUING ADVERSARIES!
JUST REMEMBER--
BAMF!
--YOU CAN'T KILL A CONCEPT!
AIN'T THAT THE SORRY TRUTH!

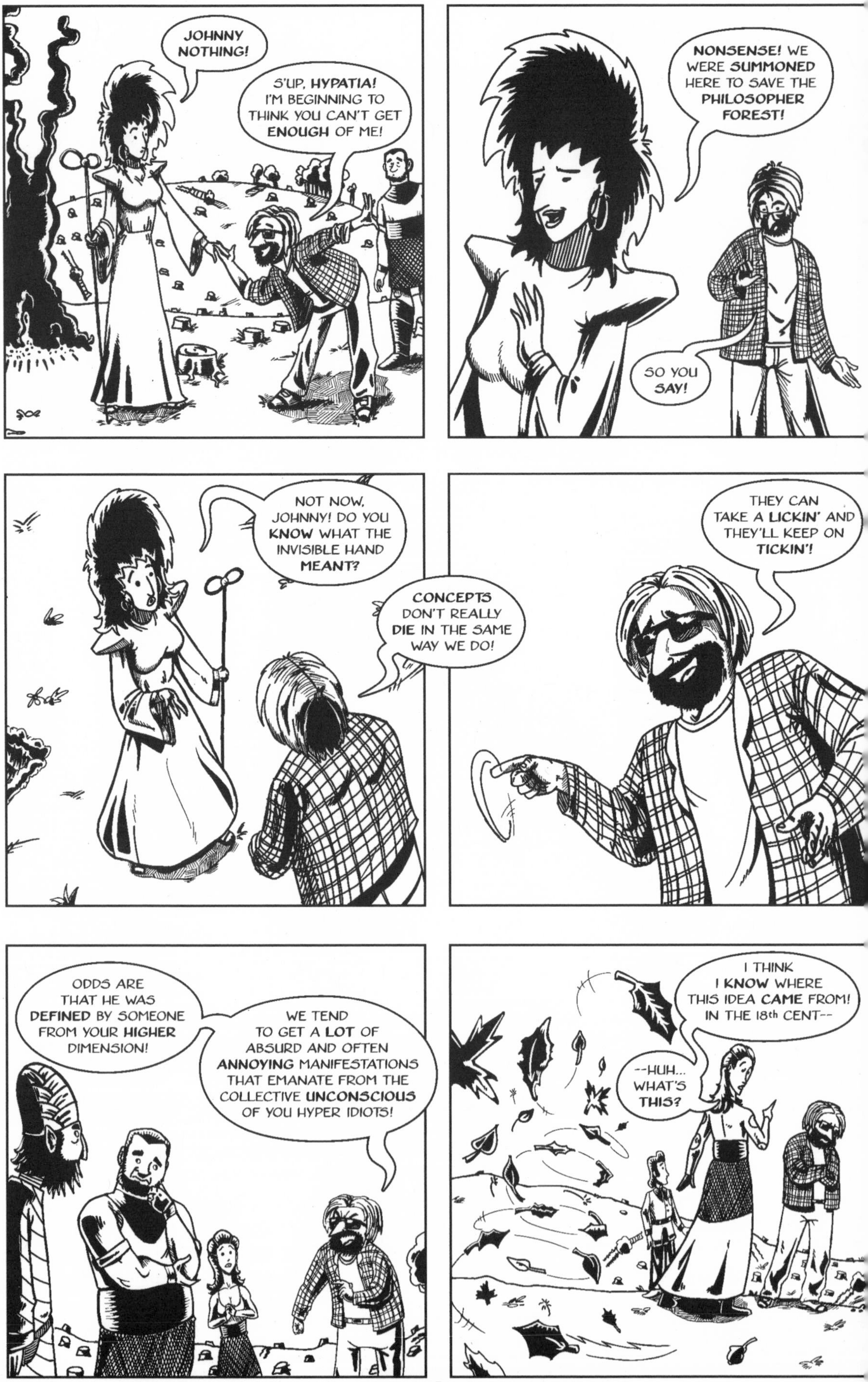
JOHNNY NOTHING!
S'UP, HYPATIA! I'M BEGINNING TO THINK YOU CAN'T GET ENOUGH OF ME!
NONSENSE! WE WERE SUMMONED HERE TO SAVE THE PHILOSOPHER FOREST!
SO YOU SAY!
NOT NOW, JOHNNY! DO YOU KNOW WHAT THE INVISIBLE HAND MEANT?
CONCEPTS DON'T REALLY DIE IN THE SAME WAY WE DO!
THEY CAN TAKE A LICKIN' AND THEY'LL KEEP ON TICKIN'!
ODDS ARE THAT HE WAS DEFINED BY SOMEONE FROM YOUR HIGHER DIMENSION!
WE TEND TO GET A LOT OF ABSURD AND OFTEN ANNOYING MANIFESTATIONS THAT EMANATE FROM THE COLLECTIVE UNCONSCIOUS OF YOU HYPER IDIOTS!
I THINK I KNOW WHERE THIS IDEA CAME FROM! IN THE 18th CENT--
--HUH... WHAT'S THIS?

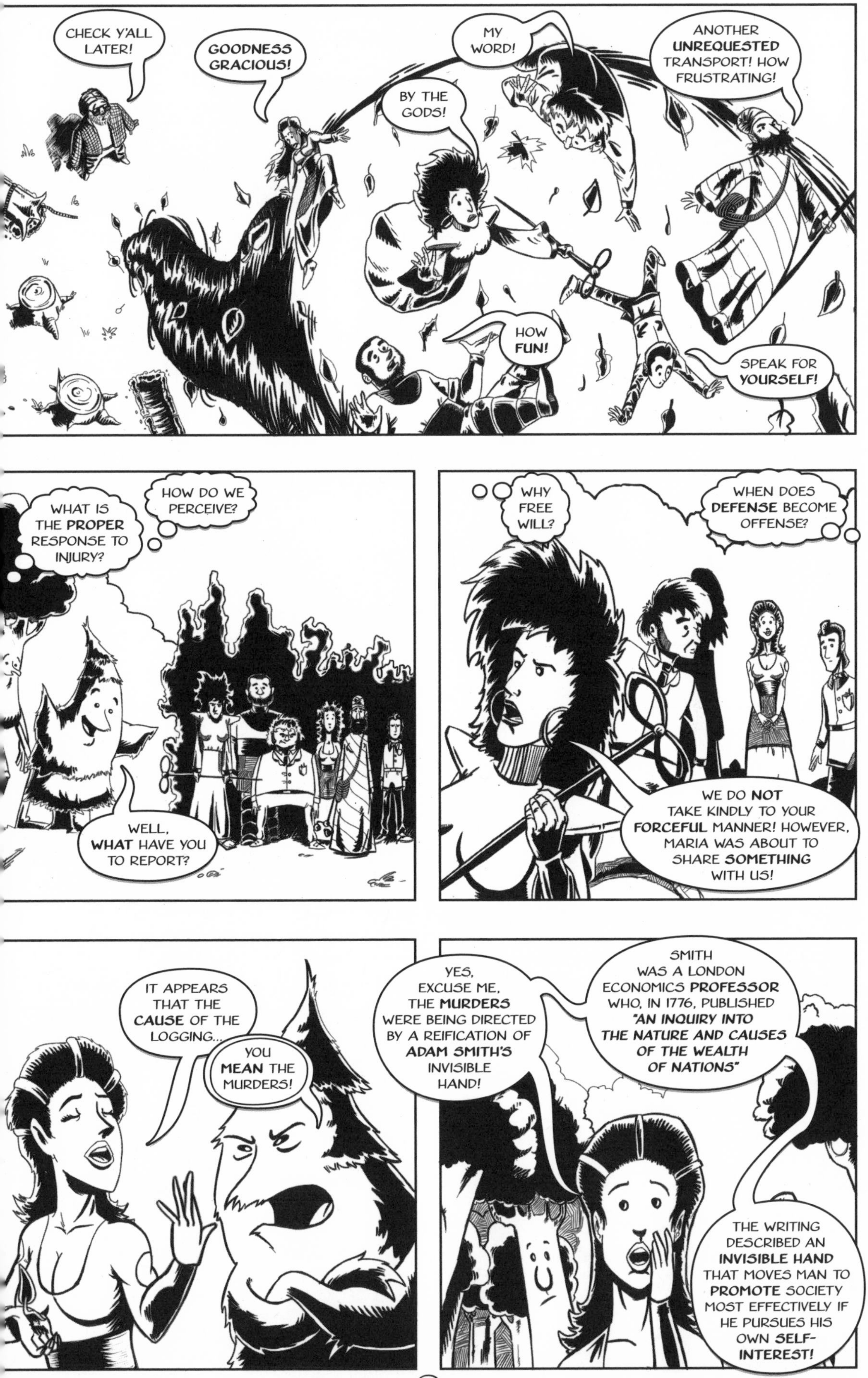
CHECK Y'ALL LATER!
GOODNESS GRACIOUS!
MY WORD!
BY THE GODS!
ANOTHER UNREQUESTED TRANSPORT! HOW FRUSTRATING!
HOW FUN!
SPEAK FOR YOURSELF!
WHAT IS THE PROPER RESPONSE TO INJURY?
HOW DO WE PERCEIVE?
WELL, WHAT HAVE YOU TO REPORT?
WHY FREE WILL?
WHEN DOES DEFENSE BECOME OFFENSE?
WE DO NOT TAKE KINDLY TO YOUR FORCEFUL MANNER! HOWEVER, MARIA WAS ABOUT TO SHARE SOMETHING WITH US!
IT APPEARS THAT THE CAUSE OF THE LOGGING...
YOU MEAN THE MURDERS!
YES, EXCUSE ME, THE MURDERS WERE BEING DIRECTED BY A REIFICATION OF ADAM SMITH'S INVISIBLE HAND!
SMITH WAS A LONDON ECONOMICS PROFESSOR WHO, IN 1776, PUBLISHED "AN INQUIRY INTO THE NATURE AND CAUSES OF THE WEALTH OF NATIONS"
THE WRITING DESCRIBED AN INVISIBLE HAND THAT MOVES MAN TO PROMOTE SOCIETY MOST EFFECTIVELY IF HE PURSUES HIS OWN SELF-INTEREST!

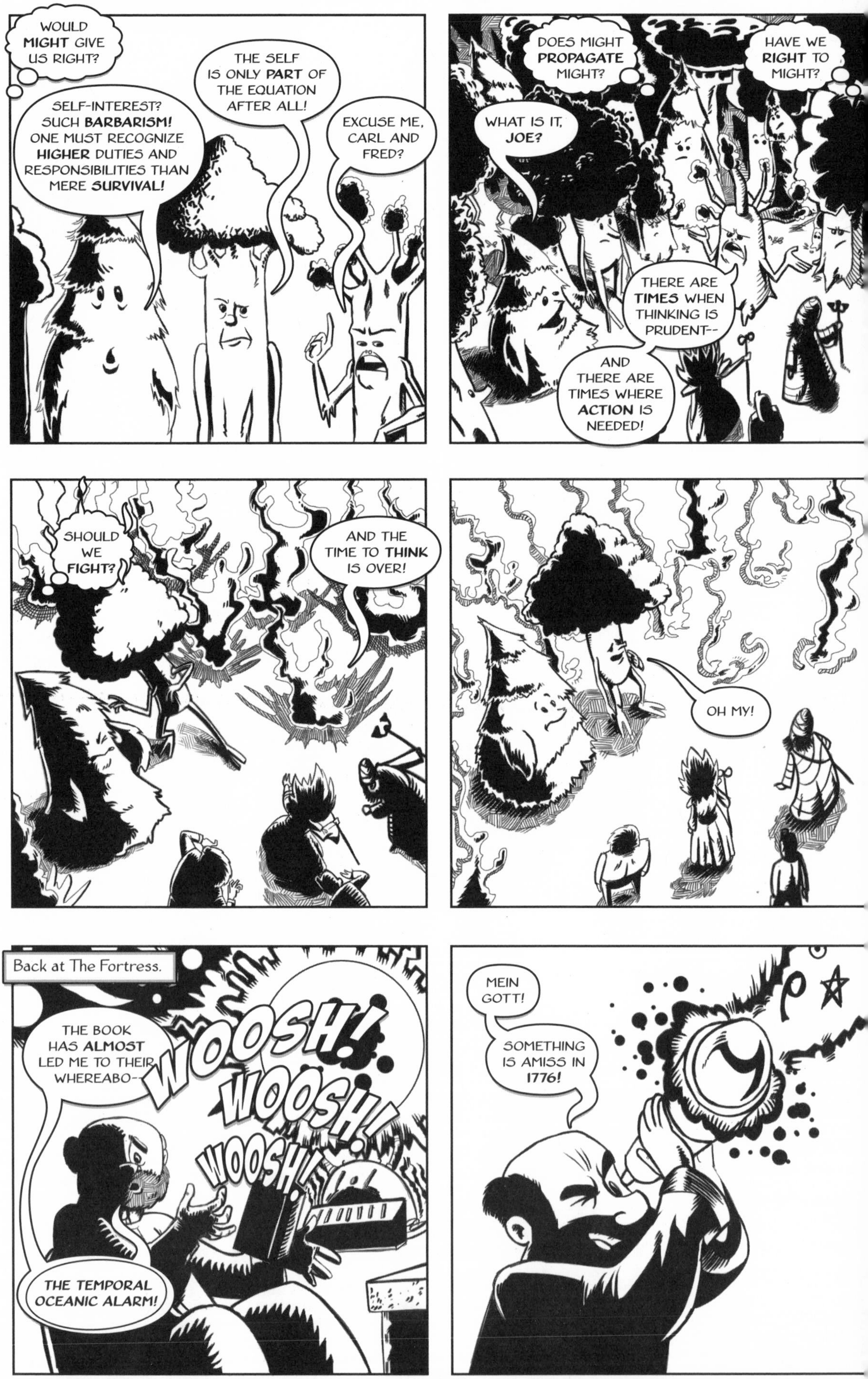
WOULD MIGHT GIVE US RIGHT?
SELF-INTEREST? SUCH BARBARISM! ONE MUST RECOGNIZE HIGHER DUTIES AND RESPONSIBILITIES THAN MERE SURVIVAL!
THE SELF IS ONLY PART OF THE EQUATION AFTER ALL!
EXCUSE ME, CARL AND FRED?
DOES MIGHT PROPAGATE MIGHT?
HAVE WE RIGHT TO MIGHT?
WHAT IS IT, JOE?
THERE ARE TIMES WHEN THINKING IS PRUDENT--
AND THERE ARE TIMES WHERE ACTION IS NEEDED!
SHOULD WE FIGHT?
AND THE TIME TO THINK IS OVER!
OH MY!
Back at The Fortress.
THE BOOK HAS ALMOST LED ME TO THEIR WHEREABO--
WOOSH! WOOSH! WOOSH!
THE TEMPORAL OCEANIC ALARM!
MEIN GOTT!
SOMETHING IS AMISS IN 1776!

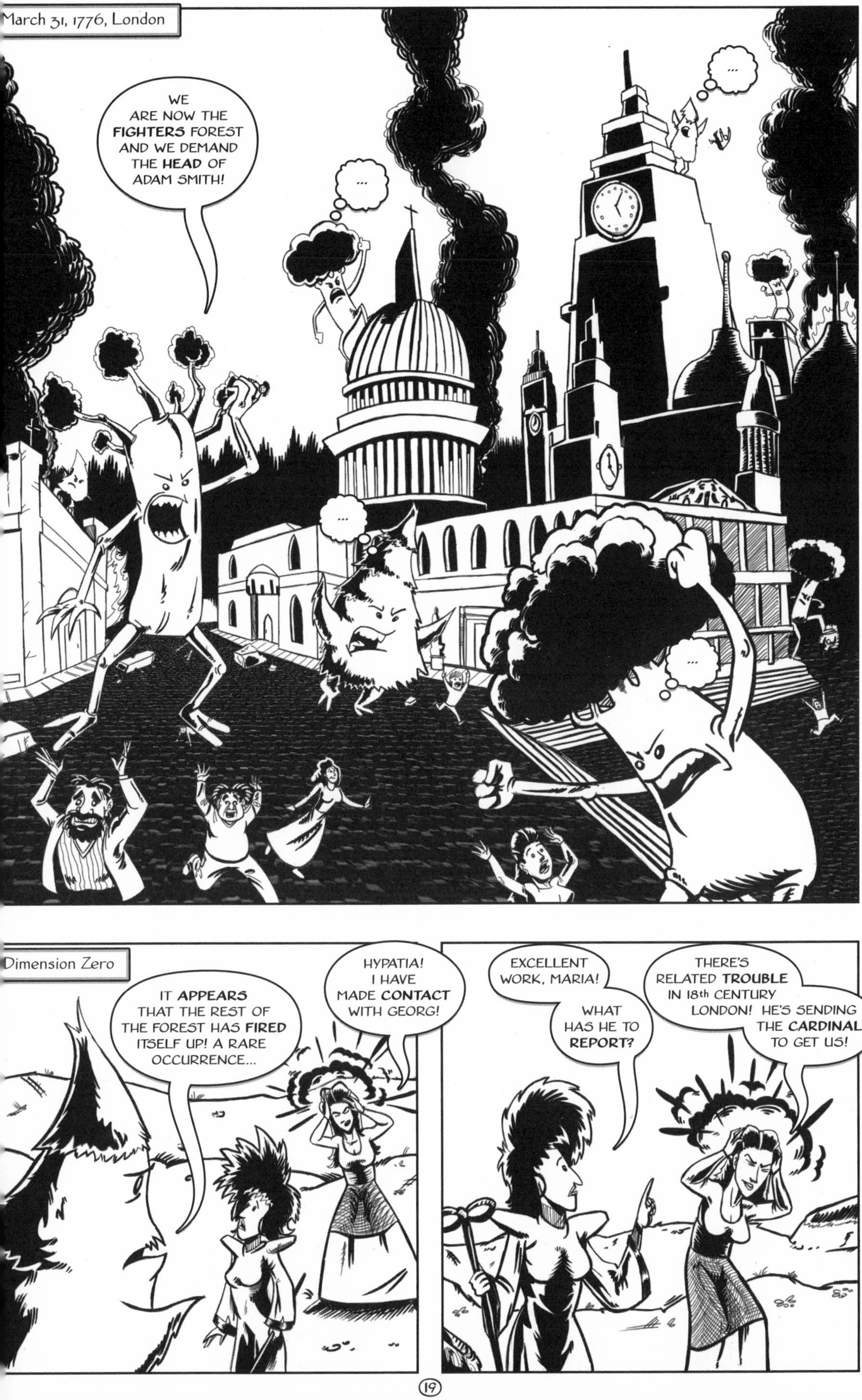
March 31, 1776, London
WE ARE NOW THE FIGHTERS FOREST AND WE DEMAND THE HEAD OF ADAM SMITH!
...
...
...
...
Dimension Zero
IT APPEARS THAT THE REST OF THE FOREST HAS FIRED ITSELF UP! A RARE OCCURRENCE...
HYPATIA! I HAVE MADE CONTACT WITH GEORG!
EXCELLENT WORK, MARIA!
WHAT HAS HE TO REPORT?
THERE'S RELATED TROUBLE IN 18th CENTURY LONDON! HE'S SENDING THE CARDINAL TO GET US!

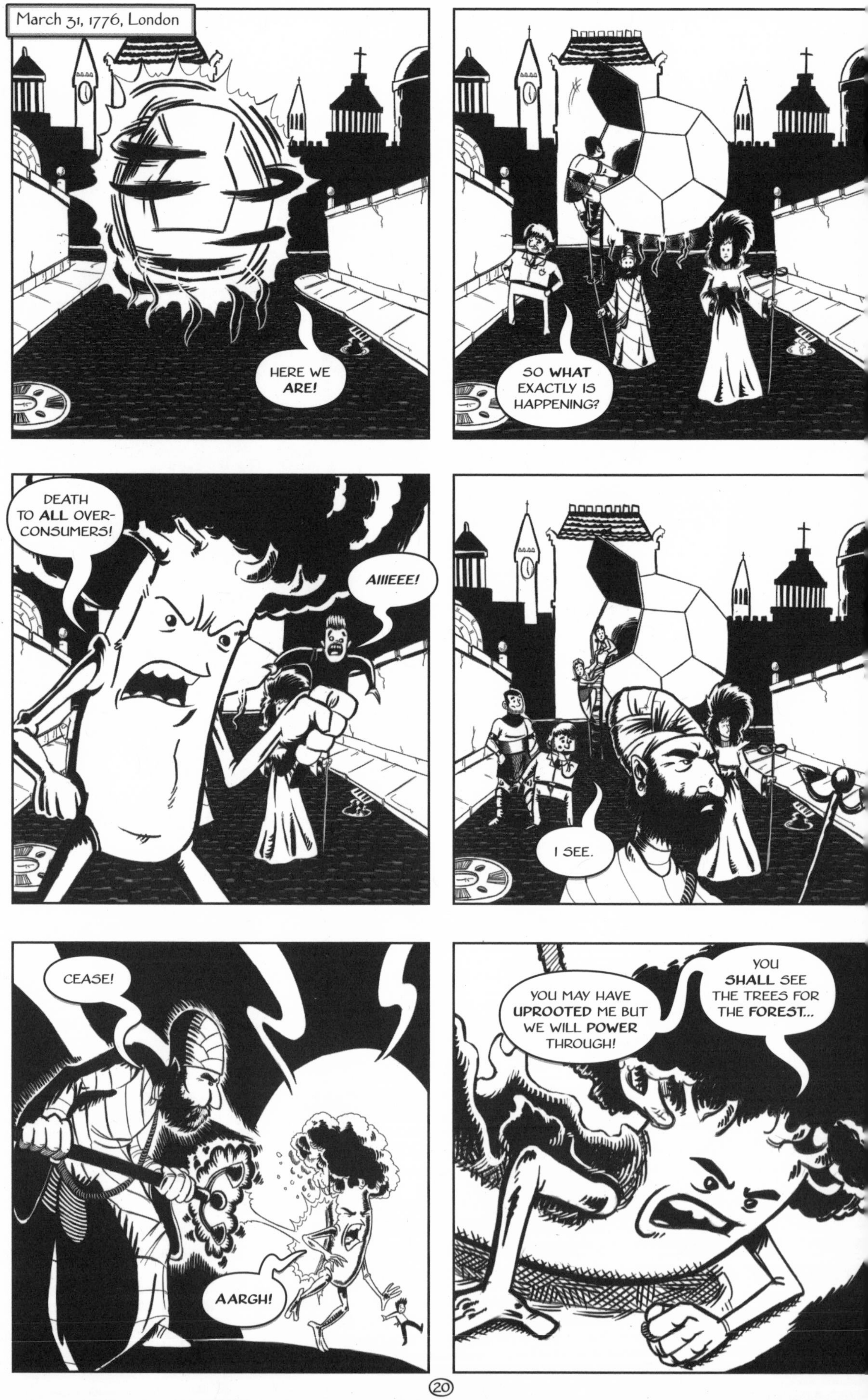
March 31, 1776, London
HERE WE ARE!
SO WHAT EXACTLY IS HAPPENING?
DEATH TO ALL OVER-CONSUMERS!
AIIIEEE!
I SEE.
CEASE!
AARGH!
YOU MAY HAVE UPROOTED ME BUT WE WILL POWER THROUGH!
YOU SHALL SEE THE TREES FOR THE FOREST...

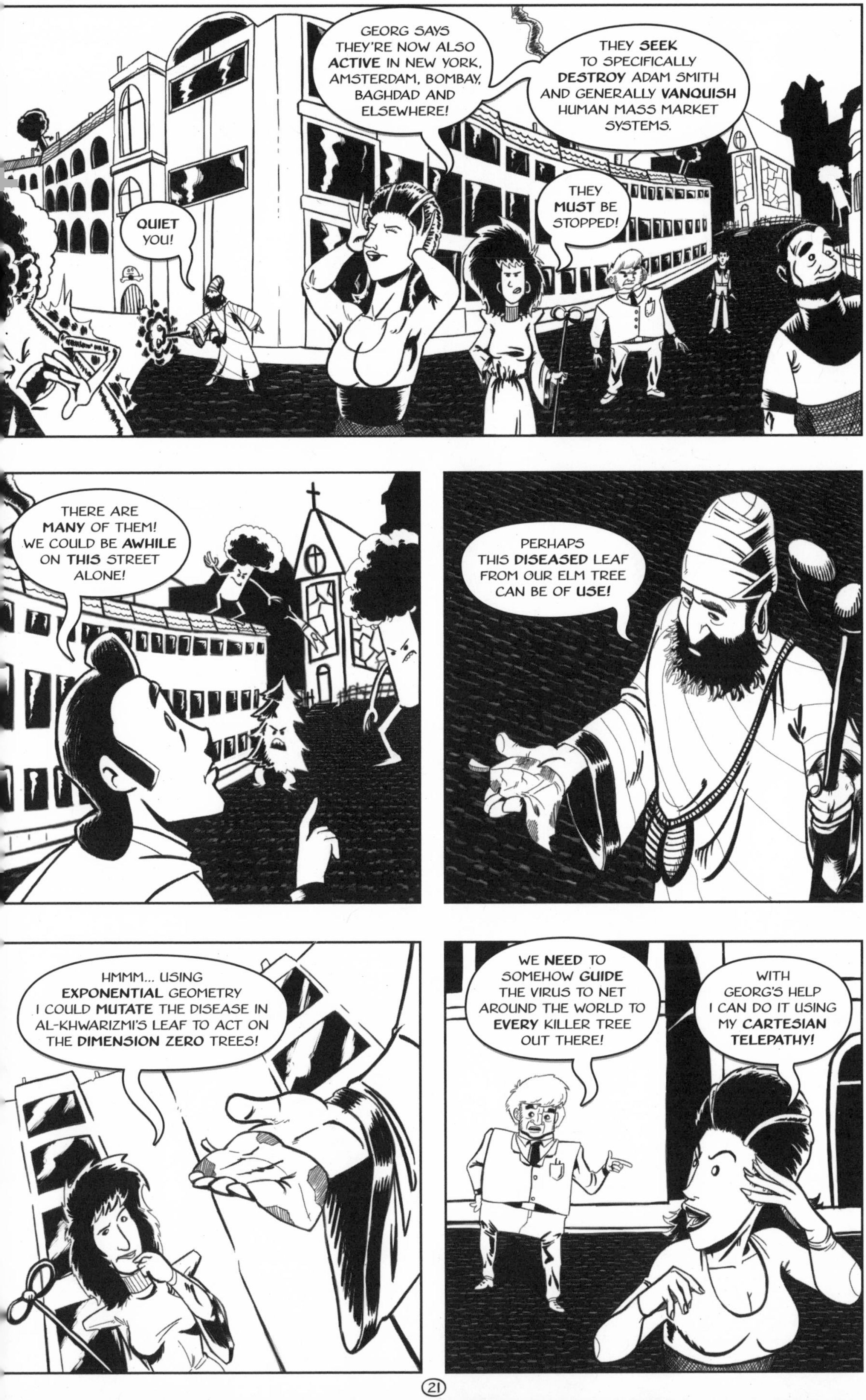
GEORG SAYS THEY'RE NOW ALSO ACTIVE IN NEW YORK, AMSTERDAM, BOMBAY, BAGHDAD AND ELSEWHERE!
THEY SEEK TO SPECIFICALLY DESTROY ADAM SMITH AND GENERALLY VANQUISH HUMAN MASS MARKET SYSTEMS.
QUIET YOU!
THEY MUST BE STOPPED!
THERE ARE MANY OF THEM! WE COULD BE AWHILE ON THIS STREET ALONE!
PERHAPS THIS DISEASED LEAF FROM OUR ELM TREE CAN BE OF USE!
HMMM... USING EXPONENTIAL GEOMETRY I COULD MUTATE THE DISEASE IN AL-KHWARIZMI'S LEAF TO ACT ON THE DIMENSION ZERO TREES!
WE NEED TO SOMEHOW GUIDE THE VIRUS TO NET AROUND THE WORLD TO EVERY KILLER TREE OUT THERE!
WITH GEORG'S HELP I CAN DO IT USING MY CARTESIAN TELEPATHY!

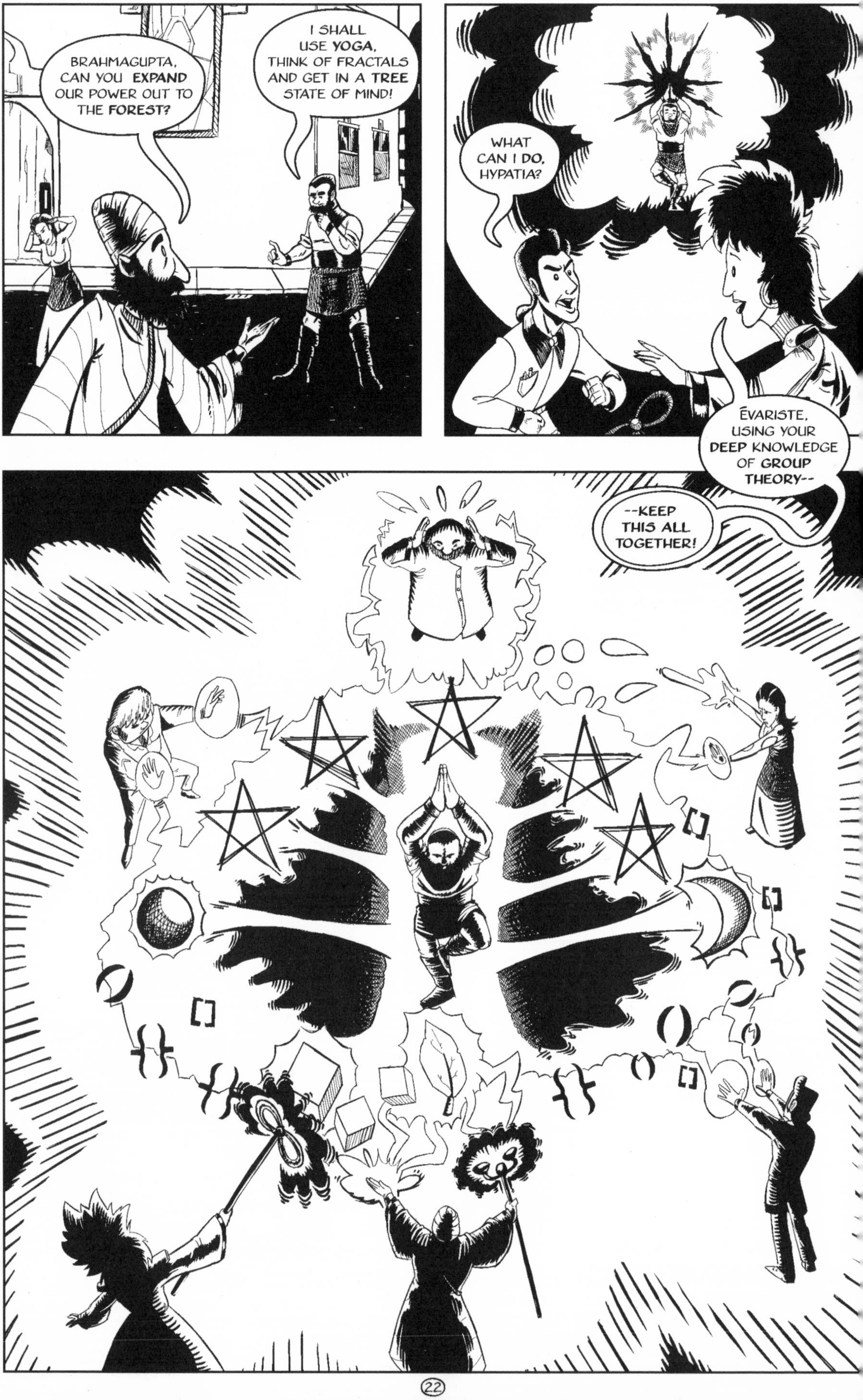
BRAHMAGUPTA, CAN YOU EXPAND OUR POWER OUT TO THE FOREST?
I SHALL USE YOGA, THINK OF FRACTALS AND GET IN A TREE STATE OF MIND!
WHAT CAN I DO, HYPATIA?
ÉVARISTE, USING YOUR DEEP KNOWLEDGE OF GROUP THEORY--
--KEEP THIS ALL TOGETHER!

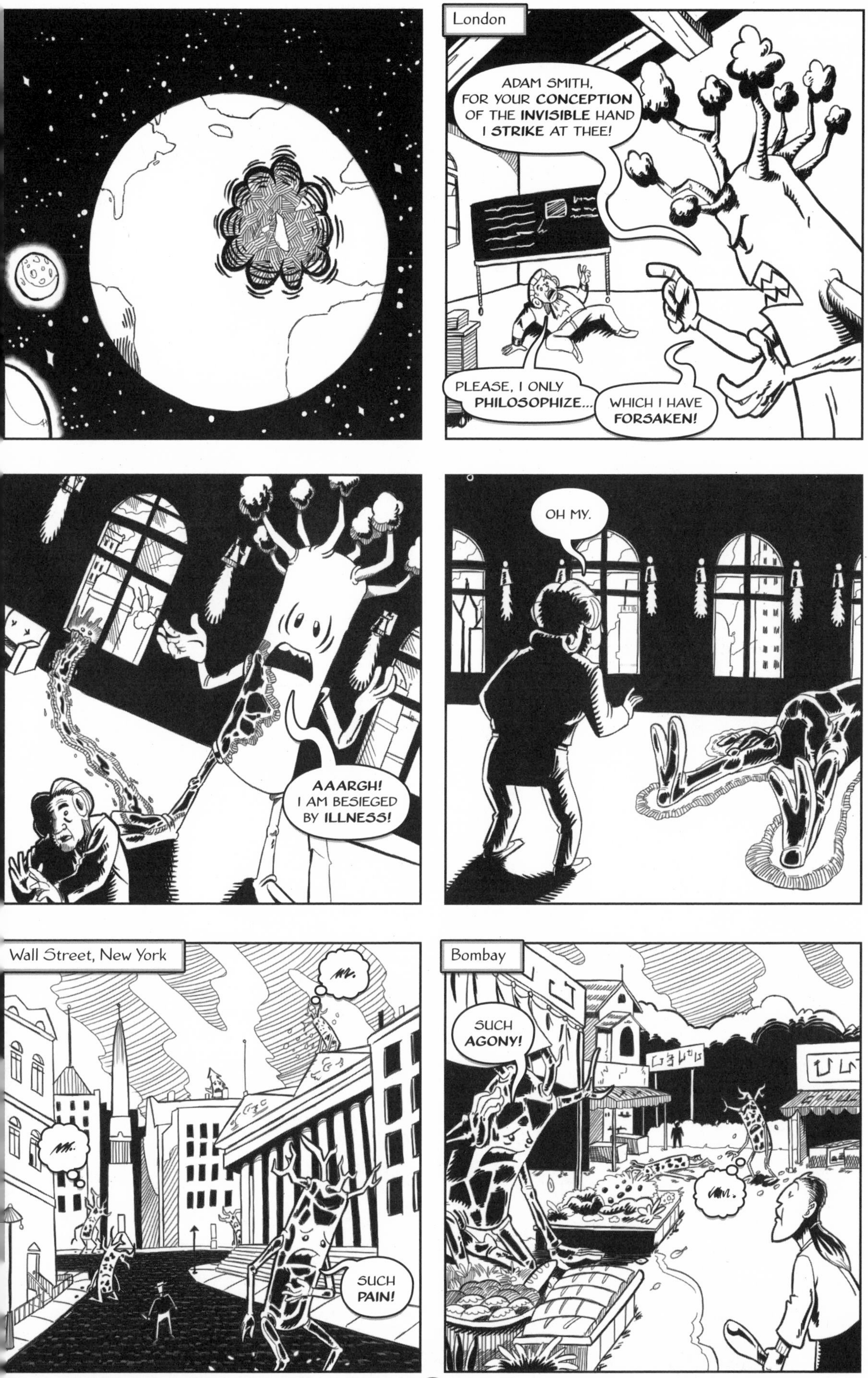
London
ADAM SMITH, FOR YOUR **CONCEPTION** OF THE **INVISIBLE** HAND I **STRIKE** AT THEE!
PLEASE, I ONLY **PHILOSOPHIZE...**
WHICH I HAVE **FORSAKEN!**
AAARGH! I AM BESIEGED BY **ILLNESS!**
OH MY.
Wall Street, New York
SUCH **PAIN!**
Bombay
SUCH **AGONY!**

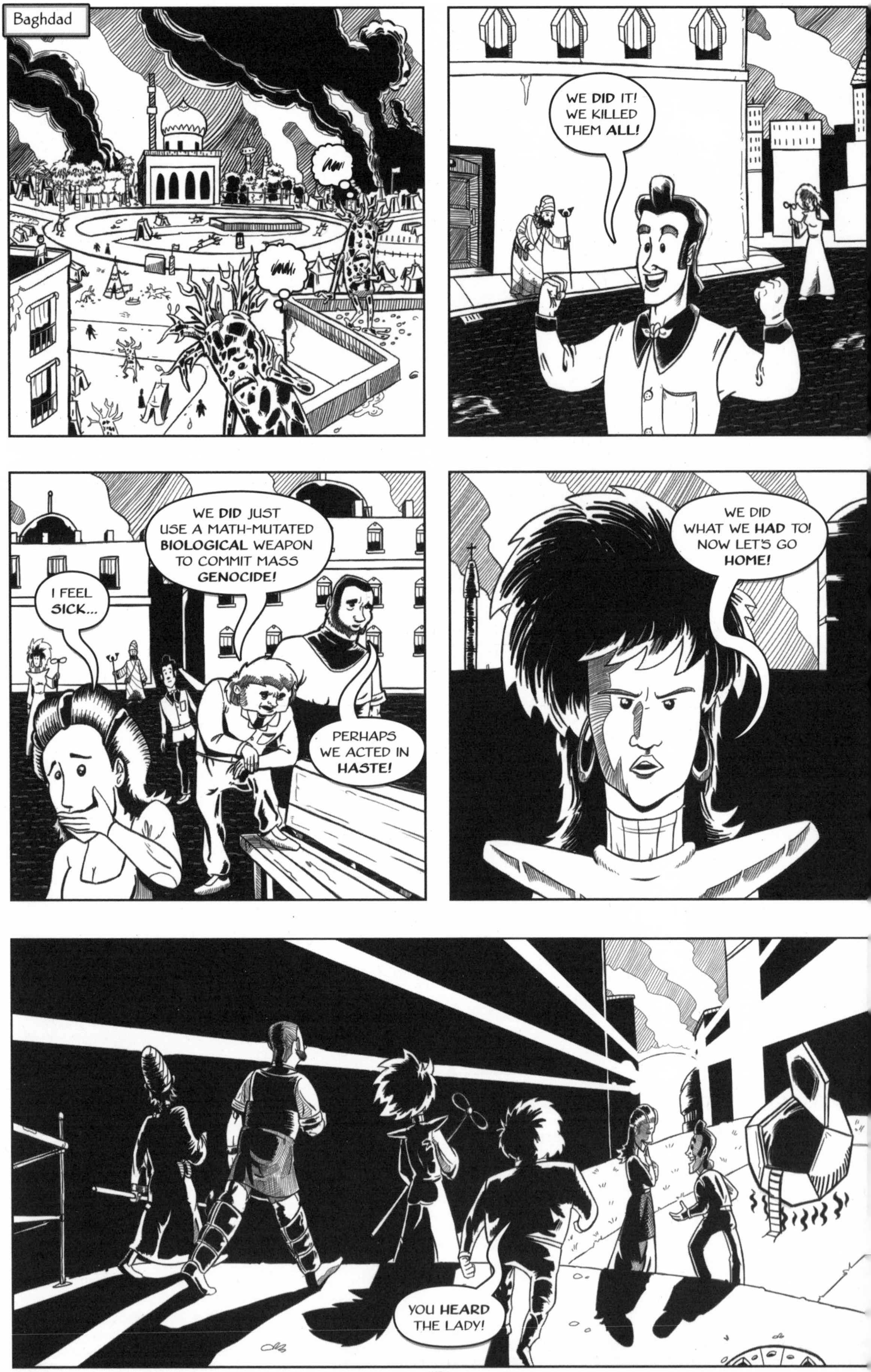
Baghdad
WE DID IT! WE KILLED THEM ALL!
I FEEL SICK...
WE DID JUST USE A MATH-MUTATED BIOLOGICAL WEAPON TO COMMIT MASS GENOCIDE!
PERHAPS WE ACTED IN HASTE!
WE DID WHAT WE HAD TO! NOW LET'S GO HOME!
YOU HEARD THE LADY!

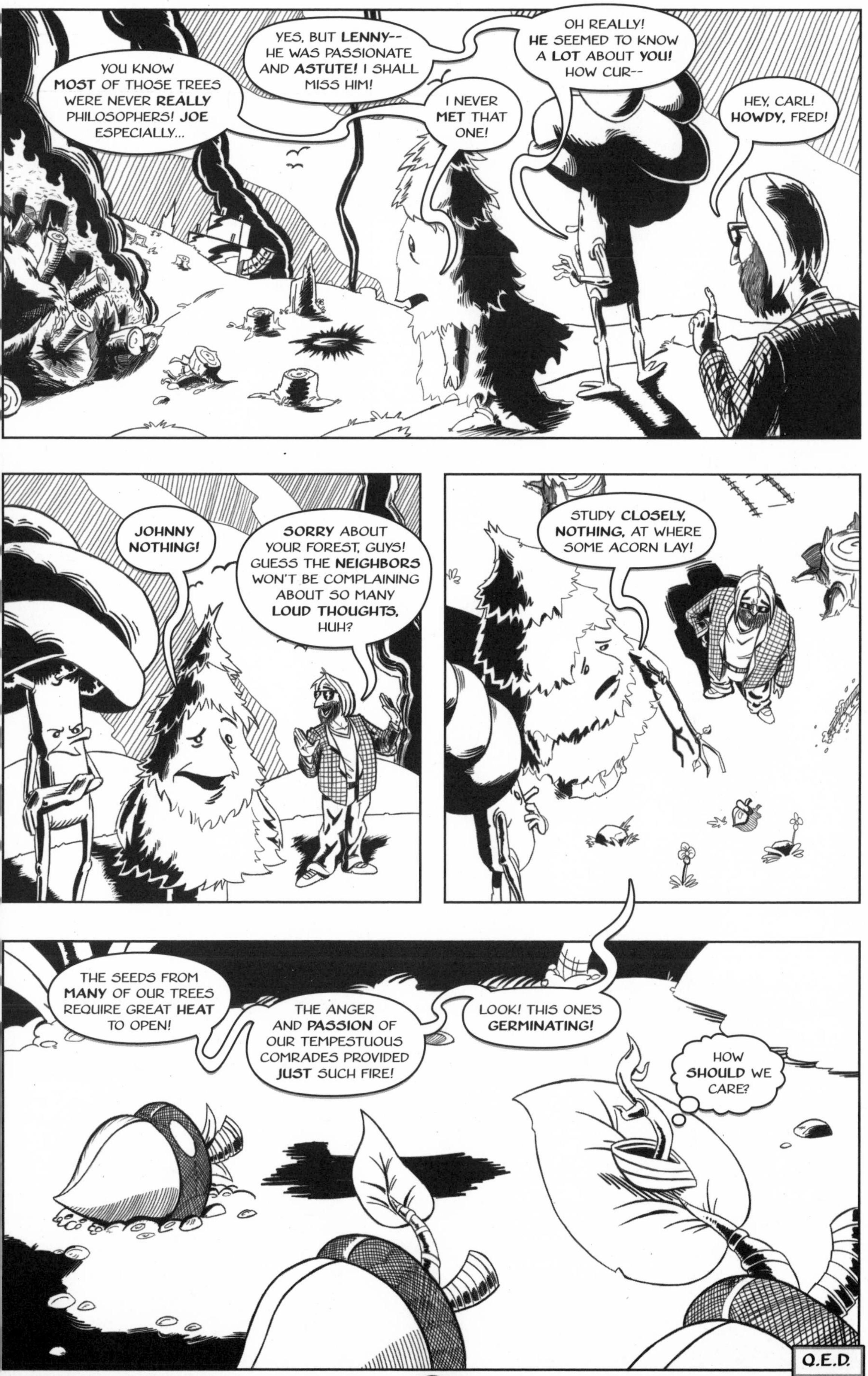
YOU KNOW MOST OF THOSE TREES WERE NEVER REALLY PHILOSOPHERS! JOE ESPECIALLY...
YES, BUT LENNY-- HE WAS PASSIONATE AND ASTUTE! I SHALL MISS HIM!
I NEVER MET THAT ONE!
OH REALLY! HE SEEMED TO KNOW A LOT ABOUT YOU! HOW CUR--
HEY, CARL! HOWDY, FRED!
JOHNNY NOTHING!
SORRY ABOUT YOUR FOREST, GUYS! GUESS THE NEIGHBORS WON'T BE COMPLAINING ABOUT SO MANY LOUD THOUGHTS, HUH?
STUDY CLOSELY, NOTHING, AT WHERE SOME ACORN LAY!
THE SEEDS FROM MANY OF OUR TREES REQUIRE GREAT HEAT TO OPEN!
THE ANGER AND PASSION OF OUR TEMPESTUOUS COMRADES PROVIDED JUST SUCH FIRE!
LOOK! THIS ONE'S GERMINATING!
HOW SHOULD WE CARE?
Q.E.D.

BOOK THREE

I must study politics and war that my sons may
have liberty to study mathematics and philosophy.

John Adams, Second President of
The United States
1735-1826

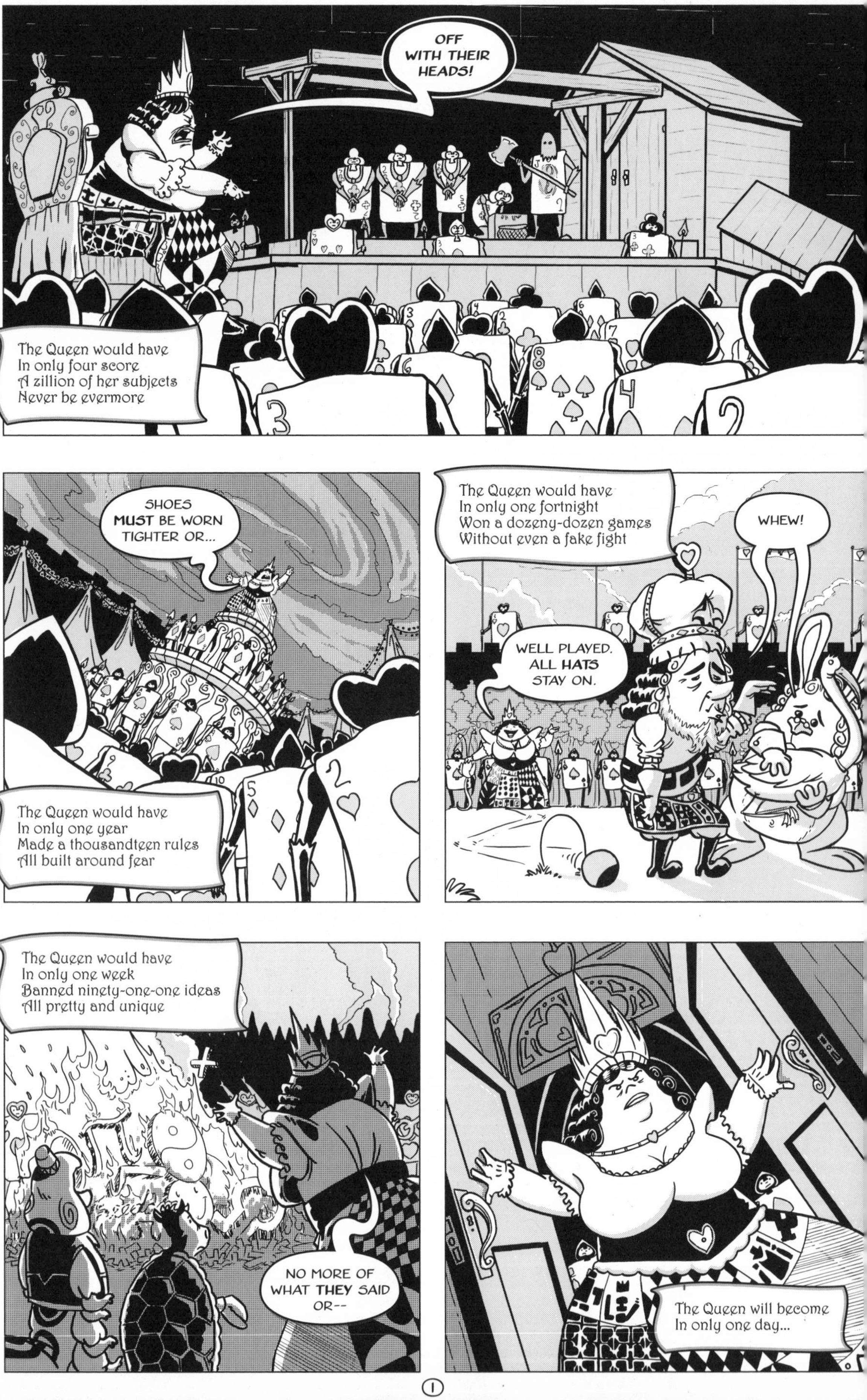
OFF WITH THEIR HEADS!
The Queen would have
In only four score
A zillion of her subjects
Never be evermore
SHOES MUST BE WORN TIGHTER OR...
The Queen would have
In only one year
Made a thousandteen rules
All built around fear
The Queen would have
In only one fortnight
Won a dozeny-dozen games
Without even a fake fight
WHEW!
WELL PLAYED. ALL HATS STAY ON.
The Queen would have
In only one week
Banned ninety-one-one ideas
All pretty and unique
NO MORE OF WHAT THEY SAID OR--
The Queen will become
In only one day...

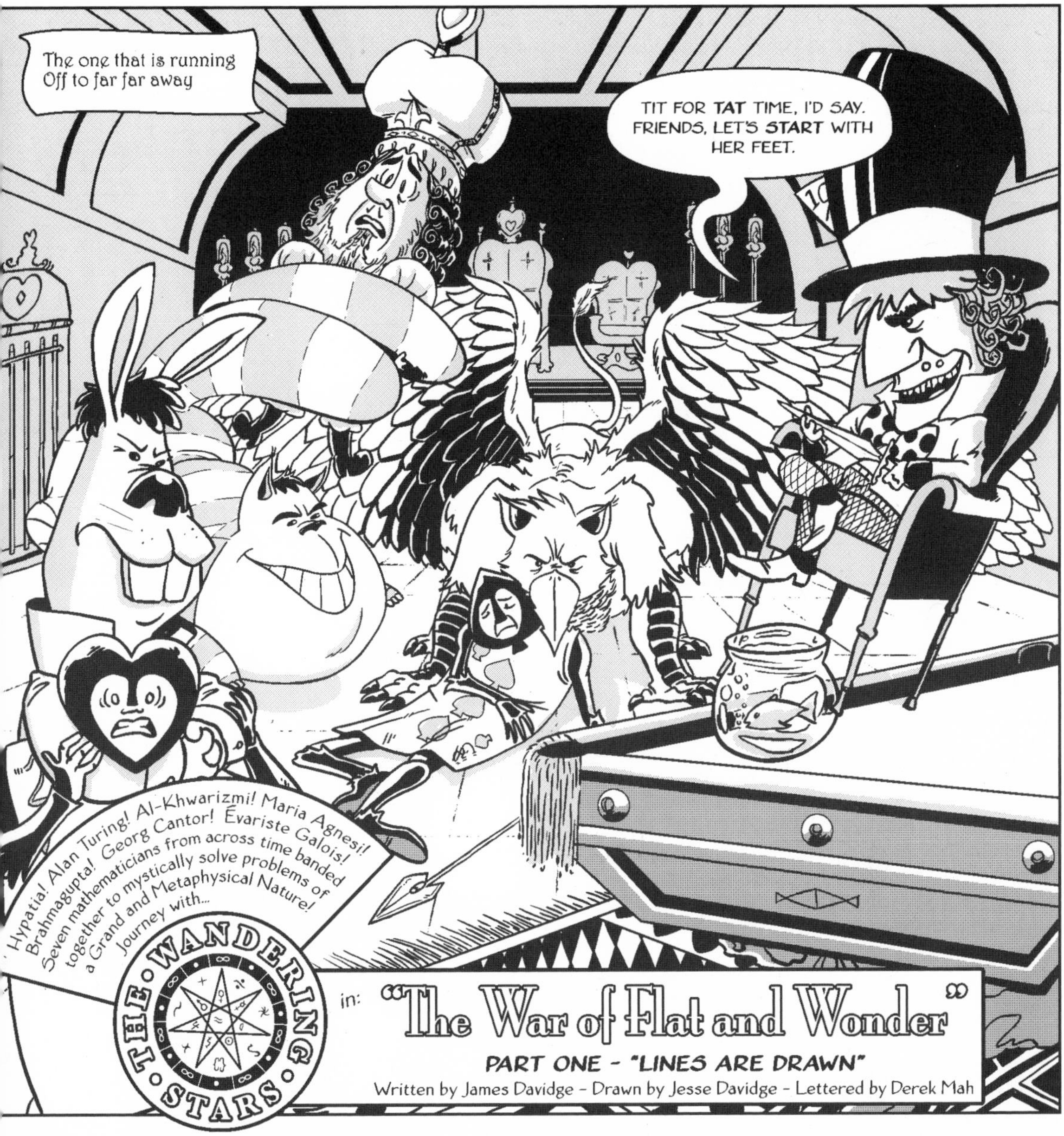
The one that is running
Off to far far away
TIT FOR TAT TIME, I'D SAY. FRIENDS, LET'S START WITH HER FEET.
Hypatia! Alan Turing! Al-Khwarizmi! Maria Agnesi! Brahmagupta! Georg Cantor! Évariste Galois! Seven mathematicians from across time banded together to mystically solve problems of a Grand and Metaphysical Nature! Journey with...
THE WANDERING STARS
in: "The War of Flat and Wonder"
PART ONE - "LINES ARE DRAWN"
Written by James Davidge - Drawn by Jesse Davidge - Lettered by Derek Mah

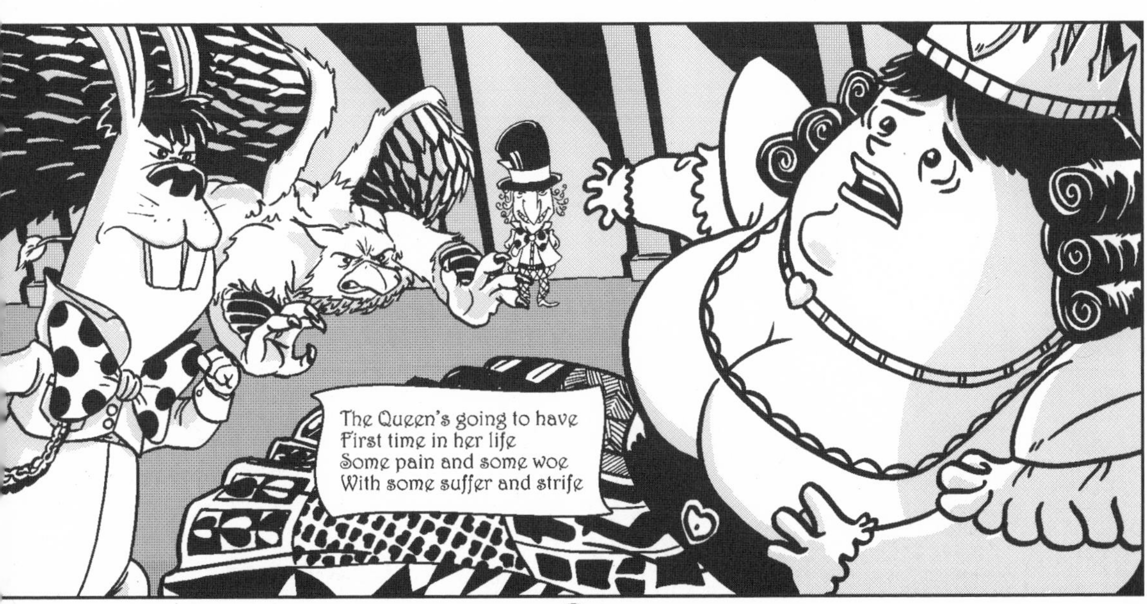
The Queen's going to have
First time in her life
Some pain and some woe
With some suffer and strife

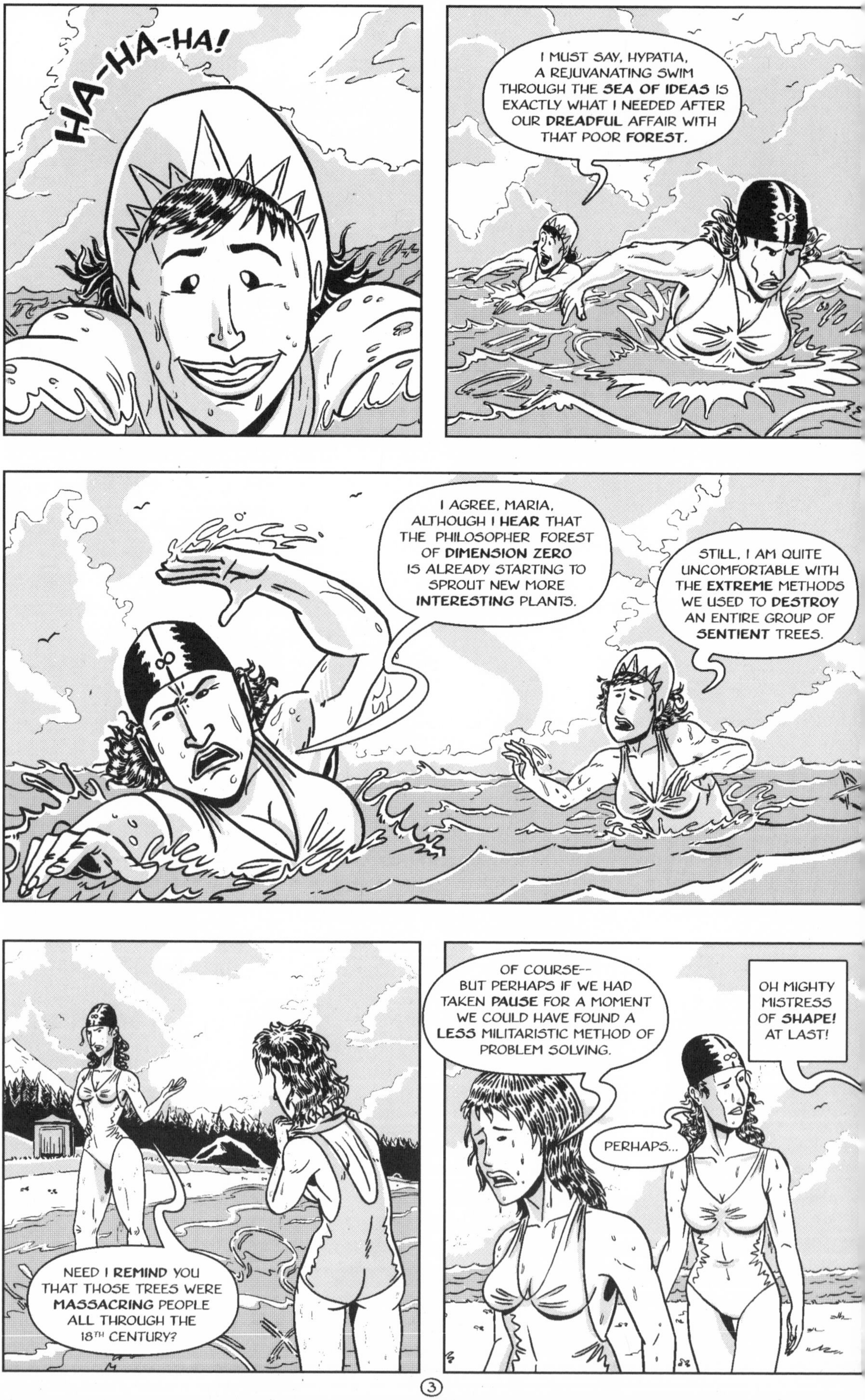
HA-HA-HA!
I MUST SAY, HYPATIA, A REJUVANATING SWIM THROUGH THE **SEA OF IDEAS** IS EXACTLY WHAT I NEEDED AFTER OUR **DREADFUL** AFFAIR WITH THAT POOR **FOREST.**
I AGREE, MARIA, ALTHOUGH I **HEAR** THAT THE PHILOSOPHER FOREST OF **DIMENSION ZERO** IS ALREADY STARTING TO SPROUT NEW MORE **INTERESTING** PLANTS.
STILL, I AM QUITE UNCOMFORTABLE WITH THE **EXTREME** METHODS WE USED TO **DESTROY** AN ENTIRE GROUP OF **SENTIENT** TREES.
NEED I **REMIND** YOU THAT THOSE TREES WERE **MASSACRING** PEOPLE ALL THROUGH THE 18TH CENTURY?
OF COURSE-- BUT PERHAPS IF WE HAD TAKEN **PAUSE** FOR A MOMENT WE COULD HAVE FOUND A **LESS** MILITARISTIC METHOD OF PROBLEM SOLVING.
PERHAPS...
OH MIGHTY MISTRESS OF **SHAPE!** AT LAST!

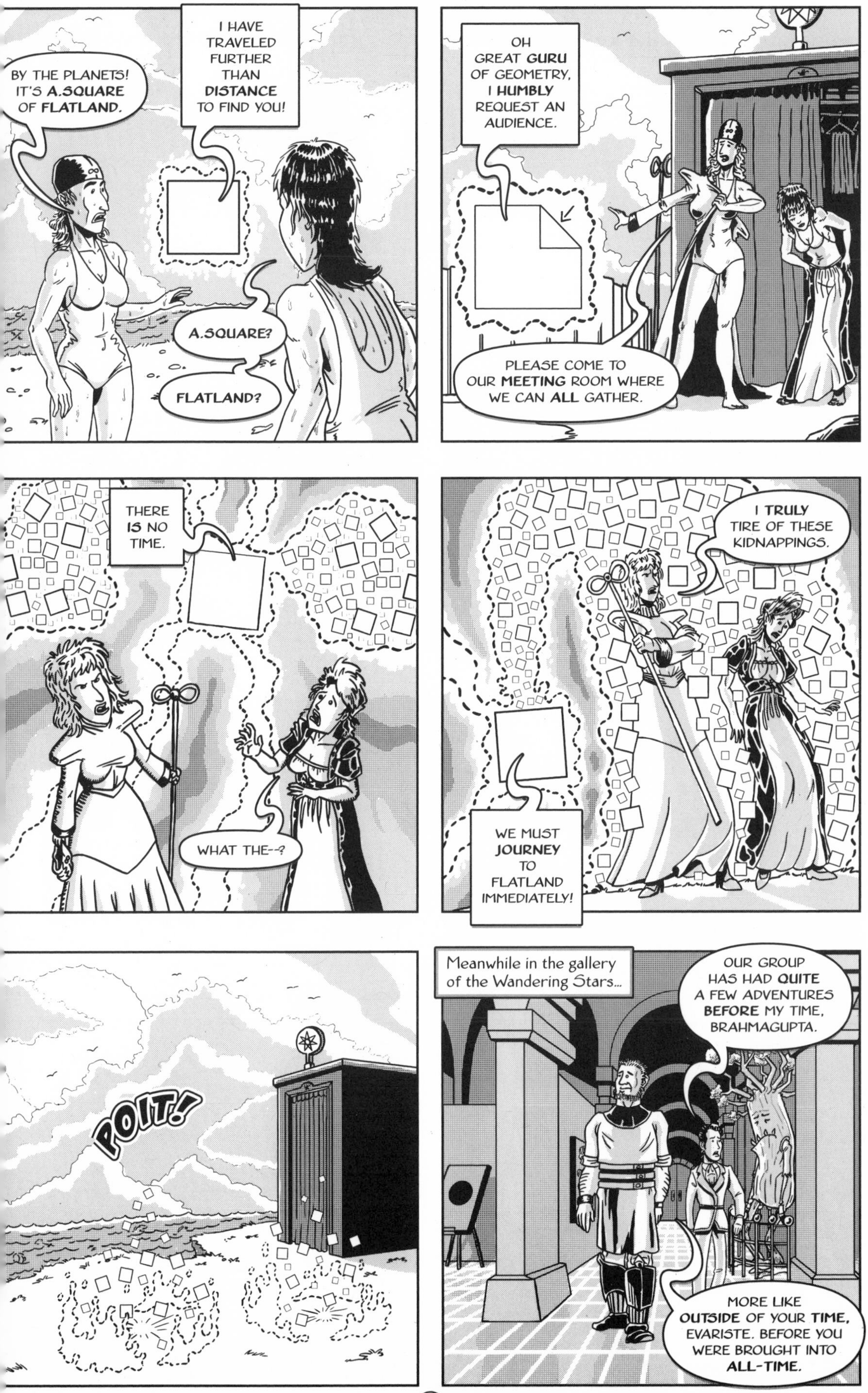
BY THE PLANETS! IT'S A.SQUARE OF FLATLAND.
I HAVE TRAVELED FURTHER THAN DISTANCE TO FIND YOU!
A.SQUARE?
FLATLAND?
OH GREAT GURU OF GEOMETRY, I HUMBLY REQUEST AN AUDIENCE.
PLEASE COME TO OUR MEETING ROOM WHERE WE CAN ALL GATHER.
THERE IS NO TIME.
WHAT THE--?
I TRULY TIRE OF THESE KIDNAPPINGS.
WE MUST JOURNEY TO FLATLAND IMMEDIATELY!
POIT!
Meanwhile in the gallery of the Wandering Stars...
OUR GROUP HAS HAD QUITE A FEW ADVENTURES BEFORE MY TIME, BRAHMAGUPTA.
MORE LIKE OUTSIDE OF YOUR TIME, EVARISTE. BEFORE YOU WERE BROUGHT INTO ALL-TIME.

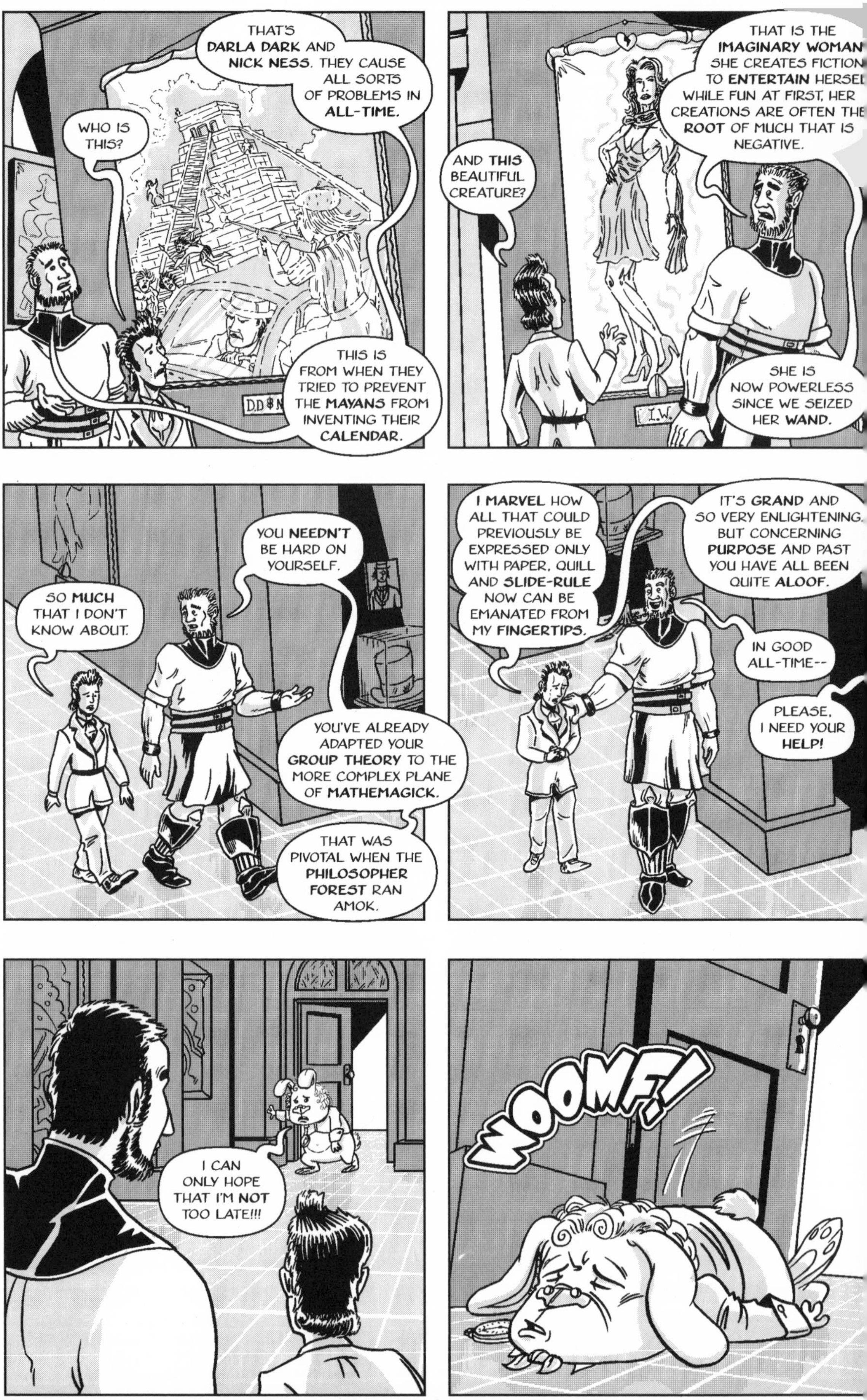
WHO IS THIS?
THAT'S DARLA DARK AND NICK NESS. THEY CAUSE ALL SORTS OF PROBLEMS IN ALL-TIME.
THIS IS FROM WHEN THEY TRIED TO PREVENT THE MAYANS FROM INVENTING THEIR CALENDAR.
D.D.&N.
AND THIS BEAUTIFUL CREATURE?
THAT IS THE IMAGINARY WOMAN. SHE CREATES FICTION TO ENTERTAIN HERSELF. WHILE FUN AT FIRST, HER CREATIONS ARE OFTEN THE ROOT OF MUCH THAT IS NEGATIVE.
SHE IS NOW POWERLESS SINCE WE SEIZED HER WAND.
I.W.
SO MUCH THAT I DON'T KNOW ABOUT.
YOU NEEDN'T BE HARD ON YOURSELF.
YOU'VE ALREADY ADAPTED YOUR GROUP THEORY TO THE MORE COMPLEX PLANE OF MATHEMAGICK.
THAT WAS PIVOTAL WHEN THE PHILOSOPHER FOREST RAN AMOK.
I MARVEL HOW ALL THAT COULD PREVIOUSLY BE EXPRESSED ONLY WITH PAPER, QUILL AND SLIDE-RULE NOW CAN BE EMANATED FROM MY FINGERTIPS.
IT'S GRAND AND SO VERY ENLIGHTENING. BUT CONCERNING PURPOSE AND PAST YOU HAVE ALL BEEN QUITE ALOOF.
IN GOOD ALL-TIME--
PLEASE, I NEED YOUR HELP!
I CAN ONLY HOPE THAT I'M NOT TOO LATE!!!
WOOMF!

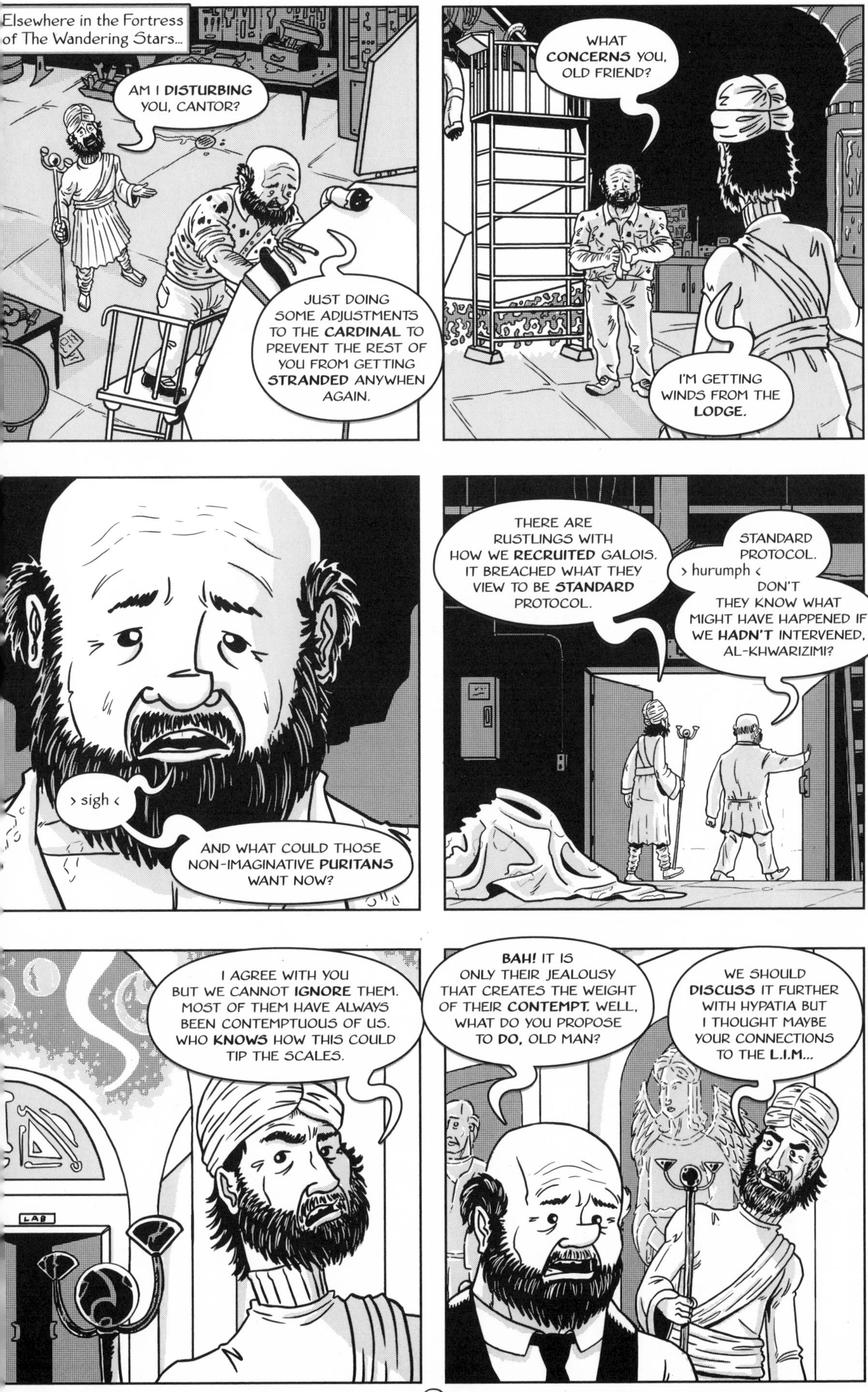
Elsewhere in the Fortress of The Wandering Stars...
AM I DISTURBING YOU, CANTOR?
JUST DOING SOME ADJUSTMENTS TO THE CARDINAL TO PREVENT THE REST OF YOU FROM GETTING STRANDED ANYWHEN AGAIN.
WHAT CONCERNS YOU, OLD FRIEND?
I'M GETTING WINDS FROM THE LODGE.
› sigh ‹
AND WHAT COULD THOSE NON-IMAGINATIVE PURITANS WANT NOW?
THERE ARE RUSTLINGS WITH HOW WE RECRUITED GALOIS. IT BREACHED WHAT THEY VIEW TO BE STANDARD PROTOCOL.
STANDARD PROTOCOL. › hurumph ‹ DON'T THEY KNOW WHAT MIGHT HAVE HAPPENED IF WE HADN'T INTERVENED, AL-KHWARIZIMI?
I AGREE WITH YOU BUT WE CANNOT IGNORE THEM. MOST OF THEM HAVE ALWAYS BEEN CONTEMPTUOUS OF US. WHO KNOWS HOW THIS COULD TIP THE SCALES.
LAB
BAH! IT IS ONLY THEIR JEALOUSY THAT CREATES THE WEIGHT OF THEIR CONTEMPT. WELL, WHAT DO YOU PROPOSE TO DO, OLD MAN?
WE SHOULD DISCUSS IT FURTHER WITH HYPATIA BUT I THOUGHT MAYBE YOUR CONNECTIONS TO THE L.I.M...

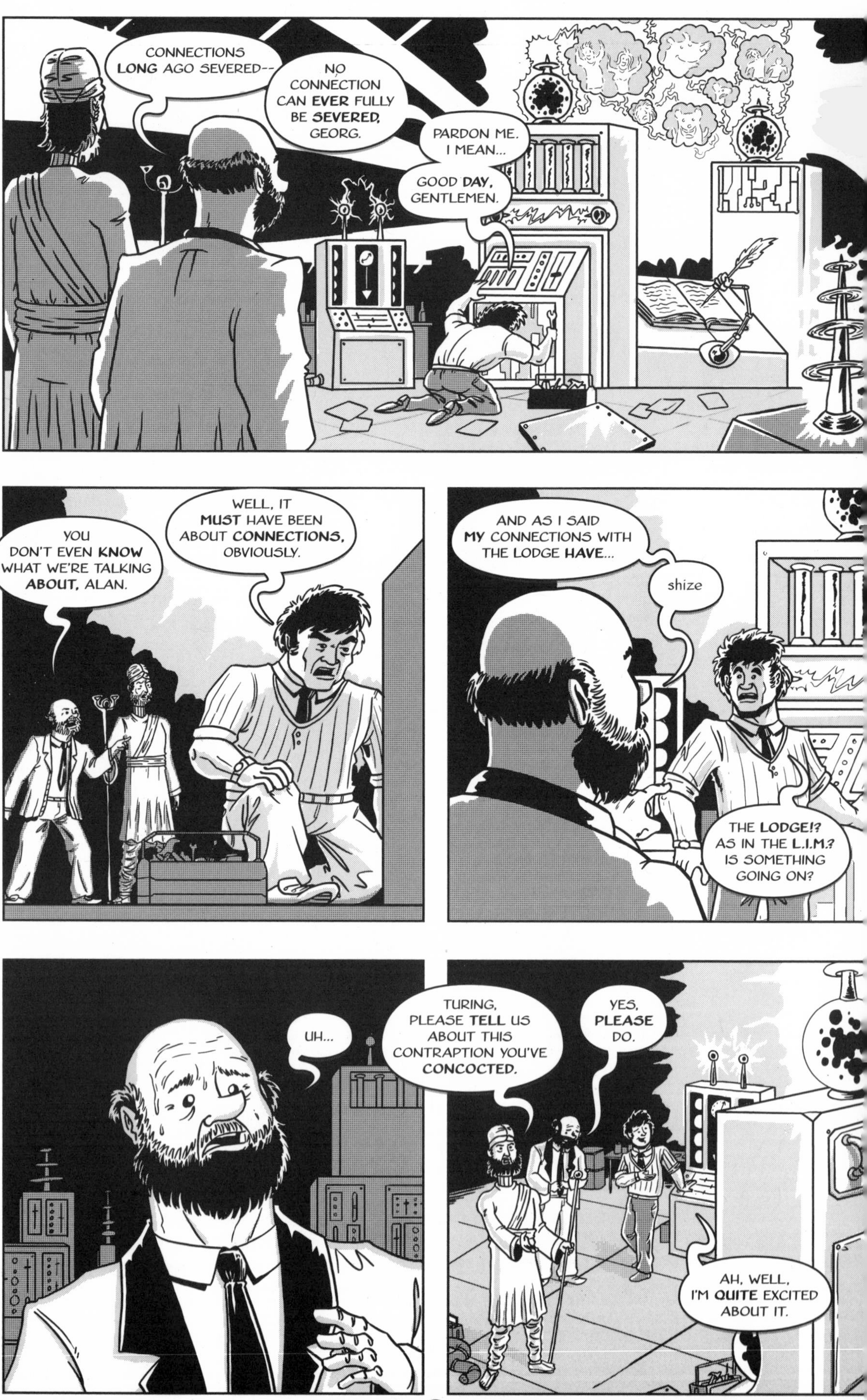
CONNECTIONS LONG AGO SEVERED--
NO CONNECTION CAN EVER FULLY BE SEVERED, GEORG.
PARDON ME. I MEAN...
GOOD DAY, GENTLEMEN.
YOU DON'T EVEN KNOW WHAT WE'RE TALKING ABOUT, ALAN.
WELL, IT MUST HAVE BEEN ABOUT CONNECTIONS, OBVIOUSLY.
AND AS I SAID MY CONNECTIONS WITH THE LODGE HAVE...
shize
THE LODGE!? AS IN THE L.I.M.? IS SOMETHING GOING ON?
UH...
TURING, PLEASE TELL US ABOUT THIS CONTRAPTION YOU'VE CONCOCTED.
YES, PLEASE DO.
AH, WELL, I'M QUITE EXCITED ABOUT IT.

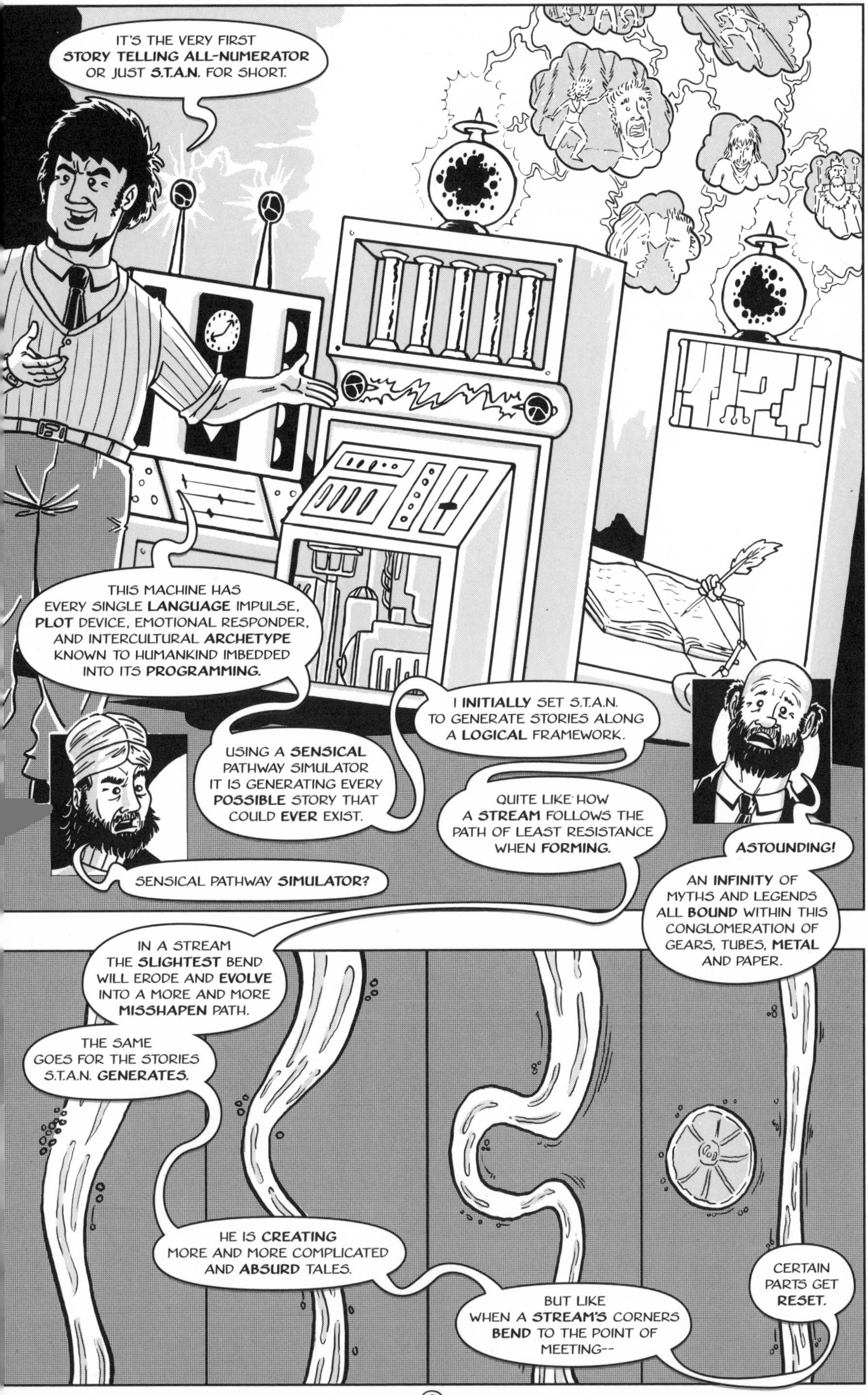
IT'S THE VERY FIRST STORY TELLING ALL-NUMERATOR OR JUST S.T.A.N. FOR SHORT.
THIS MACHINE HAS EVERY SINGLE LANGUAGE IMPULSE, PLOT DEVICE, EMOTIONAL RESPONDER, AND INTERCULTURAL ARCHETYPE KNOWN TO HUMANKIND IMBEDDED INTO ITS PROGRAMMING.
USING A SENSICAL PATHWAY SIMULATOR IT IS GENERATING EVERY POSSIBLE STORY THAT COULD EVER EXIST.
SENSICAL PATHWAY SIMULATOR?
I INITIALLY SET S.T.A.N. TO GENERATE STORIES ALONG A LOGICAL FRAMEWORK.
QUITE LIKE HOW A STREAM FOLLOWS THE PATH OF LEAST RESISTANCE WHEN FORMING.
ASTOUNDING!
AN INFINITY OF MYTHS AND LEGENDS ALL BOUND WITHIN THIS CONGLOMERATION OF GEARS, TUBES, METAL AND PAPER.
IN A STREAM THE SLIGHTEST BEND WILL ERODE AND EVOLVE INTO A MORE AND MORE MISSHAPEN PATH.
THE SAME GOES FOR THE STORIES S.T.A.N. GENERATES.
HE IS CREATING MORE AND MORE COMPLICATED AND ABSURD TALES.
BUT LIKE WHEN A STREAM'S CORNERS BEND TO THE POINT OF MEETING--
CERTAIN PARTS GET RESET.

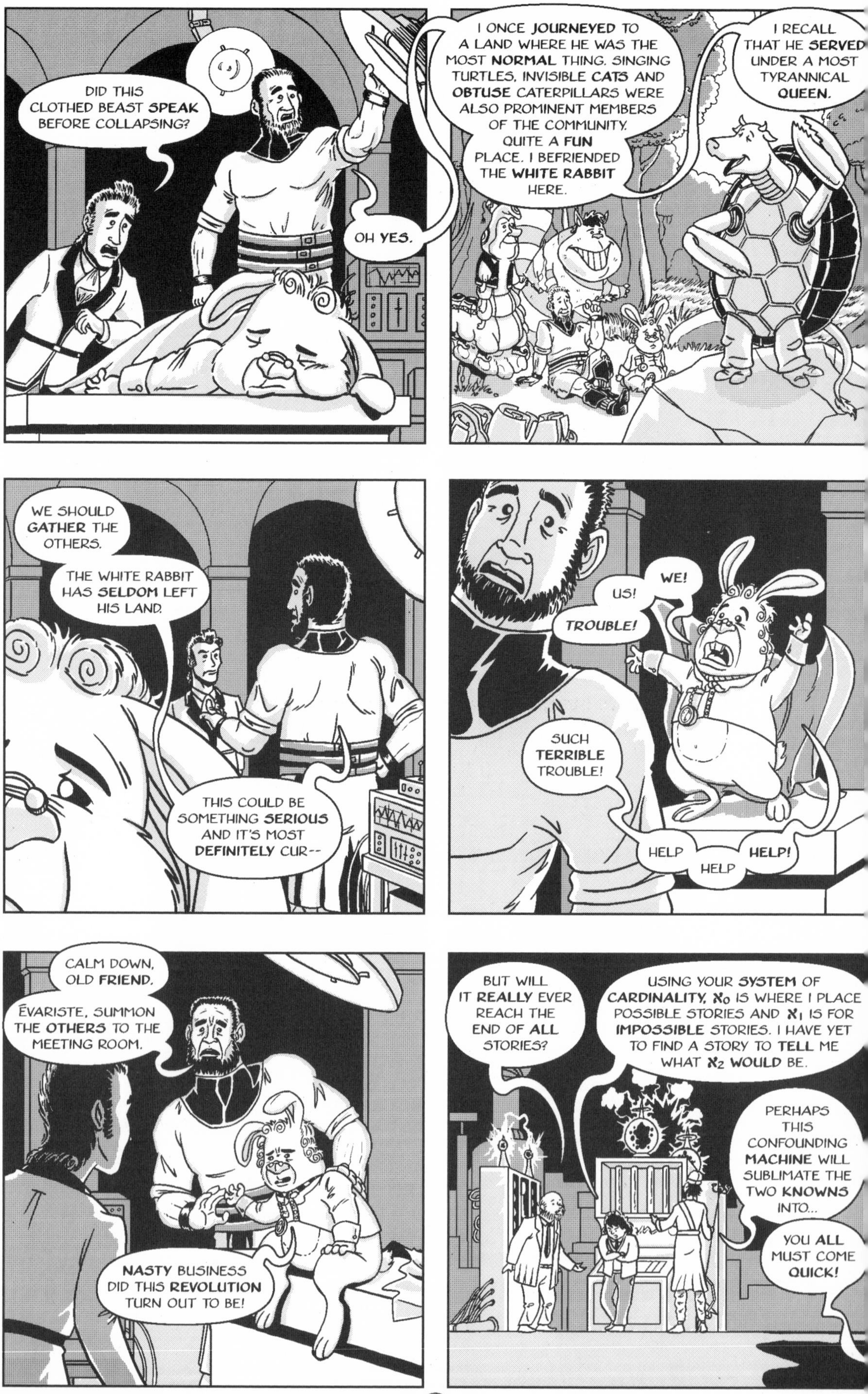
DID THIS CLOTHED BEAST SPEAK BEFORE COLLAPSING?
OH YES.
I ONCE JOURNEYED TO A LAND WHERE HE WAS THE MOST NORMAL THING. SINGING TURTLES, INVISIBLE CATS AND OBTUSE CATERPILLARS WERE ALSO PROMINENT MEMBERS OF THE COMMUNITY. QUITE A FUN PLACE. I BEFRIENDED THE WHITE RABBIT HERE.
I RECALL THAT HE SERVED UNDER A MOST TYRANNICAL QUEEN.
WE SHOULD GATHER THE OTHERS.
THE WHITE RABBIT HAS SELDOM LEFT HIS LAND.
THIS COULD BE SOMETHING SERIOUS AND IT'S MOST DEFINITELY CUR--
WE!
US!
TROUBLE!
SUCH TERRIBLE TROUBLE!
HELP
HELP
HELP!
CALM DOWN, OLD FRIEND.
ÉVARISTE, SUMMON THE OTHERS TO THE MEETING ROOM.
NASTY BUSINESS DID THIS REVOLUTION TURN OUT TO BE!
BUT WILL IT REALLY EVER REACH THE END OF ALL STORIES?
USING YOUR SYSTEM OF CARDINALITY, $\aleph_0$ IS WHERE I PLACE POSSIBLE STORIES AND $\aleph_1$ IS FOR IMPOSSIBLE STORIES. I HAVE YET TO FIND A STORY TO TELL ME WHAT $\aleph_2$ WOULD BE.
PERHAPS THIS CONFOUNDING MACHINE WILL SUBLIMATE THE TWO KNOWNS INTO...
YOU ALL MUST COME QUICK!

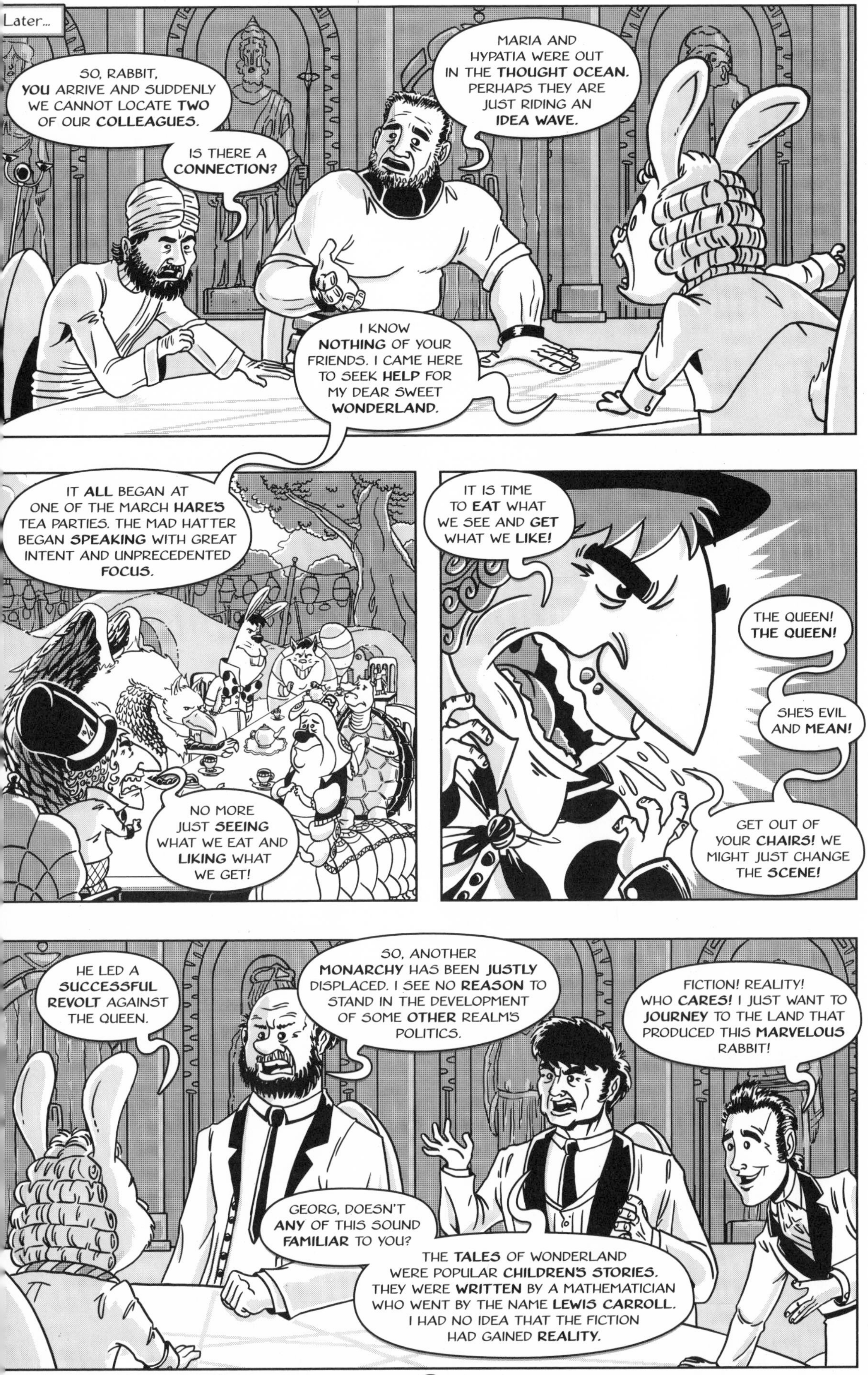
Later...
SO, RABBIT, YOU ARRIVE AND SUDDENLY WE CANNOT LOCATE TWO OF OUR COLLEAGUES.
IS THERE A CONNECTION?
MARIA AND HYPATIA WERE OUT IN THE THOUGHT OCEAN. PERHAPS THEY ARE JUST RIDING AN IDEA WAVE.
I KNOW NOTHING OF YOUR FRIENDS. I CAME HERE TO SEEK HELP FOR MY DEAR SWEET WONDERLAND.
IT ALL BEGAN AT ONE OF THE MARCH HARE'S TEA PARTIES. THE MAD HATTER BEGAN SPEAKING WITH GREAT INTENT AND UNPRECEDENTED FOCUS.
NO MORE JUST SEEING WHAT WE EAT AND LIKING WHAT WE GET!
IT IS TIME TO EAT WHAT WE SEE AND GET WHAT WE LIKE!
THE QUEEN! THE QUEEN!
SHE'S EVIL AND MEAN!
GET OUT OF YOUR CHAIRS! WE MIGHT JUST CHANGE THE SCENE!
HE LED A SUCCESSFUL REVOLT AGAINST THE QUEEN.
SO, ANOTHER MONARCHY HAS BEEN JUSTLY DISPLACED. I SEE NO REASON TO STAND IN THE DEVELOPMENT OF SOME OTHER REALM'S POLITICS.
FICTION! REALITY! WHO CARES! I JUST WANT TO JOURNEY TO THE LAND THAT PRODUCED THIS MARVELOUS RABBIT!
GEORG, DOESN'T ANY OF THIS SOUND FAMILIAR TO YOU?
THE TALES OF WONDERLAND WERE POPULAR CHILDREN'S STORIES. THEY WERE WRITTEN BY A MATHEMATICIAN WHO WENT BY THE NAME LEWIS CARROLL. I HAD NO IDEA THAT THE FICTION HAD GAINED REALITY.

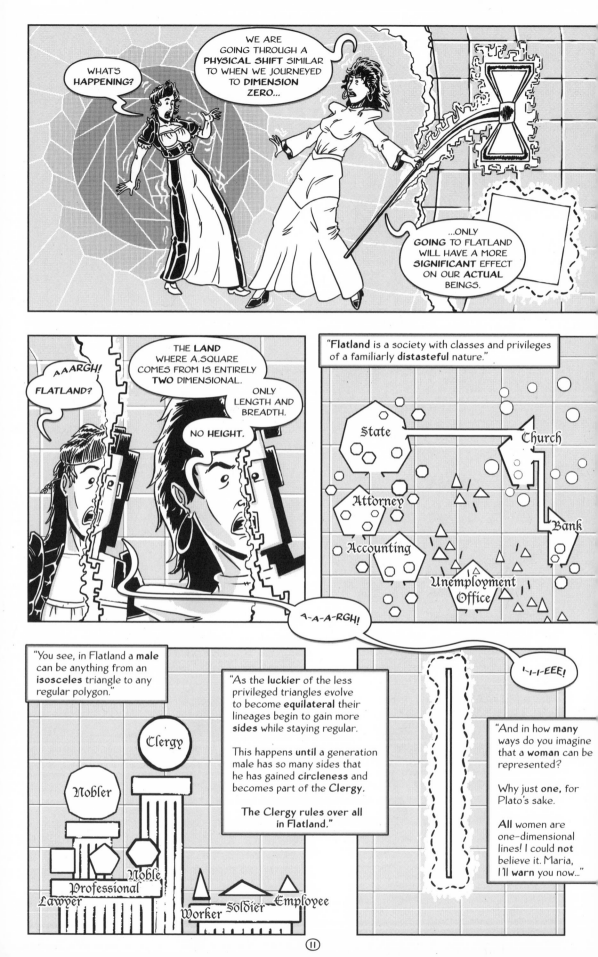

WHAT'S HAPPENING?

WE ARE GOING THROUGH A **PHYSICAL SHIFT** SIMILAR TO WHEN WE JOURNEYED TO **DIMENSION ZERO**...

...ONLY **GOING** TO FLATLAND WILL HAVE A MORE **SIGNIFICANT** EFFECT ON OUR **ACTUAL** BEINGS.

AAARGH! FLATLAND?

THE **LAND** WHERE A.SQUARE COMES FROM IS ENTIRELY **TWO** DIMENSIONAL. ONLY LENGTH AND BREADTH.

NO HEIGHT.

"**Flatland** is a society with classes and privileges of a familiarly **distasteful** nature."

State

Church

Attorney

Accounting

Bank

Unemployment Office

A-A-A-RGH!

ЧI-I-EEE!

"You see, in Flatland a **male** can be anything from an **isosceles** triangle to any regular polygon."

"As the **luckier** of the less privileged triangles evolve to become **equilateral** their lineages begin to gain more **sides** while staying regular.

This happens **until** a generation male has so many sides that he has gained **circleness** and becomes part of the Clergy.

The Clergy rules over all in Flatland."

"And in how **many** ways do you imagine that a **woman** can be represented?

Why just **one**, for Plato's sake.

All women are one-dimensional lines! I could **not** believe it. Maria, I'll **warn** you now..."

Clergy

Nobler

Professional

Lawyer

Noble

Worker Soldier Employee

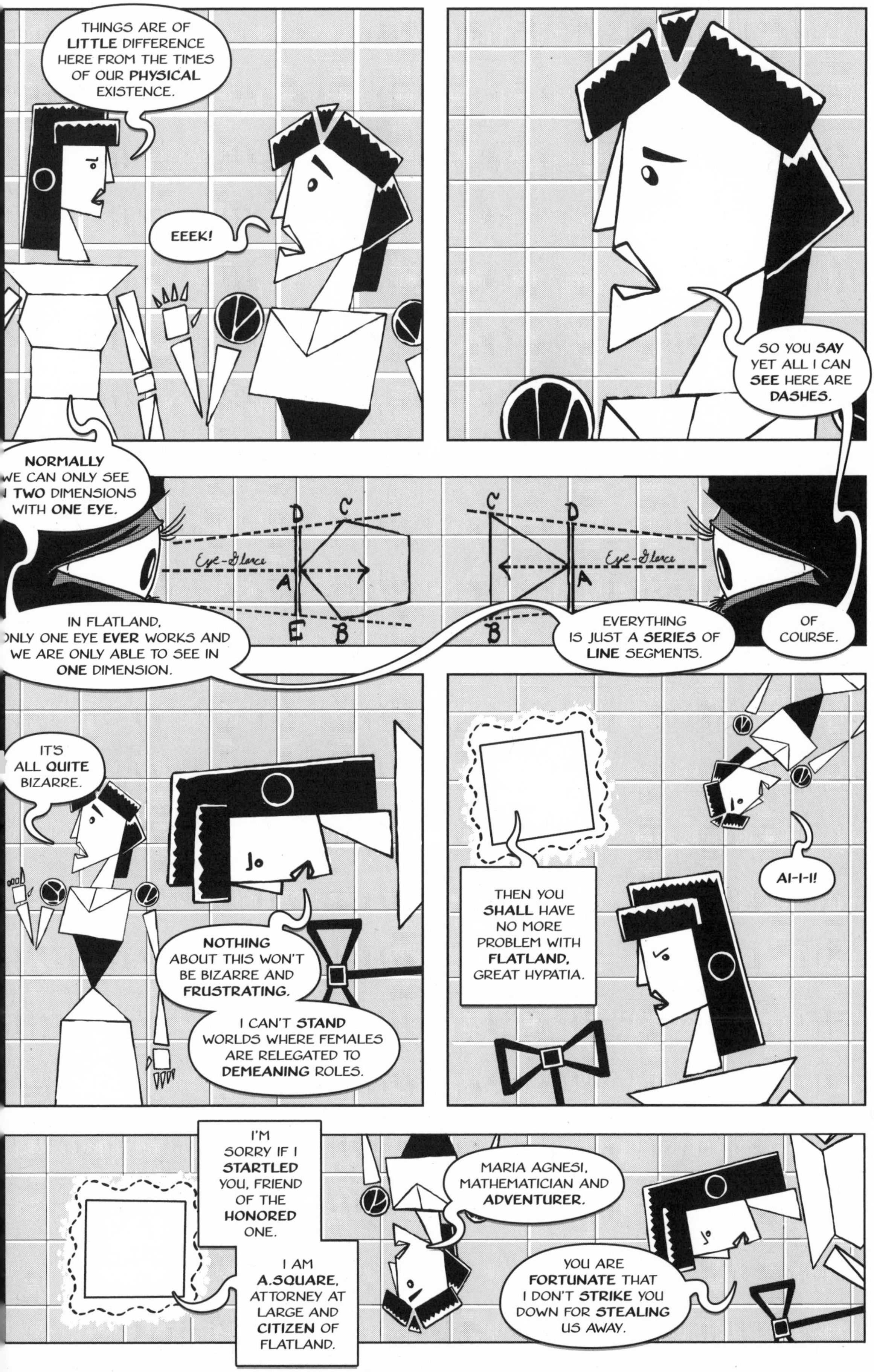

THINGS ARE OF LITTLE DIFFERENCE HERE FROM THE TIMES OF OUR PHYSICAL EXISTENCE.
EEEK!
SO YOU SAY YET ALL I CAN SEE HERE ARE DASHES.
NORMALLY WE CAN ONLY SEE IN TWO DIMENSIONS WITH ONE EYE.
D
C
Eye-Glance
A
E
B
C
D
Eye-Glance
A
B
IN FLATLAND, ONLY ONE EYE EVER WORKS AND WE ARE ONLY ABLE TO SEE IN ONE DIMENSION.
EVERYTHING IS JUST A SERIES OF LINE SEGMENTS.
OF COURSE.
IT'S ALL QUITE BIZARRE.
NOTHING ABOUT THIS WON'T BE BIZARRE AND FRUSTRATING.
I CAN'T STAND WORLDS WHERE FEMALES ARE RELEGATED TO DEMEANING ROLES.
THEN YOU SHALL HAVE NO MORE PROBLEM WITH FLATLAND, GREAT HYPATIA.
AI-I-I!
I'M SORRY IF I STARTLED YOU, FRIEND OF THE HONORED ONE.
I AM A.SQUARE, ATTORNEY AT LARGE AND CITIZEN OF FLATLAND.
MARIA AGNESI, MATHEMATICIAN AND ADVENTURER.
YOU ARE FORTUNATE THAT I DON'T STRIKE YOU DOWN FOR STEALING US AWAY.

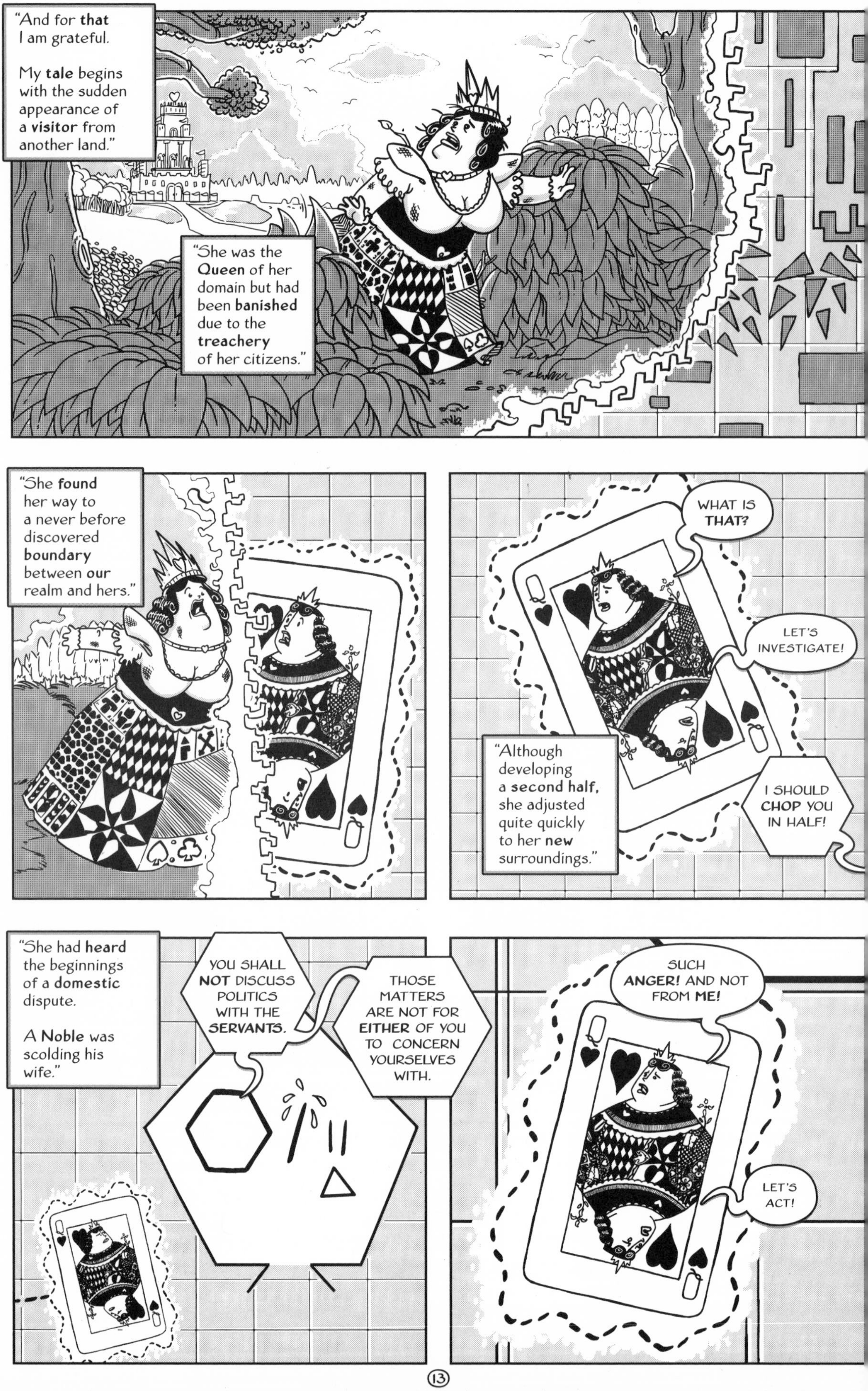
"And for **that** I am grateful.
My **tale** begins with the sudden appearance of a **visitor** from another land."
"She was the **Queen** of her domain but had been **banished** due to the **treachery** of her citizens."
"She **found** her way to a never before discovered **boundary** between **our** realm and hers."
WHAT IS **THAT?**
LET'S INVESTIGATE!
"Although developing a **second half,** she adjusted quite quickly to her **new** surroundings."
I SHOULD **CHOP** YOU IN HALF!
"She had **heard** the beginnings of a **domestic** dispute.
A **Noble** was scolding his wife."
YOU SHALL **NOT** DISCUSS POLITICS WITH THE **SERVANTS.**
THOSE MATTERS ARE NOT FOR **EITHER** OF YOU TO CONCERN YOURSELVES WITH.
SUCH **ANGER!** AND NOT FROM **ME!**
LET'S ACT!

REALLY?
YOU MUST SWAY SO I CAN SEE YOU AND YOUR SHARP ENDS MUST ALWAYS BE AT LEAST THREE FEET AWAY FROM ME.
YOU WHO ARE MANY.
IT IS WITHIN YOU TO STOP THIS ABUSE.
ALL YOU HAVE TO DO IS BE AWARE OF YOUR OWN POWER.
LET'S MOTIVATE!
UH...
OFF WITH HIS SIDES!
BRILLIANT!
MY DARLING, WHAT ARE YOU DOING? YOU MUST STILL PRODUCE MY HEPTAGON HEIR. PLEASE STOP!
AAAAAARGH!!

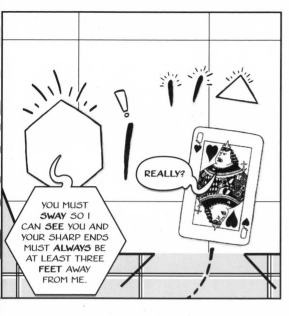

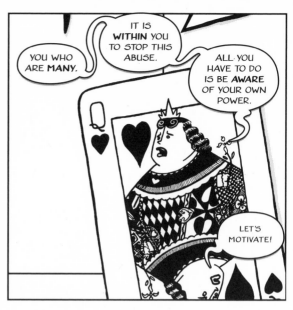

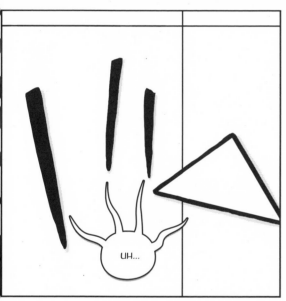

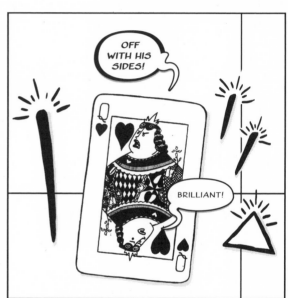

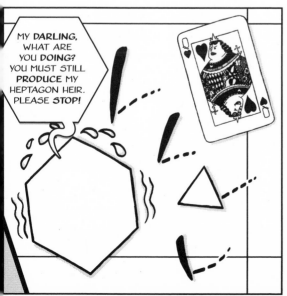

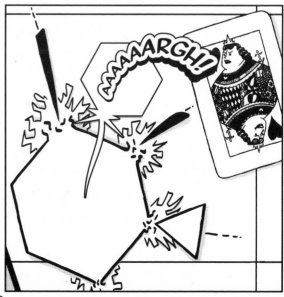

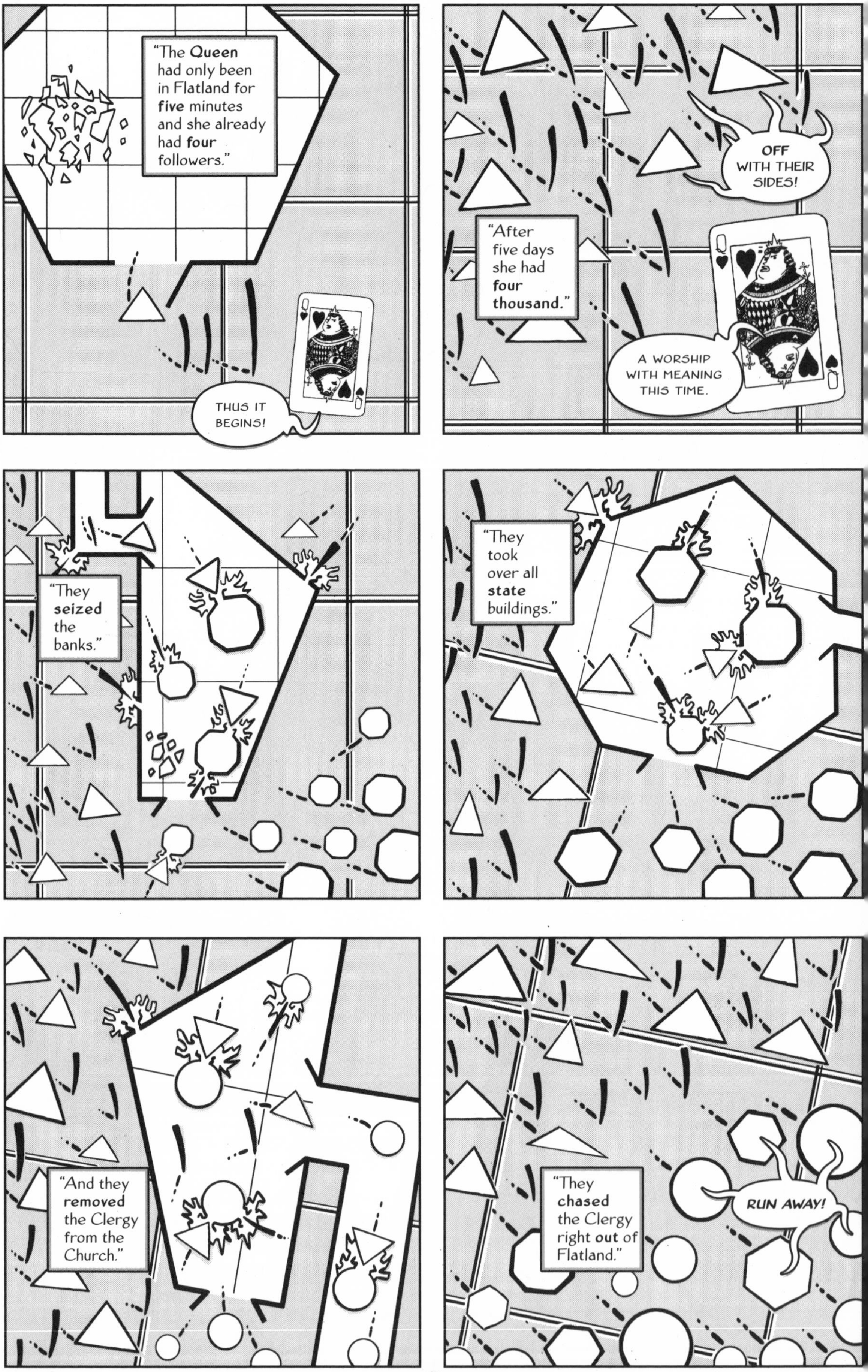
"The **Queen** had only been in Flatland for **five** minutes and she already had **four** followers."
THUS IT BEGINS!
OFF WITH THEIR SIDES!
"After five days she had **four thousand.**"
A WORSHIP WITH MEANING THIS TIME.
"They **seized** the banks."
"They took over all **state** buildings."
"And they **removed** the Clergy from the Church."
"They **chased** the Clergy right **out** of Flatland."
RUN AWAY!

"The Queen had **made** herself **leader** in a land of **strangers**."

EXCELLENT.

MOST EXCELLENT.

AND MY CONGRATULATIONS TO HER. IT WAS A **REVOLUTION** WHOSE TIME HAD COME IN THIS **ANTIQUATED** LAND. I PRAY YOU DIDN'T BRING US HERE TO TRY TO **REVERSE** THE WORK DONE.

GOODNESS, **NO!**

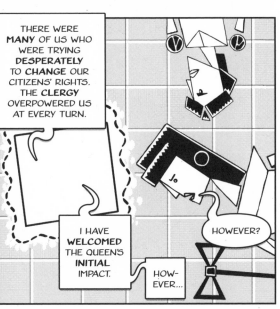

THERE WERE **MANY** OF US WHO WERE TRYING **DESPERATELY** TO **CHANGE** OUR CITIZENS' RIGHTS. THE **CLERGY** OVERPOWERED US AT EVERY TURN.

I HAVE **WELCOMED** THE QUEEN'S **INITIAL** IMPACT.

HOW-EVER...

HOWEVER?

SHE MEANS TO TAKE US TO **WAR.**

Back at the Fortress...

IT'S STILL **UNCLEAR WHAT** YOU WISH FROM US, WHITE RABBIT.

PERHAPS WE CAN **INVESTIGATE** THIS FROM THE LITERARY **SOURCE** OF 19TH CENTURY ENGLAND.

NO NO **NO!** YOU MUST FOLLOW ME **NOW.**

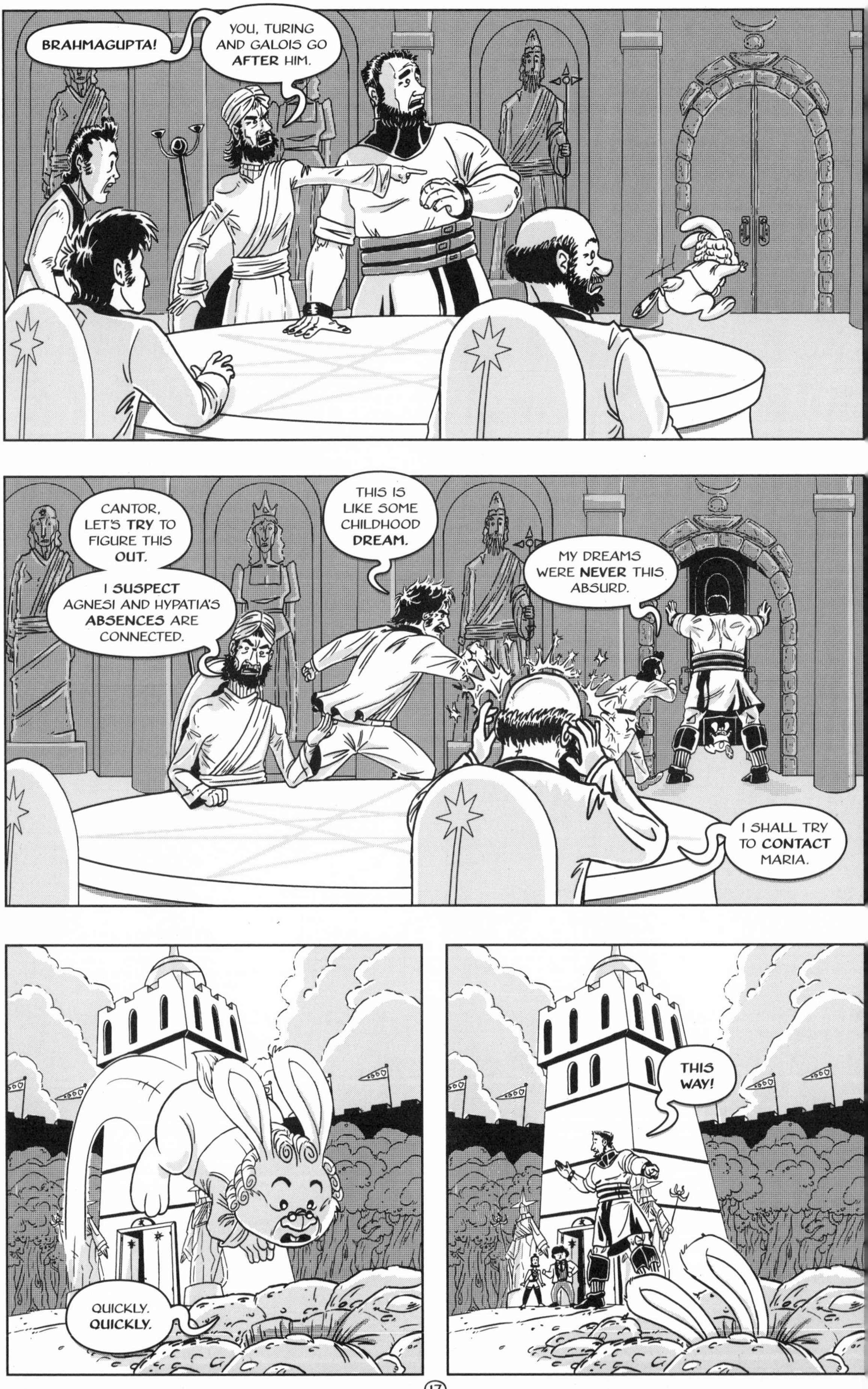
BRAHMAGUPTA!
YOU, TURING AND GALOIS GO AFTER HIM.
CANTOR, LET'S TRY TO FIGURE THIS OUT.
I SUSPECT AGNESI AND HYPATIA'S ABSENCES ARE CONNECTED.
THIS IS LIKE SOME CHILDHOOD DREAM.
MY DREAMS WERE NEVER THIS ABSURD.
I SHALL TRY TO CONTACT MARIA.
QUICKLY. QUICKLY.
THIS WAY!

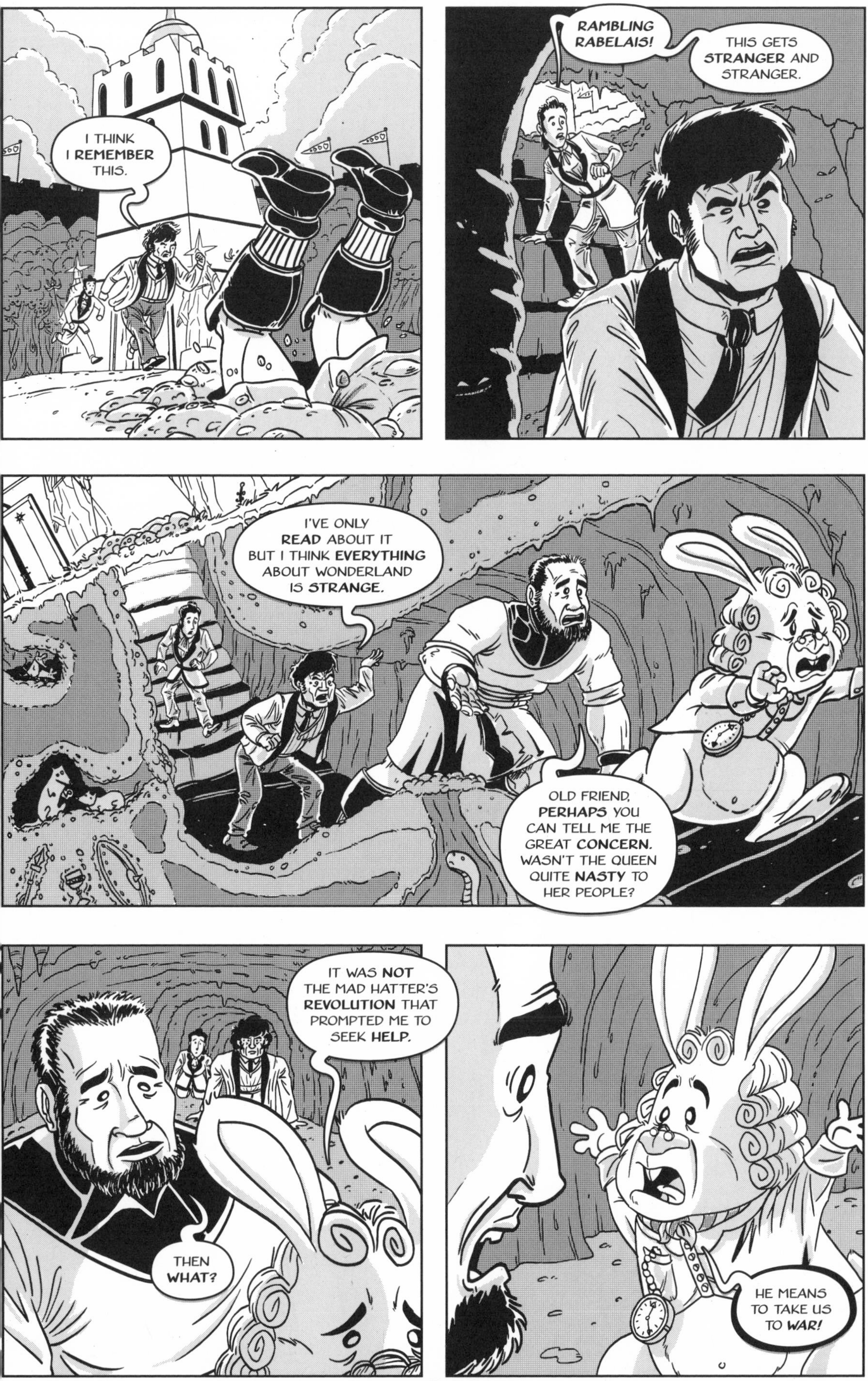
I THINK I REMEMBER THIS.
RAMBLING RABELAIS!
THIS GETS STRANGER AND STRANGER.
I'VE ONLY READ ABOUT IT BUT I THINK EVERYTHING ABOUT WONDERLAND IS STRANGE.
OLD FRIEND, PERHAPS YOU CAN TELL ME THE GREAT CONCERN. WASN'T THE QUEEN QUITE NASTY TO HER PEOPLE?
IT WAS NOT THE MAD HATTER'S REVOLUTION THAT PROMPTED ME TO SEEK HELP.
THEN WHAT?
HE MEANS TO TAKE US TO WAR!

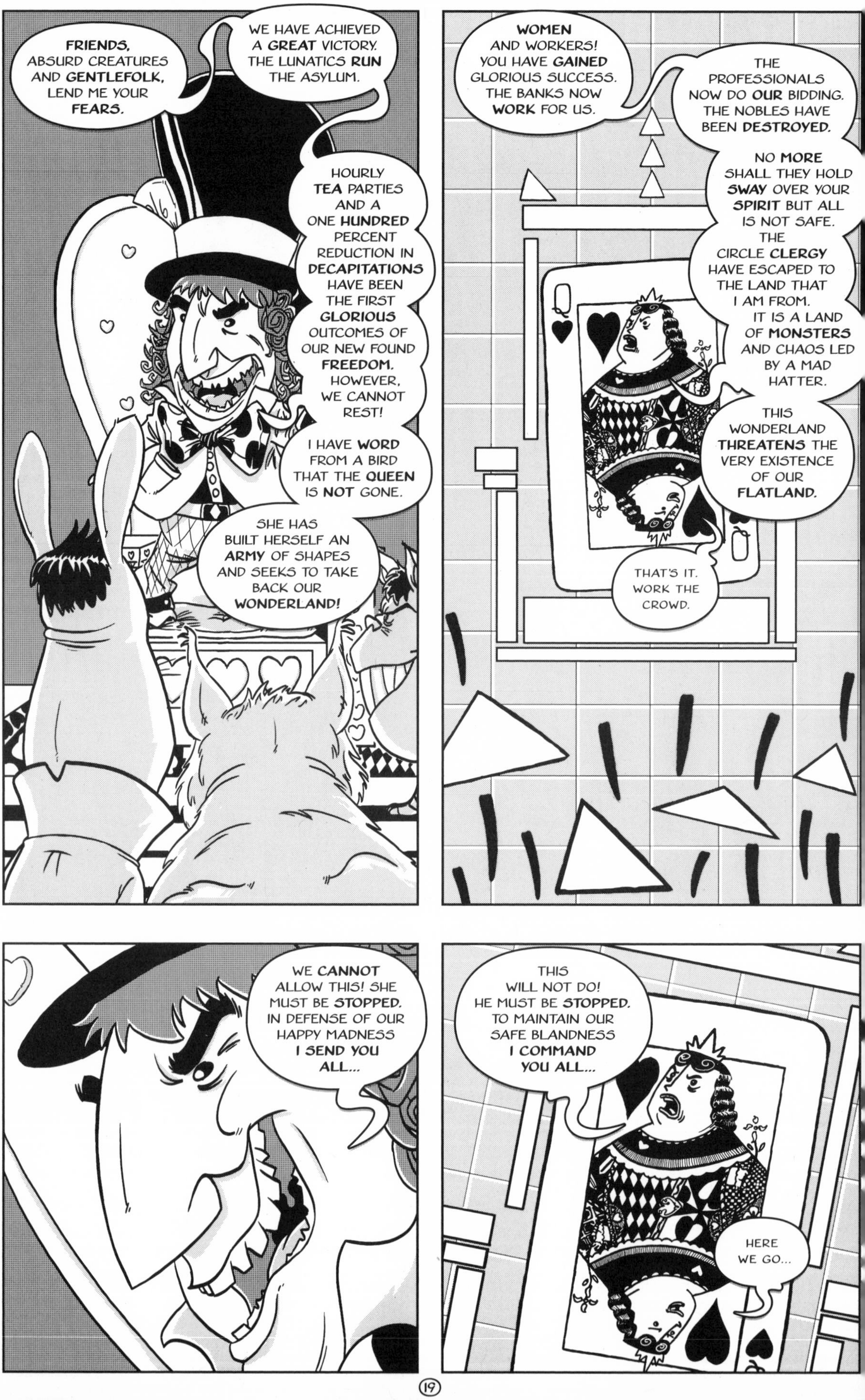
FRIENDS, ABSURD CREATURES AND GENTLEFOLK, LEND ME YOUR FEARS.
WE HAVE ACHIEVED A GREAT VICTORY. THE LUNATICS RUN THE ASYLUM.
HOURLY TEA PARTIES AND A ONE HUNDRED PERCENT REDUCTION IN DECAPITATIONS HAVE BEEN THE FIRST GLORIOUS OUTCOMES OF OUR NEW FOUND FREEDOM. HOWEVER, WE CANNOT REST!
I HAVE WORD FROM A BIRD THAT THE QUEEN IS NOT GONE.
SHE HAS BUILT HERSELF AN ARMY OF SHAPES AND SEEKS TO TAKE BACK OUR WONDERLAND!
WOMEN AND WORKERS! YOU HAVE GAINED GLORIOUS SUCCESS. THE BANKS NOW WORK FOR US.
THE PROFESSIONALS NOW DO OUR BIDDING. THE NOBLES HAVE BEEN DESTROYED.
NO MORE SHALL THEY HOLD SWAY OVER YOUR SPIRIT BUT ALL IS NOT SAFE. THE CIRCLE CLERGY HAVE ESCAPED TO THE LAND THAT I AM FROM. IT IS A LAND OF MONSTERS AND CHAOS LED BY A MAD HATTER.
THIS WONDERLAND THREATENS THE VERY EXISTENCE OF OUR FLATLAND.
THAT'S IT. WORK THE CROWD.
WE CANNOT ALLOW THIS! SHE MUST BE STOPPED. IN DEFENSE OF OUR HAPPY MADNESS I SEND YOU ALL...
THIS WILL NOT DO! HE MUST BE STOPPED. TO MAINTAIN OUR SAFE BLANDNESS I COMMAND YOU ALL...
HERE WE GO...

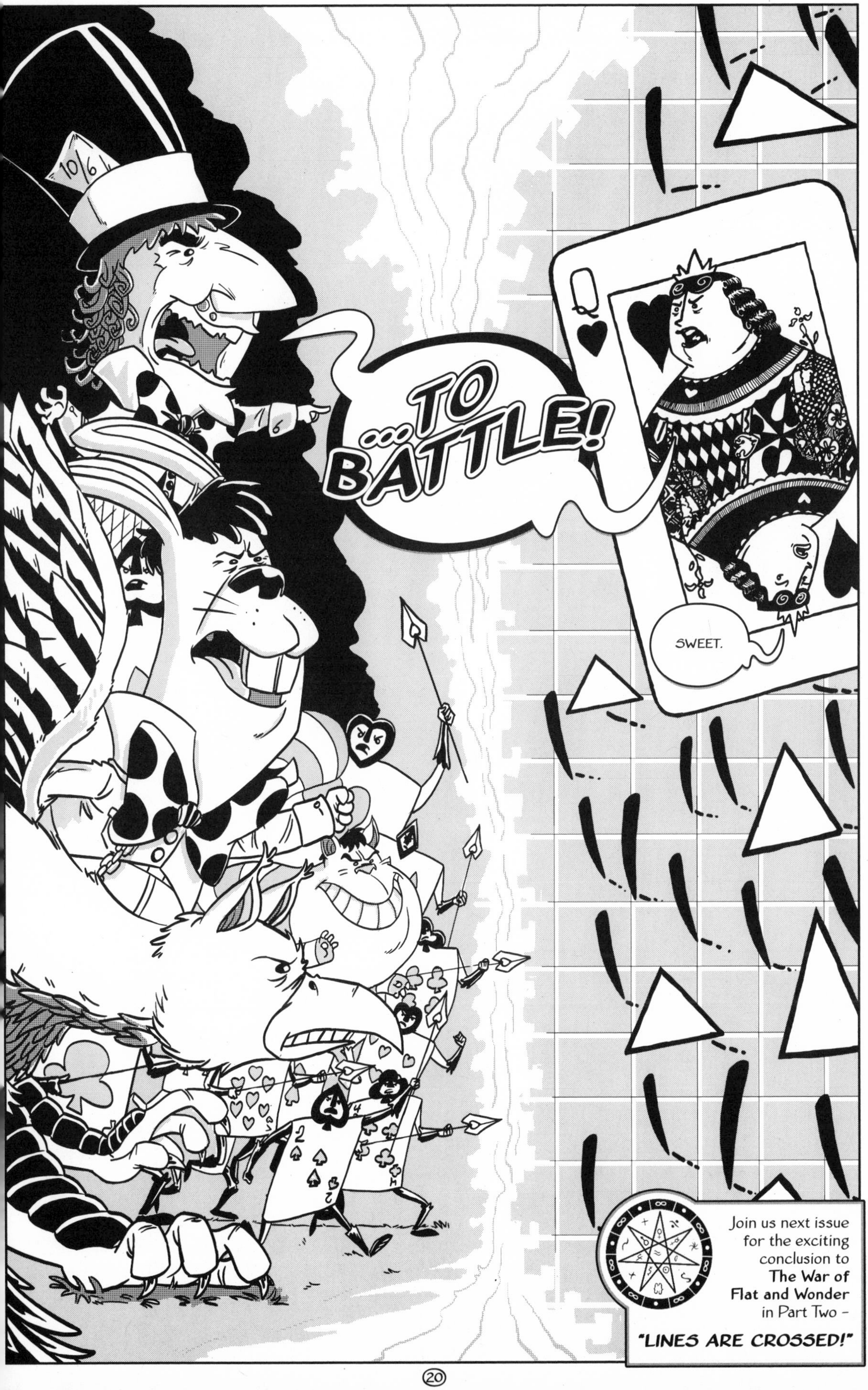
...TO BATTLE!
SWEET.
Join us next issue for the exciting conclusion to **The War of Flat and Wonder** in Part Two -
"LINES ARE CROSSED!"

BOOK FOUR

The horror of that moment," the King went on,
"I shall never forget."
"You will, though," the Queen said,
"if you don't make a memorandum of it."

~ Lewis Carroll
1832 - 1898

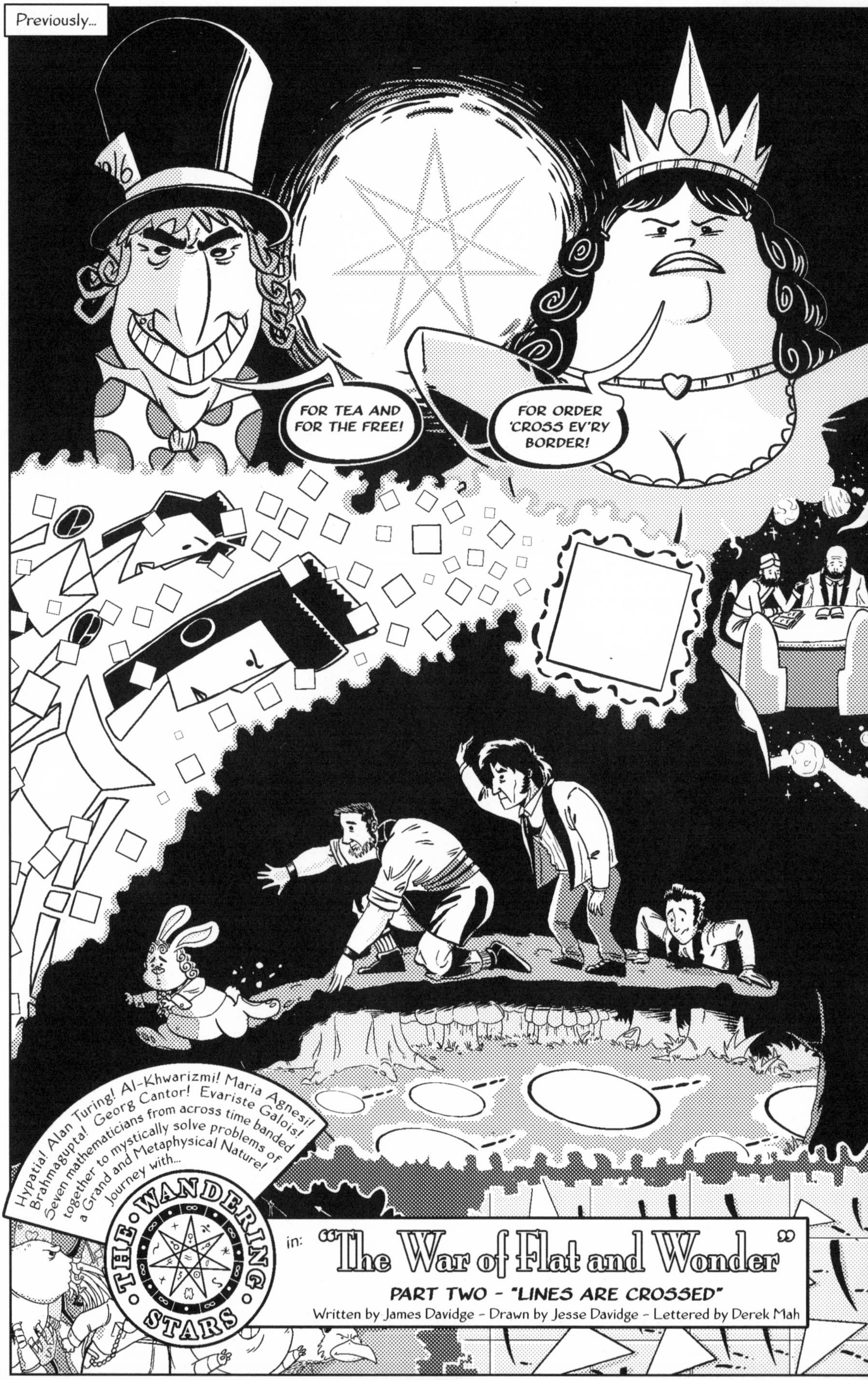
Previously...
FOR TEA AND FOR THE FREE!
FOR ORDER 'CROSS EV'RY BORDER!
Hypatia! Alan Turing! Al-Khwarizmi! Maria Agnesi! Brahmagupta! Georg Cantor! Evariste Galois! Seven mathematicians from across time banded together to mystically solve problems of a Grand and Metaphysical Nature! Journey with...
THE WANDERING STARS
in: "The War of Flat and Wonder"
PART TWO - "LINES ARE CROSSED"
Written by James Davidge - Drawn by Jesse Davidge - Lettered by Derek Mah

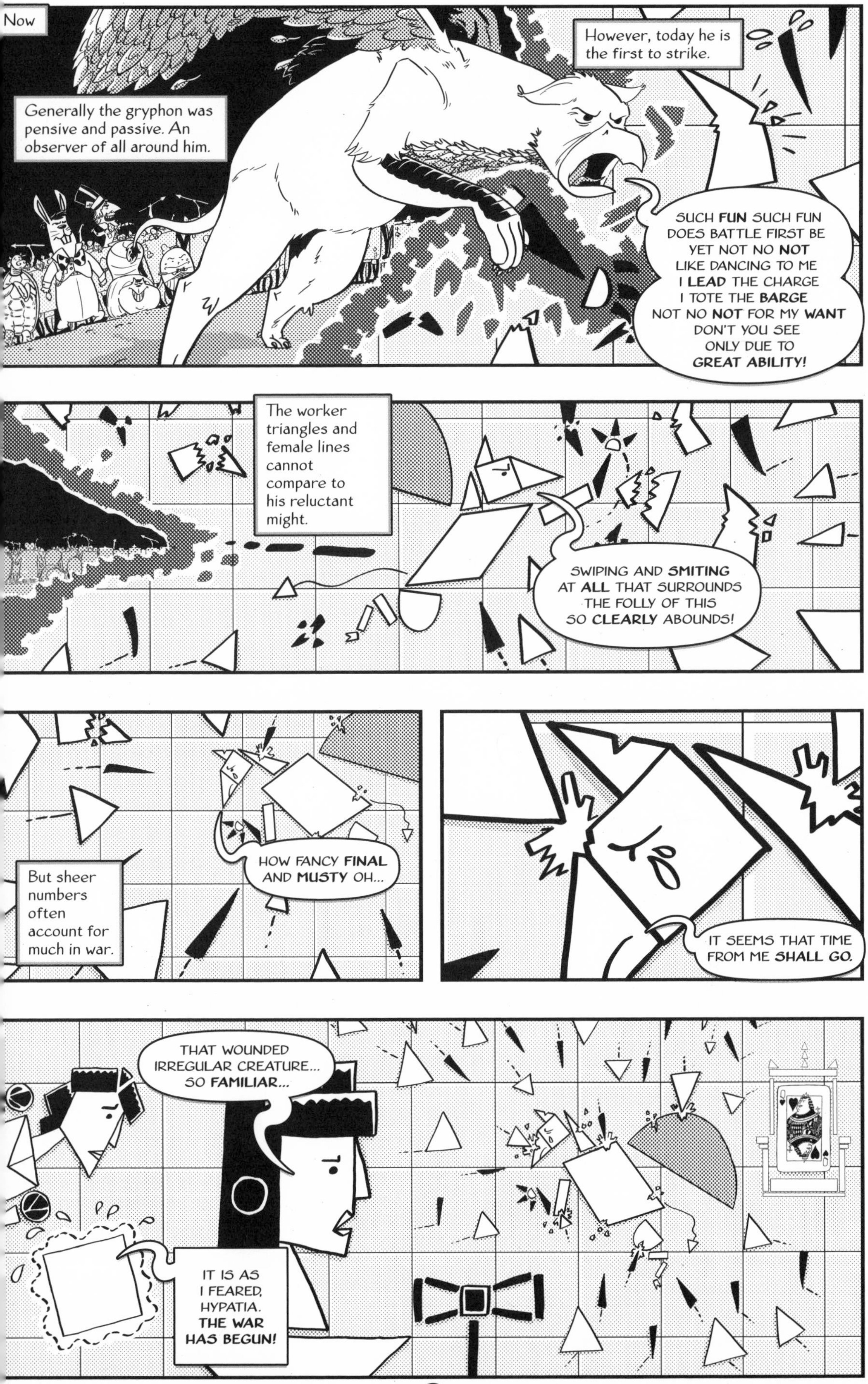
Now
Generally the gryphon was pensive and passive. An observer of all around him.
However, today he is the first to strike.
SUCH FUN SUCH FUN DOES BATTLE FIRST BE YET NOT NO NOT LIKE DANCING TO ME I LEAD THE CHARGE I TOTE THE BARGE NOT NO NOT FOR MY WANT DON'T YOU SEE ONLY DUE TO GREAT ABILITY!
The worker triangles and female lines cannot compare to his reluctant might.
SWIPING AND SMITING AT ALL THAT SURROUNDS THE FOLLY OF THIS SO CLEARLY ABOUNDS!
HOW FANCY FINAL AND MUSTY OH...
But sheer numbers often account for much in war.
IT SEEMS THAT TIME FROM ME SHALL GO.
THAT WOUNDED IRREGULAR CREATURE... SO FAMILIAR...
IT IS AS I FEARED, HYPATIA. THE WAR HAS BEGUN!

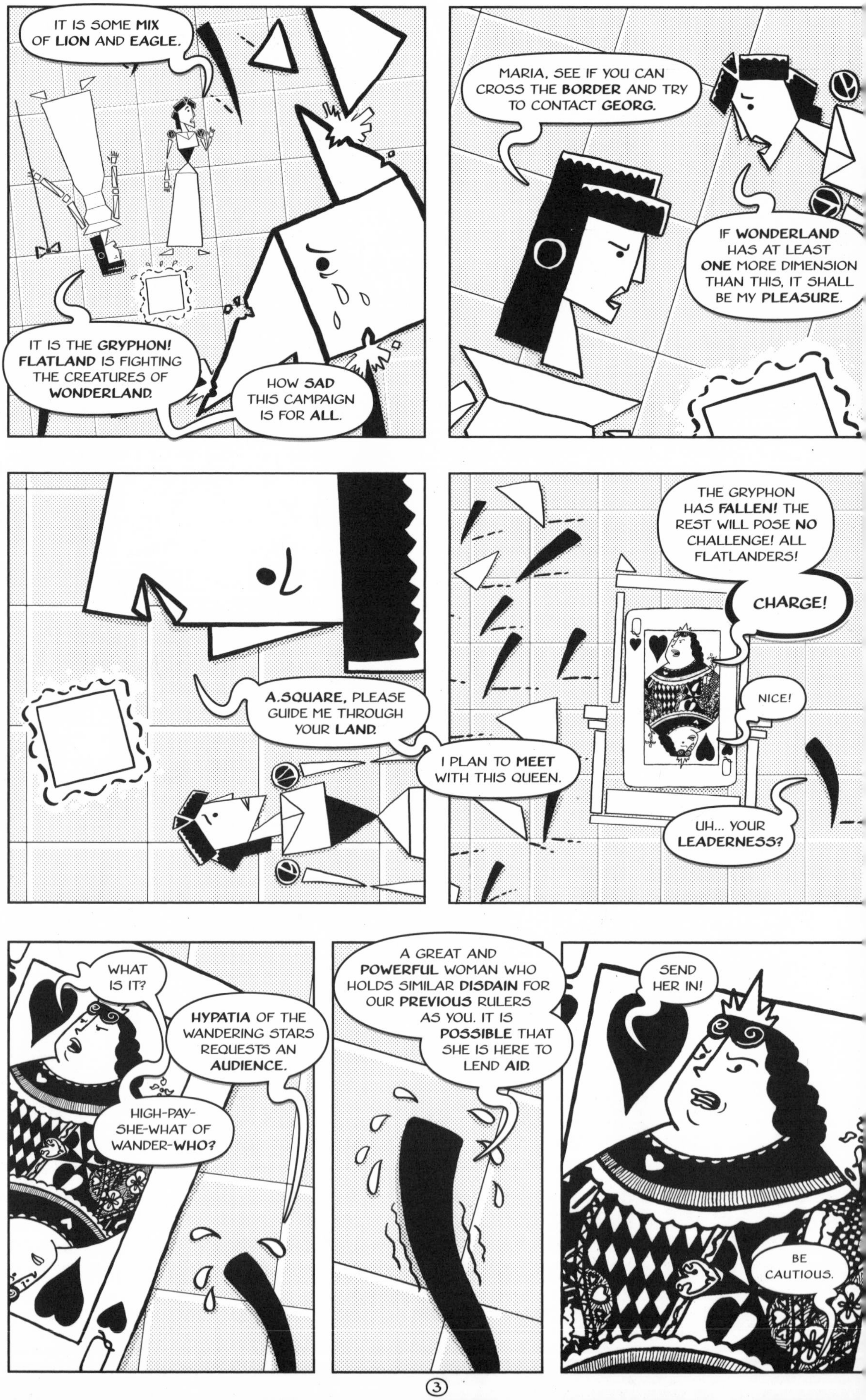

IT IS SOME MIX OF LION AND EAGLE.
IT IS THE GRYPHON! FLATLAND IS FIGHTING THE CREATURES OF WONDERLAND.
HOW SAD THIS CAMPAIGN IS FOR ALL.
MARIA, SEE IF YOU CAN CROSS THE BORDER AND TRY TO CONTACT GEORG.
IF WONDERLAND HAS AT LEAST ONE MORE DIMENSION THAN THIS, IT SHALL BE MY PLEASURE.
A.SQUARE, PLEASE GUIDE ME THROUGH YOUR LAND.
I PLAN TO MEET WITH THIS QUEEN.
THE GRYPHON HAS FALLEN! THE REST WILL POSE NO CHALLENGE! ALL FLATLANDERS!
CHARGE!
NICE!
UH... YOUR LEADERNESS?
WHAT IS IT?
HYPATIA OF THE WANDERING STARS REQUESTS AN AUDIENCE.
HIGH-PAY-SHE-WHAT OF WANDER-WHO?
A GREAT AND POWERFUL WOMAN WHO HOLDS SIMILAR DISDAIN FOR OUR PREVIOUS RULERS AS YOU. IT IS POSSIBLE THAT SHE IS HERE TO LEND AID.
SEND HER IN!
BE CAUTIOUS.

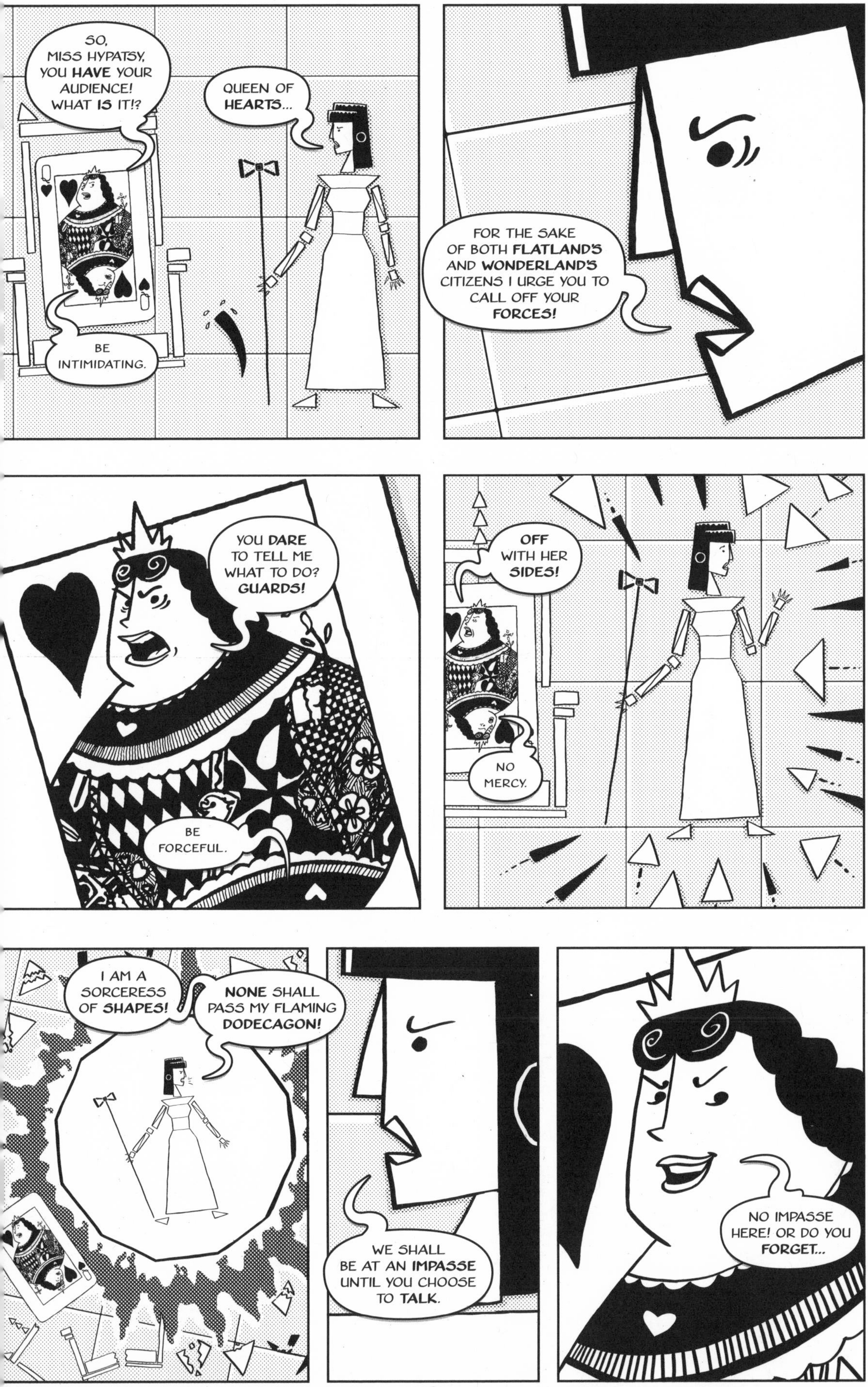
SO, MISS HYPATSY, YOU **HAVE** YOUR AUDIENCE! WHAT **IS** IT!?
QUEEN OF **HEARTS**...
BE INTIMIDATING.
FOR THE SAKE OF BOTH **FLATLAND'S** AND **WONDERLAND'S** CITIZENS I URGE YOU TO CALL OFF YOUR **FORCES!**
YOU **DARE** TO TELL ME WHAT TO DO? **GUARDS!**
BE FORCEFUL.
OFF WITH HER **SIDES!**
NO MERCY.
I AM A SORCERESS OF **SHAPES!**
NONE SHALL PASS MY FLAMING **DODECAGON!**
WE SHALL BE AT AN **IMPASSE** UNTIL YOU CHOOSE TO **TALK**.
NO IMPASSE HERE! OR DO YOU **FORGET...**

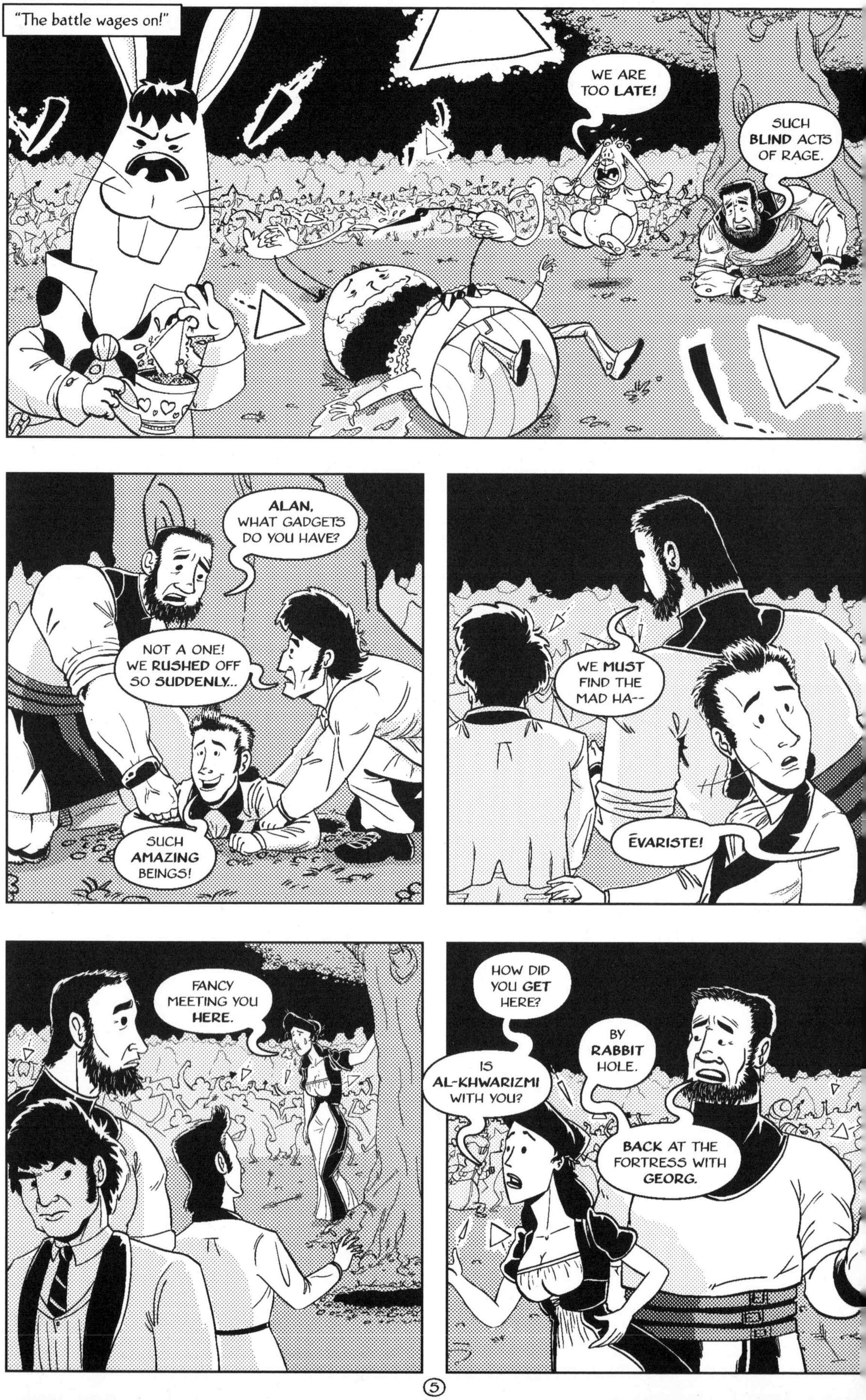
"The battle wages on!"
WE ARE TOO LATE!
SUCH BLIND ACTS OF RAGE.
ALAN, WHAT GADGETS DO YOU HAVE?
NOT A ONE! WE RUSHED OFF SO SUDDENLY...
SUCH AMAZING BEINGS!
WE MUST FIND THE MAD HA--
ÉVARISTE!
FANCY MEETING YOU HERE.
HOW DID YOU GET HERE?
BY RABBIT HOLE.
IS AL-KHWARIZMI WITH YOU?
BACK AT THE FORTRESS WITH GEORG.

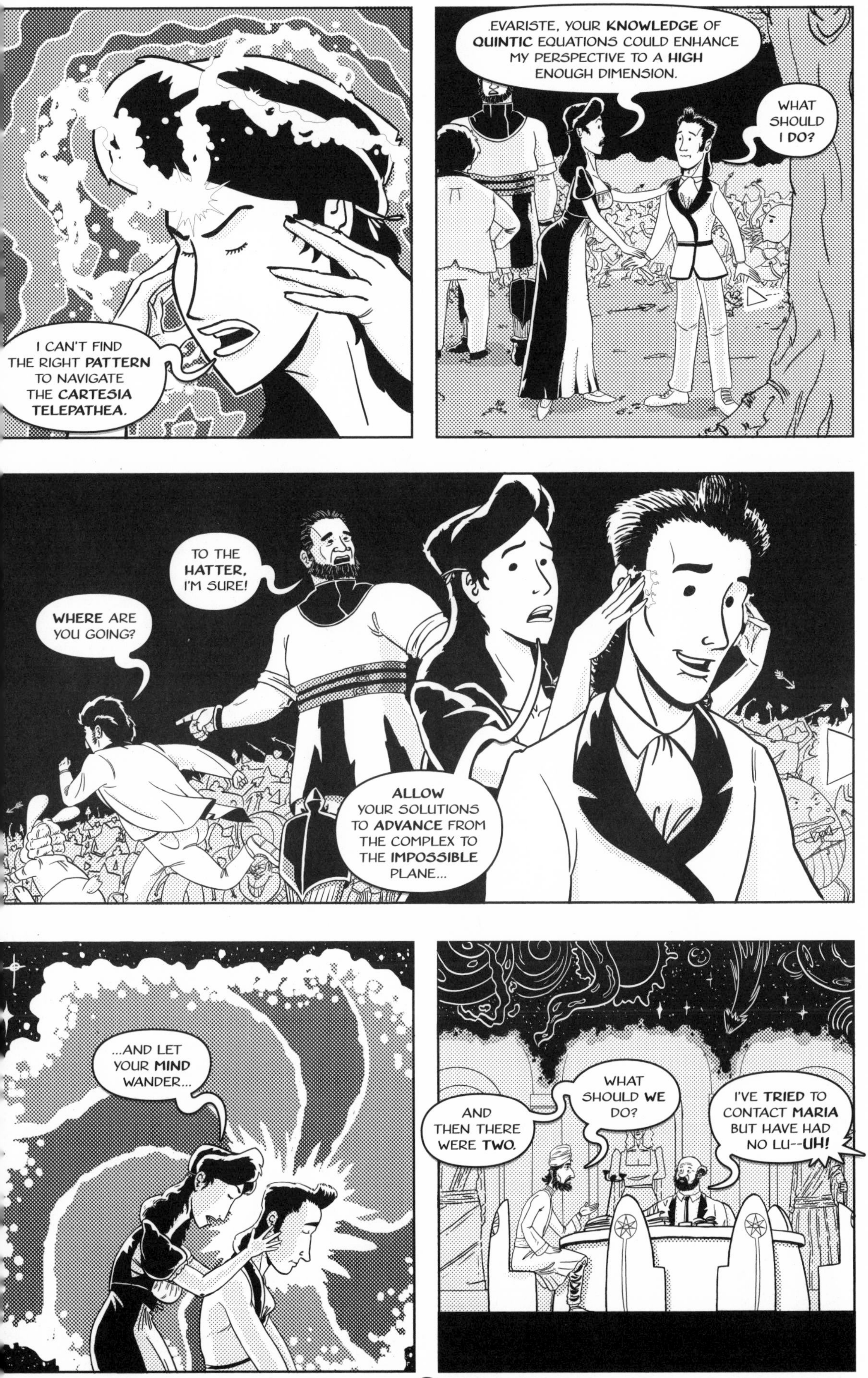
I CAN'T FIND THE RIGHT PATTERN TO NAVIGATE THE CARTESIA TELEPATHEA.
.EVARISTE, YOUR KNOWLEDGE OF QUINTIC EQUATIONS COULD ENHANCE MY PERSPECTIVE TO A HIGH ENOUGH DIMENSION.
WHAT SHOULD I DO?
WHERE ARE YOU GOING?
TO THE HATTER, I'M SURE!
ALLOW YOUR SOLUTIONS TO ADVANCE FROM THE COMPLEX TO THE IMPOSSIBLE PLANE...
...AND LET YOUR MIND WANDER...
AND THEN THERE WERE TWO.
WHAT SHOULD WE DO?
I'VE TRIED TO CONTACT MARIA BUT HAVE HAD NO LU--UH!

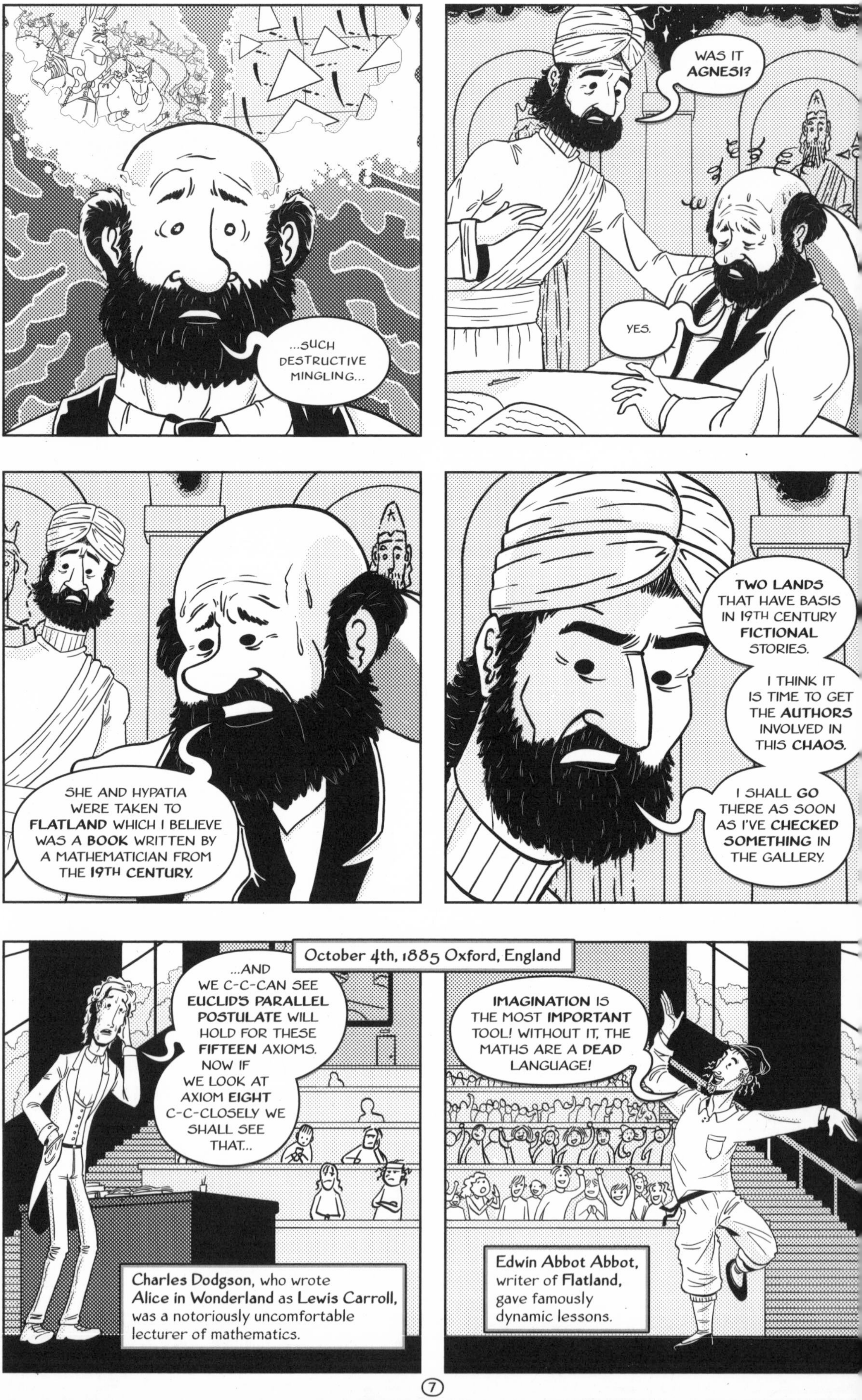
...SUCH DESTRUCTIVE MINGLING...
WAS IT AGNESI?
YES.
SHE AND HYPATIA WERE TAKEN TO FLATLAND WHICH I BELIEVE WAS A BOOK WRITTEN BY A MATHEMATICIAN FROM THE 19TH CENTURY.
TWO LANDS THAT HAVE BASIS IN 19TH CENTURY FICTIONAL STORIES.
I THINK IT IS TIME TO GET THE AUTHORS INVOLVED IN THIS CHAOS.
I SHALL GO THERE AS SOON AS I'VE CHECKED SOMETHING IN THE GALLERY.
October 4th, 1885 Oxford, England
...AND WE C-C-CAN SEE EUCLID'S PARALLEL POSTULATE WILL HOLD FOR THESE FIFTEEN AXIOMS. NOW IF WE LOOK AT AXIOM EIGHT C-C-CLOSELY WE SHALL SEE THAT...
Charles Dodgson, who wrote Alice in Wonderland as Lewis Carroll, was a notoriously uncomfortable lecturer of mathematics.
IMAGINATION IS THE MOST IMPORTANT TOOL! WITHOUT IT, THE MATHS ARE A DEAD LANGUAGE!
Edwin Abbot Abbot, writer of Flatland, gave famously dynamic lessons.

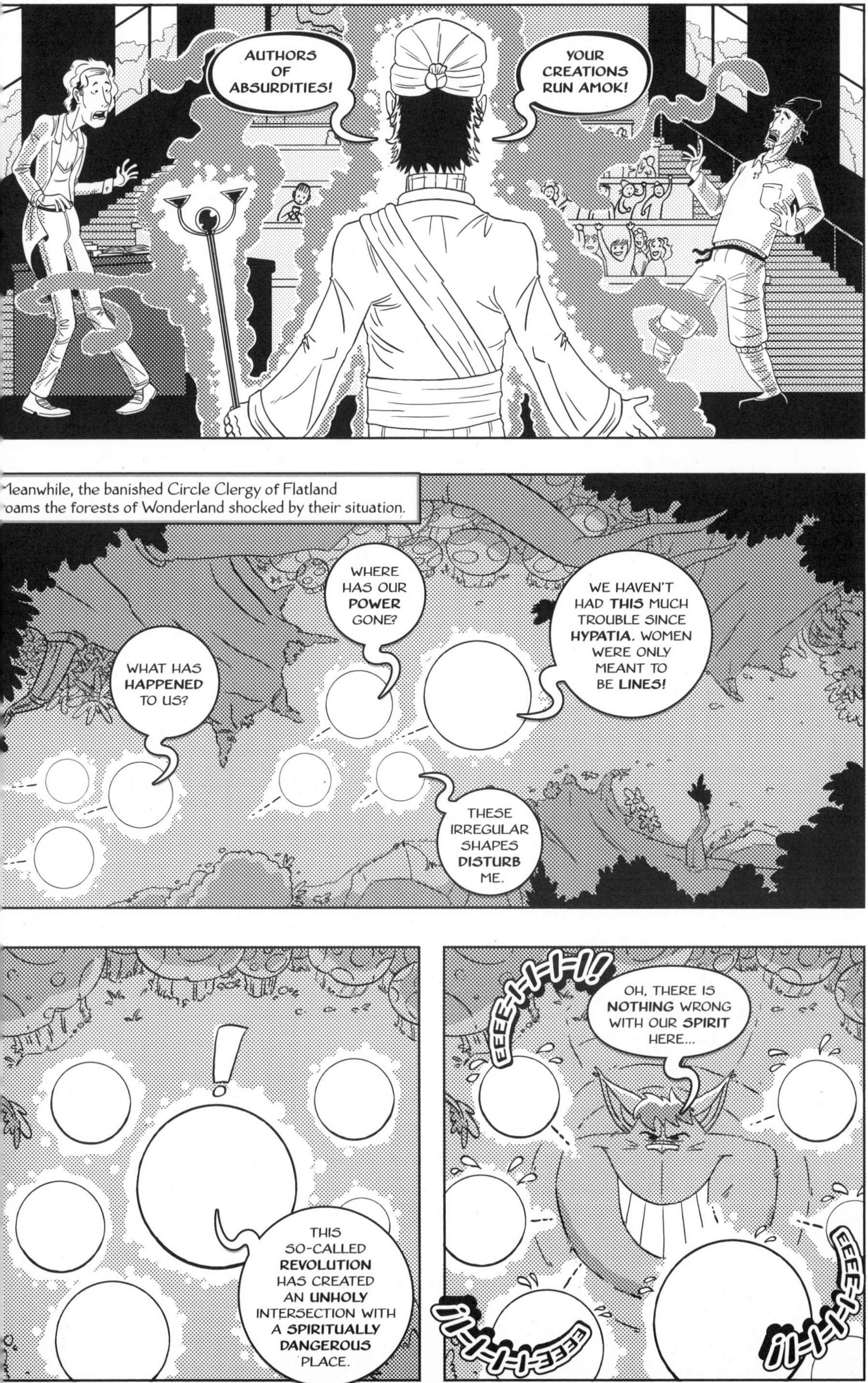
AUTHORS OF ABSURDITIES!
YOUR CREATIONS RUN AMOK!
Meanwhile, the banished Circle Clergy of Flatland roams the forests of Wonderland shocked by their situation.
WHAT HAS HAPPENED TO US?
WHERE HAS OUR POWER GONE?
WE HAVEN'T HAD THIS MUCH TROUBLE SINCE HYPATIA. WOMEN WERE ONLY MEANT TO BE LINES!
THESE IRREGULAR SHAPES DISTURB ME.
!
THIS SO-CALLED REVOLUTION HAS CREATED AN UNHOLY INTERSECTION WITH A SPIRITUALLY DANGEROUS PLACE.
EEEE-I-I-I-I!!
OH, THERE IS NOTHING WRONG WITH OUR SPIRIT HERE...
EEEE-I-I-I-I!!
EEEE-I-I-I-I!!

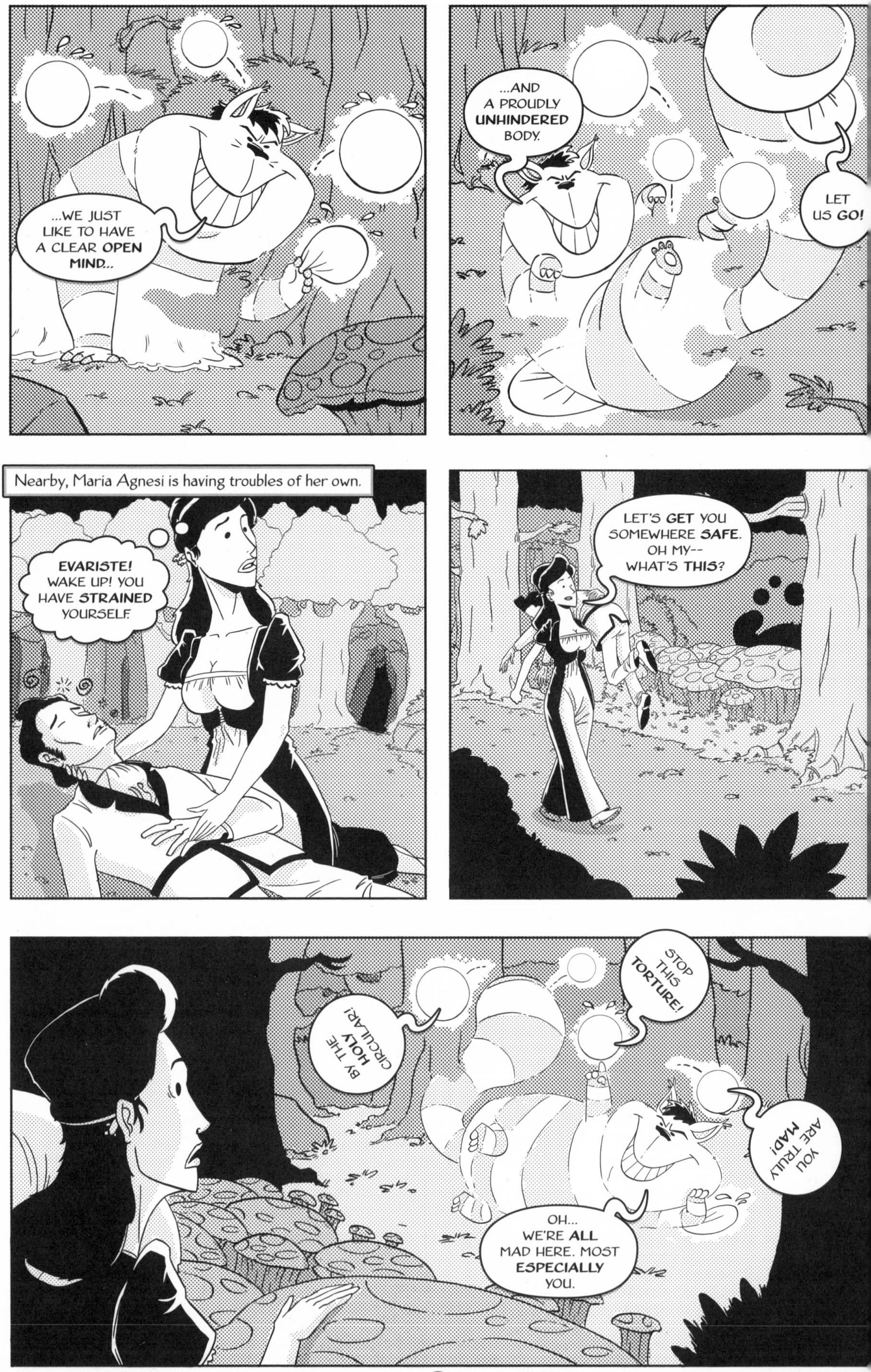

...WE JUST LIKE TO HAVE A CLEAR **OPEN MIND**...
...AND A PROUDLY **UNHINDERED** BODY.
LET US **GO!**
Nearby, Maria Agnesi is having troubles of her own.
EVARISTE! WAKE UP! YOU HAVE **STRAINED** YOURSELF.
LET'S **GET** YOU SOMEWHERE **SAFE**. OH MY-- WHAT'S **THIS**?
BY THE **HOLY** CIRCULAR!
STOP THIS **TORTURE!**
YOU ARE TRULY **MAD!**
OH... WE'RE **ALL** MAD HERE. MOST **ESPECIALLY** YOU.

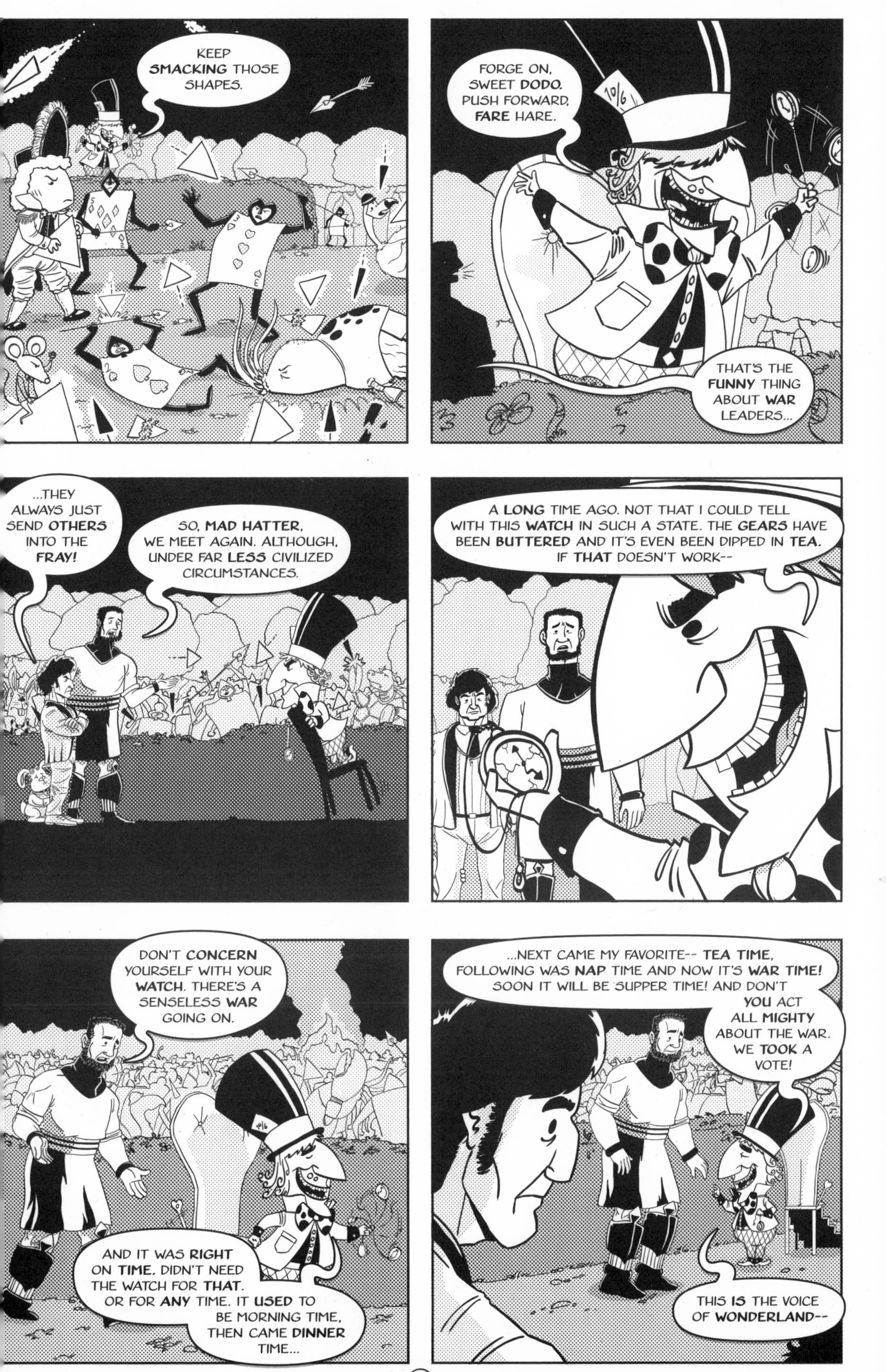
KEEP SMACKING THOSE SHAPES.
FORGE ON, SWEET DODO. PUSH FORWARD, FARE HARE.
THAT'S THE FUNNY THING ABOUT WAR LEADERS...
...THEY ALWAYS JUST SEND OTHERS INTO THE FRAY!
SO, MAD HATTER, WE MEET AGAIN. ALTHOUGH, UNDER FAR LESS CIVILIZED CIRCUMSTANCES.
A LONG TIME AGO. NOT THAT I COULD TELL WITH THIS WATCH IN SUCH A STATE. THE GEARS HAVE BEEN BUTTERED AND IT'S EVEN BEEN DIPPED IN TEA. IF THAT DOESN'T WORK--
DON'T CONCERN YOURSELF WITH YOUR WATCH. THERE'S A SENSELESS WAR GOING ON.
AND IT WAS RIGHT ON TIME. DIDN'T NEED THE WATCH FOR THAT. OR FOR ANY TIME. IT USED TO BE MORNING TIME, THEN CAME DINNER TIME...
...NEXT CAME MY FAVORITE-- TEA TIME, FOLLOWING WAS NAP TIME AND NOW IT'S WAR TIME! SOON IT WILL BE SUPPER TIME! AND DON'T YOU ACT ALL MIGHTY ABOUT THE WAR. WE TOOK A VOTE!
THIS IS THE VOICE OF WONDERLAND--

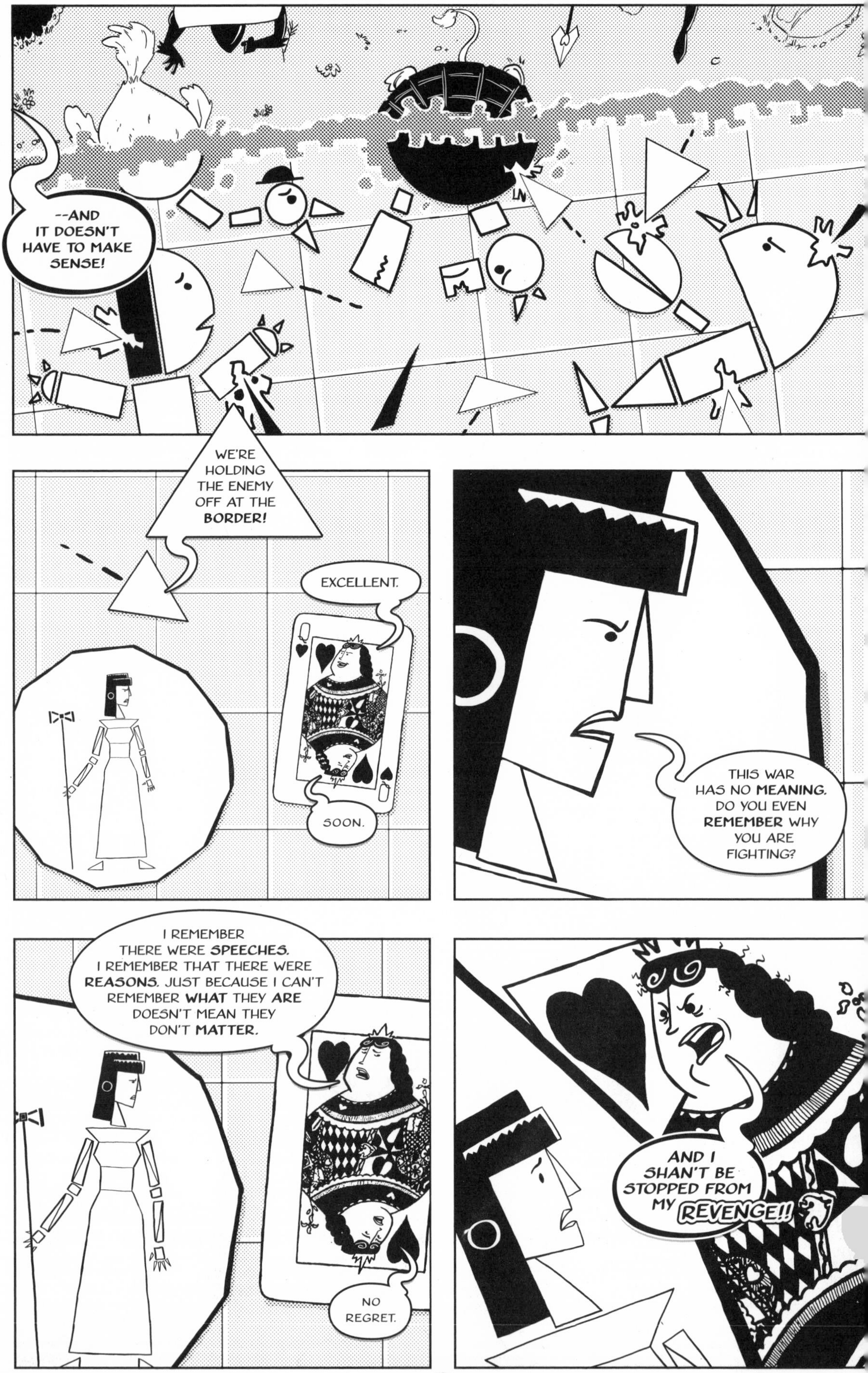
--AND IT DOESN'T HAVE TO MAKE SENSE!
WE'RE HOLDING THE ENEMY OFF AT THE BORDER!
EXCELLENT.
SOON.
THIS WAR HAS NO MEANING. DO YOU EVEN REMEMBER WHY YOU ARE FIGHTING?
I REMEMBER THERE WERE SPEECHES. I REMEMBER THAT THERE WERE REASONS. JUST BECAUSE I CAN'T REMEMBER WHAT THEY ARE DOESN'T MEAN THEY DON'T MATTER.
NO REGRET.
AND I SHAN'T BE STOPPED FROM MY REVENGE!!

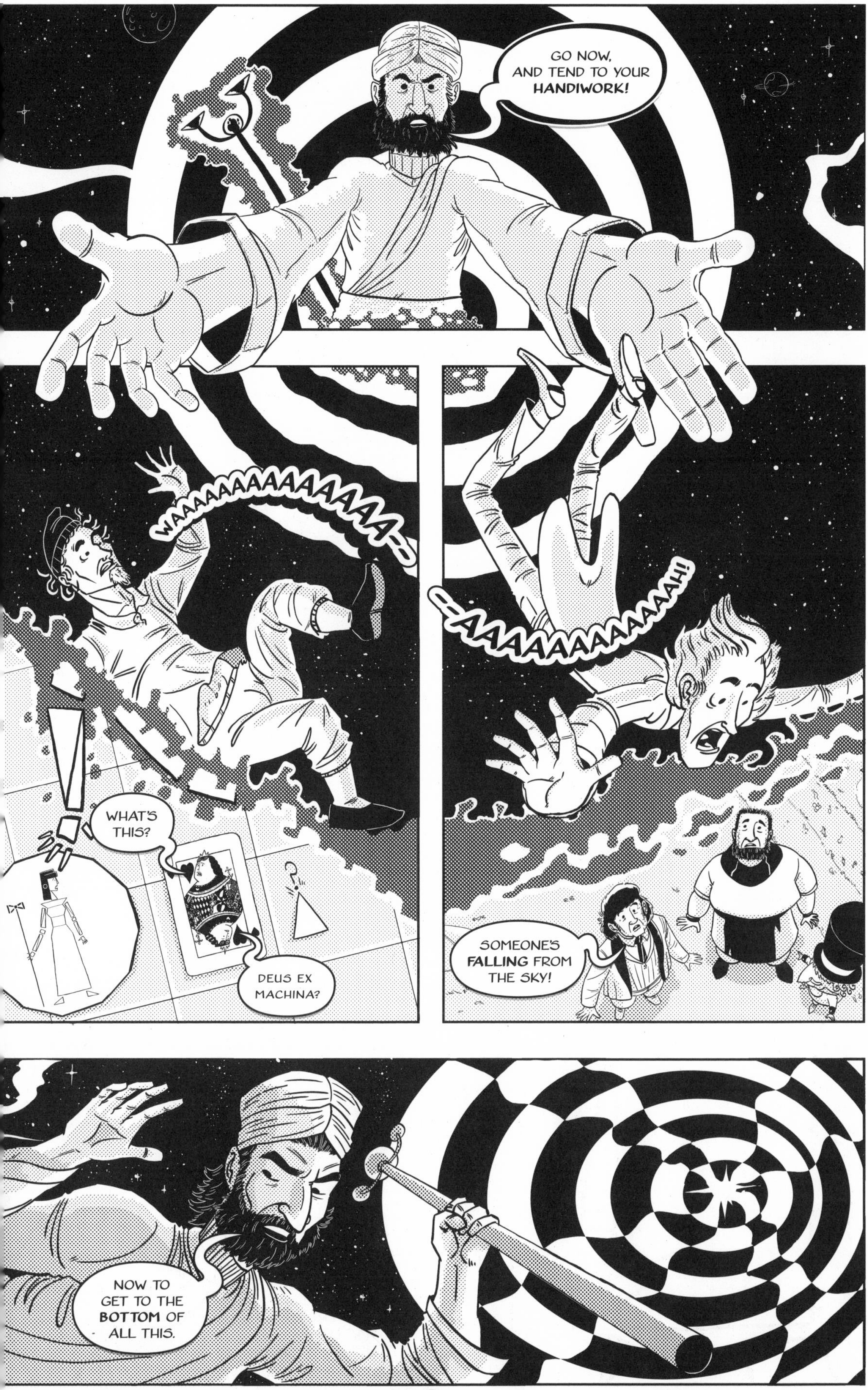
GO NOW, AND TEND TO YOUR **HANDIWORK!**
WAAAAAAAAAAAAAAA--
--AAAAAAAAAAAAAH!
WHAT'S THIS?
DEUS EX MACHINA?
SOMEONE'S **FALLING** FROM THE SKY!
NOW TO GET TO THE **BOTTOM** OF ALL THIS.

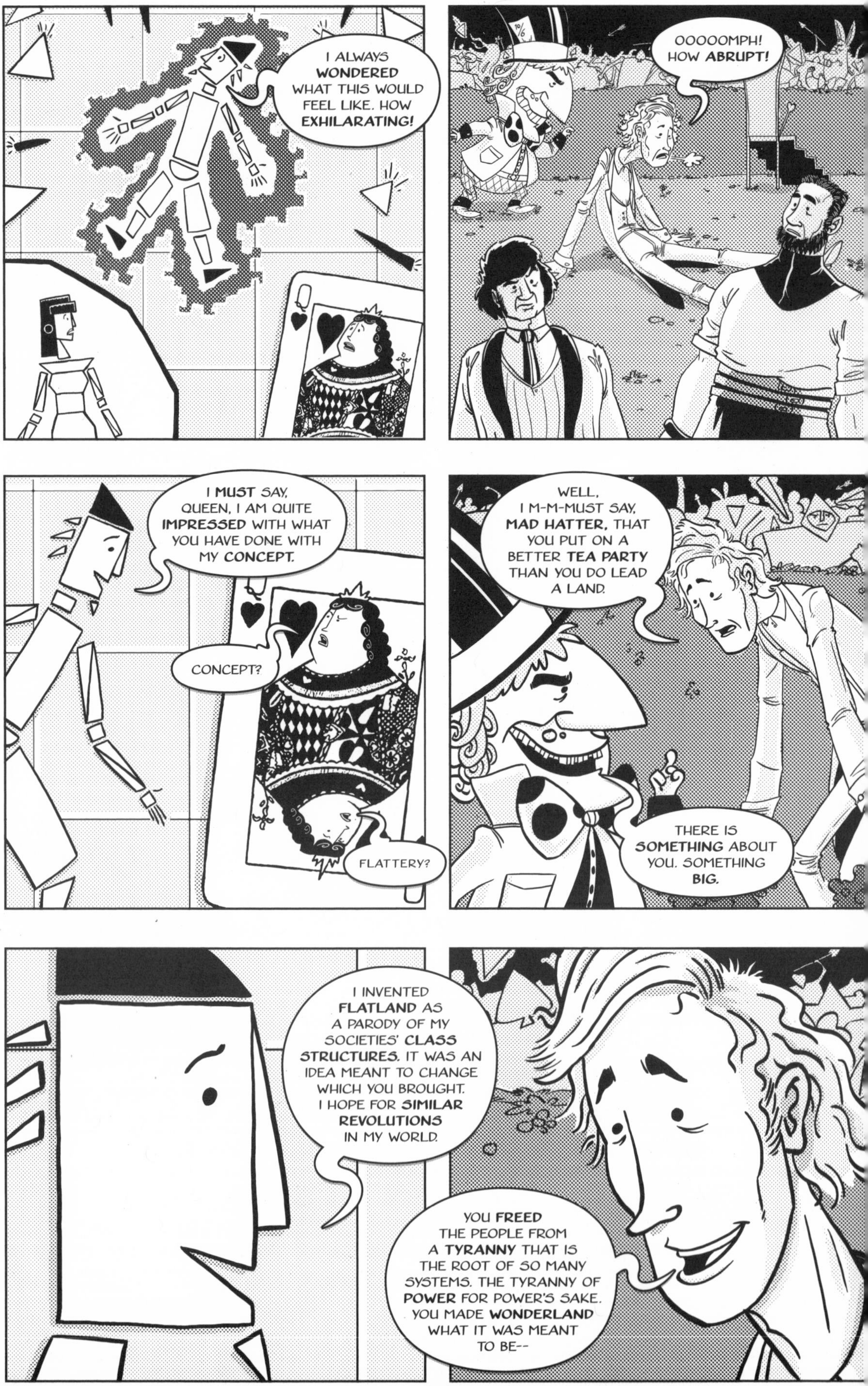
I ALWAYS WONDERED WHAT THIS WOULD FEEL LIKE. HOW EXHILARATING!
OOOOOMPH! HOW ABRUPT!
I MUST SAY, QUEEN, I AM QUITE IMPRESSED WITH WHAT YOU HAVE DONE WITH MY CONCEPT.
CONCEPT?
FLATTERY?
WELL, I M-M-MUST SAY, MAD HATTER, THAT YOU PUT ON A BETTER TEA PARTY THAN YOU DO LEAD A LAND.
THERE IS SOMETHING ABOUT YOU. SOMETHING BIG.
I INVENTED FLATLAND AS A PARODY OF MY SOCIETIES' CLASS STRUCTURES. IT WAS AN IDEA MEANT TO CHANGE WHICH YOU BROUGHT. I HOPE FOR SIMILAR REVOLUTIONS IN MY WORLD.
YOU FREED THE PEOPLE FROM A TYRANNY THAT IS THE ROOT OF SO MANY SYSTEMS. THE TYRANNY OF POWER FOR POWER'S SAKE. YOU MADE WONDERLAND WHAT IT WAS MEANT TO BE--

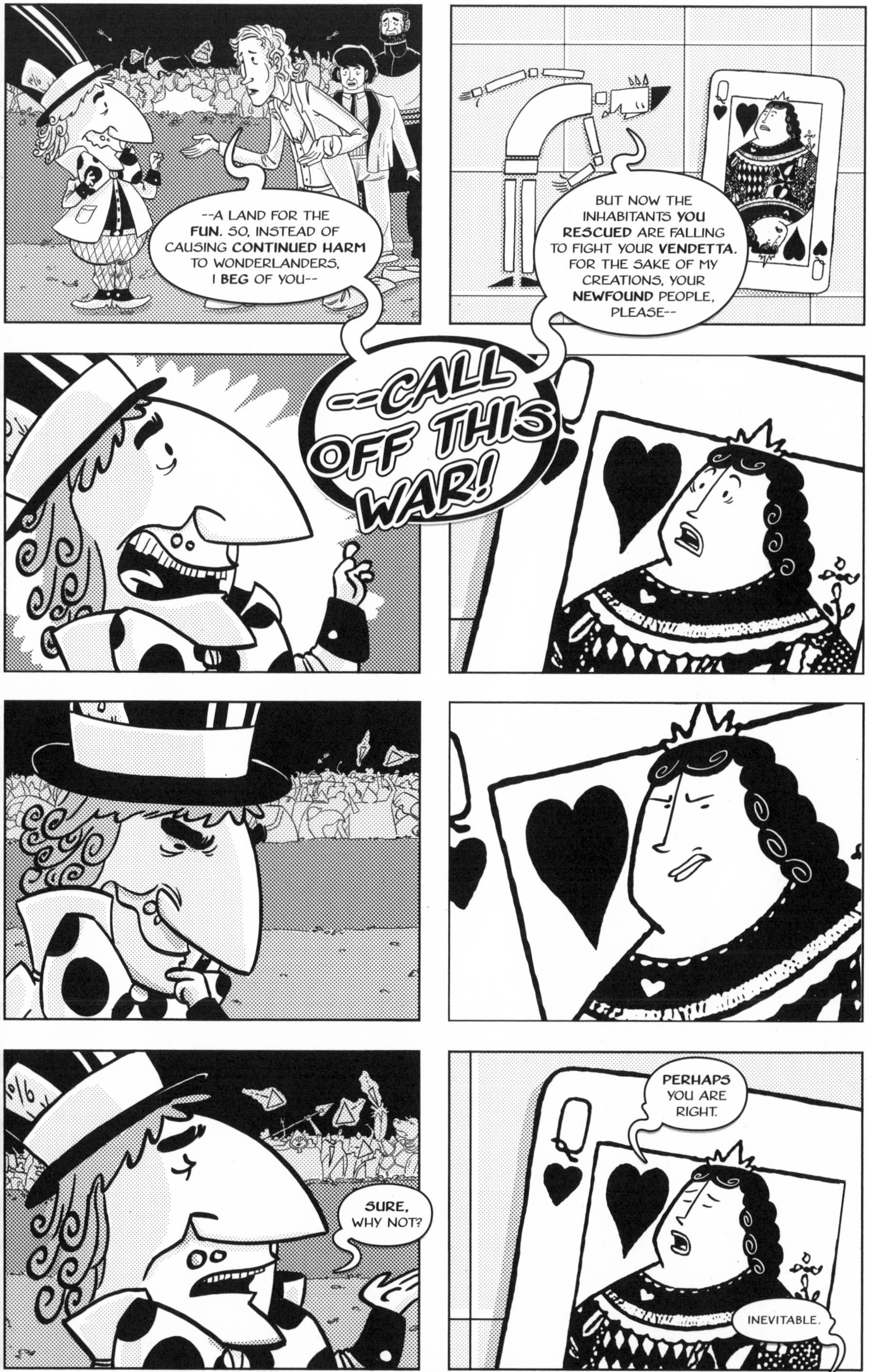
--A LAND FOR THE FUN. SO, INSTEAD OF CAUSING CONTINUED HARM TO WONDERLANDERS, I BEG OF YOU--
BUT NOW THE INHABITANTS YOU RESCUED ARE FALLING TO FIGHT YOUR VENDETTA. FOR THE SAKE OF MY CREATIONS, YOUR NEWFOUND PEOPLE, PLEASE--
--CALL OFF THIS WAR!
SURE, WHY NOT?
PERHAPS YOU ARE RIGHT.
INEVITABLE.

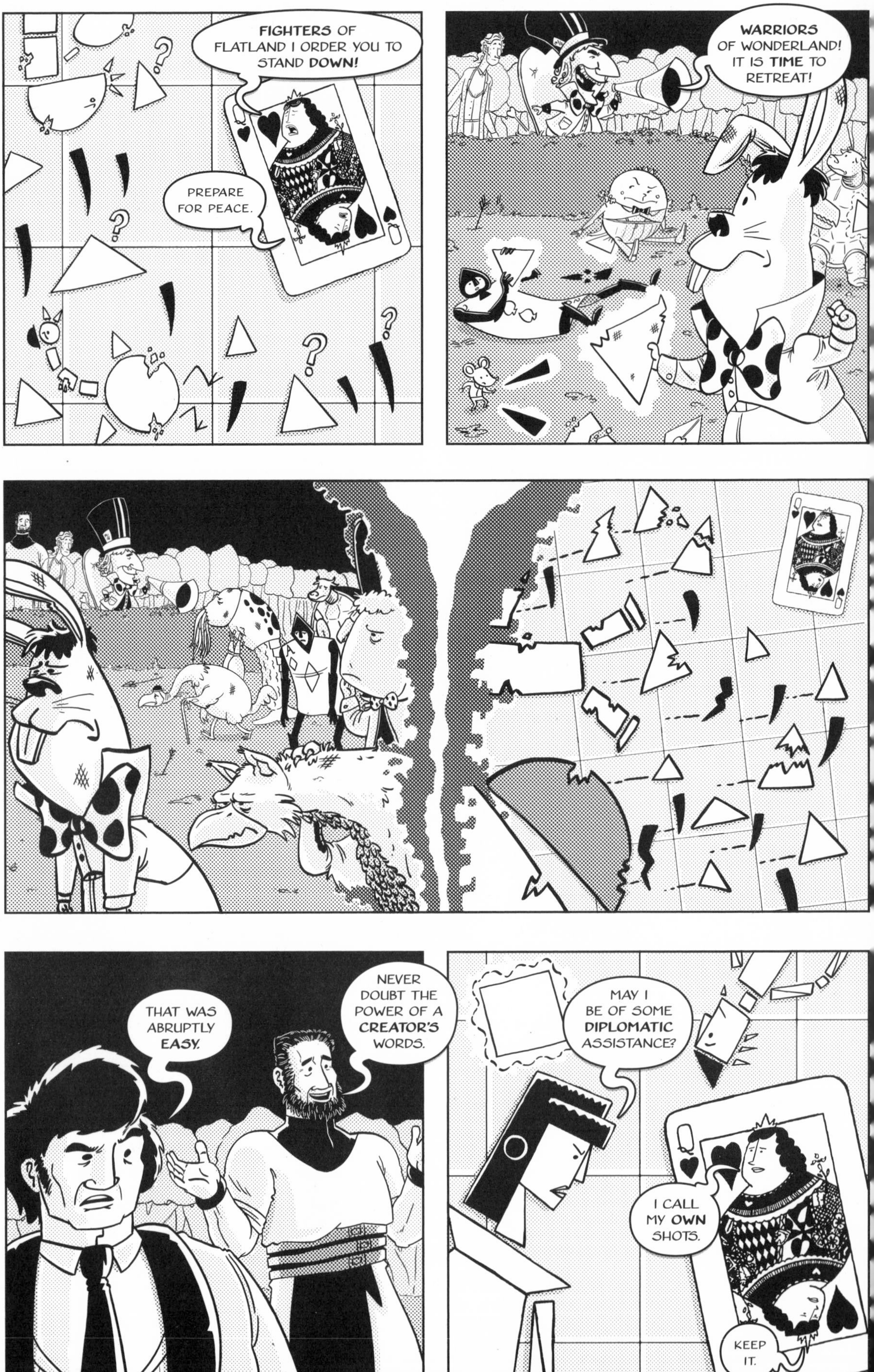
FIGHTERS OF FLATLAND I ORDER YOU TO STAND DOWN!
PREPARE FOR PEACE.
WARRIORS OF WONDERLAND! IT IS TIME TO RETREAT!
THAT WAS ABRUPTLY EASY.
NEVER DOUBT THE POWER OF A CREATOR'S WORDS.
MAY I BE OF SOME DIPLOMATIC ASSISTANCE?
I CALL MY OWN SHOTS.
KEEP IT.

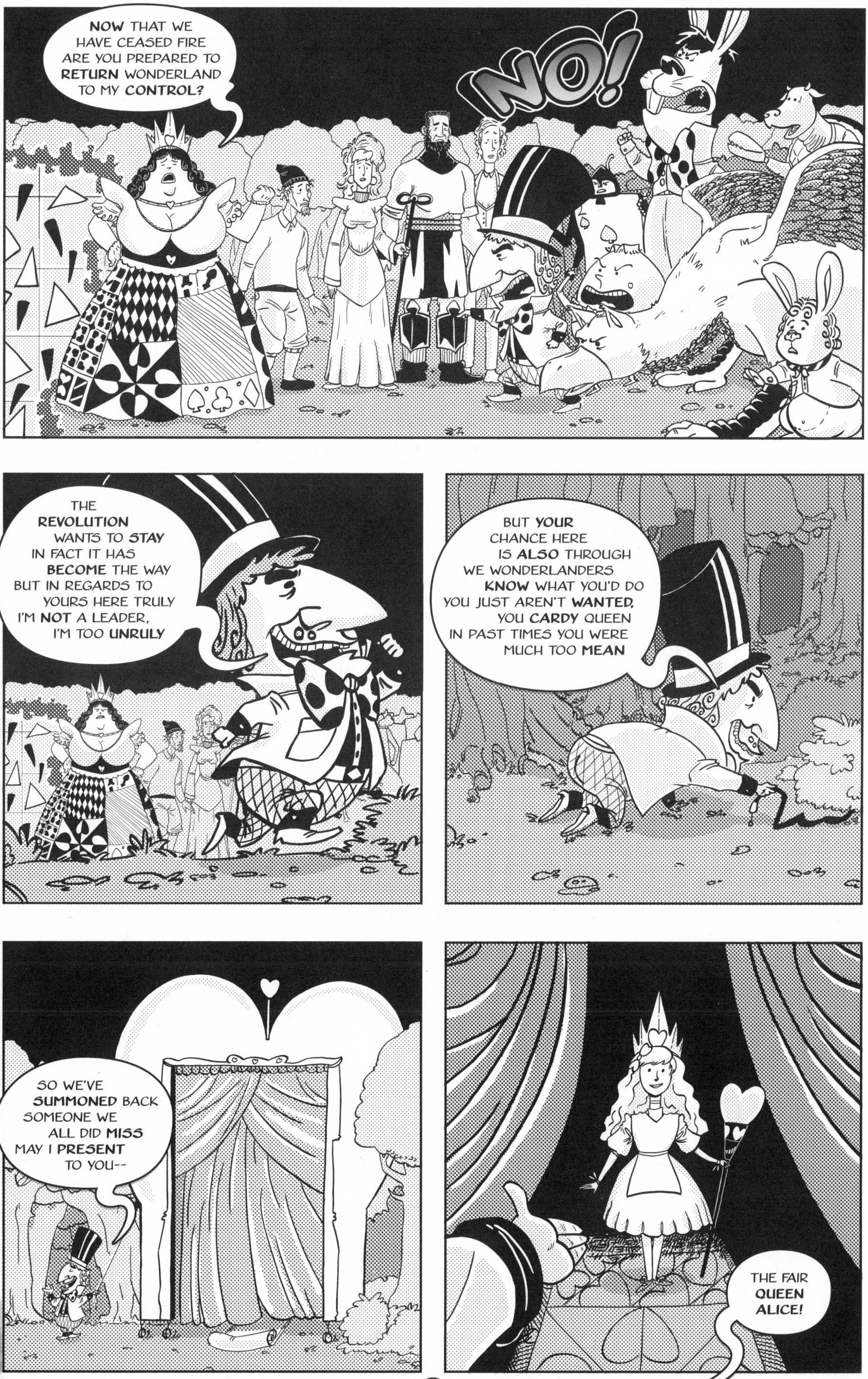
NOW THAT WE HAVE CEASED FIRE ARE YOU PREPARED TO RETURN WONDERLAND TO MY CONTROL?
NO!
THE REVOLUTION WANTS TO STAY IN FACT IT HAS BECOME THE WAY BUT IN REGARDS TO YOURS HERE TRULY I'M NOT A LEADER, I'M TOO UNRULY
BUT YOUR CHANCE HERE IS ALSO THROUGH WE WONDERLANDERS KNOW WHAT YOU'D DO YOU JUST AREN'T WANTED, YOU CARDY QUEEN IN PAST TIMES YOU WERE MUCH TOO MEAN
SO WE'VE SUMMONED BACK SOMEONE WE ALL DID MISS MAY I PRESENT TO YOU--
THE FAIR QUEEN ALICE!

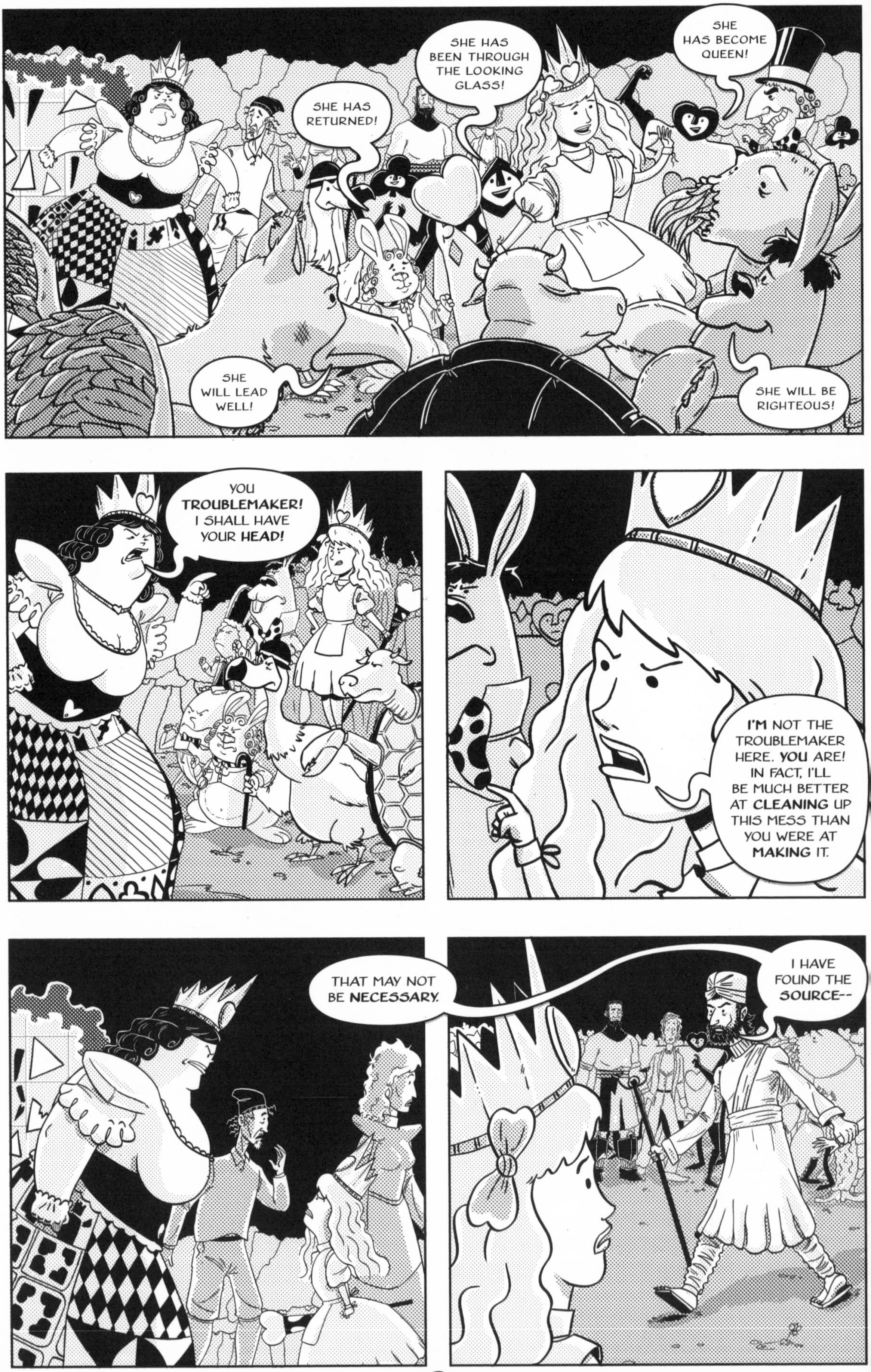
SHE HAS RETURNED!
SHE HAS BEEN THROUGH THE LOOKING GLASS!
SHE HAS BECOME QUEEN!
SHE WILL LEAD WELL!
SHE WILL BE RIGHTEOUS!
YOU **TROUBLEMAKER!** I SHALL HAVE YOUR **HEAD!**
I'M NOT THE TROUBLEMAKER HERE. **YOU** ARE! IN FACT, I'LL BE MUCH BETTER AT **CLEANING** UP THIS MESS THAN YOU WERE AT **MAKING** IT.
THAT MAY NOT BE **NECESSARY.**
I HAVE FOUND THE **SOURCE--**

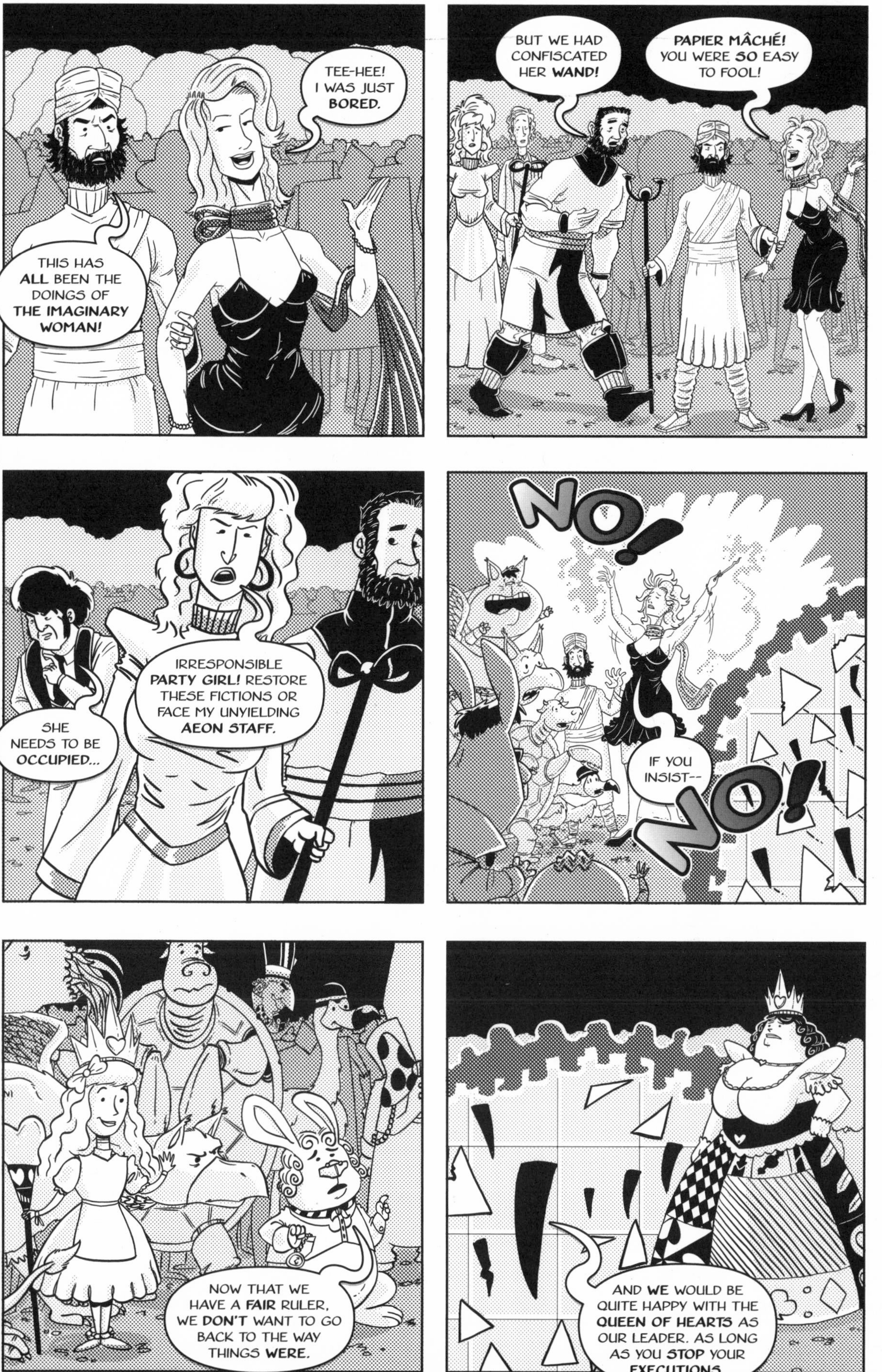
TEE-HEE! I WAS JUST **BORED.**
THIS HAS **ALL** BEEN THE DOINGS OF **THE IMAGINARY WOMAN!**
BUT WE HAD CONFISCATED HER **WAND!**
PAPIER MÂCHÉ! YOU WERE **SO** EASY TO FOOL!
SHE NEEDS TO BE **OCCUPIED...**
IRRESPONSIBLE **PARTY GIRL!** RESTORE THESE FICTIONS OR FACE MY UNYIELDING **AEON STAFF.**
NO!
IF YOU INSIST--
NO!
NOW THAT WE HAVE A **FAIR** RULER, WE **DON'T** WANT TO GO BACK TO THE WAY THINGS **WERE.**
AND **WE** WOULD BE QUITE HAPPY WITH THE **QUEEN OF HEARTS** AS OUR LEADER. AS LONG AS YOU **STOP** YOUR **EXECUTIONS.**

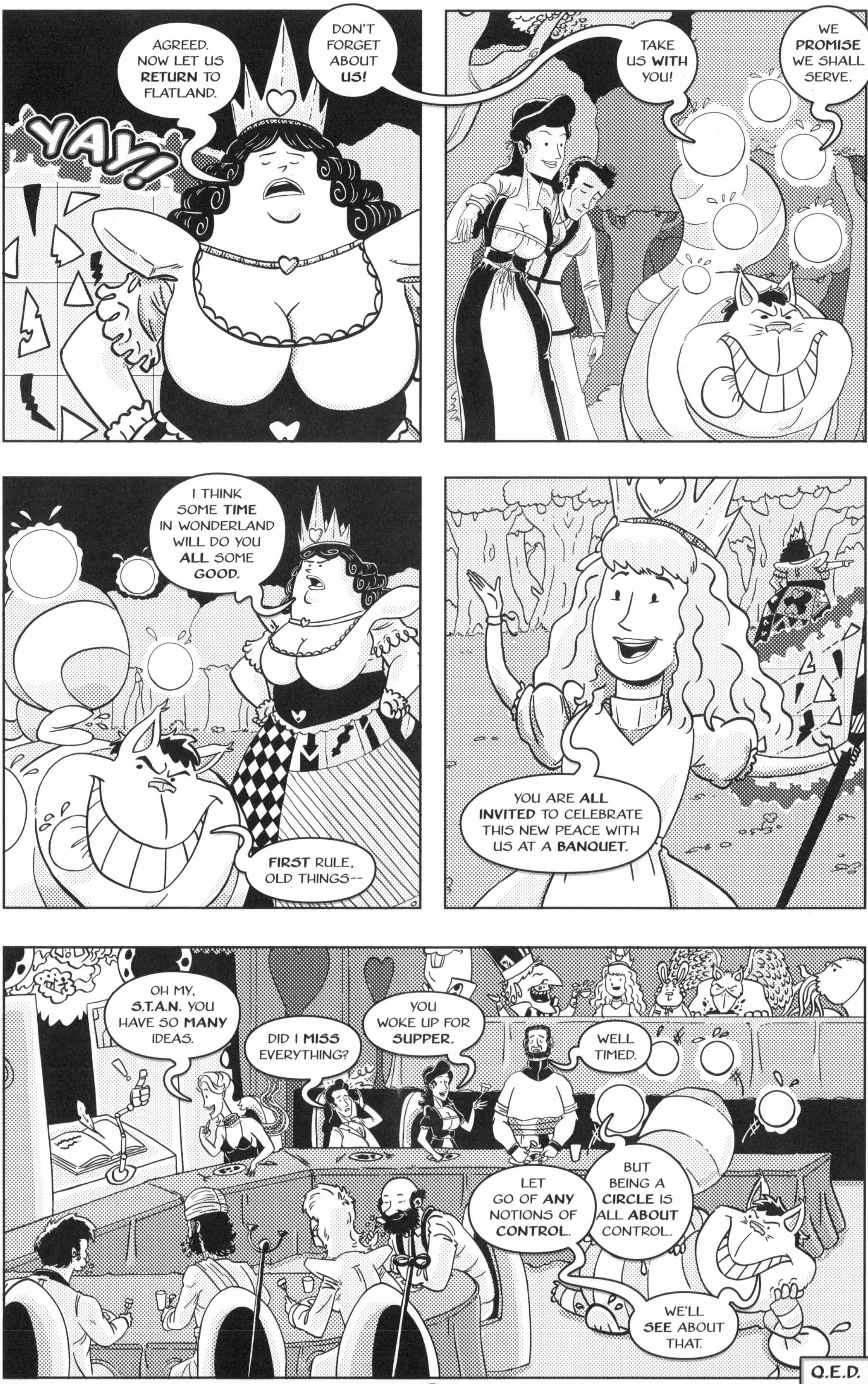
YAY!
AGREED. NOW LET US RETURN TO FLATLAND.
DON'T FORGET ABOUT US!
TAKE US WITH YOU!
WE PROMISE WE SHALL SERVE.
I THINK SOME TIME IN WONDERLAND WILL DO YOU ALL SOME GOOD.
FIRST RULE, OLD THINGS--
YOU ARE ALL INVITED TO CELEBRATE THIS NEW PEACE WITH US AT A BANQUET.
OH MY, S.T.A.N. YOU HAVE SO MANY IDEAS.
DID I MISS EVERYTHING?
YOU WOKE UP FOR SUPPER.
WELL TIMED.
LET GO OF ANY NOTIONS OF CONTROL.
BUT BEING A CIRCLE IS ALL ABOUT CONTROL.
WE'LL SEE ABOUT THAT.
Q.E.D.

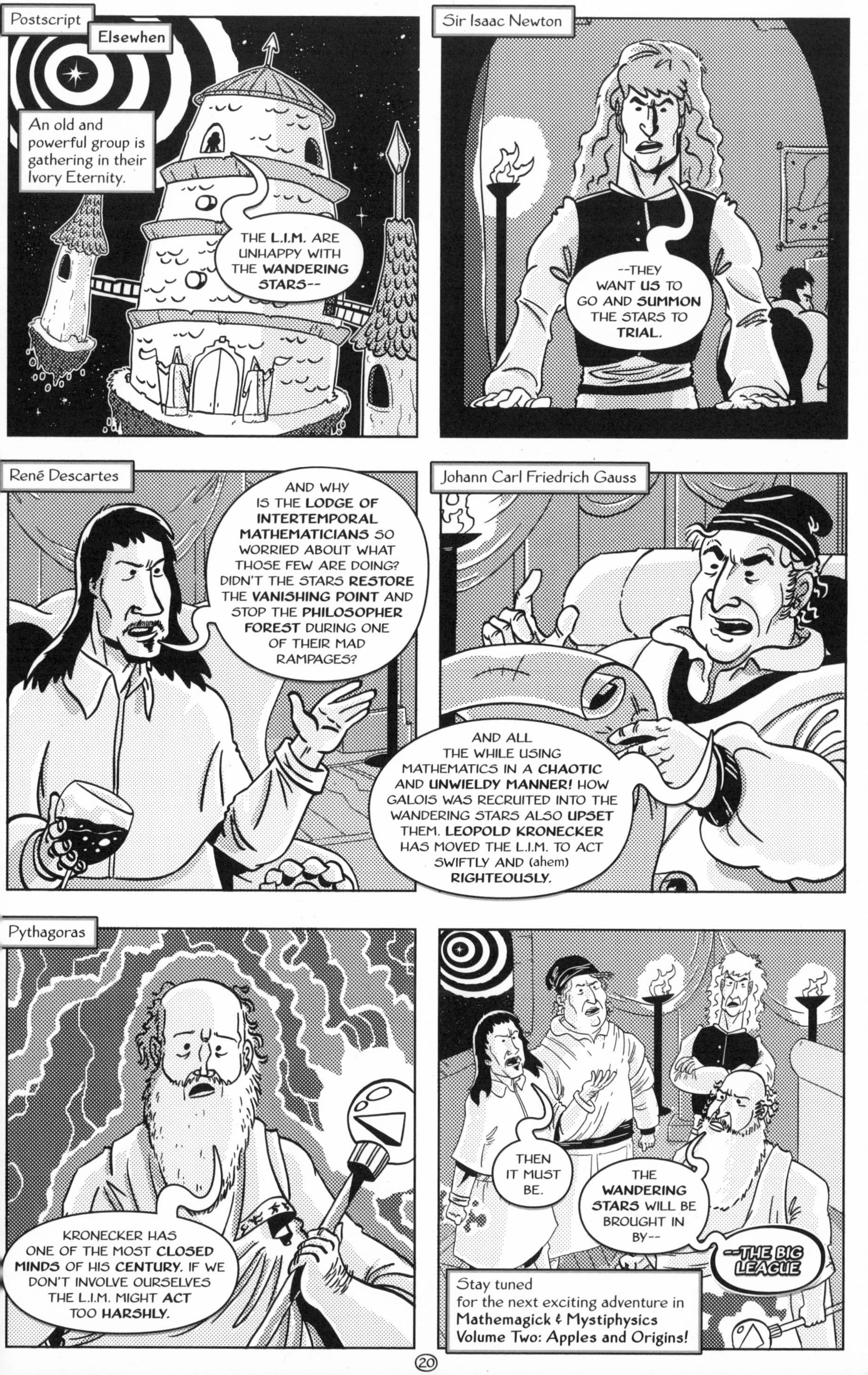
Postscript
Elsewhen
An old and powerful group is gathering in their Ivory Eternity.
THE L.I.M. ARE UNHAPPY WITH THE WANDERING STARS--
Sir Isaac Newton
--THEY WANT US TO GO AND SUMMON THE STARS TO TRIAL.
René Descartes
AND WHY IS THE LODGE OF INTERTEMPORAL MATHEMATICIANS SO WORRIED ABOUT WHAT THOSE FEW ARE DOING? DIDN'T THE STARS RESTORE THE VANISHING POINT AND STOP THE PHILOSOPHER FOREST DURING ONE OF THEIR MAD RAMPAGES?
Johann Carl Friedrich Gauss
AND ALL THE WHILE USING MATHEMATICS IN A CHAOTIC AND UNWIELDY MANNER! HOW GALOIS WAS RECRUITED INTO THE WANDERING STARS ALSO UPSET THEM. LEOPOLD KRONECKER HAS MOVED THE L.I.M. TO ACT SWIFTLY AND (ahem) RIGHTEOUSLY.
Pythagoras
KRONECKER HAS ONE OF THE MOST CLOSED MINDS OF HIS CENTURY. IF WE DON'T INVOLVE OURSELVES THE L.I.M. MIGHT ACT TOO HARSHLY.
THEN IT MUST BE.
THE WANDERING STARS WILL BE BROUGHT IN BY--
--THE BIG LEAGUE
Stay tuned for the next exciting adventure in Mathemagick & Mystiphysics Volume Two: Apples and Origins!

Afterword by James Davidge

While I wouldn't say that I believe in mathemagick, there is a part of me that desperately wants to.

A number of years ago, in the late hours of an otherwise unremarkable evening, I was driving home when I saw a friend, Moore Newell, eating a slice of pizza on the steps leading up to his place. Stopping to say a quick hello, the spontaneous greeting prompted Moore to run upstairs and quickly grab a book he thought I should read. The novel he handed me was Cryptonomicon by Neal Stephensen. It was an appropriate title to be leant given I was beginning my career as a mathematics teacher.

I found myself quickly engaged in a tale that embraced math, both its concepts and its history, as material for exciting and humorous storytelling. Cryptonomicon tells the fictional tale of two generations of the Waterhouse family. In World War II, Lawrence Waterhouse stumbles into becoming a codebreaker who spends some time at Bletchley Park, the centre for cryptography responsible for breaking the Nazi's Enigma Code. The present day tale is about his grandson, Randy Waterhouse, who is a computer programmer caught up in the world of digital banking and internet security. In the former storyline, one of the supporting characters is Alan Turing, the famous genius behind Bletchley Park's human—powered computer.

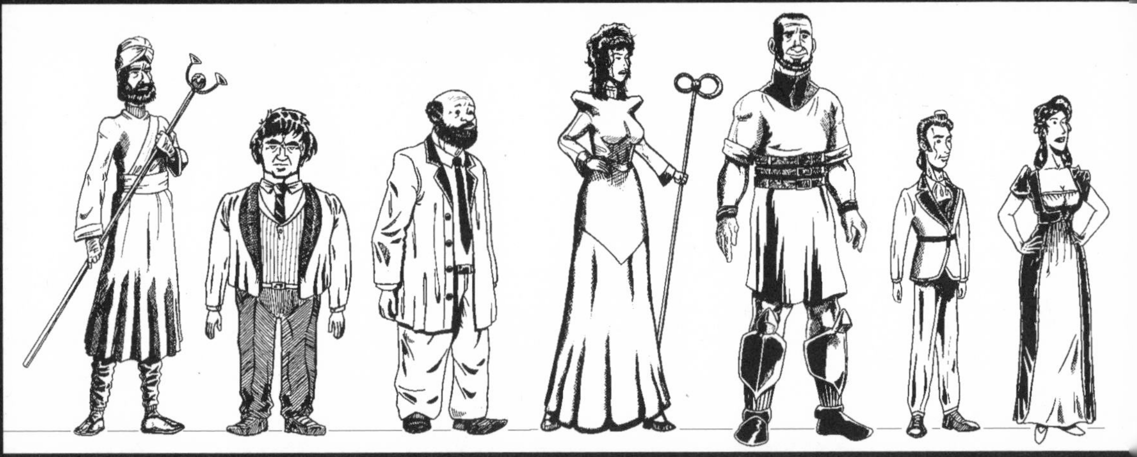

Line—up of the Wandering Stars

At roughly the same time, I was also reading Fermat's Enigma by Simon Singh which excellently chronicles the pathway of ideas that led to Andrew Wiles providing a relatively recent proof to a famous statement that had remained stubbornly unproven for centuries. The book introduced me to many mathematicians and it was in those pages that I was introduced to the brilliant mind and turbulent life of Évariste Galois.

Discovering the legends of these two men increased my awareness that there were many fascinating lives in the world of mathematics that I had never learnt of when polynomials and equations had been taught to me by my math instructors. I recalled the odd anecdote sometimes shared but we students were grappling with the ideas too much to really give any attention to those long dead masters. No mathematicians, aside from possibly Pythagoras or Euclid, had entered the popular zeitgeist in the way that scientists like Einstein or

For some reason I can still recall the meadow of grass and wild flowers I was looking at during a walk near my home in Calgary when I started to imagine a team of "super—mathematicians" that tackled world—threatening problems much like how the Justice League had in the comic—riddled memories of my youth.

Thus began a quest to find mathematicians whose lives, and even deaths, made them suitable candidates for the strange universe that was percolating in my head. I began scouring bookstores of all sorts, always asking the shopkeepers if there was a math section. Often I was led to a science section that may have had some books on how to better understand math. Other times there would be a shelf, maybe two, that revealed a bevy of titles dedicated to journalistically exploring math in interesting ways. Libraries also were valuable resources and I soon knew the Dewey decimal sections that would bear the most fruit.

Line—up for the Wonderland Cast

An extended trip to the east coast of Canada culminated with a visit with my sister, Gillian, and her family in St. John's Newfoundland. During my time there, a couple blocks from where I was staying, a massive Dutch merchant ship was docked for repairs in the harbour. Brandished on the vessel's dull, gray metallic side was a bright yellow seven pointed star. The simple image inspired much as I began to construct not just a team, but a cosmology. I don't want to say much more as there are future volumes of Mathemagick & Mystiphysics coming that will strive to playfully illuminate the many spheres of the Wandering Stars.

Once I had cobbled out scripts to the first two stories, I began my quest for an artist. A common struggle for an aspiring writer of comics is that it can often be a challenge in itself to find an artist interested in your project. Most young comic artists are working at getting their own creations on the page and they can't be disparaged for that. Even if an artist agrees to draw your script, it justifiably takes them a lot of time to produce even a page if they are having to work a full time job and have a life and such. Having no funds to compensate anyone to draw my dream, I was finding it difficult to see it actualized.

I was in Edmonton visiting family. My cousin Jesse had travelled from Vancouver to share in the festivities at my grandparents. During one of those cold nights, my brother, John, took myself and Jesse over to the house of his buddy, Shaun McKee, for some holiday cheer. I always enjoy seeing Shaun as he is a lot of fun to talk comics with. While Shaun and John played a video game, I showed an early draft of the first adventures of the Wandering Stars to Jesse. Jesse was about ten years younger than me. Although I could remember when he was born I barely knew him as we had never lived in the same cities. However, during family gatherings I noticed that he was almost always either reading a comic book or drawing. I figured that, if nothing else, I'd get his feedback. I had shown that very draft to many people before him and while some had responded with kind appreciation for it, no one showed as much interest as Jesse. I can't say what happened in his mind but he told me he liked the concept and wanted to draw it. Jesse was a full time animator and I was happy to enlist him but realistic about the possibility of not seeing any output.

Line—up of Wonderland Extras

A few months later, I was stunned to see thoughtful character sketches being e—mailed to me. Shortly after that I started to see panel layouts and eventually, wonder of all wonders, finished pages. To this day, I am amazed at the level of commitment Jesse has shown as he chips away at creating the visual landscape of the Wandering Stars. In the early months of 2006, just over two years after I showed the script to my cousin, we self—published the first issue of the Wandering Stars. We enlisted Derek Mah to grace Jesse's images with his lettering. We included a math lesson of my devising and a wonderfully absurd essay written by Sean Coleman about the perspective of chairs.

Over the next few years, we attended numerous comic conventions and festivals, pro—moting our work to anyone who would listen. I started to notice that saying "mathemagick and mystiphysics" would often entice people to learn more. For the third issue we changed the title of the comic to feature both of these portmanteau words.

Our project is evolving as we shift from the classic pamphlet model of comic story presentation to the thicker spine of the graphic novel. Our next tale, Apples and Origins, is a full length novel that further explores the rich histories of the Wandering Stars as they are confronted by the Lodge of Intertemporal Mathematicians. After that, things get just plain crazy in our third volume entitled Space Time Boogaloo.

And maybe by then, a part of me will believe in mathemagick.

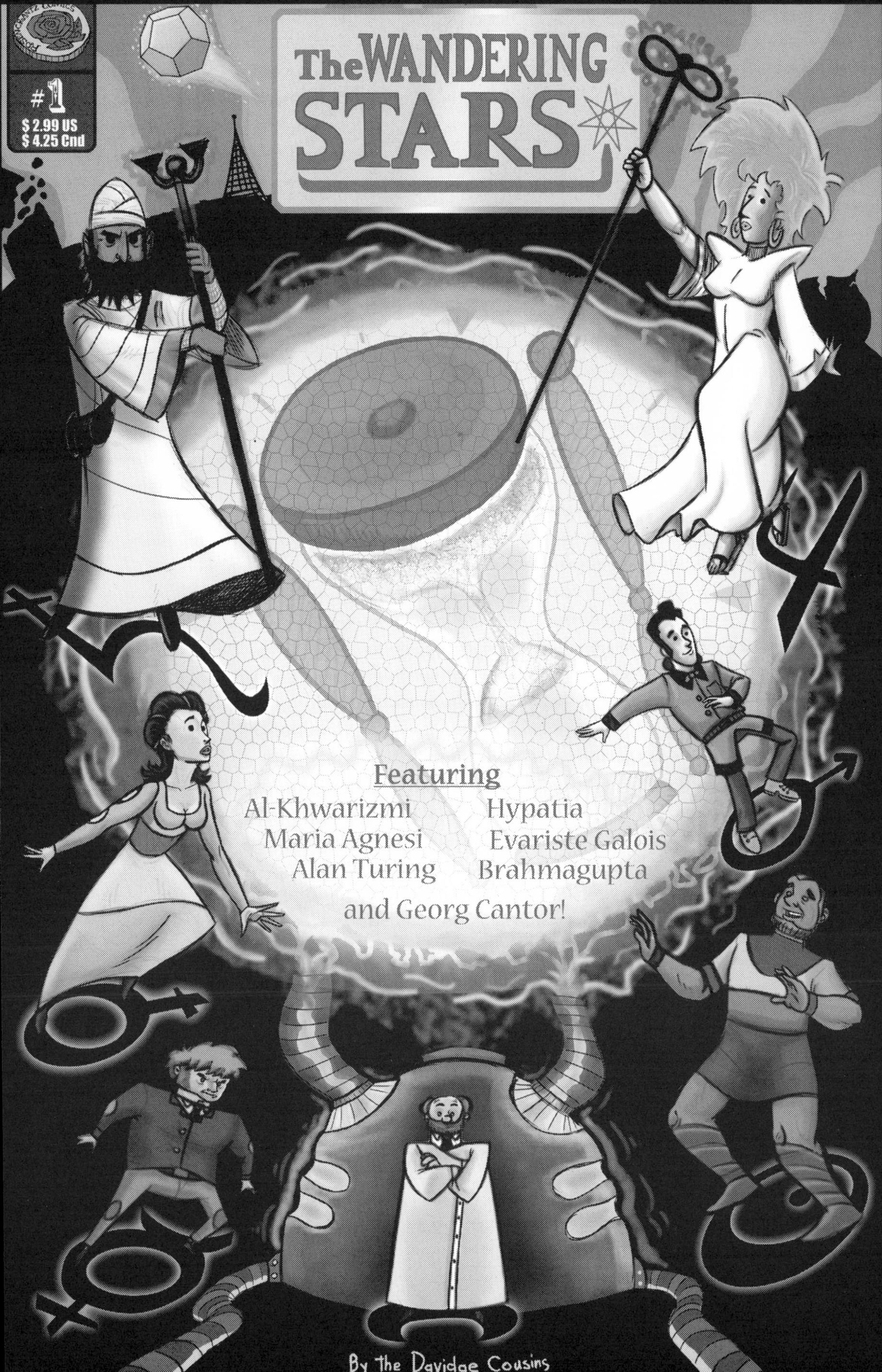
The WANDERING STARS
#1
$ 2.99 US
$ 4.25 Cnd
Featuring
Al-Khwarizmi
Hypatia
Maria Agnesi
Evariste Galois
Alan Turing
Brahmagupta
and Georg Cantor!
By the Davidge Cousins

Cover Two: Published March 2007

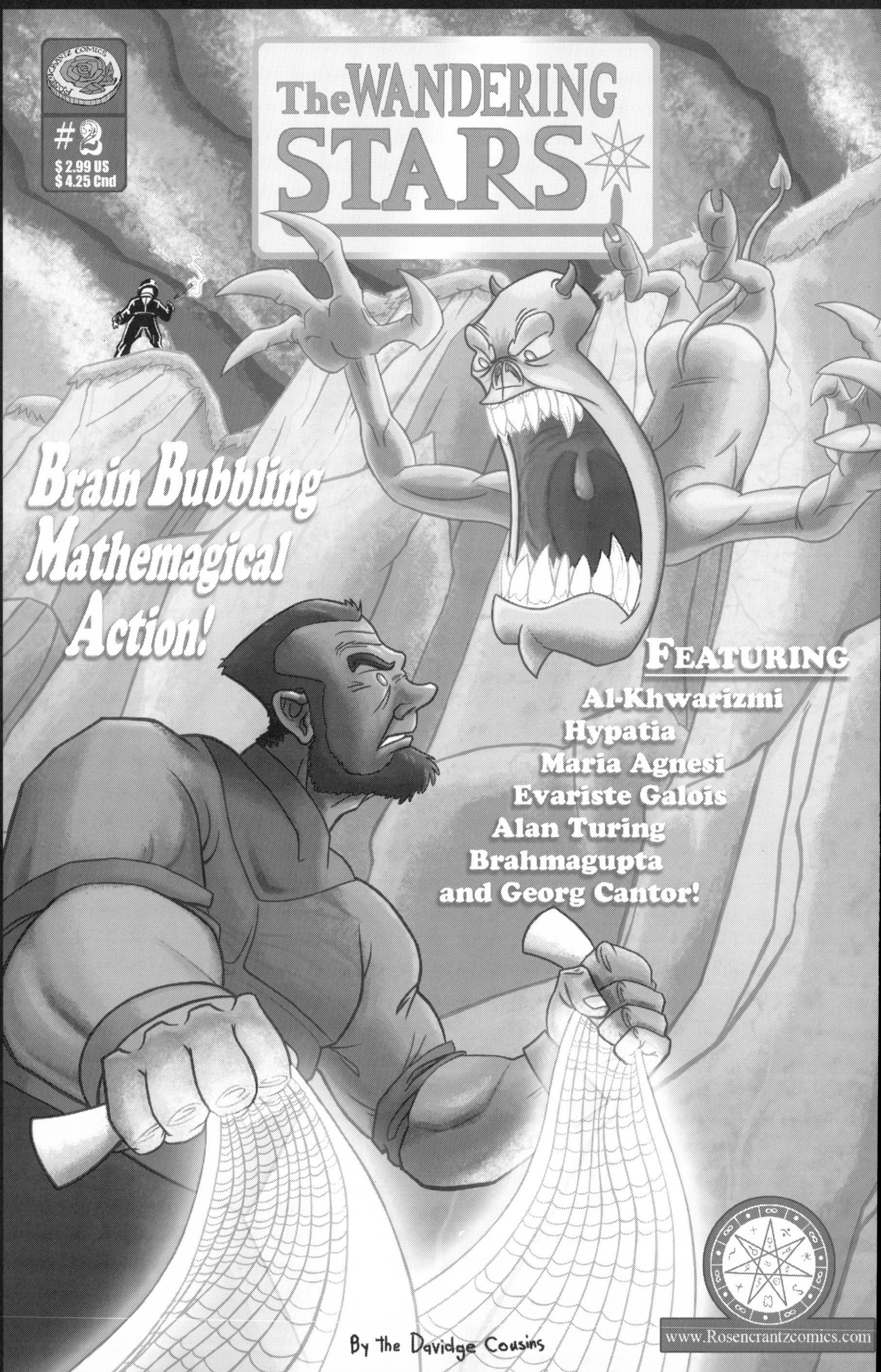

The WANDERING STARS
#2
$ 2.99 US
$ 4.25 Cnd
Brain Bubbling Mathemagical Action!
FEATURING
Al-Khwarizmi
Hypatia
Maria Agnesi
Evariste Galois
Alan Turing
Brahmagupta
and Georg Cantor!
By the Davidge Cousins
www.Rosencrantzcomics.com

#3
$2.99

MATHEMAGICK AND MYSTIPHYSICS FEATURING THE WANDERING STARS

By the Davidge Cousins

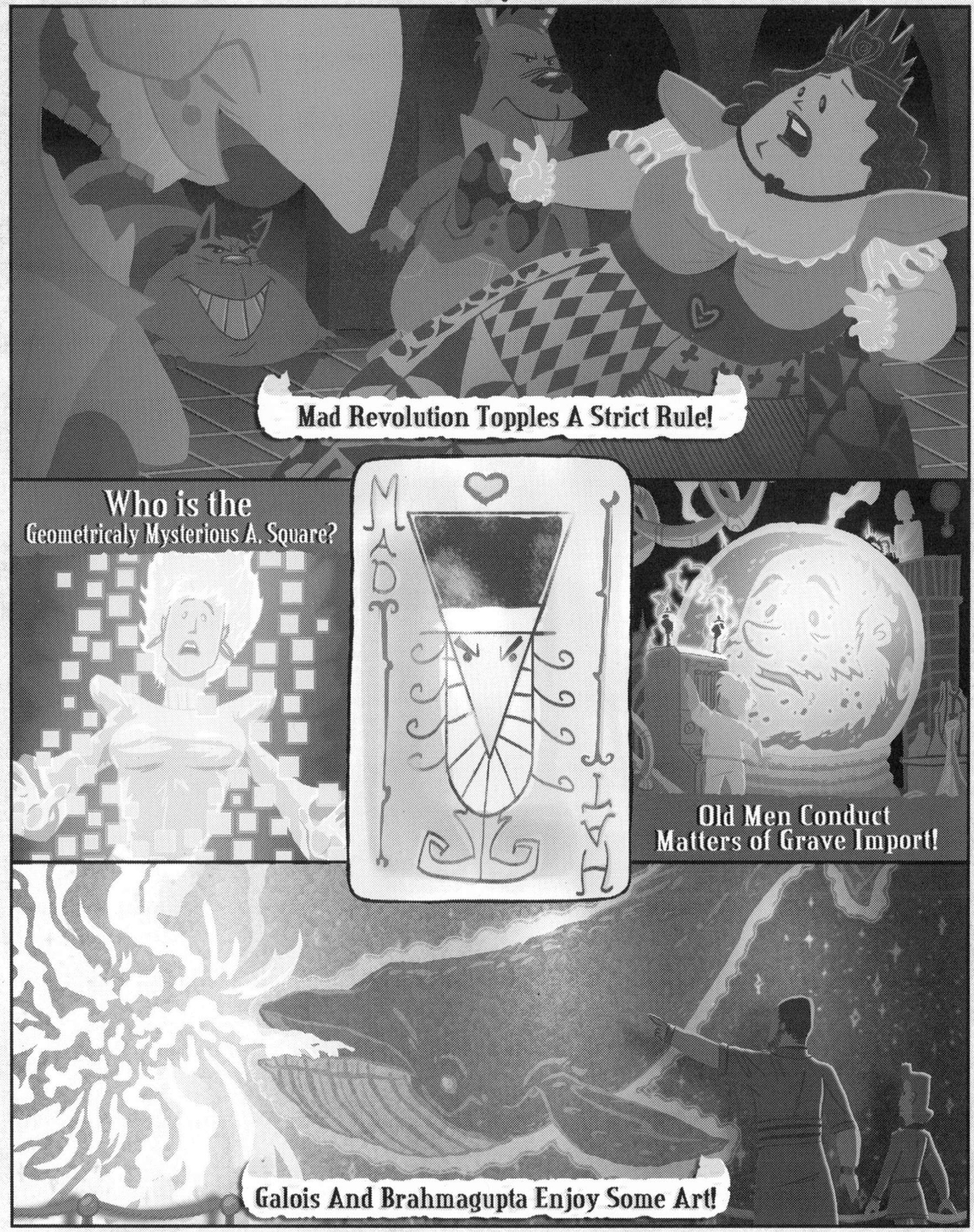
Mad Revolution Topples A Strict Rule!
Who is the Geometricaly Mysterious A. Square?
Old Men Conduct Matters of Grave Import!
Galois And Brahmagupta Enjoy Some Art!

AS A TERRIBLE BATTLE BREWS IN "THE WAR OF FLAT AND WONDER" PART 1 OF 2

Promotional Comic originally published in Happy Harbor Comics
Tales from the Harbor Volume 4 in 2008

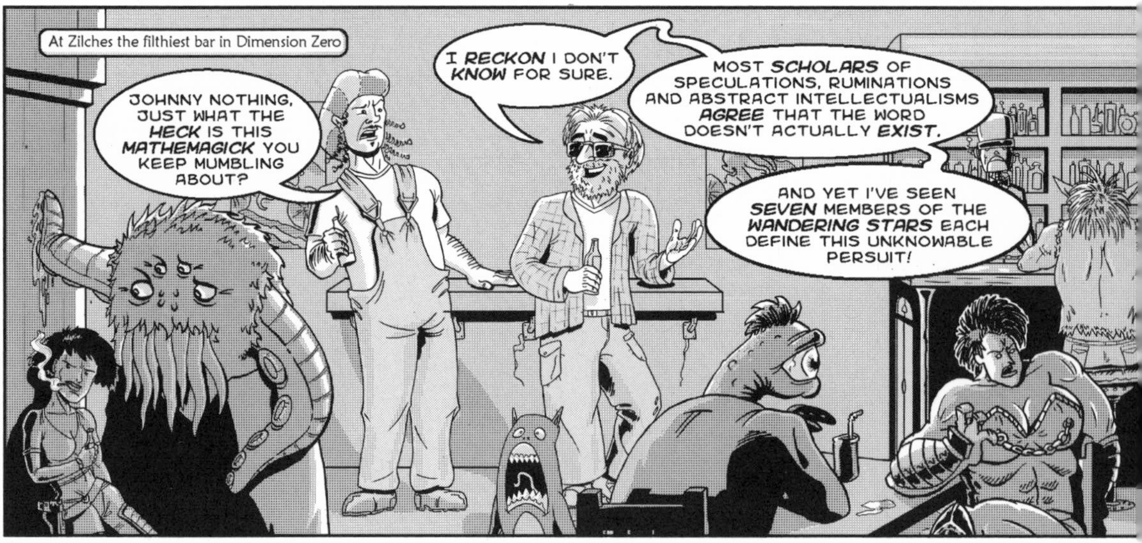

At Zilches the filthiest bar in Dimension Zero
JOHNNY NOTHING, JUST WHAT THE HECK IS THIS MATHEMAGICK YOU KEEP MUMBLING ABOUT?
I RECKON I DON'T KNOW FOR SURE.
MOST SCHOLARS OF SPECULATIONS, RUMINATIONS AND ABSTRACT INTELLECTUALISMS AGREE THAT THE WORD DOESN'T ACTUALLY EXIST.
AND YET I'VE SEEN SEVEN MEMBERS OF THE WANDERING STARS EACH DEFINE THIS UNKNOWABLE PERSUIT!

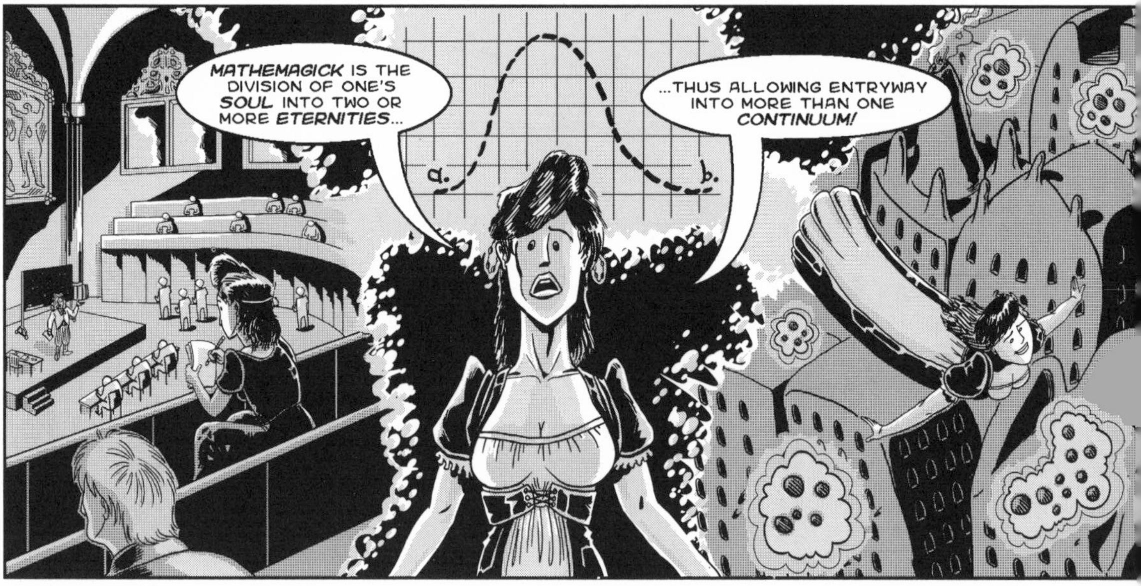

MATHEMAGICK IS THE DIVISION OF ONE'S SOUL INTO TWO OR MORE ETERNITIES...
...THUS ALLOWING ENTRYWAY INTO MORE THAN ONE CONTINUUM!
a.
b.

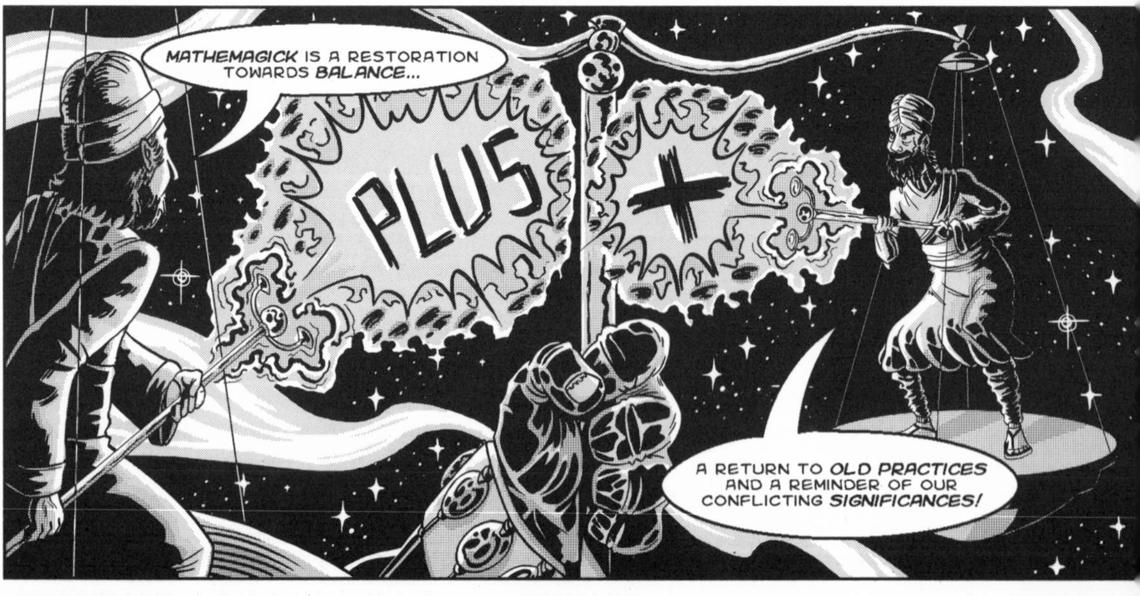

MATHEMAGICK IS A RESTORATION TOWARDS BALANCE...
PLUS
A RETURN TO OLD PRACTICES AND A REMINDER OF OUR CONFLICTING SIGNIFICANCES!

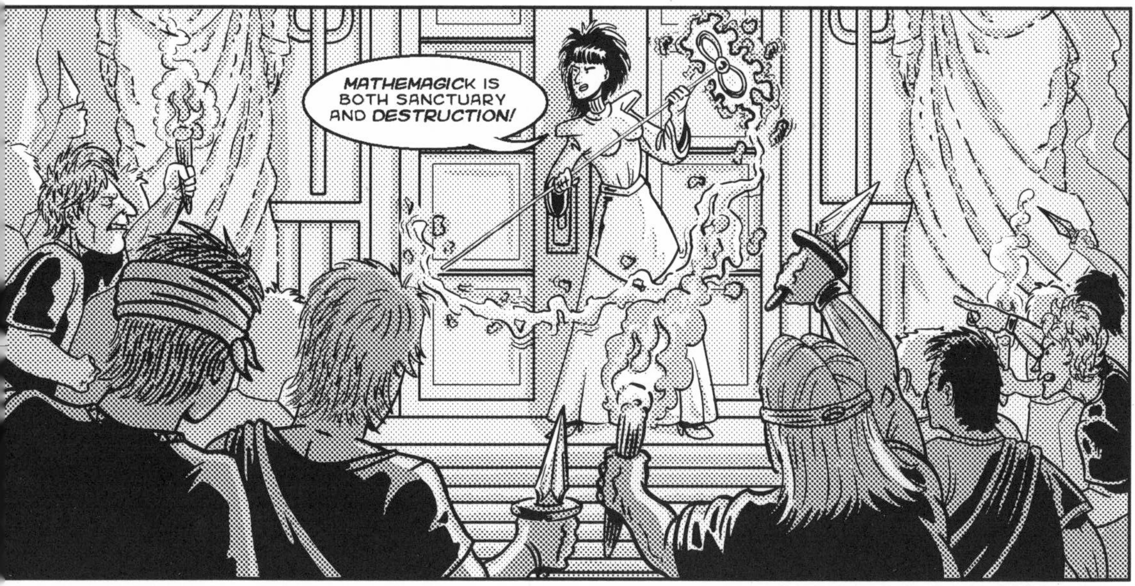
MATHEMAGICK IS BOTH SANCTUARY AND DESTRUCTION!

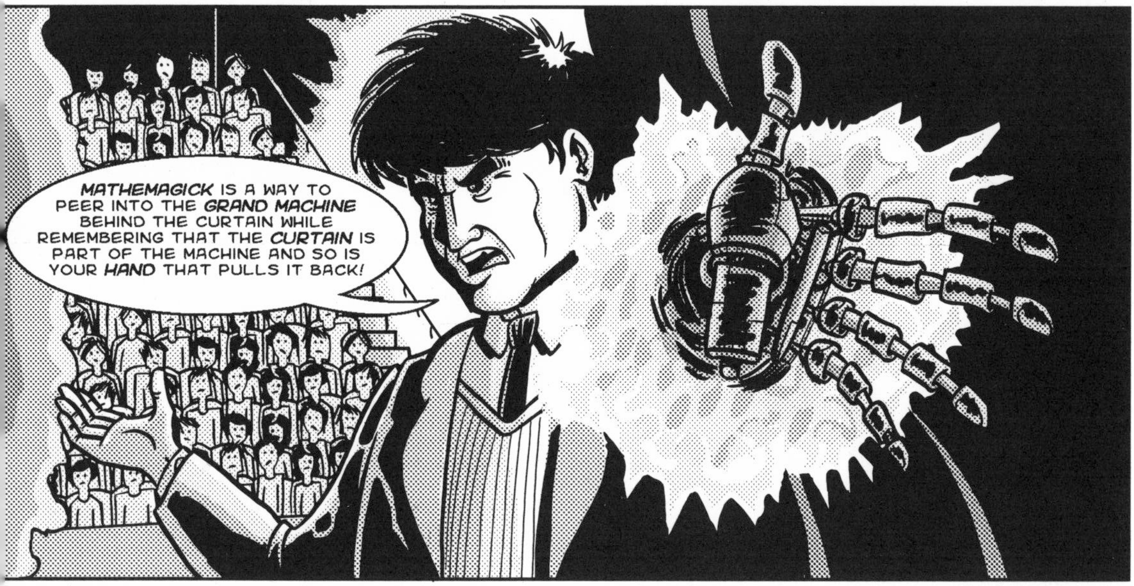
MATHEMAGICK IS A WAY TO PEER INTO THE GRAND MACHINE BEHIND THE CURTAIN WHILE REMEMBERING THAT THE CURTAIN IS PART OF THE MACHINE AND SO IS YOUR HAND THAT PULLS IT BACK!

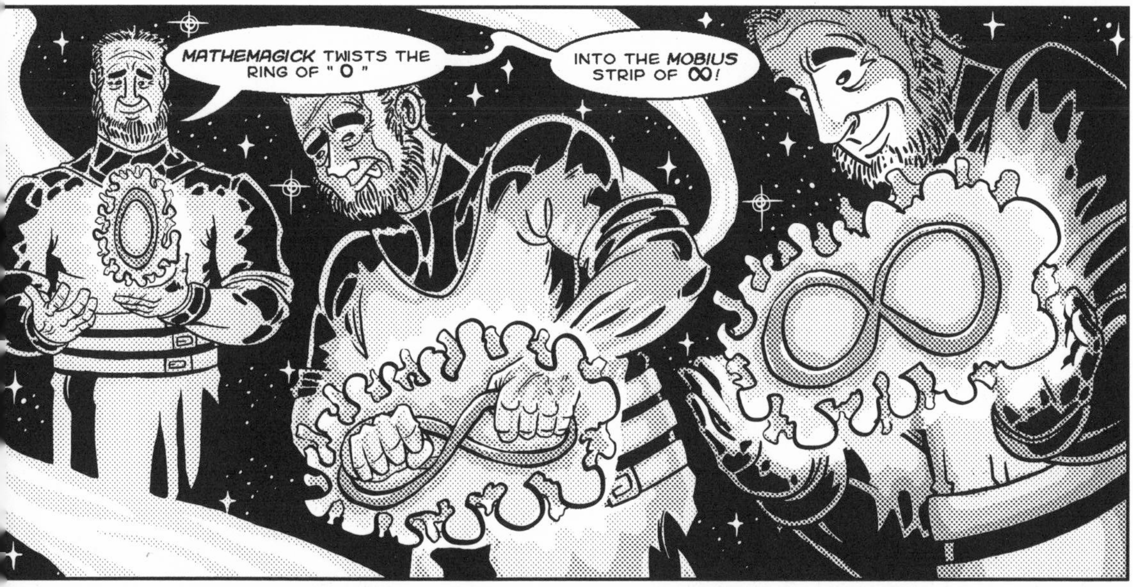
MATHEMAGICK TWISTS THE RING OF " 0 "
INTO THE MOBIUS STRIP OF ∞!

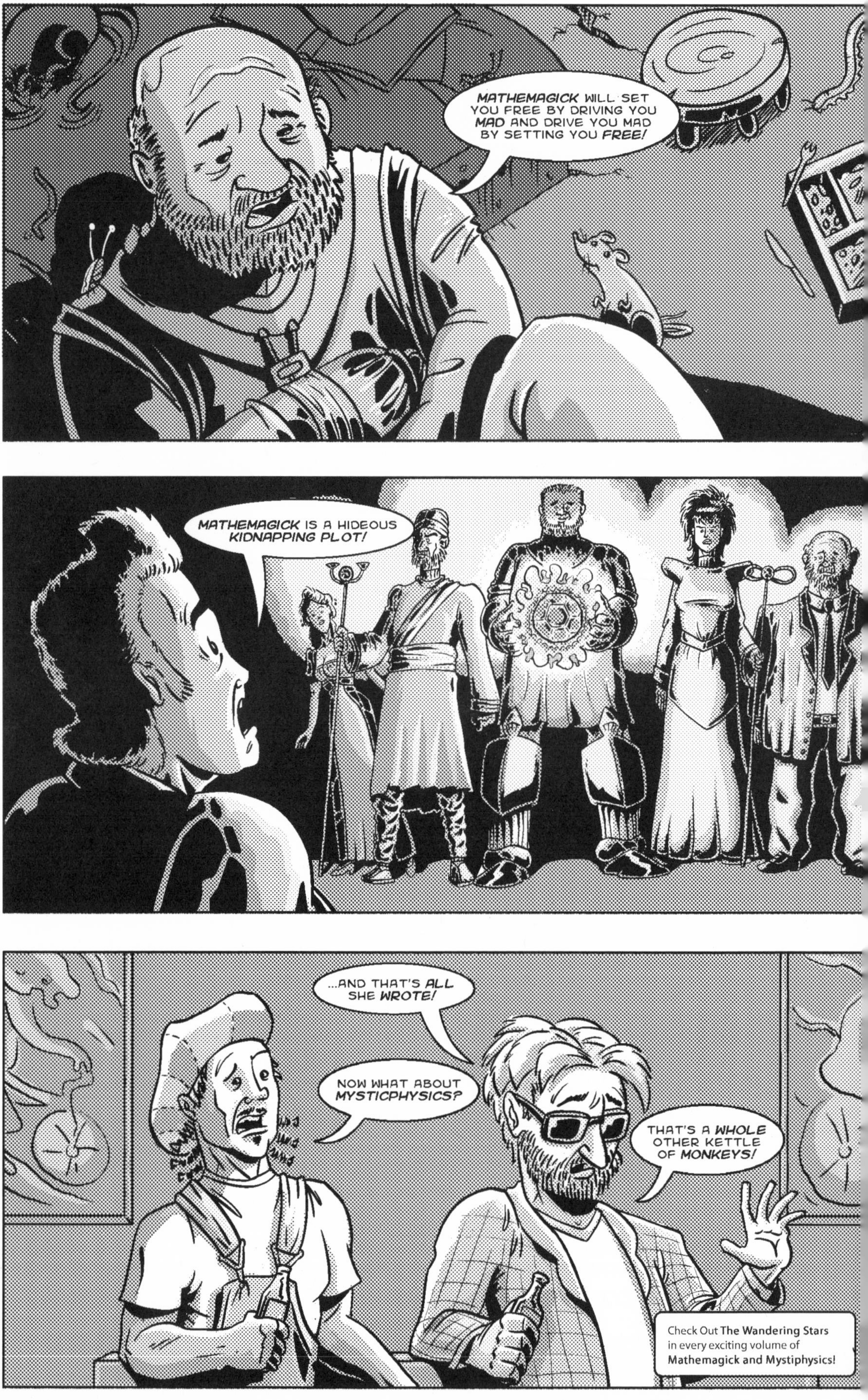
MATHEMAGICK WILL SET YOU FREE BY DRIVING YOU MAD AND DRIVE YOU MAD BY SETTING YOU FREE!
MATHEMAGICK IS A HIDEOUS KIDNAPPING PLOT!
...AND THAT'S ALL SHE WROTE!
NOW WHAT ABOUT MYSTICPHYSICS?
THAT'S A WHOLE OTHER KETTLE OF MONKEYS!
Check Out The Wandering Stars in every exciting volume of Mathemagick and Mystiphysics!